Also by Ann Aguirre

The Only Purple House in Town

Fix-It Witches
Witch Please
Boss Witch
Extra Witchy

I Think
I'm in
Love
with an
ALIEN

ANN AGUIRRE

sourcebooks
casablanca

Published by Sourcebooks Casablanca, an imprint of Sourcebooks
P.O. Box 4410, Naperville, Illinois 60567-4410
(630) 961-3900
Fax: (630) 961-2168
sourcebooks.com

Cataloging-in-Publication data is on file with the Library of Congress.

Printed and bound in the United States of America.
VP 10 9 8 7 6 5 4 3 2 1

For those we have lost but never forgotten

GROUP CHAT
OCTOBER 21 | 17:37

[JazzyPlum has entered the chat]

[SquidHead has entered the chat]

[Seeker has entered the chat]

[Jeneticist has entered the chat]

[FarfromHome has entered the chat]

[Stargazer has entered the chat]

FarfromHome: Why are we here?

Stargazer: Don't be rude. Thanks for hosting, J.

Seeker: Are you talking to Jazzy or Jeneticist?

Stargazer: Jazzy is JP. Try to keep up.

Jeneticist: Okay, I sent you all chat invites because they locked our forum thread.

SquidHead: It was over a thousand replies. Loading time was probably slowing the server.

JazzyPlum: Now we can continue the convo! And any others that strike our fancy.

Stargazer: Yay! I always wanted to be part of a cool group chat.

FarfromHome: Then you're still waiting.

Seeker: I'm happy to be here. I've been feeling a little...

Jeneticist: Isolated? It feels like I never see anyone face-to-face these days.

Seeker: Yeah. You get it.

JazzyPlum: Are we going to resume the discussion from the forum? Or...

SquidHead: Or what?

Stargazer: We could do intros!

FarfromHome: I'm not putting my info in a random group chat.

Seeker: Maybe just one fun fact to start?

Jeneticist: I love that! I'll go first. I volunteered for a SETI-type program in college and monitored transmissions. I was so hoping I'd find...something. That proves we're not alone.

Seeker: You're not alone. You have us.

SquidHead: Also, that's not a surprise to anyone who's talked to you on the Aliens Among Us forum.

JazzyPlum: I'll go next. I play the violin.

SquidHead: Wow, that's so cool. Are you a professional musician?

JazzyPlum: Maybe I'll answer that next time. ☺

Seeker: It *is* more than one fact. My turn? Let's see. I love to travel, especially what most people would consider extreme tourism.

Jeneticist: Whoa. You mean like parachuting into a disaster zone?

Seeker: Not quite to that extent, but I definitely go off the beaten path.

Stargazer: Remind me never to let you plan my holidays.

JazzyPlum: 🦔

Stargazer: I'll take a shot. I'm a second dan black belt in judo.

SquidHead: Our muscle has entered the chat. Me next! I work in tech, 100% remote. I'm in charge of some pretty important code. That's all I'm at liberty to say.

FarfromHome: You design websites, got it.

SquidHead: Hey!

JazzyPlum: FFH is teasing you.

FarfromHome: Am I?

Jeneticist: You're also the only one who hasn't shared a fact.

FarfromHome: I am the smartest person any of you will ever encounter.

Stargazer: You sure seem to think so.

SquidHead: Are you in Mensa?

Seeker: What's Mensa?

JazzyPlum: An organization for people with a high IQ.

Jeneticist: This was fun! I have to get going, but I'll send the picture I mentioned in the forum thread when I find it in my digital files.

Seeker: Talk to you soon, J.

Jeneticist: ☺

1

JENNETTE

I HAVE A *HUGE* CRUSH on someone I've never even met.

Depending on your definition, it might not be the first time either. Do fictional characters count? If they do, then I've fallen many times, usually with aliens in video games. Why romance humans when I can experience the glorious fantasy of hooking up with a sexy purple person with three eyes and head tails? I've got a soft spot for monsters in certain romance novels too. Trust me, horns and tails are no obstacle.

But this is a real person, someone I've been talking to online for about six months. Seeker is part of a group chat that I started, funneling invitations through direct messages on the Aliens Among Us website. I staunchly believe that online friends are every bit as important as in-person connections. These days, my in-person friends are a bit scarce. My high school friends aren't in town anymore, and my college friends have scattered, which leaves me with work acquaintances.

I'm a bit lonely, actually. But sometimes, the streams can cross. Or at least I hope that's true. Because my online friends agreed to go to Rellows, Utah, which is a *really* special place. They've been hosting Outer Space Con—a.k.a. Space Con—since the seventies. It's a quirky little town and I can't wait to explore all the strangeness it has to offer.

My phone rings. Glancing at the number makes me sigh as I answer, "Hi, Mom."

"You're not really going off alone to meet a bunch of strangers from the internet, right? Tell me Glynnis got that wrong."

Glynnis is my little sister and she's never once opted not to tattle on me. Not since I stole some chocolate chip cookies that were meant for the school bake sale when I was seven. This time, however, I was counting on how regularly she reports in. It saves me making the phone calls anyway.

"It will be fine. I have my own room."

At the silliest motel in the world. There are only twenty rooms, and each is decorated in a different space theme. Unless you get lucky like I did, it requires reserving a year in advance to stay in the Jupiter room; apparently, it takes *two* years to stay in Uranus.

The housing situation quickly becomes untenable during Space Con since Rellows doesn't have the infrastructure to support the sheer volume of visitors that descend on the town annually. There's an RV park that fills up completely, and people are permitted to pitch tents on a vacant lot on the outskirts of town for the duration of the con. From all the reading I've done, locals rent rooms in their houses and even set up sheds and outbuildings to accommodate the sudden influx of tourists.

Pictures online make it look like Mardi Gras got drunk and had a baby with San Diego Comic-Con, only that baby was an alien. And I cannot freaking *wait* to immerse myself in the weirdness.

Attending this con is the reason I was born. Well, that and my job. But honestly, I got into astronomy because of my mild obsession with confirming that we're not alone in the universe.

The long pause tells me that my mother is trying to find something supportive to say. Recently, she read a how-to book on the value of positive reinforcement, and since she used to nitpick constantly, this is a good change. I let her sort through objections until she finally settles on, "Well, I'm glad to see you trying new things. Even if I don't agree with the risks you're taking. Why don't you invite your sister? Just in case."

I count to ten silently. "Because Glynnis isn't interested in Space Con. If she went, she would be bored."

She'd also complain the whole *time.*

Mom offers another terrible suggestion. "Why don't you invite Nina then? You never talk about her anymore."

That hurts.

"We lost touch," I remind her. "She's busy. New life in Sacramento."

Besides, even if I had someone to go with me, I'd still rather make an impression on my own. I don't need Glynnis telling my online friends what a humongous dork I am. And seeing Nina after all these years would be beyond awkward too. If my Aliens Among Us friends still like me once we've hung out in person, then I can remove the *online* qualifier and they'll just be friends, right? I've always found it difficult to bond with people because I can be a little obsessive about things that interest me. So it makes sense to befriend people with similar hobbies who won't get tired of theoretical talk about what kinds of aliens would live on an aquatic planet with heavy gravity.

I have some extremely specific ideas.

"I want you girls to get closer. I won't be around forever. Your poor father..."

My dad died last year. Lung cancer. He was only sixty-eight too. My parents were both older when I was born, forty for my dad, thirty-eight for my mom. She had a whole career as a teacher for a long time, and they thought she couldn't have kids, when suddenly, she thought she was going through early menopause, and surprise! Nope, it was me. My sister stunned everyone by coming along two years later, and my parents were both befuddled to suddenly have two daughters when they'd basically given up on babies.

"Are you still running with the Whiskey Tango Foxtrots?" I ask pointedly.

My mom joined a senior group called WTF, and they're constantly challenging themselves. First they did water aerobics together, then it was dance class, and now they're low-impact jogging. I love the idea, but since my mom got in shape thanks to their activities, allusions to her imminent demise don't hold much weight anymore.

"Three times a week," she answers, seeming not to get the connection. "And then we eat a big pancake breakfast."

I laugh because my mom is truly living her best life. "Sounds awesome."

At least we're not talking about Glynnis or Space Con anymore. Thankfully, the diversion seems to have worked. Mom chatters on, sharing the tea on various ladies in her circle. "And *then* I found out Lulu is dating a forty-eight-year-old. Imagine! She's sixty-two!"

"Get it, Lulu."

"Jennette!" Then my mom giggles. "You know what? I saw

selfies of them together and he doesn't look *too* young. It's the beard, I think. They make a cute couple."

Forty-eight is certainly old enough to do whatever he wants. And apparently, he wants to do Lulu. I've met her a couple of times, and she reminded me of Blanche from *The Golden Girls*, with similar Southern charm and a flirtatious manner.

A few minutes later, Mom hangs up without remembering that she needed to finish scolding me about Space Con and random internet strangers.

As of yesterday, I'm officially on vacation, and I'm leaving in a little while. From Ontario, Oregon, to Rellows, Utah, it takes between seven and eight hours, depending on how fast I drive and how often I stop along the way. I'm the type who absolutely will stop for a cool roadside stand or to investigate a giant ball of twine or a "unique bones" museum housed in a former gas station. I could have flown, but it's easier to pack all my costumes and prosthetics and special effects makeup in the back of my Scion xB. Truthfully, the suitcase dedicated to cosplay is bigger than the one for my regular clothes and toiletries.

I check everything for the tenth time before I'm satisfied. Time to load the xB. It's a boxy little beauty, light blue and low mileage. I bought it pre-owned several years ago, supposedly from someone who only used it to run errands and go grocery shopping, so it has less than fifty thousand miles even though it's an older model. And there's plenty of room for everything I'm taking to Space Con.

My neighbor waves as I drag the last suitcase out the front door. Nancy will be taking care of my cats and houseplants while I'm gone. She's in her forties, recently divorced, and just moved into the other side of the duplex. But I've known her much longer, as she handled property management for her ex.

Technically, she's my landlady too since she got the building as part of her separation agreement, but she's more interested in my cats than my personal business. To be fair, Scotty and Spock are the best cats in the world. I will tolerate no disagreements. Scotty is a plump orange and white lad while Spock is a sleek gray Abyssinian mix with sensitive ears. They're both neutered and they couldn't be cuddlier if they were lapdogs.

Right now, they're both on the top tier of the cat condo by the window staring out at me wistfully. Scotty puts a wee, pink-beaned paw on the window while Spock tries to mind meld me. *Come back inside, human. We need you to open our cans.* I almost run back inside for one more snuggle session. *No. I must be strong. Space Con or bust!*

Circling back to my original point, I invited everyone in the group chat and they all agreed it sounded like a good time, thank goodness. But I held my breath waiting for Seeker's response. He's the one I'm dying to meet.

Unless I've forgotten how it goes, we've totally been flirting for the last three months, and I'm so into him it's embarrassing. I tap my phone screen and reread what he said to me last night, holding back the squee with great effort.

Seeker: Can't wait to meet you in person.

Jeneticist: Likewise. Really looking forward to it.

Seeker: I've been counting down the days since we decided to do this.

Jeneticist: OMG. Me too. 🤍

I'm like a teenager; it's been ages since I was so excited to spend time with someone. I haven't seen any pics, but I don't care. Looks are secondary to me since I don't experience visual attraction. Sure, I'm aware when people are attractive, but I admire them the same way I do a painting or sculpture. But I'm deeply, profoundly drawn to Seeker. I hoard facts about him in a notebook. Told you I'm a dork. I don't know his full name, but he said to call him Tam. Or Seeker, whichever I prefer.

I get in the car and close the door, then buckle in. After almost a year of chatting online, I'm *finally* gonna meet him in person.

2
SEEKER

THIS IS PROBABLY A POOR choice.

But I wouldn't even be *on* this planet if I wasn't prone to those. The gray market contact warned me repeatedly. Planet 97-B isn't a premium destination, they said. Don't risk it, they said. The locals are often hostile, the world is highly contaminated, and the tech situation makes it difficult for shuttles to come and go on schedule. Plus, in the past, there have been...complications. They even told me they were removing this stop from the tour, and this was the last time they would facilitate travel to this interdicted world.

With all those warnings, they might as well have bribed me to choose this place. Forbidden? Challenging? I love those things. I've never been good at following the rules, and I love pushing the boundaries of what's possible, even when I'm on vacation. It's not even that difficult to travel between planets.

A small unit I carry tricks the brain and optical nerve, mirroring what different life-forms expect to see. I adjust for the dominant being at each new destination, and if the locals have their own tech, there's a complementary function that disrupts surveillance equipment. This permits me to experience a different reality, albeit briefly.

The vacation to Planet 97-B was supposed to be a quick trip before I chose a course that would please my family, especially Oona. When I realized I was marooned on this planet, I assessed my situation and swiftly assimilated what I needed to know about working in "web development." It was simple to spoof credentials and receive digital payments with their basic security protocols. Now I receive payment as a "contractor" and I'm constantly relocating my domicile. There seem to be very strange regulations regarding who can live where and for how long.

Consequently, I'm packing up my belongings because this will be my last day here in this "studio apartment." Which is entirely a misnomer. There's no studio; it's a compact living space, similar to second-class accommodations on an interstellar cruiser. Those alloys tend to be better quality, however. This unit is substandard, but I received a discount for paying for thirty days.

That's the local vernacular. For some reason, they demarcate time in a most irregular fashion. The local calendar perplexes me, but I've learned to pretend that it makes sense. A year is twelve months, which is an unusual number. Multiples of ten divide more neatly. Then each month has a seemingly random number of days. Some are thirty, others thirty-one, and one outlier has twenty-eight. Or twenty-nine, every fourth year. It's truly a remarkably complicated system. And don't even get me started on how there are twenty-four hours in a day, or sixty minutes in an hour. It all seems incredibly random.

But I've memorized the vagaries of the human schedule and I'm absolutely making the best of this. Since I'm living among the locals like a research scientist, perhaps I'll formalize my findings and get my name in the scholarly journals: *My Time on 97-B by Tamzir Jaarn*. I can envision the academic accolades I'll receive already, assuming I can make it back.

It's not all bad here.

I created credentials on a platform called Aliens Among Us. I thought I'd be quietly entertained by how wrong they were, but as it turns out, they were an incredibly passionate and earnest group, and I got drawn in. At first, it amused me to offer "theoretical" answers about things I knew to be true in the larger universe. But the thoughtful responses kept me coming back. It staved off the loneliness. Before, I wouldn't have understood the weight—knowing that I'm the only one of my kind on this tiny little ball of dirt and water.

When Jeneticist invited me to join a group chat, as it's called, I accepted. Because I've become curious about her. Perhaps even fond? If it's appropriate to use the word. I've never known anyone who shines so bright even at such a remove. She radiates warmth like a star, and I enjoy sharing ideas with her. The others, as well, of course, but there's no point in pretending that I feel the same about *everyone* in the chat.

Enough reflection. I should get underway.

There are instructions for vacating the premises. I was advised to put my towels and linens in the hygiene machine, which is not for biological matter, only inorganic material. To me, it makes sense to cleanse everything at once. But they use water on 97-B in unusual ways. That resource is scarce on many planets and cleaning occurs through other means.

A final glance assures me I have left behind no traces in the small space I'm vacating. Nobody will be able to tell a nonhuman person was staying here. I hoist my belongings and make my way out into the city.

The stench is shocking. Too many bodies, actual biological waste, methane, carbon monoxide, rotting sweetness, and stagnant water. Do humans have no sense of smell? I'm surprised one of them hasn't invented tech to address this contamination. I have ideas—bioengineered tardigrades who feed on specific types of pollution, for example.

I move past tall, crumbling edifices without drawing notice. To avoid rigorous security checks, I've opted to travel slowly over land. Ground transport here is inefficient, but air travel is worse. And all the methods create toxins that further pollute the environment. So many problems could be solved by joining the Galactic Union, but before that offer will be put forth, 97-B must develop reliable interstellar travel on their own. It's the minimum requirement, though there are rumors that certain planets have been helped along by collectives who wanted to open up travel to those destinations. If 97-B was cleaner, it might earn such favor from the travel bureau.

Now, I use a token I spoofed to gain access to a local transport vehicle. From there, I make my way to a larger staging area. As usual, when I'm surrounded by humans I worry about the bandwidth on my personal camo unit. Will it affect all brains equally? Or will someone see me as I truly am? Sometimes it seems to falter where small children are concerned, possibly because their neurological functions aren't fully developed.

And then the little one will say, "Mommy, that's a monster!" and point in my direction. When the parental figure sees only a normal person, they shush the child and hurry them away with a mumbled apology. Sometimes they even lecture.

"It's unkind to point, Abigail. We respect everyone, even if they look a little different. Remember what we talked about?"

Today, however, I stow my belongings in the underside of the vehicle, and everyone shuffles onboard without anyone glancing more than once in my general direction. It takes twelve hours, and I change conveyances once in a seedy station in the middle of nowhere. As I settle into my seat for the last part of the journey, an elder human settles into the space next to me with an audible groan.

"Hope you don't mind, but I find it's best to pick my neighbor before somebody unpleasant chooses me. If the bus doesn't fill up, I'll move over."

I'm pleased with the translation device. When I first arrived, there were odd skips and colloquial failures. But I've trained it on entertainment programs until it's no longer offering archaic idioms.

"You're welcome to sit with me," I say politely.

The elder spends a good deal of time arranging personal belongings and then turns to me with an expression I find challenging. Lips and eyes convey meaning, but not to me. I've done most of my communication remotely.

"Where are you headed? If it's not too nosy. If it is, then never mind."

"Rellows, Utah."

"You're going to that outer space convention? I'm visiting my cousin in Provo. I've been meaning to check on her, but traveling gets tough at my age."

I make an encouraging sound, and the elder tells me about their life until the vehicle starts. Eventually, they taper off and begin making odd noises. It would appear they have fallen asleep in the middle of a sentence. How curious.

Four more hours, and I will finally meet Jen. One moment of connection in a desert of loneliness.

The others don't know this, but this will be my first and last moment with all of them. Once the gathering ends, I have some plans percolating and I'm getting off this rock, one way or another.

GROUP CHAT
OCTOBER 24 | 18:44

Jeneticist: Here are the photos I promised. I took them in college.

Stargazer: Wow, these are gorgeous. Professional quality.

JazzyPlum: There's something so mysterious, but also rather lonely. About the stars.

FarfromHome: Loneliness is for the weak-minded.

SquidHead: You never get lonely?

Seeker: Call me weak-minded then.

Jeneticist: Maybe we can help.

Seeker: Never mind. I don't want to derail the discussion with my personal issues.

Stargazer: Well, I feel like we're getting to be friends. You can talk to us if you're going through a tough time, Seeker.

JazzyPlum: I second that!

FarfromHome: They don't speak for me.

SquidHead: Every party needs a pooper, that's why we invited you, FFH.

Jeneticist: I wasn't trying to form a support group, but there's no reason we can't do both. Talk about aliens *and* boost each other when we need it.

Seeker: Thank you. I'll keep that in mind.

Stargazer: Getting back to the photos, if Seeker doesn't want to go into detail right now, I'm wondering if you work at an observatory, J.

JazzyPlum: Oh good question! I'm curious too.

Jeneticist: That was the dream, but right now, I'm an adjunct professor of astronomy at a community college. I also do some online math tutoring to pay the bills.

Seeker: Then you're interested in the sciences.

Jeneticist: Definitely. I really only tap my creative side when I'm applying biological knowledge to try and predict what type of life would arise on what type of world.

SquidHead: Oh, that's so fun! I actually wrote a simulator that helps with the probability. It's like Spore, but for aliens. And I haven't released it.

JazzyPlum: [Shut up and take my money.gif]

Stargazer: 🛸

Jeneticist: Uh, you've been holding out on us, Squiddy. As your extremely loyal pals, why don't we have beta-testing privileges?

SquidHead: Are y'all really interested?

FarfromHome: I will probably regret saying this, but...yes. Absolutely. I want to play your "evolve an alien" simulator.

Seeker: Honestly, so do I. It sounds fun.

SquidHead: Okay, here's the link. You can download files for Linux, Windows, or Apple.

Jeneticist: I'm so excited about this game! Uh, can you romance the aliens by any chance?

Stargazer: An excellent question.

SquidHead: It's a simulator. I haven't written any dialogue or storylines.

Seeker: I'm curious to see the science behind the algorithm. You based it on biological data?

SquidHead: Absolutely.

JazzyPlum: I love Spore! Already downloading.

FarfromHome: As am I.

Jeneticist: Me too! I'll be back after playing a bit.

3
JENNETTE

I CAN'T BELIEVE I'M HERE.

Rellows, Utah greets me with a lime-green sign: WELCOME TO RELLOWS. A colorful UFO rotates on top of it, and I'm mildly amazed that nobody has stolen or vandalized the installation. Lights sparkle in the distance, houses full of people who live here year-round. GPS guides me smoothly to the motel on the other side of town. The glowing UFO says RELLOWS INN, and a marquee letter sign underneath reads: EARTHLINGS ACCEPTED. ALIENS WELCOME. NO VACANCY.

The parking lot is quite full, even though Space Con officially kicks off tomorrow. It takes over the whole town, and I can't wait to experience *everything*. I park my car and hop out to survey the motel. It's been painted recently, a pastel seafoam green, and there's a mural on the side depicting aliens arriving in a starburst of rainbow colors. The building is cement block, L-shaped with rooms facing the parking lot. I head for the office on the right; it's a small space with a desk, a couple of chairs, and an honest-to-God beaded curtain that separates the front from the back.

The door jingles as it closes behind me, and a round little old lady pops out from the back. "You caught me eating my macaroni and cheese!" she says cheerfully.

"Sorry about that. I'm checking in. I'm in the Jupiter room, Jennette Hammond."

"What a pretty name. My aunt shared it. Pity about her. Such a pity."

Uh.

If I ask what happened, I'm afraid she'll tell me. Judging by her expression, it must be something horrible. I'd rather not know.

The office is delightfully kitschy, full of signs with amusing slogans. *"Too Alien for Earth, Too Human for Outer Space." "I Hope Aliens Believe in Me." "The Sky Is Not the Limit."* And my personal mantra of eternal hope: *"Aliens Are Out There, Be Ready."* Everything here is carefully curated, creating a vibe that welcomes people like me. Smiling slightly, I wait while she searches through a pile of papers on her desk. There doesn't seem to be a computer anywhere in the reception area. How fascinating.

"Here's your paperwork," she declares triumphantly.

They take reservations online, but it seems like everything else is done on paper. Just as I'm wondering if she'll do something weird with my credit card like photocopy it, she produces a tablet with a card-reading attachment. I've seen vendors at cons use these before, so I swipe it and show her my ID, which she hands back after a brief glance.

"You print out your reservations?" I ask.

"Just the form for you to fill out with your license plate info."

Oh, I've done this at other hotels. I provide the info and sign off on my authorization of charges, and then she hands me a weighty key with a Jupiter key chain. Okay, that's adorable.

"There are maps of the area in the rack. Water and coffee are available twenty-four seven. Ice and vending machines are in the outbuilding near Room 20. Oh, you'll find a few brochures for local restaurants in your room. Enjoy your stay and let me know if you need anything."

By coincidence, I've parked closer to my room, Room 16, than the office. I unload my bags and lock up, then make my way to the suite that will be mine for the duration of Space Con. I unlock the door and realize the photos didn't do the place justice. The walls are mostly gray, with an accent wall behind the bed done in stripes that roughly match Jupiter's tones. Though the furnishings are minimalist and IKEA-inspired, they allow me to focus on the little decorative touches.

The art is a blend of paintings and actual telescopic photos of Jupiter, along with some space-themed objects like a rocket ship telephone. I even like the padded armchair that must have time traveled from the seventies to achieve that shade of burnt sienna, matching the bedspread and curtains to an impressive degree.

There's a mini fridge and a microwave next to the desk, which gives me some options. I don't need to eat out for every single meal, though I probably will. Underfoot, the carpet is plush and gray, old-fashioned shag. I'm both pleased and relieved that the theme doesn't continue in the bathroom. It's the usual motel beige.

All told, it's nicer than I expected and very clean.

I stash my suitcases in the small closet and stretch, rolling my neck and shoulders. It was a long drive, and I'm tired, but I'm also hungry and wired, so close to meeting everyone that I can taste it. I also didn't come all this way to hide in my room.

Before I do anything else, however, I text my mother.

Me: Made it to the hotel safely. Getting some dinner.

Mom: Thanks for letting me know. Send pics if you spot any famous people.

Me: I will.

Mom: Have fun!

A remarkably efficient exchange. This is also why I prefer to text. My mom receives proof that I'm not stranded in a ditch. I don't spend forty minutes hearing why every life choice I've ever made is a terrible mistake. Really, it's a win-win for both of us.

Just in case, I check the chat, and sure enough, there are messages from JazzyPlum and SquidHead. Like me, they've arrived and are making plans to meet up at Bob's Diner. Based on the time stamp, I can catch them if I get in the car now.

I don't take time to second-guess myself. After running my fingers through my wavy hair and making sure I don't have smudges on my face, I rush back to the car.

It's a mile and a half to the diner, which is packed at this hour. They went by the book for the diner atmosphere with plenty of chrome, red vinyl, black-and-white floor tiles, and tiny little "jukeboxes" at each table that play mood music at a low volume.

I've never sent any candids, so I'm wondering how I'll recognize Jaz or Squid. Then my phone pings.

SquidHead: I'm sending a pic. Don't judge my lack of hair.

OMG, so nervous.

I scan the restaurant and spot a lanky bald man. He's the tallest person I've ever met, at least six-foot-six and maybe more. I'm pretty sure this is the right person, but then I'm positive when he produces a squid-faced tentacle alien plushie from behind his back.

A woman converges on us then. Jaz is in her late thirties, with short hair in a pixie cut. She has light brown eyes, golden skin, and a winning smile. She's got a table for four already. I wave both hands in excitement, trying not to be a total dork as I rush over.

"Jaz?" I say cautiously.

"Jen?"

"Yes!"

I stand there grinning ridiculously for a few seconds, and then she says, "Are you a hugger?"

And I admit, "Normally, I'm not, but I kinda want to hug *you*."

Jaz beams. "Me too! Let's do it."

It's a quick one, just a little squeeze, but something about it feels odd. I don't have any time to linger on that impression because as we pull back, she turns to the man waiting patiently to be acknowledged.

"Squiddy!" Jaz exclaims.

We check preferences and then exchange another round of awkward little hugs. Then I sit down to Jaz's left, letting Squid take the right. I feel like dancing in my chair like a little kid; that's how happy I am to be meeting my online friends in real life.

"First," I say. "Are we sticking to online nicknames?"

Jaz taps her fingers on the Formica tabletop, seeming to think it over. "To be honest, I don't much like my given name. So I'd rather be Jaz. If that's okay with everyone else."

"Definitely!" I glance at SquidHead. "How about you?"

"Much as I enjoy this guy…" He makes the plushie dance on the tabletop. "My name is a tad less embarrassing. It's Tad, by the way. And yes, that was a little joke."

"Jen works for me, both ways. Short for Jennette."

The waitress hurries over with a harried smile, clad in an iconic pink diner dress with ruffled white apron. I think I've seen this uniform in multiple eighties sitcoms. "Did you decide what you want? Or do you need another minute?"

"I haven't even looked at the menu," I admit.

Jaz adds, "Give us five minutes, please. We're just getting settled."

"I'd love some iced tea if that's an option," Tad says.

We add our drink orders quickly and the server jots them down. "Coming right up."

The menu offers typical diner fare like burgers, chicken tenders, and patty melts. I decide on a Reuben sandwich as Jaz and Tad debate the merits of the Tex-Mex bean burger versus the mushroom Swiss melt. I'm hungry enough that everything sounds good. When the waitress stops by again, we place our order. Watching a man devour perfectly golden french fries lightly dipped in ketchup, I let my mind wander a little. *So hungry.*

Suddenly Tad says, "Oh, there he is now." He gets up and waves, impossible to miss at his height.

"Wait, who's joining us?" I ask.

"Seeker!" Jay says. "Did you miss that part of the convo?"

Oh my God. I didn't plan for this tonight. I should have changed my clothes and put on some makeup.

I'm not *ready* to meet my online crush right this second.

4
SEEKER

I'M ALWAYS NERVOUS WHEN ENTERING a new environment.

Will technology keep me safe?

And where is the nearest exit if it malfunctions? Pausing, I memorize the escape route before I move away from the front of the diner. The other humans have shared identifying markers about themselves in the communication hub, and I recognize SquidHead first, exceptionally tall and entirely lacking in cranial fur. He lifts an appendage tentatively as I thread my way toward them.

Two female humans are present. Based on qualifying characteristics, one of them is JazzyPlum. She is slight with short cranial fur. The other woman is Jeneticist. There is no explanation for my certainty, but she feels familiar, possibly because we've been chatting privately outside of the group. She is the smallest of three, but also the roundest. Humans come in all shapes and sizes.

As I move toward them, I ready my explanations. I don't have any belongings other than what I'm carrying with me, but I have gleaned enough of their consumer culture to grasp that they will find that strange, so I should dodge any discussion of what I own and refer to a practice called "minimalism" if they become insistent.

"You must be…" The male hesitates, tilting his cranium to assess me thoroughly.

"Seeker." The one who isn't Jen seems to have no doubt who I am, which I find curious.

In our chats, I've given no clues regarding my appearance, mostly because the technology I developed is inconsistent. Due to differences in brain chemistry, I might look different to Jeneticist, JazzyPlum, and SquidHead. If they compare notes, they'll find it strange. The camouflage isn't meant to withstand prolonged scrutiny; that's why I've spent the last 363 days in relative isolation.

And why I'm risking my safety to meet the beings who kept me sane and grounded during the loneliest and most difficult period of my existence.

"And you're Jeneticist?" I guess.

"Jennette. Jen works." She gets to her feet, showing teeth.

Human smiles are deceptive. Some Terran mammals display teeth for aggression, but that's not the human custom. It's a welcoming demonstration, a promise that they won't use those teeth in a hostile fashion. Not that I think they could do much harm with them. Their chewing apparatuses are generally blunt and square, more akin to the mouths of herd-grazing herbivores than dangerous predators.

"And I'm Jaz," the other female says.

"Sit down, take a load off," SquidHead invites. "I'm Tad, by the way."

"Tamzir. But you can call me Seeker. I'm used it."

Everyone settles at the table. The vacant seat is across from Jaz, between Jen and Tad, who studies me with an expression I can't scan. "Is that derived from Arabic?" he asks.

"I have no idea how my parents found my name," I say truthfully.

That's because there is a consecration ceremony and then the gestational parent embarks upon a period of isolation and deep meditation so that their subconscious mind can provide the answer. What they experience during those moments is private and sacred, and they emerge like an insect from a chrysalis, profoundly changed by the experience. I can't share any of that information or a single true thing about my lived experience. I suffer a surge of wrenching melancholy.

Ah. It seems it's possible to be lonely among other beings as well.

"Well, I like it," Jen says. "It has a lovely ring to it."

"Thank you."

"Are you hungry?" Jaz asks. "We already ordered, but—"

"I'm fine. I ate before I came over. I'm here because I wanted to be social."

Dodging meals with humans will prove difficult. I'm subsisting on protein drinks I've sourced after carefully analyzing the ingredients and contents. It's suboptimal, but I can't be too selective. My own food ran out a long time ago.

"Some water then?" Jen offers.

I incline my head gratefully. Intensive study of humans via their entertainment programs has taught me the basics of their body language, though I still don't understand how, when, and why I should move my appendages when I speak. There doesn't seem to be a standard in this regard. Gestures are personal and instinctive, it seems.

"So where's everyone staying?" Tad inquires.

"I'm at the Rellows Inn," Jen says at once. "In the Jupiter room."

Jaz displays excitement in the form of a controlled twitch movement. "Wow! I tried to reserve there after you invited us to meet you here, but they were already booked up."

"I got lucky," Jen admits. "There was a cancellation and I snagged it."

Tad says, "I borrowed my brother's camper. Hooked it to the back of my car and brought my lodgings with me. I'm out at the RV park outside town."

"That's genius," Jaz says. "I'm at a standard motel, but I felt fortunate to get a room at all. I had no idea the competition was so fierce! It's worse than Comic-Con."

Jen turns to me, seeming intent on including me in their conversation. "What about you, Seeker?"

I refrain from acknowledging that I don't plan to stick around. In the most literal sense, I am passing through. My emergency beacon ran out of power a while ago, and I haven't been able to adapt it to communicate with local tech. So far, anyway. I'll keep trying.

To leave, I may have to repurpose technology from 97-B. Some asset hoarders are trying to assemble ships capable of reaching the lunar surface, but their designs are lackluster, and they seem to explode more than successfully launch. It's a baffling waste of supplies, but it might be my only hope. According to my research, there will be an attempted launch on the coast in four days. With such a concentration of technology and resources, perhaps I'll be able to scavenge something I can use.

I am weighing my options, but I cannot tarry indefinitely, simply hoping that my situation will improve.

But they're all staring, waiting for an answer. "I found a tiny place online, but it's only for a couple of nights."

Put kindly, it's more of a storage facility than a residence. There's no area for food preparation and the sleeping area is elevated, tucked beneath the roof. Hygiene facilities appear rudimentary. But it doesn't signify. I'll be leaving soon anyway.

"It must be grim," Tad says. "Well, you can crash with me for the rest of the week if you want. If this is like other cons I've attended, we'll only be there to sleep and wash up."

Jaz asks, "Do you have an extra bed?"

"I do! The dining table turns into a bunk."

"How fascinating," I say.

"Oh, it's a clever design." Tad shows enthusiasm, judging me interested in mobile lodgings such as the one he's using.

The conversation hits a lull when another human trundles up, overladen with a shocking number of dishes. I would help her, but my companions show no willingness to assist. Their customs seem strange to me. One can only provide aid if there will be compensation involved? I don't understand that mindset at all.

They do appear to appreciate her service, at least.

"This looks fantastic," Jaz says.

"Thank you so much," Jen adds.

Tad can't tear his gaze away from his meal. "You're an angel. I'm starving."

She pauses, taking a second look at me. "Whoa. I can't believe you're here. In person! Batman is my favorite superhero!"

I've had this happen a couple of times before. Usually, they think I'm some celebrity. And if I let her continue, she'll make the rest of the table overly curious. "I'm not famous. I just look like…" *Whoever you think I am.*

"Oh. Sorry about that. Anything else?"

"Just some water," Jen says quickly.

Kind of her. Since I don't eat in public, I wasn't certain of the request protocols. I can safely consume water, and hydration is important for many body types. In fact, I have only encountered one being for whom water was toxic. On an interesting evolutionary track, he was. It would be incredibly difficult for him to find pure liquid hydrogen. Of course, he wouldn't have been able to adapt to the levels of oxygen in this environment, even with respiratory therapy.

"Coming right up!" the server says.

"I wonder which Batman she thought you were." Jen frowns, tilting her head. "You don't look like *any* of them, to be honest."

Tad glances up from his plate. "Have any Black actors played Batman?"

Jen blinks, seeming confused by the question. "Uh—"

"So we're missing FarfromHome and Stargazer," Jaz cuts in.

I have the feeling she interrupted to save me, but I'm unsure why I have that impression. Tad returns to eating as if he hasn't received sustenance in a long time. Since he's quite elongated, perhaps he metabolizes food more rapidly than a smaller being. "I wonder what they're like," he mumbles around a mouthful of food.

"Chew and swallow before you speak," Jen suggests.

"Oops. Sorry. I didn't have lunch. Or breakfast."

"Why not?" Jaz asks.

"I was driving."

Jen laughs. "Oh, you're one of *those* men."

"What sort?" he asks.

Jen and Jaz share a look, then Jen does a low, gruff voice. "'Can't stop. Driving. Can't eat. Driving.'"

Tad grins a bit, showing only a hint of teeth. "That checks out."

"I wouldn't have thought that about you," Jaz says.

"How well do we really know each other?" I ask, conscious that I'm keeping a huge secret. It felt ironic at first. Now I'm just a bit sad that I can't tell the truth.

"Everyone wears masks," Jaz puts in.

She nibbles at the edges of her meal, seeming...hmm. I don't know how she seems. Human faces are interesting to me and mobile, certainly, but I don't always understand what I'm seeing, despite many hours logged studying them like an observational scientist. But now that I'm paying closer attention, Jaz doesn't appear as emotive as Jen or Tad.

Jen nods. "It's because we want people to like us and not realize that we're all secretly bundles of hidden anxiety."

"What are you anxious about?" Tad asks. He's devoured most of his food already.

I sip my water. It has an unusual tang, metallic.

"I was *so* nervous about meeting all of you in person." For some reason, Jen glances at me when she says this.

If I'm reading the situation correctly, she wants reassurance. Which means I only need to be honest. "Truly? But I've wanted to meet you for a while. And you're everything I hoped you'd be and more."

PRIVATE CHAT
OCTOBER 26 | 19:29

[Jeneticist has joined the conversation]
[Seeker has joined the conversation]

Jeneticist: Hey, I hope you don't mind the private message.

Seeker: Not at all. Is something bothering you?

Jeneticist: No, but I've been thinking about what you said before. About how you're feeling. And I just wanted to check in. But I didn't want to do that in the main chat.

Seeker: You're concerned about me?

Jeneticist: I am, but I don't want to be nosy.

Seeker: It would only be intrusive if I requested you to desist and you persisted.

Jeneticist: So this is okay?

Seeker: I'm pleased that you care about my well-being. It's... been a while since that was the case. I've lost touch with so many.

Jeneticist: Totally get that. I had one group of friends in high school, but we drifted. I made new ones in college, but then everyone scattered after graduation. I still talk to some of them online, but they all think I'm a bit weird, frankly.

Seeker: I question their discernment. To me, you seem like a person of uncommon wit and sensitivity.

Jeneticist: Gosh. You're making me blush. 😊

Seeker: Is that good?

Jeneticist: That depends on your intentions.

Seeker: I just want to communicate with you. And the others, of course.

Jeneticist: Now that we have the private chat going, feel free to ping me anytime. I can listen if you need a friendly ear or we can get to know each other better.

Seeker: I'm looking forward to that.

Jeneticist: Me too. 🐹

Seeker: There's nothing particularly wrong. I just feel cut off.

Jeneticist: A bit trapped, maybe?

Seeker: That's more accurate than you know.

Jeneticist: I think we all feel that way sometimes. I don't want to be teaching Astronomy 101 to students who are only there to complete the science prereq.

Seeker: If you could be doing anything else instead, what would it be?

Jeneticist: Do I have to be realistic with this answer?

Seeker: No. I said anything.

Jeneticist: The nerd in me wants to say that I dream of traveling on an alien ship, but I'd be super scared.

Jeneticist: I don't cope well with changes in my routine and being that far from my family would suck. I might be open to leaving my hometown someday, but not my solar system.

Jeneticist: So...I want to meet some aliens without leaving Earth!

Seeker: An intriguing answer.

Jeneticist: You think so? To me it seems like I've already limited myself a bit.

Seeker: There's nothing wrong with knowing yourself well.

Jeneticist: Wait a minute, I'm supposed to be cheering *you* up! Making you feel less isolated and whatnot.

Seeker: You have. 😍

Jeneticist: Careful with those heart eyes. I might think you're flirting.

Seeker: Hmm. I can neither confirm nor deny those allegations.

Jeneticist: Tease. Gonna do another run in Squiddy's game now. It's so strange. And fun!

Seeker: I wonder if your alien would like my alien...

Jeneticist: 🤭

5

JENNETTE

MY HEART FLUTTERS.

He didn't just *say* that, right? With no preamble. Yet it doesn't feel like a line or a come-on, like bullshit he's trying to see if he's got a shot at a con hookup. Tad shoots him an impressed look and Jaz grins at me, raising her brows.

"My man Seeker with the smooth moves," Tad says. "I need to learn from you."

He seems puzzled. "Learn what?"

Okay, he probably doesn't mean that how it sounded. My pulse steadies as I apply myself to my food. I should have realized he isn't declaring a romantic interest the second we meet in person. That would be weird.

He's a little older than I thought he would be, possibly even forty, but I can't think of a good way to ask. In a friend group, it really doesn't matter how old everyone is, provided they get along well and have a lot to talk about. It only matters if we date, and I admit that's one of my fantasies—that we get together at some point. I steal another surreptitious look, admiring his shaggy dark hair, touched with silver at the temples. His face is long and narrow, with a strong jaw and nose. His eyes are deep brown. If I saw him without knowing who he was, I probably wouldn't spare him a second look.

The silence is a bit extended now. I think Tad is surprised that Seeker doesn't get the joke, but I've been in his situation. Sometimes I don't get humor that's obvious to other people. Jaz is on her phone, maybe typing a message.

I answer for Tad. "He's saying he needs help in the charm department."

"Was that a charming thing to say?" Seeker asks. "I was only being honest."

Tad laughs. "There he goes again. I doubt I could learn those instincts in a thousand years. In fact, if there was an Olympic event for putting my foot in it, I'd win the gold every time."

"I'm sure you're not that bad," Jaz says, tucking away her cell phone.

"We like you as you are," I add.

Tad just shakes his head, making a dismissive motion. "I'd rather talk about the game. You've been playing for a while now, and I've been busy with the day job. So, what's the verdict? Should I think about releasing it?"

"Definitely," Jaz says. "The UI could use a bit of polish, but the overall concept is sound. And fun."

"Maybe there could be more in the endgame," I suggest.

"Like what?" Seeker asks.

"Like a wrap-up regarding what became of the aliens you created? Maybe you could do an 'if, then' sort of algorithm and generate a random outcome based on certain evolutionary paths?"

"They conquered twelve planets before going to war with superior technology and were obliterated?" Tad suggests.

"Exactly. So the game doesn't just randomly end."

"I like that addition," Jaz says. "It *could* use a bit of something when we come to the end of the evolutionary path."

Right now, it just displays a dark screen with the words: *Your alien is fully evolved. Thanks for playing.*

Tad seems thoughtful. "Hmm. I might be able to do something like that, based on the choices that were made during the evolutionary process."

I'm focused on him and Jaz, trying to hide how much I'd rather be staring at Seeker, who appears to be listening with complete focus. I wonder if he stares at his phone like that when we're messaging each other. His dark eyes are trained on me, more than the others.

I can't let myself be misled again. It doesn't mean that he's *into* me, even if he regards me with that deceptive intensity.

Besides, he's too old for me. Probably.

Soon, we wrap up the meal and split the bill. Tad pays and I give him cash, as does Jaz. Then the four of us stand up, preparing to go our separate ways. We wind up outside the diner, and Tad has car keys in hand, but Seeker and Jaz don't seem to have any. He's quieter than I expected, given how much he talks online. Maybe he's like me, better in a virtual setting.

"Do you have a ride?" I ask him.

"I walked over," he replies.

"I need a shower," Jaz says, offering a little fluttery wave. "I'm staying nearby."

"And I'm longing to stretch out," Tad asks. "We can catch up tomorrow after we've rested. Meet up with Stargazer and FFH."

"Sounds great," Jaz agrees.

They both head out, leaving me to offer Seeker a ride. I hope this isn't intentional matchmaking. I'd be so embarrassed if they could tell I have a crush. I try to make this sound casual.

"If you give me the address, I can drop you off."

"That would be very kind. It's been a long day."

I get the sense that he's understating the situation. I don't know why I think that, but he doesn't strike me as someone who complains for the sake of it. "My car is this way. We can put your rucksack in the back."

It's an interesting bag. It seems to be a military duffel, but judging by its age, it can't belong to Seeker personally. He might have gotten it from a relative or thrifted it. He shoulders it easily, so that means he travels light.

"What a lovely color," he says as we reach my car.

Which is how I felt when I found my xB back in the day. "Thanks. I dread having to change vehicles. I really love this car."

"Then why change? Will it become impossible to repair?"

Sometimes he asks questions that make me feel like he's new here. But then, I look for signs of alien life everywhere I go, so of course I'd think that.

"It can be challenging to find parts once they discontinue a model."

If he's never owned a car, he wouldn't know that. People in big cities all over the world go their entire lives on public transit. Seeker might be one of those types. Which explains why he doesn't know about car maintenance or upkeep.

"Oh, I see," he says. "I don't have a driving license or a personal vehicle."

English isn't his primary language, but he doesn't have a recognizable accent. I unlock the car, stow his bag, and we both climb in. Maybe I'm fixating on minuscule details, just as Glynnis says I do. He certainly intrigues me, no doubt about that.

"Give me the address?"

He recites it from memory and I input it into my phone. *Two miles away.* Does that mean he walked all the way there, just to sip water and sit with us for half an hour?

"I hope it's not out of your way?"

"Not at all," I lie. In fact, I'm a mile and a half in the other direction, but I have a car, so it doesn't matter. "Did you hike into town from there?"

I have to know.

"No, I came from the bus station. It wasn't far."

Oh. That means he didn't even stop off at his rental. I tell myself it's not because he was so eager to see me, only that he wanted to meet people before crashing for the night. I slide a glance at his profile as I start the car. Everything he packed for the week is in that single duffel bag? He's not a cosplayer; that much is certain. I envy his ability to travel light.

Rellows is gearing up for the huge week-long party. There are banners everywhere, signs advertising special sales. They don't have a venue large enough to house the behemoth Space Con has become, so it's held at the county fairgrounds with overflow events in various spaces around town. They're talking about building a community center that would have conference rooms and an event hall, but I doubt it would be big enough either. The town can't support a hotel of a suitable size the rest of the year.

"Did you travel a long way?" I ask, breaking the silence as I drive.

"It seemed so."

An odd response, I think. Not a yes or a no. I've only traveled via Greyhound once, and it was the longest six hours of my life. He must've really wanted to meet us to put himself through that. The realization colors my words, and I can't help but feel flattered, even if he came to see all of us, not me personally.

"You can rest up tonight before our adventures begin tomorrow," I say cheerfully.

"Is that a promise?"

Ugh, I'm so bad at this. That sounds flirtatious, maybe even suggestive. But I got my hopes up earlier and it turned out to be nothing. *He doesn't have a crush on you,* I tell myself. *It's not mutual. Unrequited feelings are what you do.*

I finally figure out what to say, the perfect note of lightness. "To have adventures? Absolutely. We can sample all the delights Space Con has to offer."

"As long as I'm guaranteed more time in your company," Seeker says seriously.

My silly heart flutters. Again.

6
SEEKER

"DO YOU WANT TO MAKE plans to meet up tomorrow?" Jen asks.

"Let's do that."

In the enclosed space of her personal vehicle, Jen smells good. Her scent feels…bright, sparking on my senses like a sunrise. I caught hints of it in the restaurant, but it was loud and overwhelming in there, with so much sensory information that I couldn't focus on her. Now that I can, I experience a frisson of pleasure.

That is probably not an appropriate observation, however. When I have logged another human saying that someone smells appealing, they were usually engaged in intimate behavior. In visual entertainment, it's usually a prelude to exploratory mouth-to-mouth contact. Kissing. My people have nothing similar, but it seems just as intimate as exchanging genetic material. I don't entirely understand the purpose, but perhaps it's to ensure that the prospective partner's alkaline balance is palatable? I remain uncertain why humans would need to taste one another to determine if they're suitable together.

"Do you have a ride to the fairgrounds?"

"I intended to walk," I tell her.

She checks something on her personal communication device.

Her *phone*, I remind myself. Then she turns to me while shaking her head. "Okay, that's way too far. It's four miles! And you'll pay a fortune in Ubers. I'll pick you up tomorrow morning."

"What time?"

"Is nine okay?"

I incline my head. "I'll see you then. Thank you for offering to provide transportation. And…" I shouldn't say this. But I do anyway. "I'm *so* glad to meet you."

"Likewise." She's smiling, her chin slightly lowered.

Jen waits until I let myself into the small residence, using the code that was provided to me. It's a level of advancement that surprises me faintly. I paid digitally for this short-term rental and I have communicated directly with no humans. Yesterday, I received a numeric PIN that will work for the duration of my stay.

Inside, it's even smaller than I expected; it's a rectangle, and it doesn't smell pleasant. The lights work at least, but I'm glad I won't be staying more than a couple of nights. Though Tad offered to let me share his accommodation, I won't be here that long. The two nights I've reserved should be long enough for me to assuage my curiosity about the humans who kept me company during this long, self-imposed exile.

That is the truly uncomfortable aspect.

I made my choices, despite multiple warnings. But I never imagined the tour company would simply abandon me here. I was on time for the rendezvous, but I waited and waited atop that mountain for a shuttle that never arrived. That fresh despair washes over me, the way I felt trudging back down that desolate slope. Being stranded in an alien land is worse than I imagined.

I can't let down my guard or appear too strange. My life depends on blending in.

Though I had a passing familiarity with the customs, I didn't study for what was meant to be a brief sojourn. For the past 363 days, I have paid critical attention to their media and news coverage, trying to assimilate as best I can. But the truth never leaves me—I am alone here. Unwanted. Unwelcome. And if the humans knew the truth, they would destroy me.

I've seen the films. Secret government labs devoted to cutting up aliens and experimenting on them.

But if I'm safe anywhere on this planet, it would be Rellows, Utah during Space Con. Here, people spend the week dressing up as aliens, so I might not even attract a second glance if I went without camouflage technology. Not that I plan to risk it.

I assess my surroundings, judging what I have leased. Since I subsist on the same protein mixture for every meal, it doesn't impact me. I'm getting low on the powder I sourced, but it should last another week if I'm careful.

I deposit my bag on the floor and close the window coverings. This "tiny house," as it was listed on the rental site, sits outside of town and there is plenty of privacy, as it's apart from the main dwelling and fenced in with its own private garden. I won't be out there more than necessary. Much of the local flora impedes my respiratory function, an issue I'd need to address if I planned to stay.

Then I unpack the few things I brought from off-world. My personal tech. Hygiene items that would mystify humans who encountered them. A musical instrument, four pipes conjoined, a gift from my gestational parent, Oona. They wanted me to focus on creating beauty instead of endlessly seeking ephemeral, if electrifying moments. And I planned to do that—to settle down after one last adventure, the most challenging yet.

Why didn't I listen? The representative at the tour agency explained all the risks at length. I just didn't think anything disastrous could happen to *me*. After all, I survived on a planet that was essentially an active volcano, running for my life the entire time. I was exultant when I made the final shuttle off-world, and I've been trying to recapture that thrill ever since.

Everyone I know must fear for my safety by now, but I have no way to contact anyone beyond Planet 97-B. For a while, I tried, using scrap parts sourced from old tech, but range? Range is the problem. If I boosted the signal enough, it would also be scanned by the local authorities, attracting attention I neither want, nor can afford. I'm snared in a wretched trap of my own making.

It's a risk, but I power down the tech camo. There's no need for it in private, and all devices require downtime. It's versatile, adaptive tech; I should know. I invented it. Well, perhaps that's a specious claim, more accurate to say I upgraded from the older versions available and released my update after extensive testing. It's proven popular with scientists who blend in among more primitive life-forms to observe their behaviors up close.

Residual royalties from each use allow me to do as I like without worrying about my next invention. In the Galactic Union, we don't hoard resources as they seem to on 97-B. Once someone hits a threshold of wealth, their assets are redistributed to those who need them. It's a sensible system.

Right now, my biggest fear is that the technology will degrade, and I'll have no means to repair it. Then I'll be helpless. But I do have a plan.

Using the old phone I repaired, I skim the article again. *Billionaire Visionary Poised to Make History.* After a history of spotty launches for the last fifteen years, Owen Lusk has designed and built the most advanced ship in the world. Due to launch for its maiden voyage in just six days, the reclusive Lusk agreed to speak to Connie Brightway regarding his mission. "We'll establish the first Mars colony within five years," Lusk predicted. "And in ten more, I'll have a hundred thousand people in a self-sustaining colony on Mars. I have extensive plans for aeroponics and a specially engineered microbe that will accelerate the terraforming. It may take decades, but Mars will provide a refuge for humanity."

It seems to me that they should focus on fixing the planet they've poisoned instead of squandering resources to steal another. But the relevant aspect of that article is the launch. Is it possible I could find something useful on-site? Building a shuttle from salvage would take a long time, but I might find usable components. The idea poses an incredible challenge, one I'm not entirely sure I can surmount. And I still need to adapt and charge the emergency beacon, or leaving won't do me any good.

If I can access the launch site. If I can fix the beacon. There are so many variables that I don't feel confident about my chances, especially on my own. But waiting has become untenable. I feel so guilty. I told Oona I'd be home soon, that I'd focus on creating beauty.

I swore that I would take one last trip, then stop living with such reckless abandon. To settle down and make everyone proud.

But now I've gotten myself in such a disastrous predicament

that all numerical probability points to me perishing here. I've run so many simulations, and none of them give me good odds at stowing away on that ship. In fact, the statistics indicate the vessel will explode before it leaves the stratosphere.

I'm so tired of living without hope for the future, and I desperately want to see Jen again. It was difficult to go inside my domicile without watching the red glow of her vehicle's receding lights. Seeing that brightness fade felt like the crushing weight of loneliness that only her presence amends. It sounds melodramatic, but she's been a constant ever since she reached out to me privately. Because she was *worried* about my welfare, sensed something awry in my communications.

Not in the sense that I don't belong, although I don't.

But because she cares. Considering how many blessings and opportunities I've squandered, I don't merit her kindness, but I'm starved for it. Her gentleness nourishes my spirit, but I tell myself that I'll only stay for two days. We'll make some memories and then I'll be on my way, because staying here would mean my demise.

I can't exist in this limbo any longer.

PRIVATE CHAT
NOVEMBER 10 | 21:13

Seeker: Are you busy?

Jeneticist: Not at the moment. What's up?

Seeker: Just wondering how you are. Making sure you're well.

Jeneticist: Aw. 😍

Jeneticist: That's sweet! Is it because I've been scarce in the group chat this week?

Seeker: I was a little worried. Normally, you're very...

Jeneticist: Chatty? You can say it. I text more than I talk in real life, though.

Seeker: In person you're more of a listener?

Jeneticist: You could say that. I mean, if I know someone well or really like them, I'll talk more. But normally, I nod and smile. I'm always worried about people judging me.

Seeker: I would say their opinions don't matter, but sometimes they do. For social reasons or matters pertaining to professional advancement.

Jeneticist: Exactly. I'm so glad you get it.

Seeker: I'm a bit of an outsider, but I understand societal conventions.

Jeneticist: An outsider?

[five minutes later]

Seeker: Sorry, I had something to deal with.

Jeneticist: It's okay. You don't have to answer if you don't want to. If it's too personal.

Seeker: No, I want to tell you.

Jeneticist: I'm listening.

Seeker: You could say I've always been...searching for something. And I've never been able to find it. So I substitute experiences for that elusive sense of "yes, this is where I belong."

Jeneticist: Wow. You don't fit in with your family?

Seeker: I think they must be disappointed in me, although they've never said so.

Jeneticist: Maybe not. You seem pretty flipping awesome to me.

Seeker: Do I?

Jeneticist: You're deflecting. Just say thank you.

Jeneticist: That's what I had to learn to do when people paid me compliments that felt untrue or unwarranted. I have to believe they see something I don't and that they're sincere in their praise.

Seeker: That is an astute observation.

Jeneticist: I'm definitely not flattering you.

Seeker: Then...thank you. For seeing something that I don't. 🫶

Jeneticist: Thanks for checking in, by the way. It's nice to have someone reach out, wondering how I am.

Seeker: Is that not the norm?

Jeneticist: It's easy to get caught up in your day-to-day and not touch base with people. I've been grading end-of-term papers and just been buried in work.

Seeker: Is that why you've been quiet in chat?

Jeneticist: Yeah. I'll be done soon, thankfully. Then I get a break.

Seeker: Any exciting plans?

Jeneticist: I intend to talk to you more. Does that qualify? 😊

Seeker: It does. Definitely.

Jeneticist: I was wondering...

Seeker: What?

Jeneticist: Never mind. I'm not feeling brave enough today. One day maybe I'll ask.

Seeker: And I'll be here when you do.

7

JENNETTE

I WAKE UP SMILING.

It's not a surprise, because I fell asleep with a silly grin on my face while hugging the spare pillow to my chest. I've been nursing this secret daydream about how Tamzir and I hit it off in person, how our relationship might develop if he likes me even a fraction as much as I like him. Sure, he's older than I expected, but I haven't clicked with anyone like this…well, ever. And it's not like he's old enough to be my father. That's not the only challenge, though. Long-distance relationships can be tricky.

I might be up for it. If he is. But none of my fantasies can come true if I don't get out of bed.

Normally, I'm slow to get moving, which is why I set multiple alarms on my phone. But it's not even eight and I'm wide awake. Time to partake of the free breakfast in the dining room adjacent to the office and then get ready for what could be the best day of my life. I go out in pajamas and slippers, as most of the other guests have done, and find a simple spread. Cereal, milk, coffee, basic fruit and pastries, a few yogurt cups, a pot of oatmeal, some instant eggs, and bread to be toasted.

I go with yogurt, fruit, and a pastry, then head back to my room. I have less than half an hour to get cleaned up and put on my first costume. But it's an easy one; I'm dressing up as Liz from *Roswell*, which means I can wear normal clothes. I'll just do more makeup than I'd normally wear and change my style to match hers, which means chunky ankle boots, a bracelet, and a gray tank top with my cutoffs. I won't be putting on the leather jacket, however. It's supposed to be hot as hell later.

With speed that comes from practice, I put together the look quickly and grab my backpack and car keys. I can't wait to see Seeker and, even more, to share all the fun of Space Con with him. I hope he's not the type to get intimidated by crowds. I can be a bit nervous too, but it helps that we'll be outside. That should make it easier to find some space if I need it. Cons that are held in hotels and convention centers can be a real challenge.

As I step outside, I send a message.

Me: On my way!
Seeker: All preparations complete for pickup.

Sometimes I wonder if Seeker is like this with everyone or if he's simply prone to communicating with me as if I'm his superior officer on the Starship *Enterprise*. As I hop into my car, I check the urge to respond with a quote from Captain Janeway. I don't know what shows he's seen, and I'd rather get moving.

I drive across town singing along with my playlist. I tend to get obsessed with songs, so I have just a few that I play on loop. It used to annoy people I hung out with, but there's nobody to complain when I play "Shake It Out" by Florence + the Machine twice. "Love Me More" by Sam Smith has just started playing when I reach my destination.

The place Seeker's chosen to stay strikes me as a bit odd—well outside of town, a tiny house separated even from the main property. To me, it looks like the homeowners repurposed a shed, likely to capitalize on Space Con. That little hut probably stands empty most of the time, and then they charge a fortune for this week alone. But maybe he left his reservations until it was too late to get something better. Someone who's new to Space Con wouldn't realize just how chaotic the town becomes. I know because I've wanted to go for like ten years. I have extensive notes in my phone related to all the panels and activities I want to check out today.

Seeker emerges and he strides toward my car, climbing in without hesitation.

In daylight, he looks a little different. The strange thing is, I can't put my finger on the change. His eyes are…lighter, maybe? Not as deep a brown as I thought. And he looks a little *younger* too. That's confusing because, if anything, it would make sense for him to look younger at night, not in the sunlight. Maybe he's in his thirties, not forties? Late thirties isn't such a big gap. We're both adults, right?

I have the oddest sense that his face doesn't look the same, as if there have been minute shifts, cheekbones slightly higher, nose a touch wider. I study him for a beat too long, and he returns my scrutiny with an intensity that makes my pulse skitter.

"I don't know who you are," he says.

I blink. "What?"

"Your costume. I was hoping I could figure it out, but—"

"*Oh.*" That's why he was staring so hard. "I'm Liz from *Roswell.* I have more complicated costumes, but I don't want to work that hard on day one."

Wait until he sees me as an Orion from the original *Star Trek.* Since I don't paint my whole body—just my face and hands—it doesn't take six hours, at least. I favor green tights and shiny boots, a tight minidress, and a bouffant wig. The trick is finding green body paint that doesn't rub off on everything.

"You look happy," he says then.

For some reason, that compliment settles into my chest with a warm glow. It's better, somehow, than hearing I'm pretty or well dressed. Those are cosmetic, superficial observations, but for him to read my body language, my expression? It means that he's interested in me as a person. And he's correct. Actually, I'm *beyond* happy, orbiting somewhere among the constellations, all starshine and jubilation.

"Thanks for noticing," I answer in a warm tone. "You don't like dressing up?"

"Perhaps I'm already in costume."

"Yeah? Who are you dressed as then?" I intend it as a gentle tease, because if I'm pretty sure I'd recognize it if he was dressed up as anyone other than himself. I've consumed a lot of media and entertainment about aliens over the years.

He surprises me by glancing away, angling his face toward the window without responding. Even over chat, Seeker gave me a melancholy impression, and it's reinforced by meeting him in person. To me, he vibes like someone carrying an immense burden, one so profound that it bows his shoulders, but he can't—or won't—share the weight with anyone.

Maybe I'm reaching, inventing reasons why he sometimes seems so sad. Sometimes people have mental health issues that impact their mood. I've talked to him in chat for months, but sometimes it feels like I don't know him at all. At least not the way I want to.

I skip over the pause, changing the subject. "Are you excited for all the cool stuff?"

"I am. What do you want to do first?"

"You'll let me choose our itinerary?" That's so nice. I should mention finding the others, but I'm basking too much in the one-on-one right now, and I don't want to ruin the moment.

"I'm utterly in your hands."

See, just when I think I'm imagining the chemistry between us, he drops a comment like that. My face flushes; I can feel the heat in my throat and cheeks beneath my makeup. Hopefully, he won't notice.

"Awesome! Then let's find a place to park and see if we can make it to the roundtable at the top of the hour. There are supposed to be some unreleased recordings. Never-been-heard-before audio files! We have to check that out."

"Recordings?" A flicker of something sparks in his voice.

I steal a glance from the corner of my eye and realize that Seeker's expression never changes. He doesn't smile. But his *tone* conveys emotion. Something about that puzzles me, but before I can get a handle on it, I make the turn into the county fairgrounds. The lot is already chock full of cars, early birds eager to get started.

"Yeah, I can't wait to hear what they've got." I won't let myself get too hyped, however. I add, "It'll probably be asteroseismology or something."

There are tents erected in addition to the stationary buildings and food trucks at the edge of the lot. It already smells like corn dogs and fried dough, with just a hint of cinnamon and sugar. The idea that you can get a corn dog and churros before going to talk to people who are sure they've been abducted by aliens is rather delightful. Space Con has something for everyone—the types who swear they saw a light in the sky and went somewhere else, those like me, who live for the theoretical aspects, and still others who just want to dress up like aliens, meet celebrities who have *played* aliens, and take pictures with them.

"That's the sound of singing stars."

I shouldn't be surprised he knows that. I smile as I open the car door and grab my bag. "Let's pick up our badges and hit the ground running."

"As you wish."

That *has* to be a *Princess Bride* reference, right? This will be the best day ever.

8
SEEKER

WHEN THEY CHECK THE IDENTIFICATION that I spoofed so I can receive certain benefits while I'm stranded on 97-B, I try not to reveal my tension.

But they only give the card a cursory look, then hand over the "badge" that grants me access to all the joy this festival offers. Beside me, Jen bounces as if she cannot contain her enthusiasm, and once we have our documents, she's off, racing across the obstacle course of bodies and temporary structures. I keep pace as best I can, always aware that if the tech camo fails, I'll be in severe danger.

The roundtable is held in a building on the other side of the property. Most of the seats are taken when we slip inside, but Jen finds us space near the back. Experts are already speaking about the recordings she mentioned as we get settled. The space is airless, and later in the day it will become sweltering. While Jen gazes at the speakers in rapt attention, I study *her*.

She is graceful like a planetary curve, softness incarnate. She is warm tones and gentle laughter. I find her features strange, but less so than I did when I first landed on this world. I have become accustomed to the way humans look, less so to the way they smell.

They're constantly emitting chemical signals, but they don't seem to do this intentionally. To me, their moods shine like colors, and I can't unknow the information.

One of the experts at the front of the hall is desperate and nervous, an acrid tang discernable all the way at the back. Another has indulged in some recreational fumes that cling to their raiment and head fur, dispersing tiny whiffs of rotting sweetness. They give a brief introduction but I don't dedicate my full attention.

The nervous one says, "Without further ado, we'll just play the recording for you. Please hold all questions until the track ends."

A low whooping sound begins, and I still, scarcely daring to breathe.

That's an emergency beacon, similar to the one I'll use if I can adapt it and charge it using local tech. The sequence runs three times and then cuts off abruptly. Around me, I hear humans speculating on what that could have been. They're anatomically incapable of detecting all the tones, and it's rather remarkable that they've acquired this evidence at all. I wonder what they'd say if I confirmed their hope of what it portends.

Yes, this suffices as evidence that there are aliens among you.

"We'll take questions now. Raise your hand if you wish to speak." The expert who smells sickly-sweet recognizes a woman with spirals of brightly colored head fur.

"How did you attain this recording?" she asks.

"And how do we know it's not fake?" someone shouts.

I've noticed that humans skew toward thinking *everything* is fake, probably because they swindle each other with shocking regularity. Like other beings I've known, humans are impulsive and difficult to govern. I collect that's why their society has so many laws.

The anxious one replies, "We received the recording via an anonymous email."

The other continues, "NASA has created sound files by changing digital data recorded by telescopes in space, allowing us to know how a star or a black hole sounds. While we can't guarantee that's the case, we suspect this must be something similar."

A man in a cap waves a limb urgently and is recognized. "Respectfully, there's no way. There's an organized pattern in that file. It's timed and it repeats. I'd be very surprised if it wasn't intentional. Stars don't sound like that at all."

Clever human. He's correct.

I wonder what they'd do if I gave them all the information they claim to desire. Chances are, they wouldn't even believe me. I listen as people expound on theories and argue why those ideas are impossible. The experts provide context for their receipt of the audio file, but I'm more interested in who recorded it, and the how and why as well. It's an interesting discussion in parts, but since I already know the answer to the central question they're debating, it's difficult for me to sustain any lasting sense of intrigue.

I find myself watching Jen instead, tracking minute shifts in her expression. The way she leans forward when a question captivates her. She's far more fascinating than open discourse.

"Did you enjoy it?" she asks as the session ends.

Before I can respond, someone calls our names. "Jen! Tamzir! I was about to message you two! Have you found Stargazer or FFH yet?"

It's Jaz, closely shadowed by Tad. I realize he's the man in the hat who objected to the sound file as a natural phenomenon. I probably should have recognized him, but I was distracted, and I've never seen him in a hat. Also, he was sitting down, which disguises his impressive height.

"Not yet," Jen says.

"This is the first thing we've attended," I add.

"Where are you headed next?" Tad asks.

I glance at Jen. She's supposed to be guiding me around. I have no idea what I ought to be doing here. In fact, it would probably be safer if I hid in my dwelling until it's time for me to travel to the coast.

"Can't decide between 'Aliens in Hollywood' and 'Writing Fan Fiction about Aliens,'" she says, showing her phone to Jaz.

"Oooh, good choices. Do you want to write alien fan fiction?" Jaz asks.

Jen shrugs, but she seems a little embarrassed. "I don't know. I just thought it might be interesting."

"Question: Is the first one about the types of aliens in various films, or are they speculating which actors are actually aliens?" Tad asks.

"I'm interested in both of those panels," Jaz says immediately.

"I think it's the former," Jen replies, skimming the description on her phone. "Yep, it compares some of the most famous aliens in various films."

"We should go get seats," I say.

Jen nods enthusiastically. "Good point! I hate entering a panel that's already started. It's so rude."

I ask out of idle curiosity, "Did you two make plans last night?"

Tad shakes his head. "I guess we're fated to be friends. I saw Jaz first thing this morning and we decided to check out this session."

She nudges Tad lightly. "Let's join them. I didn't have anything concrete on my agenda anyway."

"I'm flexible," he says.

Now our duo has become a quartet. I shouldn't mind, but now that I have only one fourth of a chance at occupying Jen's attention, I feel mildly aggrieved. I'm here primarily because of her.

"Just a sec. I'm texting Star and FFH to let them know where we're headed," Jen says.

She focuses on her phone and then she sets out, threading through the crowd with the same level of concentration that she applies to all tasks. Tad and Jaz hurry after her, which amuses me. Jen probably wouldn't see herself that way, but she's undoubtedly the leader of our little band.

The "Aliens in Hollywood" panel is in a larger building because one of the panelists portrayed an alien in visual entertainment that I haven't consumed. Or at least that's what Jaz is speculating as we find seats. We're early enough to get some together and two more humans rush toward us, signaling with both arms. I cannot discern much about their appearance because they are both in disguise, one blue and sleek, the other clad in armor with many composite weapons strapped to their body. Even their cranial structure has been altered—and in a fashion I find most interesting, as this alien reminds me of the locals in the Tau Ceti cluster.

"Nook neh," the second one says.

Those sounds impart no meaning. I have heard nothing like

that in my time on this planet, and while I struggle to identify what language is being spoken, Jen laughs.

"Nobody here speaks Klingon. You must be FFH."

"Stargazer, actually."

"I'm FFH." The blue alien doesn't step closer or offer a traditional greeting.

"It's surprising to find the two of you together," Tad observes. "You bicker like it's your hobby in the group chat!"

"We just happened to rock up at the same time," Stargazer explains.

"Acquit me of spending more time with this one than I must," FFH adds.

"Yikes," Jaz says.

"That's kind of hostile," Tad points out.

The introductions happen quickly. Stargazer reminds us that her name is Poppy, and it seems she's said it before. I don't recall, but she spends most of her time trying to aggravate FarfromHome. To my knowledge, they haven't given their name yet, online or in person.

"You can call me Ravik," FFH says, as if in response to my thought.

"Is that your Viking name?" Poppy seems to enjoy poking at the least-friendly member of our social collective.

"Shh. They're starting." With a smile, Jen motions everyone into silence, as we're about to start the next round of obsessing over aliens.

This will be the most surreal day ever.

GROUP CHAT

NOVEMBER 16 | 15:10

Stargazer: Here's a pic of a cake I baked for my cousin's birthday! 🎂 🍰

Jeneticist: Is that vanilla?

JazzyPlum: Oooh, strawberries too. This looks so yummy.

Seeker: Was there a party?

SquidHead: How old is your cousin?

Stargazer: She's 21. And just a little family thing. If I could get the writing on top right next time, that would be awesome.

FarfromHome: You should get her something useful instead of encouraging a sugar addiction.

Jeneticist: Ugh. I bet you get people socks, FFH.

JazzyPlum: No way! They definitely strike me as a gift card type.

Seeker: Gift-giving seems like it should be thought-intensive and personal.

SquidHead: Exactly! I never buy something that I would like. I spend a long time figuring out what the other person would love.

JazzyPlum: Aw. I want a gift from you, Squiddy! 💟

SquidHead: Well, if we're still chatting when your birthday rolls around, I'll make it happen.

Jeneticist: OK, I'm curious. What's your favorite gift that you've ever received?

FarfromHome: Who are you asking?

JazzyPlum: Everyone, I think?

Jeneticist: Yep! But nobody has to answer if they'd rather not.

Stargazer: This is easy. My mom sent me to the Scottish Highlands to plant trees during my gap year after high school. It was an amazing trip, and there was no pressure to come home. I wandered around Europe until my visa ran out.

Seeker: Do experiences and travel count as a gift?

SquidHead: In my book they do.

FarfromHome: I'd agree.

JazzyPlum: That sounds like the best time!

SquidHead: This will sound shallow after the first two answers, but my granddad bought me my first car and then he helped me fix it up.

Jeneticist: That's not shallow! It's sweet.

SquidHead: I'm glad you think so, J.

Jeneticist: For me, it's got to be when my high school friends chipped in and bought me my first telescope. I was so happy! I put it on the balcony of my college apartment.

Seeker: And you've been watching the sky ever since.

Jeneticist: Yep. I still have it, to be honest. I've used more powerful telescopes, but I have a soft spot for the one they got me.

Stargazer: Are you planning to answer, FFH?

FarfromHome: I've never received a gift.

JazzyPlum: Are you serious?

SquidHead: Whoa.

Stargazer: Okay, now I feel bad for FFH. Are you okay?

Jeneticist: Let's not jump to conclusions or pressure them to share. Maybe they were raised in a religion that doesn't celebrate holidays.

Seeker: Which one is that?

JazzyPlum: I think Jehovah's Witnesses don't.

SquidHead: Quakers too.

Stargazer: Right, let's give FFH some space. If they wanted to talk about gifts or lack of them, they would.

FarfromHome: I don't need your intervention.

Jeneticist: We haven't heard from Seeker yet. Are you abstaining?

Seeker: No, I was trying to decide. And I think it's the song my mother wrote, celebrating the occasion of my birth.

Jeneticist: I'd love to hear it.

Seeker: Perhaps one day.

SquidHead: This has been great, but I'm starving.

Stargazer: Me too! Talk to y'all later.

JazzyPlum: Take care!

9

JENNETTE

UGH.

Colin McFarland might have played one of the sexiest aliens ever on *Nebula Odyssey*, but I'm sick of the man. He's monopolized the panel, talking over scientists who have interesting information that pertains to the fictional aliens being discussed. I love that sort of thing, people with technical expertise offering it to paths of possibility, showing others how something like this could come to pass, like a dome city on a greenhouse planet or a city in the clouds populated by bird people.

I've been incredibly conscious of Seeker beside me. And something about his proximity resonates as…unusual. It's not the fact that I have a crush on him, either. But he's not warm. Not in the way I expect. And it goes along with the surprising stillness of his expression. I don't understand why my brain is obsessing over little inconsistencies with someone I like so much.

When the talk finally concludes, I navigate to the front of the room, intending to compliment the biologist who offered some truly fascinating and memorable theories regarding potential paths for evolution. She might get a kick out of Tad's game, actually. But before I can say a word, Colin McFarland strides around the table with a huge smile.

"You must be here for me," he declares.

"What?" Why does he think that?

I try to signal Dr. Patel but she's already packing up her belongings. She doesn't realize that I came to tell her that her portion of the presentation was one of the most technically impressive and creative takes on the potential for alien life that I've ever seen.

"No, I—"

"Don't be shy, honey. Normally, I charge twenty bucks for photos, but I'll let you take a selfie with me for free. Come here." He wraps a meaty arm around my shoulders, dragging me against his side.

Wow. Colin smells. Not in a good way, either. It's a fermented cocktail of booze and old sweat, with just a whisper of baby wipes, as if he made a half-hearted attempt to swipe his pits before he showed up. He practices a few smiles before setting on a particular shit-eating grin and tilts his head toward mine.

Please, someone save me.

I should elbow him in the side and get him to let go of me, but I freeze up in tense situations, and I loathe being stared at. If I make an issue of this, Colin's fans will come for me on social media. I can imagine the vitriol now. As a weirdo in high school who only had a few close friends, I have powerful, paralyzing memories of how it feels to be hated online. I endured some social media attacks and ostracism, and I'm not eager to revisit that portion of the program.

Reluctantly, I get my phone out. Dr. Patel is gone, off to her next panel or an ice-cold lemonade. I'm so disappointed that I could cry.

Suddenly Seeker is next to me. "Are you all right?"

Colin answers for me. "She's great. Getting some one-on-one time with her idol, right? How many people will get this lucky today?" He drops his voice. "Play your cards right and you could get my spare room key too. How's that sound?"

My right hand curls into a fist. I can't bring myself to tell Colin off, banshee-shrieking at top volume, but I don't *want* this photo. Not even slightly. I hold out a hand to Seeker, though I'm not even sure what I'm trying to do. He pulls me away from Colin and I let out a breath. His support makes me a little braver. Just enough.

I take a breath and protest. "That's enough. Don't be gross."

People who love *Nebula Odyssey* would be so disappointed to learn how disgusting McFarland is, quite unlike the smooth-talking alien charmer, Darak Sai. Without waiting for a reply, I march out of the building while the rest of the group hurries after me. I feel a little shaky because I hate conflict, but sometimes speaking up is necessary.

Jaz reaches me first. "Are you okay? That looked—"

"Did he just sexually harass you?" Poppy demands.

I hesitate. "A little bit?"

"There's no such thing as just 'a little bit,'" Tad says angrily.

"You have to report him," Poppy says.

Much as I don't want to make a big deal of this, she's right. If he did that to me with fifty people looking on, how does he behave when he's alone with a starstruck fan? My stomach roils, but I'm committed. Space Con has signs posted about what we should do if we experience something that makes us uncomfortable, so I follow the procedure and find a volunteer in a yellow polo shirt. Her name tag reads, *Hi! I'm Sarah, and I'm here to help.*

"I need to file a report," I say softly.

She escorts me to the small tent set up for handling such issues. The day is heating up, and people swarm around outside, heading off to have fun. I hate that I'm holding up the group and spending more time on that asshole, but it has to be done. It takes almost an hour to complete the process. She's extremely supportive and documents everything.

Sarah wears a grim expression. "We won't invite him back," she promises. "And I'm so sorry he did this. We're getting in touch with his management and canceling the rest of his appearances here."

"Wow." I honestly didn't expect such swift action. "Thank you."

"I hope this didn't ruin your experience at Space Con."

"Not at all. I appreciate how you're handling this."

The others are all outside, waiting. Seeker seems to have worn a track pacing. He volunteered to come inside with me, but I opted to face it on my own. And I feel…stronger. That's the only word. Even if something leaks and I end up being reviled on social media with people saying I'm nowhere near cute enough for Colin to creep on me, I don't care.

"You okay?" Poppy asks.

"Yeah. They're terminating the rest of his sessions," I say.

"Wow. That's awesome!" Poppy punches the air as if we've won a major victory.

"I didn't realize what it's like," Tad says in a sober tone. "I mean, you hear things, of course. But I'm a big goober, and nobody bothers *me*."

"Is it customary to have such attention forced upon you?" Seeker asks.

"It happens more than it should," Poppy admits.

Ravik has been very quiet. "I do not care for this place at all," they finally say.

I'm not sure if they mean the tent where I made my report, the fairgrounds, or Rellows in general. Heck, Ravik might feel that way about Earth. Sometimes I do too.

"I stopped attending cons for a while because it was so bad," Jaz says.

"It tends to be famous people now," Poppy adds.

Since I've never been propositioned before, I can only nod. This was awful, and I could use a hug, but I'm not close enough to anyone here to ask. At least I don't feel shaky anymore, and I can take comfort in knowing I did the right thing.

"Let's move on," I say then. "I don't want this to ruin the rest of the day."

"They're selling box lunches now. Anyone else hungry?" Tad asks.

I could eat. And I don't have a panel circled for this brick of time. Tad forges ahead, clearing the way for the rest of us as he navigates to the parking lot where all the food trucks have set up. It's surprising there are so many of them, but from what I've read, business owners drive hundreds of miles to participate.

Only three of us get a meal, however. Jaz says she's not hungry, and the box lunches aren't vegan, so Ravik passes as well. Seeker makes no explanation, so it's just Tad, me, and Poppy tucking into the deli sandwiches. There are also chips, fruit, and big cookies. We luck into a picnic table nearby, recently vacated by a woman with four kids, all of whom are wearing glittery alien antennae, and two of whom are sobbing.

"I never understood why people drag little ones to this sort of thing," Poppy says. "They won't remember it, and it's so much work."

"Maybe she couldn't get a sitter?" I suggest.

"Could be," Jaz agrees.

Tad tilts his face toward the sky. It's even hotter now, unsurprising since this is July. His bald head is turning pink, and he dons the hat he had on earlier. Seeker and Ravik remain unaltered, though Jaz doesn't seem to notice the heat either. She's on her phone, sipping now and then at a bottle of water. She's a very dainty, delicate person, the kind who makes me feel awkward in my own skin, like I'm altogether too much. It's nothing she's done, of course. Just my own insecurity.

I'm determined not to let this hiccup ruin the day.

As I finish my food, I say, "I've been making all the decisions. Someone else pick a panel, okay?"

"Does it have to be a panel?" Ravik asks.

"Not at all," I say quickly.

"Well, there's a game demo that starts in half an hour. I'd love to get a closer look. But I don't want to force anyone…" Tad's voice trails off.

The game must be science fiction if it's being featured here, but to be honest, I don't play a lot of them. There are three other things I'd rather be doing, but I don't want to be the dissenting voice. Happily, Jaz says, "I'd like to go with you."

"I'm out," Poppy says.

"Probably not as good as your game," Ravik says, startling everyone with the praise.

Somehow, before I work out exactly how, we break off into twos. Poppy is going with Ravik, though they don't seem that interested in her company. And Seeker stays beside me, watching me with an intensity that makes me nervous and excited in the same breath.

"What's next for us then?" he asks, as if we'll be inseparable for the rest of the con.

Lord help me, I want that *so* much.

10
SEEKER

I HAVE NEVER EXPERIENCED ANYTHING like this crushing fury.

The sensation blazes hot and cold by turns, a sickness I can't purge until I act on it. However the authorities discipline the human who made Jen smell of fear and discomfort, it won't be sufficient. I must do *something*.

Jen has been unfailingly kind to me. She deserves another level of restitution. And when she excuses herself to "use the facilities," I make my move. Delving into my bag, I produce a small piece of tech that will do the job. I adjust the setting swiftly; this is a risk, but Colin McFarland deserves worse. I follow the crowd and the smell; his staff are trying to explain the sudden cancellation of his autograph sessions, claiming that he's been taken ill and regrets being unable to meet his wonderful fans.

With my acute hearing, I detect him nearby, hidden in one of the smaller tents. He's cursing whoever reported him, talking to someone on the phone. "Well, fucking *find out*. I want to know who screwed me over. They won't get away with this! It's ridiculous."

I step inside silently and unleash the nanite, small enough as to be undetectable to humans. It arrows to McFarland without hesitation and I glide away, out of sight but still within audible range. It won't hurt him, but it *will* scramble his customary filters. I hear the thud of him dropping the phone midconversation, and then he stumbles out of the tent.

"Who do you bitches think you are?" he yells.

A few people turn. From the murmur in the crowd, they recognize him. A few have their phones out, ready to capture a scandal unfolding in real time.

"None of you deserve my time, you get that? You're a bunch of disgusting, desperate lowlifes! And—yeah, so what if I grab your asses? You love that shit. You go home and get off to it. If you didn't want me touching your tits, you wouldn't put them in my face and constantly tell me how much you love me."

His team rushes him and one of the large security types focuses on shutting McFarland up, but he's still shouting. "You're asking for it! You all secretly want it!"

"Posted, you son of a bitch!" a young-looking human says.

"Canceled," another adds.

As I take silent satisfaction in the outcome, Jen joins me. "What's going on?"

Before I can reply, a human in a striped costume is eagerly replaying the video. "Check this shit out. He totally had a meltdown."

Jen watches the clip with wide eyes. "Holy crap."

"I know, right? I put it on social with hashtags SpaceCon and DarakSaiSayBye."

"Okay, that's clever." She swaps amused looks with the other human. "Give me a sec, I'll share it."

"Got fifty shares already. By the end of the day, the whole world will know how trashy he is."

Delicious satisfaction suffuses me. The tech camo can't update my emotional state, however. That's one of its limitations. While it makes me appear human, it can't process subtleties or emotional nuance.

"It's too bad," Jen says with a sigh. "His character was so awesome, you know?"

"Totally. Enjoy the rest of your con!" the fan in the striped costume says.

As the other human departs, Jen turns to me with a conflicted expression. "Do you think I contributed to his breakdown?"

"Don't be absurd." *I did this.* "Perhaps he has some chemical dependency? I understand that famous people often struggle with addictions."

My tension eases when she appears to accept that as a reasonable explanation. "Good point. I can't say I'm sorry that they're hustling him out of here. But I hope he gets the help he needs."

"You're a genuinely kind person," I say.

Jen ducks her head, waving away my statement with both hands. "Don't be silly. Anyway, it's your turn to pick our next activity."

She will find it strange if I have no preference. And I cannot admit that I traveled all this way primarily to meet *her*—to carry away some bright memories because she illuminated the darkest moments of my exile. So I scrutinize my phone and pick a session that I think will interest *her*.

"Alien innovations that could be real?" she says. "Nice! I had this one on my list. Let's go check it out."

She already seems to have memorized the map and leads the way with confidence. Being surrounded by so many humans is a trifle disconcerting, and the smells are overwhelming. Not just bodies but emotions too—and ambient odors as well. I gaze up at the sky and nearly lose track of Jen in the crowd. Rushing, I catch up just as she darts into a long building. Our event is in one of the smaller spaces at the back. Folding chairs have been set up, and they're about half full when we pick our seats in the middle, but on the aisle.

"I don't like being completely hemmed in," Jen whispers.

The panel starts with introductions and credentials. I don't bother learning them, but I do listen to the earnest discussion. There's amusement in the debates regarding which inventions could be possible with enough time, resources, and research. I know of no civilization that has perfected transporters. Inorganic matter is easier, but when you add complex biological systems to the equation, the results can be…messy. To say the least.

A special guest in the panel displays photos of some perfect spheres that hit the planet as part of a meteorite dubbed 2N2 by the scientific community. Most fragments burned up on entry, but these artifacts are unusual for their symmetric shape, unusual durability, and intriguing composition: beryllium, lanthanum, and uranium. They're also quite beautiful, in hues of gold and copper with a deep shimmer in their cores.

And I know what they are.

The Norelians use these as a power source. They're also the ones who left me stranded on 97-B. So these humans are speculating with fascination over what amounts to used-up batteries, put in terms they'd understand. I keep quiet for obvious reasons while they go back and forth on the topic.

My mind returns to the launch that's happening soon. I wish the news covered more of what's used in human ships, but they're quite proprietary about their technology. They don't share information freely and data is kept secure. I would need to do some major intrusion to find out, but it might be worth the effort, if I can acquire parts for a shuttle. But how many launches would I need before I'd have enough?

A good while later, the moderator says, "That's it for formal discussion. Let's open to some Q&A in the last ten minutes."

People in the audience line up to ask things, which I find intriguing. I can't imagine wanting to know something so badly that I'd get in a queue over it. Though I do enjoy mental challenges, I prefer finding my own solutions. For me, that's part of the satisfaction.

A human male of middling height asks the first question. "Dr. Lovell, you've taken a lot of criticism for entertaining the possibility that these objects have an interstellar origin. How do you rebut the claim that these came from Earth as a result of coal consumption?"

"I've written an article on the subject," the scientist says in a curt tone. "And I did a side-by-side analysis, but the most relevant aspect is that the chemical composition simply does not match. It's not coal ash."

"That's just what they want us to think!" someone calls out.

Jen laughs softly.

Dr. Lovell relaxes. "Precisely."

More and more, I wish I could tell Jen who I am. And what I know.

How would she react? In my experience, all beings possess the capacity to be mercurial. It frightens me to imagine her turning from me in fear. Or worse, betraying me those who mean me harm. What if this is a truth she can't process?

As we attend more workshops, I weigh the risks and wonder if I'm mentally unwell for even contemplating taking such an immense risk on someone I haven't known for that long. Months in human terms, digitally. Days here in Rellows. It's such a fragile foundation, so how can I be certain she won't react badly? But I can't leave without help.

In fact, I'm not certain I can leave at all.

With effort, I compartmentalize these grim thoughts as I follow where Jen leads. She doesn't realize that's what I'm doing, I think, but I take pleasure in her eagerness, her boundless joy. Perhaps I've become desensitized to smaller delights through my habit of chasing colossal adventures. I will savor these moments and replay them later for more detailed review.

We pass from the small tent to a shocking blaze of color on the horizon. That is something I will miss about 97-B. The sky is glorious. I understand the science behind this rare beauty, the spectrums of light and the wavelengths and the high clouds that create the brightest hues. I perceive more than humans do, so it's even more majestic to me. I've been to many worlds and seldom felt the need to stare at the sky as I do here.

I admire the colors and spectrums and feel faintly homesick for the beauty I took for granted and the family I may not see again. When I quarreled with Oona, when I said that I might never come back, I didn't mean it. They were words spoken hastily and from a place of pressure. And now, from me, my family has only silence. That last interaction haunts me. I didn't know it would be the last communication we had.

"I wonder where everyone else is," Jen says.

She follows my gaze when I don't respond and takes a deep breath, a slight smile curving her mouth. This means she's happy, entirely present in this moment. "Wow," she whispers, her hand gently brushing against me.

It must be confusing when that happens. The tech camo can't create sensory impressions; it can only confuse her about what she's experiencing. Her mind will whisper that there's something...not right about it, but her eyes can't help her resolve the conflict.

She's not touching skin, at least not in the way she understands it.

My body temperature conforms to my surroundings, not a set median. If the external temperature drops low enough, I'll fall into a resource-conservation state similar to the reptiles on this world. Humans call that brumation. I read a fascinating story about a human who had a turtle as a domestic companion and thought the creature had perished. They interred it according to local customs, and three months later, the animal crawled out of the ground and came looking for food. They must have been so startled yet so delighted, a true amalgamation of emotions.

That's how I feel about Jen, brightness illuminating my bleak prospects.

"Incredible," I agree.

But I'm not looking at the sunset anymore. I care about this human woman so much more than I expected for such a short personal encounter. This isn't how I imagined it would be. I thought I'd satisfy my curiosity and feel certain that it's time to move on. Now I don't know what to do, or how to handle these feelings. Romantic bonds do form among my people, but seldom swiftly. And they are forever, so I must be cautious here.

Yearning shimmers through me as I regard her silently, steadily. Though I wondered earlier, I'm now certain I can trust her. There is no rational explanation for why I feel so sure that she's the last person who would betray me or allow me to come to harm. Yet I'm positive of it as I've been of little else in this life. The question haunts me:

Should I tell her the truth?

PRIVATE CHAT
NOVEMBER 24 | 09:18

Seeker: [Birthsong.mp3]

[five minutes later]

Jeneticist: Oh wow, this is enchanting! Is this a pan flute?

Seeker: Similar. It's a local instrument.

Jeneticist: I love this. It sounds like elves are gathering in a clearing about to celebrate the spring solstice.

Seeker: ...elves?

Jeneticist: Fantasy elves, not Keebler elves. Their soundtrack would be completely different.

Seeker: 😂I'm glad you like the song anyway.

Jeneticist: I do! Is that you playing?

Seeker: How did you guess?

Jeneticist: Just a feeling I had. Since it's an original written by your mom, I didn't think it would be a professional recording. Thanks for sharing it with me.

Seeker: Oona wants me to focus on music.

Jeneticist: Oona?

Seeker: My mother.

Jeneticist: Ah, I see. In a professional capacity?

Seeker: Correct.

Jeneticist: You don't want to?

Seeker: I had other things I was more interested in, but I'm starting to regret some of my choices.

Jeneticist: It's never too late to make a change!

Seeker: Do you really believe that?

Jeneticist: Yep. That said, it's easier to think about something than to make a big move. Inertia is a powerful force.

Seeker: Is that why you're still at the community college and tutoring online?

Jeneticist: Ouch. I'm in this picture and I don't like it.

Seeker: I don't follow. What picture?

Jeneticist: 😲

Jeneticist: Seriously, how do you NOT recognize that meme? Have you been at a research station in Antarctica or something?

Seeker: I'm not online all the time, so what? 😞

Jeneticist: Sorry, sorry.

Jeneticist: I'm avoiding the question by picking at you.

Seeker: It's fine.

Jeneticist: No, it's not. And you're right. That's why I haven't tried to get a better job.

Seeker: I'm not prone to sticking to what's comfortable, but there's nothing wrong with doing that.

Jeneticist: That feels like a pity pat.

Seeker: What now?

Jeneticist: A pity pat. "There, there. You're doing the best you can. Bronze star for effort."

Seeker: I have no idea what you're talking about.

Jeneticist: Never mind! Let's talk about you.

Seeker: What about me?

Jeneticist: Big question time. Have you ever been in love?

Seeker: As in, have I met someone I thought I wanted to share my life with for all time?

Jeneticist: Yeah. Exactly.

Seeker: I don't think so. What about you?

Jeneticist: I've had two boyfriends and one girlfriend. But it wasn't serious, and they lost patience with my "alien obsession."

Seeker: Then it wasn't right. Anyone who cares about you will accept all aspects.

Jeneticist: I hope you're right.

Seeker: Usually am. But I have some work to finish. Talk to you soon. 🛡️

Jeneticist: 🛡️

11

JENNETTE

SEEKER IS STUDYING ME.

But before he acts on whatever he's thinking about, Jaz runs toward us through the crowd. Tad trails her in deceptively casual strides.

Jaz is carrying a few extra bags; she must have found the exhibition hall. I'm curious about what she's bought, but she's practically vibrating with excitement. "Did you hear about the party? Well, party and costume contest."

"And space-themed karaoke!" Tad says with a broad smile.

"It will be 'Space Oddity' and 'Rocket Man,' forty-seven times," I predict.

But it's not a complaint, just a certainty about my own people. I belong to the Dork Tower collective, after all, and we're nothing if not consistent. I consider my own options. What would I sing at special space karaoke?

Hmm...

It has to be "We Must Believe in Magic," assuming the song's featured in the list. I first heard it watching reruns of the *Muppets* as a little kid, and the charm of the song stayed with me, sort of haunting, and despite its simplicity, it also felt epic somehow. Listening to it made me think of a crew out among the stars, setting off on an amazing voyage.

"I texted Ravik and Poppy," Jaz says. "They're meeting us at the venue."

We make our way through the crowd as a group with Tad cracking jokes and Jaz encouraging him. Seeker is quiet, enough that I'm a little worried about him, but I don't want to draw attention to his mood. If he wanted to confide in us, he would.

In passing, the smell of kettle corn makes me hungry, but I can hold out for one more session. The biggest building at the fairgrounds has been decorated to contain everyone who's interested in attending. I decide that the cash bar is genius, as are the snack stands set up at regular intervals. Part of the floor is dedicated to dancing, and people are as bad at it as you might imagine, except for the guy doing the robot. They've decorated the place like a spaceship with shiny silver streamers and strobing lights. Left to my own devices, I'd probably flee the scene immediately.

But I want to stay with everyone a bit longer. And by everyone, I mean Seeker. After all, I try not to lie to myself. It's counterproductive.

Poppy finds us first. She's not with Ravik, which doesn't surprise me at all. They might have already bailed on the social aspects—no, there they are, carefully weaving through the excited, noisy bodies nearby. Their alien look really is seamless, impressive in every detail.

Poppy's Klingon warrior prosthetics are probably starting to annoy her by now. I love dressing up, but the more complicated the costume, the quicker I want it off. I've designed incredible, involved outfits, but at peak, I wore each of them just long enough to be judged and then immediately started disrobing. Textures often bother me to the point that I could start yelling my head off, a huge issue when you'd prefer to be invisible.

"Everyone have a good day?" Poppy asks.

"Totally," Jaz says.

"Chitchat later," Tad urges. "Let's fill out our request slips and get in line for karaoke. There's a big crowd! We might not get a turn before they shut down for the night."

"Oh no," Ravik intones with mock dismay.

That makes me laugh, but I'm siding with Tad. I follow him happily, ready to throw myself into the fun. Dance like nobody's watching, isn't that what they say? For once, I can handle the attention, as this is the kindest audience I'll ever encounter. They're cheering raucously for the guy currently emulating Shatner's spoken-word rendition of "Rocket Man."

They don't have the song I wanted in the playlist, but I find "Weird Science." That'll do. I scrawl my request and hand it to the volunteer who's managing the karaoke session. Seeker appears at my shoulder.

"May I participate in your performance?" he asks.

Such a formal way to ask to sing with me. I'm already nodding, though. "Of course! Do you know the song?"

"I am reviewing it now," he says.

Like all of this is super serious, life or death, not a bit of convention fun. But he's an intense person, very focused on doing and saying the right things. It occurs to me that this probably stems from feeling socially awkward, and do I ever relate to that. I wish I could say, *Stop worrying, these are your people.* But it's a lot easier to say that than to internalize it. I know that personally as well.

We're treated to a terrible version of "Across the Universe," a decent "Mr. Roboto," and an amazing cover of "Silent Running." For a moment, we're all quiet, and then the whole room sounds off with applause and sincere cheering. The slight, timid guy with the unexpectedly incredible voice smiles, pushes his glasses up on his nose, and then acknowledges the praise with a tiny bow before rejoining the audience. I'm wondering who will have to follow that when they call Poppy and Jaz.

Jaz sounds like an angel; I think Poppy is lip-synching. If she's singing, it's not very loud. I don't know if "Defying Gravity" counts as a sci-fi song, but it has gravity in the title and it's popular. More importantly, Jaz is killing it. Since she plays violin, I shouldn't be surprised she can sing too, but I can scarcely breathe for how good she is. I'm riveted...and so is Seeker. Though he hasn't paid Jaz particular attention before, now he can't look away.

She presses one hand to her chest, absolutely nailing the crescendo, and she even ad-libs some gorgeous runs, nothing excessive. These embellishments are perfectly controlled, not over-sung, as they say on the TV singing competitions I've watched now and then. When she wraps up, everyone screams their heads off.

"Whew," the volunteer says. "I had no idea we had so much talent at Space Con! Let's hear it for Jaz! And Poppy."

Another round of applause, though it's obvious who stole that round.

"You sang beautifully," Seeker says.

Well, crap. Now I'm jealous. I don't want to be. It's petty. But I am.

Jaz smiles. "Thanks. Normally I'm too nervous to open my mouth onstage, but everyone here is so nice."

Poppy doesn't seem to mind. "I'm just glad I didn't embarrass myself."

"I don't want to sing now," Tad mumbles.

"You already put our names down," Ravik points out.

And the volunteer calls them up. No escape. The two of them are beyond awkward at first, and for reasons known only to Tad, he's put them down for "Intergalactic" by the Beastie Boys. But to my surprise, Ravik steps up and brings the swagger necessary to sell the song. Tad seems stunned but he manages to halfway match the energy and soon they're bouncing around, giving attitude and dropping the lyrics with conviction.

"Ravik! You didn't tell us about your secret ambitions to be a hip-hop star," I joke.

They give me a look, but I'm not sure how to interpret it. "Have we concluded the noisy portion of the evening's entertainment?"

"When you say shit like that, it makes me want to yell in your ear," Poppy says. She seems to enjoy poking at Ravik in person even more than she did online.

Now everyone else has gone from our little group, and they totally killed it, albeit in different styles. I'm even *more* nervous when they call our names. I don't want to be the weakest link. Despite my doubts, I head to the front with Seeker beside me. The first strains of "Weird Science" start and there's no screen with a bouncing ball for me to follow along with either. There's only a sea of unfamiliar faces.

Luckily, this is a song that demands enthusiasm, not precision.

Seeker watches me instead of the audience, taking cues from me. When I do a little dance on the line about hearts and hands, he mimics my silly moves, matching my enthusiasm. And on the next verse, when I point at someone in the crowd, inviting them to shout the chorus, he does the same. We're totally in synch.

We may not be the most talented, but it doesn't matter—we're having a blast. And so is the crowd. Their laughter and cheers echo back to us, energizing me. By the end, they're chanting "weird science" along with us. I sneak a look at my partner, but he is as impassive as ever, his face giving away nothing of his emotions. I wonder why he doesn't smile, even when he seems to be having fun. At least, I *think* he likes doing things with me.

The DJ says, "Let's give these two a hand!" and I impulsively take a bow.

Seeker does too, then follows me back toward the group. "I have never done anything like that before," he says.

"I hope I didn't push you into—"

"No. I wanted to share the experience with you." He pauses as if contemplating his next words. "There is some pressure for excellence in such matters where I'm from."

"Ah, the achievement ladder. I know people who won't do *anything* if they're not great at it."

"But…enjoyment matters," he declares.

"It definitely does." And Seeker makes everything better. "I was kind of nervous. I couldn't have done it without you."

We share a look, and I wish I could say that I see his eyes sparkle or some visual cue that means he's feeling this too. But instead, his face is still and static, almost like a photo. I frown, confused by what feels like mixed messages. The others rush in our direction, lights flashing as the next performer starts singing.

"You two have mad chemistry!" Poppy calls, waggling her eyebrows beneath the ridges of her Klingon forehead ridge.

"Definitely," Tad says. "Anyone else hungry?"

"I could eat," I admit. It's been a while. But the food trucks have all closed for the night, so there are only snacks on-site now. I add, "Should we go get dinner? I can take four people in my car if anyone needs a ride."

That said, folding Tad into my back seat will be tough. But he shakes his head. "We should just meet up. Pick a restaurant?"

Most places are staying open late, special Space Con hours, so we don't need to worry about all the eateries closing their doors at 8:00 p.m. We get out our phones and agree on a comfort-food place that looks good. Seeker follows me as we split up to find our cars.

A happy sensation washes away my minor pang of jealousy from before; I'm mildly irritated with myself over that. He's not my boyfriend. I have no right to feel any kind of way over him liking how Jaz sings. *Everyone* loved how she sounded, judging by the reaction. It's not like Seeker was alone in thinking she's good.

"Are we coming back to the party?" he asks.

"I'm not sure. Depends on how long it takes to eat, how late it is. Do you want to?"

"It doesn't matter, as long as I'm with you."

12
SEEKER

JEN STOPS WALKING, CENTERED IN a spill of golden light from one of the con's aerial illuminations.

"Okay, you've said things that sound flirty before, and I really need to...just ask. Are you doing that on purpose?"

"Doing what?" *Flirty*, what does that mean?

I quickly sort through what I've learned from watching their local entertainments. I believe it's when someone shows signs that they'd be receptive to a romantic overture. Jen thinks I'm attempting to initiate courtship with intent to mate? The idea should be laughable, but then I remember the purity of how I feel when she's nearby, how she keeps the loneliness at bay. And the way I thought she shone, before.

Perhaps it's not entirely incorrect. If I lived here. If I planned to stay. But I don't know how to respond because I don't intend to be here long enough for my answer to matter, even if I don't know how to leave. I'm still weighing the idea of infiltrating the upcoming launch to loot their tech, but the logistics are daunting. I'm not a seasoned rebel; the rules I've broken never pertained to sneaking or thievery.

"I like you," I finally reply.

Though I'm not an expert in human emotions, I note how her face changes, mouth tilting downward. "That covers a lot of ground."

I can offer her this much reassurance; honesty costs me nothing. "I enjoy spending time with you. But I won't be here long. If I would be, then—"

"You *are* flirting." Her expression shifts again, brightening. Seeming delighted, she raises her head so the waning sunset makes her eyes sparkle. "You're saying that you're into me, but you'll be traveling soon, right? And you can't get into a long-distance relationship."

That's the perfect excuse. She has *no* notion just how long-distance that relationship would be. "Exactly."

"But you're open to a con fling?"

I have no inkling what that entails and I can't open my phone to search the term. Before I can reply, she unlocks the car and gets in. I join her, feeling more confused than I've been since coming to maturity. But if Jen's offering it, this "con fling" probably isn't bad.

So I shut my door and then reply. "That is accurate."

She laughs. "Only you would react so nonchalantly to this." But she doesn't sound as if that's a bad thing. "We can see how things go. I'm enjoying our banter an awful lot, and I want to make sure we're on the same page about it."

To extrapolate from context, she wants to continue with the understanding that it cannot lead to a permanent association. So long as that remains true, I can enjoy these moments with her. And not analyze each word that we exchange. I can continue saying true things without being alarmed over how she will receive them.

"We are," I say then.

"Awesome! I was so afraid that I had a crush on you all by myself."

She wasn't certain that it was reciprocal?

I thought I had been painfully obvious in my partiality, my preference for her company. Not that I don't find the others agreeable enough. But they're not Jennette. She is the one who consistently reaches me even when my sadness has become too much to carry, when my isolation is too much for one being to bear.

She drives with casual cheer, singing along to music I do not know. I remember sharing my birthsong with her and the way she made me feel afterward. She is the best part of being stranded on 97-B and I wish—

No. There is no point in wishing for impossible things.

We arrive at the restaurant a little while later, and since we paused to chat, the others have gotten a table already. They have two chairs reserved for us and Tad is already ordering food. The dining establishment is spacious, but they have attempted to mitigate this but arranging odd articles around, like a stuffed mammal dressed in clothing and rectangular artifacts all over the walls. Amber light spills from tinted coverings, perhaps an attempt to embody their bold yellow sun.

"Over here!" Poppy bounces to her feet, signaling wildly, as if we could miss her.

"I got us an appetizer platter," Tad says. "Cheese sticks, wings, and potato skins."

"Can we not have the whole potato?" I ask.

Jen laughs as she sits down. "You never miss a beat, do you?"

I wasn't joking. For all I know, there's some reason they only eat the skin. But instead of persisting with the inquiry, I pretend I've succeeded at witty repartee and bask in their amusement as something I intentionally achieved.

Jaz draws Ravik's attention when she compliments them on their musical style from karaoke earlier. "I had no idea you were so gifted," she says.

"Gifted." Poppy snorts.

Ravik ignores her. "Mimicry is an underrated talent. I simply observed how the original performers behaved and mirrored it."

"Being here is cool as hell," Tad says suddenly. "But it's so surreal. Last week, I hadn't even seen photos of all of you. Now we're just hanging out, about to dig into some grub."

As he says this, a huge plate of food is deposited on the table by a woman wearing apparel that matches the colors on the walls. Fascinating. She says, "Let me know if you need anything else," and rushes off before we could possibly ask. Is that intentional?

I have noticed humans enjoy turning odd things into challenges. Such evidence is all over their entertainment, so it wouldn't surprise me to hear that we must also compete to receive food or liquid refreshments in a timely fashion.

"Surreal," Jen agrees.

But she sneaks a glance at me when she says this. Is that because of our discussion?

"How do you feel about con flings?" I ask the table in general.

Poppy chokes on a sip of her icy beverage. "Excuse me?"

Her reaction concerns me. Have I said the wrong thing? Jen slowly slides down in her chair while the others try to mask their reactions.

Tad recovers first. "I mean. I don't go looking for it, but if someone tells me they're into me and wanting to have a bit of fun, I'm not *against* it."

He steals a look at Jaz when he says this, but she's sawing at a brown thing on her plate with complete focus, carving it into tiny bites. I underestimated how difficult it would be to share social occasions with humans and never ingest anything. They're quite communal with their consumption, more than I expected.

Ravik remains silent, the least communicative member of the group, in chat or in person. Jen dips a tube of food into a pot of red and takes a bite. She's not looking at any of us, but I can see that her color has changed, a deeper, ruddy hue on her cheeks and ears.

Now I'm certain I've done something wrong, but she didn't tell me it was a secret.

Poppy makes a noise in her throat. "You're all making *me* find out, I take it? Fine, I can't resist. There has to be a reason you asked. So who is it? Which one of us caught your eye, huh?" She pauses, narrowing her gaze as she skims the others. "If it's me, I'll just say that's a pass. You're *way* too young for me."

At that, Jen lifts her head and stares at Poppy. I don't recognize a lot of expressions, but I've been memorizing them, and this one matches the illustration for confusion perfectly. Her mouth is pulled in and the top of her face is crinkled.

"You prefer silver foxes?" Jen asks.

Now I really don't know what they're talking about, and Poppy is confused. I can't let them discuss how I look. Time for a diversion. "Could I have a cheese stick?"

I can't eat this thing. I don't know what I'll do with it when I have it, but Jen is quick to put one on my plate, along with some of the red stuff. I swirl it around and try to decide how to dispose of it when I notice. Jaz is quietly dropping bits of food on the floor. Once might be an accident. Twice? Definitely not.

Now she's looking at me. Her expression doesn't change.

"Bathroom," she says.

I get up immediately. "Me too."

In fact, my people can go days, in human time, without needing to eliminate. Our bodies are efficiently designed. But I'm certain Jaz wants to get me alone and I need to find out why.

I follow her through the restaurant to the back hallway and she wheels on me as soon as we reach relative privacy. "Get it together!" she snaps.

"What?"

"I've never been so embarrassed in my life. You're making it so obvious that you're not *from* here that I don't know what to do. I can't keep covering for you! Humans are simple, not stupid. They'll notice!"

The enormity of what she's saying washes over me. "You're from the agency? Are you my contact? My ride?"

Jaz lets out a trill. Not human laughter, but close. "Please. I've been here for almost ten of their cycles. I clocked you as soon as you sat down. Your tech isn't as good as mine."

Well, that's a strike squarely in the self-esteem, considering that

I'm using my own upgrade. Yet hope wars with disbelief and I have to ask, "Then do you have an exit strategy?"

Her response flummoxes me. "Why would I want one? This is my home."

GROUP CHAT

DECEMBER 3 | 19:39

Stargazer: Time for another game!

Jeneticist: Sounds fun. Another virtual icebreaker?

Stargazer: I'll wait until everyone replies before explaining the rules.

Seeker: Here.

SquidHead: Me too.

JazzyPlum: I have rehearsal in forty-five minutes. I only have half an hour.

FarfromHome: I make no promises.

Stargazer: Yay! The group's all here.

Stargazer: I'm giving you two choices. Don't say I don't take your feelings into account. The first option is Finish My Sentence. One person starts and someone else finishes. I'll assign random numbers to determine the order.

Jeneticist: And the other option?

SquidHead: Better not be Never Have I Ever.

Stargazer: It's not! Could be worse, though. Confessions is the name of the game, and you share something you've never told anyone before. It shouldn't be anything illegal or that will hurt anyone involved in the game.

Seeker: Do we vote then?

Stargazer: That's the fair way to do it.

JazzyPlum: What if we tie? There's an even number of us.

Stargazer: I'm not voting to avoid a tie.

FarfromHome: That is an apt solution. I choose Finish My Sentence.

Jeneticist: Confessions.

SquidHead: Confessions redux!

Seeker: Finish My Sentence.

Stargazer: It's all down to you, Jaz.

JazzyPlum: I'm going with Confessions. I'm curious what Squiddy will say.

SquidHead: I'll try to make it juicy. 😷

FarfromHome: I would like to go first and get it over with.

Stargazer: Go ahead, fun sponge.

FarfromHome: This group is the closest I have come to friendship. I'm not sure if it counts.

Jeneticist: OMG! Of course it counts. We're friends, I promise. Feel free to contact me privately if you ever want to talk.

Stargazer: Wow. Much as I expected to be snarky, I agree with Jen.

Seeker: Likewise.

SquidHead: This was a great idea, Star. I already feel closer to you lot.

JazzyPlum: I'm here if you need anything, FFH.

FarfromHome: Why did I agree to play this game?

Jeneticist: I'll take a turn. When I was in fourth grade, I tried to leave a note on Nolan Kazinski's desk. He was in the front row. I fumbled it.

Jeneticist: The paper ended up under the teacher's desk. Mr. Mandell read it and then kindly lectured the class about how it's normal to get a crush on your teacher, but that sending love letters is a step too far.

Stargazer: Classic! Did anyone ever find out it was you?

Jeneticist: Sadly, yes. Ashley Clemmons saw me and told everyone I wanted to marry Mr. Mandell. They called me Teacher's Pet until I changed schools in junior high.

SquidHead: Aw, that sucks. Did you ever confess to Nolan?

Jeneticist: That's a negative. He dated Ashley Clemmons all through high school.

Stargazer: That's probably why she targeted you. You were coming for her man!

Seeker: I'm sorry that happened.

FarfromHome: Quite a protracted punishment for a small mistake.

Jeneticist: It's fine. I'm over it. ☺

JazzyPlum: I'm up next. I need to head out soon. I'll read everyone else's confessions later.

SquidHead: Go for it.

JazzyPlum: I have no family to speak of. I'm grateful to have all of you in my life.

Stargazer: Whoa. Not even distant cousins or whatever?

JazzyPlum: There's no one.

Jeneticist: You've got us!

SquidHead: 💯 We're here for you.

FarfromHome: What they said.

Seeker: I haven't spoken to my family in a long time, so I understand a little. And yes, that's my confession as well.

JazzyPlum: Sending hugs, Seeker. Maybe you can patch things up eventually. And I'm heading out. Sorry to miss your confessions, Star and Squid.

SquidHead: Later, Jaz. Hmm. I guess I'll go with the time I tried to rush a fraternity and got rejected. I really wanted to fit in, but they laughed in my face when I showed up and said, "Uh, no, bro. The computer science building is that way."

Jeneticist: You were too good for them!

SquidHead: Oh, they were put on probation for hazing. And I did make some friends in the computer lab.

Stargazer: You're better off. Those guys are assholes.

FarfromHome: What made you want to join?

SquidHead: Parties, mainly. And to hang around with cool people.

Seeker: You've met us now, haven't you?

Stargazer: And without binge drinking! So I guess it's down to me. I failed fifth grade. My parents divorced and I stopped doing my work.

Jeneticist: Did it have a huge impact on you? Being held back, not the divorce.

Stargazer: I was small for my age, and I'd actually started kindergarten when I was four, so after flunking, I was the same age as other kids. It turned out to be a good thing. It made my parents start paying attention to me again too.

Seeker: Thanks for telling us.

FarfromHome: This game wasn't bad.

SquidHead: Yep, I'm glad we did this. I'm off. Trivia night at Café Cruz!

Jeneticist: Have fun, Squiddy.

13

JENNETTE

I STARE AT THE WALLS without seeing all the kitsch and the license plates.

They seem to have plates from all fifty states and a few from Canada too. The Prince Edward Island one is pretty with the flags and the picture of Parliament. I'm mentally rating all the plate designs when Jaz and Seeker return from the bathroom. I'm not sure what they said to each other, but he studies her throughout the meal and she's carefully not looking in his direction. I can't explain the atmosphere change, but nobody else seems to notice.

Maybe I'm overreacting, inventing a tension that isn't there. I have no reason to be jealous; we've barely even agreed that we're flirting, let alone anything more definite. But I recall how he admired Jaz's singing, and I stifle a sigh.

"Anyone got plans for tomorrow?" I ask.

"Totally," Tad says, producing his phone. He flashes the checklist on his notes app with a sheepish expression. "I also have panels and sessions cross-referenced by probable popularity, so I know how early to get there. First, I want to check out..."

My attention wanders, and I don't check back in until the waitress returns. We order, chatting until the food arrives.

Since I'm distracted and Seeker can't stop looking at Jaz, Poppy and Tad dominate the conversation. I do try to hold up my end, but I'm too conscious of the new weirdness to focus. I expect to figure out the source of the friction, but I can't. And that bothers me.

Jaz never eats much. She rearranges her food with artistic flair, but in high school, I had a classmate with an eating disorder. That's what she did to hide her anorexia.

Did Seeker notice? Maybe he called her out on it.

Then again, I've clocked him refusing food as well. In his case, judging from where he's staying, I think he might be on a tight budget. He can't afford all these meals out, so he orders water and attends to be social. He's probably got cans of soup or cereal bars in his luggage, so he'll have that later.

Finally, Ravik says, "It's late now. I don't want to go back to the party."

"Me either," Jaz agrees. "I need some downtime."

Tad sighs. "Might be a missed opportunity, but it's only running another forty-five minutes anyway. And we have the rest of the week to cut loose."

"We need to pace ourselves," Poppy puts in.

I nod. "That's true."

I've attended a few cons before, though not Space Con, and if you dump all your energy into the first few days, you'll have nothing left for the rest of the week. Then you'll end up like I did, overwhelmed and hiding in your room because you can't face another round of small talk. Panels take the pressure off, at least, because you're passively absorbing information, so there's no need to talk if you choose not to.

Soon, we split the bill and Seeker accompanies me to my car. I take comfort in knowing that whatever happened privately with Jaz, he's still leaving with me. Damn. I really want to ask, but I'm afraid he'll lie. Things have been okay, apart from my colossal embarrassment when he asked the others if they're into con flings. Honestly, I'm a little mad about that. When you add in the bizarre dynamic with Jaz, maybe I let my imagination run away with me.

Still can't figure out what he was trying to achieve. I don't think he's a player, but some of his behavior is definitely raising red flags. Yet I don't want to spend the drive in awkward silence, so I'll keep trying.

"Did you have fun?" I ask, unlocking the car doors.

"I did. It was a long day but an enjoyable one."

Such an impersonal response. It's clear that he's thinking of something else, and I can't shake the certainty that he's hiding something. Yeah, I've been talking to everyone online for almost a year, more than six months in the group chat, but how well do I *know* any of them? I start the car, for the first time conscious that I might be alone with someone I can't trust. Dammit, I don't want to regret any of this or to be forced to admit that Mom and Glynnis had a freaking point.

"I'm glad," I say softly.

"Why are you afraid? You haven't been before." The question comes out of nowhere, showing unnerving insight into my emotional state.

Now I have his full attention, and I'm not sure I want it. While I'm ostensibly in control of the vehicle, I'm aware that I'm driving him out of town. Once I stop the car, anything could happen out there. I doubt the homeowners would notice if he overpowered me and dragged me inside.

I could deny it and act like I haven't noticed anything wrong. But I don't see the point in lying. While I have my doubts about him—and maybe Jaz too—I don't want to believe he's a threat. He won't hurt me, right?

The truth it is. Please don't let me regret this.

"You're keeping something from me," I say. "And it's big."

"Why do you assume that?"

I might as well go all in. "Something happened between you and Jaz at the restaurant. The two of you were different when you came back to the table."

"Even if that's true, it's not a reason to fear me. I'm unaware of any social contract that requires me to disclose all my personal interactions."

"Wow. Okay. You can say whatever you want to Jaz, but it's uncool to pursue both of us, unless everyone is on the same page. I thought we…" I let my voice trail off, aware that I've made some huge assumptions.

That he's completely into me and that he doesn't feel the same way about anyone else. But he's correct. Even when we had that moment and he said he likes me, then we discussed having a fling, he didn't promise it would just be me. Us.

Well, shit. I feel like such a dork.

"We're communicating at cross-purposes. I did learn something startling about Jaz, but it's not my information to share. And while I do have a secret also, I need time to think."

"Wait, now I'm confused again."

What did he learn about Jaz? Maybe she's ill?

That might explain her lack of appetite. For all I know, he heard her throwing up and she admitted to having cancer. There are so many possibilities. Seeker could be playing head games with me, but why would he bother? When I consider the vibe between them tonight, it doesn't seem like sexual tension.

Good grief.

I can't even have a con fling without complicating it. My last girlfriend left because I overthink things and suck the joy out of life. Poppy has called Ravik a fun sponge before, and I felt bad for them. And I guess I'm a bit insecure too. I always wonder what people see in me. That gets old after a while.

"Did you think I had made romantic overtures to Jaz?" Seeker asks.

I mumble in reply. "You both were so weird after going to the bathroom together."

"That's because of what she said. It was quite a bombshell."

Now I feel like a nosy jerk. Why can't I just take things as they come, be more like Tad? He seems like a happy, easygoing guy.

I could tell Seeker that my last boyfriend cheated on me with one of his students and it's why I have trust issues. But I don't want to admit that. I'd rather keep quiet about the worst of my relationships. And *now* I understand why he's holding back. He probably wants a fresh start too, not to dump his baggage in my lap and challenge me to keep liking him. That's what you do when you're trying to drive people away instead of letting them learn about you organically.

"I'm sorry I made it weird," I say. "I'm prone to overanalyzing everything."

"You haven't done anything wrong. I'm just glad we sorted it out. It would have bothered me if you had driven away with such a fearful mien."

"I'm still unclear how you knew." I wasn't fidgeting, was I? I don't think so.

"This is the turn," he says instead of addressing my statement. "Thank you for the ride. We can talk more tomorrow."

Seeker is out of the vehicle with his bag and moving toward the tiny house he's rented before I can say another word. From what he said, he doesn't have anywhere to stay from tomorrow night on. Depending on how things go, I might offer to let him crash in my room, but Tad already invited him. After the awkwardness tonight, he'll probably go with Tad to the RV.

I hope I haven't screwed things up permanently. There's no point in sitting here, however. I drive back to the Rellows Inn feeling like an abject failure. Not only did I misread the situation between Jaz and Seeker, but I questioned him about it. Even if they *were* flirting or planning to hook up, I'm not his girlfriend.

Ugh. Sometimes it's not a lot of fun being me. I let myself into my room and flop backward on my bed with a groan. I need a shower, but I can't make myself get up until my phone pings. It's a private text, not the group chat.

And it raises even *more* questions.

14
SEEKER

I STAND OUTSIDE IN THE darkness for longer than I'd like.

I need to be planning. Don't I?

Then I send a text before I can think better of it. To Jen, before I can change my mind.

Seeker: Make time for me tomorrow. I'll tell you everything.

The short conversation I had with Jaz at the restaurant changed so much. Since she's been here for ten years; she's better at blending in.

"Why didn't you leave?" I'd asked, taking advantage of the privacy.

"I *want* to be here. Things are simple. Their rules are easy to follow. I have a marketable skill, and my people are naturally talented in this sphere. We learn patterns quickly."

She's a professional musician on 97-B. I don't know what she looks like with her tech turned off, but it's fascinating that it makes her look human to me as well. What do *I* look like to her?

There was no time to ask about the particulars then, so I'd

deferred that curiosity for later. Instead, I asked the blazing question. "You don't intend to leave? Ever?"

"This is my home," she reiterated. "If you stop being stubborn, it could be yours too."

Then she pushed past me, heading to rejoin the others. I followed, reeling with the new information. And apparently, I did a bad job of covering my reaction. Now Jen seems to think I might be untrustworthy. But that's a problem for later.

I have so many questions for Jaz that I consider calling her. Or texting. But I can't trust human tech with our safety. It will have to wait until we're alone again, whenever that is. The idea of accepting my fate and trying to build a life here feels...heretical, almost. Like a scientist deciding to remain among the primates they've been researching.

I head inside the small dwelling.

My nomadic existence has been grim and lonely by choice. I've always been aware that this is temporary and I shouldn't draw attention to myself. I work enough to meet my basic needs and I do most of my shopping remotely. Apart from the people in the Aliens Among Us group chat, I have no connections here.

That should make it easier for me to leave.

But at the launch site, how am I supposed to slip past all the security and search for serviceable supplies? I can use tech to research the base, but that doesn't eliminate the physical component of breaking in. And I'm a thrill seeker, not a hardened criminal. I've only broken Galactic Union rules by venturing to planets dubbed unsafe by the travel bureau.

And so far, I've always beaten the odds.

But everyone meets their match at some point. Realistic assessment suggests that I'll get myself killed attempting to raid a billionaire's compound on my own. I have been clinging to that solution out of desperation, feeling as if I had no other options. Now, I've been presented with one that seemed impossible before. Because I can't be *myself* here. My entire existence would be a lie.

Yet Jaz has done it. So does that mean I have a second viable option?

What if I stay? There's much I need to learn, but maybe I can manage.

I'd be lying if I said Jen had nothing to do with the thoughts I'm suddenly entertaining. I want to know her, but we can't develop an honest relationship as long as I'm hiding such a massive secret.

Can I trust Jen?

Does Jaz have people in her life who know the truth and would perish to keep her safe? Because that's what it might require. And do I have the right to ask that of anyone? To expect it, even? The answers to those questions don't come, as I prepare and consume the mixture that keeps me alive.

Tomorrow, I'll confide in Jen. If anyone will understand, she will. She's desperate for confirmation I can provide. I don't know if she'll still be interested in...more, once she knows. But I'm sure we've made a real connection.

I have to be. I'm staking my life on it.

My biological needs met, I bring out the emergency beacon and tinker with it. Though I don't know what will happen tomorrow with Jen, the ritual of working on the beacon soothes my nerves. The vertical space of this domicile is compact and cozy, a safe place to nest, but little else. While I would use other materials, the ones humans provide are sufficient and I manage to rest. According to my research, humans experience an interesting state of unconsciousness called dreaming. Their minds offer up random scenes, sometimes populated with nonsensical events.

While I do rest, I don't lose connection to my conscious mind. My people are known for their ability to memory walk. I pick a comforting occasion, learning from Oona, and settle in to relive the moment.

Much later, I stir, feeling refreshed. It occurs to me that I haven't arranged for a means of transport to town. And I must vacate these premises before too much longer. I have left no traces, as I have devices dedicated to hygiene, and I will use them as long as they function. Standing in an interior deluge—no, a shower—reminds me of inclement weather, and I feel no cleaner when I dry off.

I check the habitation to ensure I haven't left anything, then collect my meager belongings. As I step outside, I spot Jen's boxy vehicle zipping down the road toward me. Even though I didn't ask her to come, she's here. That speaks volumes about how reliable she is. She understands me as no one ever has, and I can trust her.

It's time to tell her. To share the burden and try to figure out what to do.

But as she draws nearer, I spot Tad in the passenger seat. While I'm willing to risk sharing the information with Jen, I'm not ready to spill it to the whole group. It's too much of a statistical uncertainty. I need to see how Jen reacts first.

"We're meeting for breakfast," Tad says as I enter the vehicle from the rear.

I'm already out of patience with these meal gatherings because they're another way that I'm forced to hide who I am. I'll need another excuse for why I'm not ordering anything.

"I didn't know. I've already eaten."

"You can have coffee," Jen suggests.

Coffee would poison me. It probably wouldn't be fatal, but that much caffeine would be a serious hallucinogen, and there's no telling what I'd say.

"I don't drink it. Caffeine is bad for me."

"I shouldn't either," Tad says unexpectedly. "Gives me the jitters. But when I haven't slept much, I need the energy boost. I got so sick on energy drinks in college that I haven't touched them since."

Jen takes her eyes off the road briefly to smile at Tad. "You could do green tea. Just a bit of caffeine."

"It's not an issue today. I slept like a rock as soon as I got back to the RV." He half turns in the seat. "Speaking of which, are you bunking with me tonight? The offer still stands if you need a place."

I make a noncommittal noise. "Thanks for the offer."

"Everything in town is booked. I've seen pics online, but nothing prepares you for the crowds. They've got stalls on the corners, selling pastries and bottles of juice and water because the restaurants can't keep up." Jen adds, "Ravik and Poppy are getting food. We're having a picnic at Tad's place. Then we'll start planning the rest of our day."

"Sounds good," I say.

What else can I say in front of Tad? That I have important news and I need to speak with her alone? It's true, but it will make Tad wonder what's up. I don't need to set up a chain reaction of gossipy speculation.

In addition, such an ominous tone doesn't fit the day's mood. The weather is cheerful and bright, all yellow glow. If I wasn't anxious about talking to Jen, I'd love to bask in the sunshine. Heat metabolizes beautifully for me, filtering out toxins and deep cleaning my system. I don't think it works that way for humans, though I believe they get some benefits from sunlight. There are risks as well, as their skin is delicate, unlike mine.

We drive in the opposite direction from town, and I catch up silently on all the text messages I missed during my memory walk. There aren't many, just the rest of the group making plans and presuming I would pose no objections. I have a private message from Jaz, however. I hope she hasn't been unwise or indiscreet.

Jaz: Think about what I said.

Nothing overt. I relax a trifle.

If she's been here for ten human years, she knows how to live among them. I don't need to worry about her discretion. Though I'm embarrassed to admit it, the opposite might not be true.

But I'll be careful. And I'll bide my time until I can get my moment with Jen.

I've lived taking risks, and there's no reason to stop, not when the reward could be so incredible.

PRIVATE CHAT
DECEMBER 4 | 20:56

Jeneticist: What did you think of the Confession game?

Seeker: It was interesting. I learned a lot about everyone, I think.

Jeneticist: Star has the best ideas. I bet she's tons of fun in person.

Seeker: I like her well enough. But you're my favorite. 🤍

Jeneticist: I am?

Seeker: Have I made a secret of my partiality? I thought it was obvious.

Jeneticist: Wow, you just come right out and say these things. How do I know you're not saying this to *everyone* in private chat? 😛

Seeker: It's a matter of trust, I suppose. You can ask them.

Jeneticist: Didn't you see the silly face? I'm joking.

Seeker: I don't really understand all the emojis. I'm working on it, though! 🌵

Jeneticist: That's a random cactus, isn't it?

Seeker: Is there ever an appropriate interval to use that one?

Jeneticist: I do it as a distraction. I feel like that's what you just did.

Seeker: And how long have you felt this way?

Jeneticist: Are you psychoanalyzing me?

Seeker: Not even slightly. I'm just happy to be talking with you. I've started to watch my phone a bit, just in case you're messaging.

Jeneticist: Really? Me too.

Seeker: Is this where I say something clever? Because I'm just waiting for you to realize that you've got something better to do.

Jeneticist: Better than getting to know you? Perish the thought.

Seeker: You're just like the sun. I don't think you realize how much of a lifeline you've become to me.

Seeker: Was that too much?

Jeneticist: No. Not at all.

Jeneticist: Though I'm a little concerned that you're going through something difficult.

Seeker: Everyone is lonely now and then.

Jeneticist: That's certainly true.

Seeker: What about you?

Jeneticist: Work has me dealing with people all the time, students and faculty alike. So I enjoy getting some time to myself.

Jeneticist: But...I do miss having someone special, who cares especially for me.

Seeker: I don't think I've ever had that.

Jeneticist: Whoa. That's what dating sites call a red flag.

Seeker: Why?

Jeneticist: Why haven't you had a serious relationship before?

Seeker: I was always traveling. This is the longest I've ever been settled.

Jeneticist: Do you want to stick around now? Or do you think you'll always have wanderlust?

Seeker: That's a difficult question.

Jeneticist: You said before you never fit in anywhere. And that you're looking for something.

Seeker: Is it strange to say that when I communicate with you, it feels like I've found it?

Jeneticist: You're flirting again.

Seeker: That was simple truth.

Jeneticist: 🫶 ☺️

Jeneticist: Be really careful. You might get my hopes up with your sweet talk.

Seeker: Maybe I'm starting to hope for things too.

Jeneticist: I guess we'll see if there's a spark when we meet in person.

Seeker: Indeed we will.

Seeker: ⚡

15
JENNETTE

THE RV PARK IS SMALL but well-kept, greener than I expect, bits of scrub bush dotting the landscape in the distance.

Overhead, the sky is heartbreakingly blue, not a cloud in sight. It will be a scorcher later, and it's already hot enough that I can taste the shimmer of asphalt when I breathe. The office is a gray building and the bathhouse is nearby. Everything seems clean. The campers are all wedged in tight as a drum, not a single lot vacant. And the overflow area has tons of tents, but it's not crowded at this hour. Everyone must be in town, prepping for a wild day at Space Con.

Poppy, Jaz, and Ravik are already present outside Tad's pop-up trailer. I don't know how comfortable it is, but it's freaking adorable, and I don't even like camping. He has a firepit and a picnic table, essential for an al fresco breakfast. I park behind Poppy's car and hurry over to help with the food.

We've got containers of cut fruit, pastries, bottled water, and cold sandwiches. Not a gourmet breakfast, but I suspect they got what they could from the small supermarket. Local shops must make a ton of money during Space Con.

"This looks great," Tad says, rubbing his hands together.

Poppy nods. "I'm so hungry I could eat at Arby's."

I laugh. "Classic *Simpsons.*"

I serve myself some nibbles while chatting with Tad and Jaz. It takes all my self-control not to drag Seeker away to find out what he needs to tell me. Based on our private chats, he might be ready to admit he can see us together. Like, dating. I hope. If he reveals that he's got a thing for Jaz, I hope I can cover my hurt without wrecking our friendship.

Regardless, whatever it is, the news must be big. And private.

Be patient, I tell myself. *Good things come to those who wait.* Once again, Seeker isn't eating. He said he had food earlier, but I'm concerned about him. He hasn't looked away from me once, and I'm starting to get self-conscious. Does my costume look weird?

For Day Two, I put in a little more effort, as did Poppy, although Ravik is blue again, the exact same look as yesterday, and come to think of it, I don't recognize what alien they're representing. Which is unusual for me.

"You're not from Avatar," I say to Ravik. "The face isn't right. But I can't think—"

"I'm an ice planet barbarian," Ravik cuts in.

"No *way,*" Poppy gasps.

"You must really love those books," Tad says around a mouthful of food.

Jaz isn't eating either. She's tapping away at her phone. She glances up as if sensing my attention. "Sorry, I was just answering a question from someone in the orchestra."

"For our next meetup, we should go to one of Jaz's concerts," I suggest.

"I would love that," she says.

Seeker has been so quiet that I find it a bit troubling. Finally, he speaks, swirling the water in the bottle so it catches the light, almost like a prism. "Where would that be?"

"Minneapolis. We perform February through June. If you let me know ahead of time, I can get tickets."

"We can buy them," I say quickly. I don't want her thinking that I'm angling for a free concert or anything.

"I love that we're making plans past Space Con." Poppy finishes her sandwich in two huge bites. "But there's a how-to class on professional-level special effects makeup and I don't want to miss it. Who's ready to leave now?"

To my surprise, Tad, Ravik, and Jaz all jump up, but then they look at the messy campsite in dismay. "I should clean up," Tad says.

I can tell he wants to rush back to the excitement. And I'm aching for a moment with Seeker. "If you'll all fit in Tad's car, we can tidy up and head over."

Tad beams at me. "You don't mind? You're an angel!"

Now that they've eaten, the others are gone so fast that it reminds of the Road Runner with Wile E. Coyote in *The Road Runner Show* cartoons. To keep my promise, I stash the leftovers in Tad's cooler and Seeker throws away the trash. He follows me into the shadows of the camper and I take a step back, suddenly aware of how alone we are.

My pulse skitters. Not in fear. Anticipation. When he closes the door tight behind us, I lick my lips. There's only one reason he'd want privacy, right? He's planning to kiss me.

Only he checks the windows in all directions in a most unromantic manner, making me think this isn't what I imagine.

"More privacy would be better, but I hope this will do," he whispers. "I need to tell you something. And I'm so afraid of how you'll react."

"You're starting to freak me out."

"Showing you will be faster. And I doubt you'd take my word for it anyway."

There's an odd pop, as if my ears have suddenly equalized in pressure and my head feels odd. When I recover from that sensation, Seeker is gone. I don't recognize the person standing here with me, and I use the *p*-word liberally.

This being is tall and slim, with an androgynous build and skin layered in what could be scales, but it could also be a pattern. A triangular head with an elongated jaw, not teeth like a human has, but more like a lizard's maw. Sensory organs of some sort, but they're set to the side, allowing for a completely different field of vision, and there are motile spines quivering all over the skull plate. Roughly humanoid, but the joints and the curves of their spine—this looks like an alien I'd see in a science fiction movie. And the colors…unearthly gorgeous, a peacock green deepening to the darkest hue of a forest, dotted with patterning in cobalt blue and violet.

"How did you do that?" I demand. "How did you get into costume so fast?"

"I didn't." Seeker's voice sounds different now too. It's deeper and so beautifully modulated that it makes my toes curl, like he's singing the notes in harmony with himself.

"This is how I look normally. I've switched off the tech that makes me appear human."

"This isn't funny."

I've been punked before by people who thought it would be funny to prove how gullible I am. Back in college, they planted transmissions to make me think I'd gotten in touch with intelligent life. I exchanged messages for a full week before another volunteer admitted to messing with me. But I never suspected Seeker would do this.

"No, it isn't." He extends a limb. His hands aren't like mine either. Seven digits on each one, and two seem to be like opposable thumbs.

I have the ridiculous thought that those hands explain the unearthly beauty of the song he sent to me. The one that didn't sound like any music I'd ever heard…

I pause. I can't take this seriously, right? The minute I believe him, he'll say, "PSYCH," and tell everyone what a dork I am.

"What do you want from me?" I demand.

"I just want you to know who I am."

Now I have a Goo Goo Dolls song in my head, "Iris." The words slam into me as I stare at his outstretched arm. "And?"

"If you can't believe my words, touch me. Will your senses lie to you?"

I don't believe him. This is impossible. It's a trick, has to be.

But I close the distance between us anyway, my mind ticking over all the little inconsistencies I've noticed. He doesn't eat human food. When I touch him, the temperature feels wrong. And his expression doesn't change. Which could explain—oh. *Oh. Oh my God.*

When I touched him before, I knew then, didn't I?

That his skin felt wrong. Not human. But then the tech he uses kicked in, I think. Made me doubt myself. And he pulled away. But now, now he's holding on to me. And I can test the resilience for myself. His skin is more like hide with velvety patches here and there, usually where the pattern changes hues. The purples are mossy soft, and he trembles a little when I brush over the spot on his forearm. Or whatever he calls it.

"You're not human."

"I've been trapped here for almost a year. It was supposed to be a vacation," he admits in a heart-wrenching tone.

The overwhelming loneliness, how he's felt trapped? It was so much deeper and more desperate than I knew. He's lived in mortal fear every single day, I imagine.

"What can I do?"

"You're already doing it. I told you, and you're not screaming. You're still here."

I stifle the urge to pinch myself, because if I could write myself into a story, this is exactly how I'd want it to go. My entire life, I've felt like I was on an impossible quest, one that made me the target of mockery, too, and now I'm with Seeker. But I don't want this to turn into a thriller, where we're constantly imperiled by hunters or government agents who want to carve him up. God, he's beautiful. I may never let go of his hand.

"I'm not going anywhere," I promise.

"Not even to Space Con?" His face moves now. Though I can't read his expression, it's no longer supernaturally static.

"This feels more important. This is life-changing. Do you want to go back to my room so we can talk more?"

"I have a lot to say," Seeker warns.

"My time is yours."

Along with anything else you might want.

16
SEEKER

I THINK THIS IS GOING well.

If Jen intended to betray me, she would already be running for her life, screaming for aid from any humans nearby. Instead, she offers time for me to reactivate the tech camo, staring the entire time as if she cannot trust her senses. And well. Yes. That's the truth.

"I still can't get over how flawless this is," she says, shaking her head. "To be honest, I did notice discrepancies when I touched you. But I thought I must be losing it."

"I'm sorry I made you doubt yourself."

"I get it. But you could walk around here like that and people would just say, 'Your costume is amazing!' You'd have problems anywhere else."

"It's not meant to withstand intimate assessment. Shall we go?"

She inclines her head, leading the way back to her vehicle. The camper door locks behind me automatically, and I climb in, desperately hoping I've done the right thing. Having one human who knows and is on my side... My joy is indescribable. Now I no longer need to curate what I hear or parse out the truth in digestible crumbs, fashioned into a shape that will make sense by 97-B standards.

The drive is silent. Jen doesn't say much until we reach the safety of her room. She closes the blackout shades and the window coverings, and then she perches on the edge of the bed, regarding me with a look that I think signifies great interest.

"You said you had a lot to say. I can't wait to hear it." Her voice lilts with excitement. Now that I examine her closer, I can see that she's practically vibrating.

She's wanted proof that humans are not alone in the universe for her entire life. And while I know she's not been waiting for *me* specifically, it's difficult not to feel moved by her single-minded devotion. Jen has been searching for a sign among the stars for more than two decades. And at last, here I am.

"I arrived almost a year ago, on a package tour."

As she laughs quietly, her eyes crinkle. I'm accustomed to human features now, even if I once found them strange. "But something went wrong?"

"You could say that. Your planet has been interdicted from the Galactic Union because you're on the cusp of reaching the stars on your own. And there are rules against uplifting other sentient beings."

"Why?" she asks.

"Problems in the past." That's the simplest explanation. "Those who arrive in the wider galaxy without adequate resources or preparations to be self-sufficient often end up in a servitor situation. They can't survive or thrive on their own, so they make unequal agreements with a more advanced society. And those arrangements can last for eons."

"That makes sense, and it's more of an explanation than we get in the science fiction shows I watch," Jen says thoughtfully. "All the programs assume that there wouldn't be contact until a civilization develops the capacity for interstellar travel, but they never lay it out properly."

"I suspect the writer who first floated that premise may have been in contact with someone from the Galactic Union."

"Whoa. You really think so?"

"While some aspects of your early science fiction entertainments are wildly incorrect, many ideas are accurate, too much for it to be a coincidence."

"I would think it also prevents a culture from developing properly or evolving on natural lines, depending too much on another group." Then Jen shakes her head. "Never mind. I could discuss this for days, but I'd rather talk about your situation specifically."

"Thank you," I say quietly.

"That must be why you're looping me in. So you don't have to bullshit everyone for the rest of your life." She pauses, a rapid flurry of emotions shifting her mobile features faster than I can read them.

I'm still new to this, though Jen's face is more familiar to me than most. Since we met in person, I have certainly spent time attempting to learn this woman's facial topography, so when I memory walk with her, every fraction of a moment will be accurate down to each eyelash. I don't understand why humans have fur on their eyes. My people have a secondary membrane that protects our sensory organs from foreign matter.

"What?" I ask, when she doesn't continue.

"Are you leaving soon? Is that why you told me? Because you won't be able to keep in touch when you get where you're going?"

Her voice breaks a little on the word *get* and it sounds as if she may be wrestling with some strong emotion.

"The opposite. I was supposed to catch my shuttle off-world almost a year ago. I waited at a remote location in Tennessee—on top of a mountain. I was there for days past the rendezvous point, until I ran out of provisions and had to accept they weren't coming."

"Oh my God. I can't begin to imagine how you coped. I know it's not the same, but I'm imagining a vacation in another country. It's a nice visit, but then my flight home never takes off. Nobody provides any help or explanations for what's going on. I'm out of money and food. I don't speak the language fluently..."

"It's been...difficult," I say.

Understatement. This woman saved me more times than she realizes. Sometimes, I'd be asking myself, *What's the point of persevering? Nothing will change. There can be no life, no future for me here.* And then my device would ping.

Jen, reaching out. Jen, asking how I am. If I need to talk.

"There's so much you're not telling me. You don't need to censor yourself. Say whatever you need to. I don't mind if we miss the whole day at Space Con. This is far more important. *You* are." She pats the bed, which dominates the room. "Get comfortable and talk to me. Tell me how I can help."

"Being seen and known helps," I say.

But I move away from the door at last, sinking onto the sleep surface with careful motions. I don't want to frighten her. First, I deactivate the tech camo—a small device I wear on my wrist— because there's no need for it anymore. Not with Jen.

"You're beautiful." The words seem to slip out beyond her

volition, and she colors, a deep rosy flush that brightens her aspect.

I also know it heralds embarrassment.

"Thank you. I *was* considered reasonably attractive among my own people."

She faces me, folding her legs into a position that doesn't look remotely comfortable. My lower limbs wouldn't turn in that configuration, but then, our joints are different.

"Tell me about them. And your home. Your family. Customs, places you've traveled. I'd love to learn anything you care to share."

It's been so long since I let myself think of everything I left behind. If I focused on it, the loss might overwhelm me and leave me unable to function. Oona and Arlan and Betau, my birth parents, and Tivani and Morv, my creche guardians. I consider what to share and then realize I don't need to.

"I'm from a star so far away that humans haven't named it. Once, I went to an observatory here, but I couldn't find it even on a telescope."

That's how far from home I am.

"What is it like?"

"It's a peaceful, beautiful place. The lights in the sky attract visitors from all over the Galactic Union. My people are known for their artistry. We create beautiful things, lasting sensory experiences. My birth parent, Oona, crafted my birthsong, which I shared with you."

"It was haunting. And I should have known then that it didn't come from here. That sound... It wasn't a pan flute?"

"No. I have my instrument with me."

"I hope you'll play for me in person sometime."

"If you want me to." I wonder if Jen can discern my ambivalence. I'm nowhere near adept enough to garner acclaim or renown on my homeworld. In the local vernacular, my skills are "mid" at best. I was a difficult youngling, never wanting to cooperate or settle.

"Only if you enjoy it," she says with uncommon perspicacity. "Why did you leave?"

She makes it easy to open up. "I found my homeworld too predictable. Too...orderly. I wanted to be somewhere more exciting, so I left—against my family's wishes."

"That must hurt even more now."

Jen appears to understand. "It does. And I have no way to get word to them. Oona must be heartbroken while Arlan will be stoic, and Betau will be lighting the lamps to guide me home, never knowing it's not possible. I can't—"

"Can I hug you?"

I know what a hug is, but it's a human comfort. Yet I agree with a whispered, "Yes," just in case there is some magic that can slake this sorrowful homesickness. Back then, I couldn't wait to leave, but now that I realize how difficult it will be to go home again, I ache.

Jen approaches with care, then bundles me close, and our bodies *spark*. Light jumps between our flesh, demonstrating the brightness of our energy. There is sweetness to her scent, notes I can't identify, but her skin is fragrant and silken. The reassuring thump of her life force resounds in a delightfully regular pattern, and her warmth soothes me in a way I couldn't have expected since I take my cues from the natural world.

Why does this feel so good?

GROUP CHAT
DECEMBER 7 | 18:27

Jeneticist: My turn for a game!

SquidHead: Oh no, it's contagious.

JazzyPlum: I have more time today.

Stargazer: I knew I couldn't be the only fun one.

FarfromHome: Reluctantly curious.

Seeker: I can't wait to find out what you have in mind.

Jeneticist: I'm thinking Truth or Dare.

SquidHead: Ooh, spicy choice!

JazzyPlum: I'm in!

Stargazer: Count me in too.

FarfromHome: I'm not doing anything dangerous or silly.

Seeker: I'm unfamiliar with the rules, by the way.

Jeneticist: How have you never played Truth or Dare?

SquidHead: Some of us didn't get invited to parties growing up, okay?

Stargazer: OK then, quick recap. If you're picked, you choose Truth or Dare. Then you answer a question or do the dare. If you choose truth and then opt to pass on answering, you have to do TWO dares.

SquidHead: Wait, I never heard of that.

Jeneticist: Sounds good to me! But how do we prove we did the dare?

JazzyPlum: Pics or it didn't happen.

FarfromHome: What if we don't want to send photographic evidence of participating in this?

Stargazer: Then you better stick to truth. Boooooooooring.

Seeker: Fair enough. Start us off, Jen?

Jeneticist: I'll start tame. Star, Truth or Dare?

Stargazer: Dare, obviously!

Jeneticist: Oooh. Spicy. I dare you to send a sincere compliment to someone in the group via private message.

Stargazer: I thought for sure I'd be eating hot sauce and crying. You're too nice.

FarfromHome: Hmm. I find it hard to credit that you mean that, Star. But...thank you.

JazzyPlum: Oooh, wonder what she said!

Stargazer: That's for me to know and you to find out. I pick... Seeker! Truth or Dare?

Seeker: Truth.

Stargazer: Have you ever had a crush on anyone in the group chat?

SquidHead: Ugh. I knew this would happen!

Seeker: Define "crush."

FarfromHome: Even I know this.

Jeneticist: Don't tease him.

JazzyPlum: You want their attention. You think about them often.

Seeker: Oh. Then yes.

Stargazer: So sweet! Who is it?

Seeker: I don't believe I'm required to disclose that. Isn't it my turn to pick someone?

Jeneticist: It is.

Seeker: JazzyPlum, Truth or Dare?

JazzyPlum: Dare. Do your worst.

Seeker: Record yourself playing the violin and share it with the group.

JazzyPlum: Give me a minute.

[Two minutes later, JazzyPlum sends mp3]

SquidHead: Wow, that's beautiful. You're so talented.

Seeker: Definitely.

Stargazer: Is that Liszt?

JazzyPlum: It is. You have a knowledgeable ear.

Stargazer: My dad loves his music. Rhapsody No. 2!

SquidHead: It's a very moody piece. Anyway, Jaz, it's your turn.

JazzyPlum: And I'm picking you! Truth or Dare.

SquidHead: I'm doing Dare too. Have at me.

JazzyPlum: Let's see...record yourself hopping on one foot for 30 seconds. You can just show your foot, if you want.

SquidHead: Cruel and unusual, but okay.

[One minute later, a video pings the chat]

Jeneticist: Don't take this the wrong way, but your feet are huge.

SquidHead: I'm aware. And I'm picking FarfromHome. Truth or Dare?

FarfromHome: Truth, obviously.

SquidHead: Who do you like the most in the group chat?

FarfromHome: That's like asking where I want to be hit. But... fine. I'd have to say Jeneticist.

Stargazer: Really? I thought you disliked us all equally.

FarfromHome: Some more than others. To end this game, I pick Jeneticist.

JazzyPlum: Saving the best for last?

Seeker: It seems so.

FarfromHome: Truth or Dare, J?

Jeneticist: Truth.

Stargazer: Boo! You wimped out.

Jeneticist: Pffft. Go ahead, FFH.

FarfromHome: I'm thinking what to ask. Oh. What's your biggest regret?

SquidHead: Deep one.

Seeker: I'm interested in this answer as well.

JazzyPlum: Me too.

Jeneticist: I'd have to say, taking the safe job instead of holding out for my dream offer. I settled in and got comfortable. Now I don't know if I'll ever get in at an observatory.

Stargazer: Aw. It's not too late! Probably. You're not 87, right?

Jeneticist; I'm not. 🐌

Seeker: Then believe in yourself. You never know what the future holds.

FarfromHome: A thoughtful response. I expected nothing less.

JazzyPlum: That's it for me.

SquidHead: Same! Take care, everyone.

17

JENNETTE

I'M HUGGING SEEKER.

Tamzir.

I wonder if he'd prefer for me to use his name, now that I know the truth. I breathe him in because I *can*. Now that his tech isn't scrambling my brain waves and confusing my senses, I'm aware of a sharp, spicy scent that must emanate from him, like a chemical blend of cinnamon, cardamom, and saffron. Not exactly, of course, but those are the comparisons that linger in my mind.

At last, I sit back, hoping he feels better. Because there's so little I can do when he's lost so much. Yet it means everything to me that he trusts me with such a weighty secret. He's put his life in my hands, and I'm so aware of that, it hurts. In a good way.

I'll never betray that faith.

"You mentioned five family members… What does family look like where you're from?"

"To put it in terms you'll understand, it depends on the domestic partnership. My parents formed a triad, though Betau isn't sexually involved with Arlan or Oona. They all contributed genetic material when they were ready to brood young. They hatched six of us, and we were reared collectively in the creche. My creche guardians are Tivani and Morv."

Though I hate to interrupt, I have to ask, "What's a creche?"

Sure, I could extrapolate, but it would be better to get his words on the topic. Seeker pauses, likely trying to figure out how make it stack up without context. I wait patiently, still sitting close to him. And he doesn't move back.

"I suppose the closest comparison I can make on 97-B is a commune, where everyone takes responsibility for the offspring and contributes to caring and raising them. Creche guardians are an extra set of unrelated parents who focus on education."

"Oh, that's interesting." I have so many questions that I don't even know what to ask first.

"Is it? For me, it's just how things were. I find it strange how uninvolved humans are, how they seek to cut connections whenever possible. There are so many of you, but it seems to me that you push for self-sufficiency at the expense of connection."

I laugh, though there's a trace of wryness in it. I see what he means. "We do fight like hell to get free of our family's influence, and then we look for that one perfect person who can complete us. But…"

"Perhaps that's not possible. There can certainly be a special person—or people, depending on how your needs align—but it seems to me that if you expect *one* person to meet all your needs until the end of time…"

I nod. Seeker and I are on the same page. "It's setting yourself up for failure. I've always thought a relationship should be welcoming, with plenty of room for others." It's not that I'm looking for a poly arrangement per se, but I don't want to be with a *possessive* person, who gets aggro over me wanting to see friends or pursue hobbies on my own. My last boyfriend hated me spending time on cosplay.

"You would like it there," he says then.

"Don't you have a word for it? Like, we call this planet Earth."

Seeker makes an amused sound. "Yes. We call it Home. Earth translates to dirt, does it not? Or soil?"

He has a point. "In your language, though? What's the phonetic sound?" Even if the syllables don't mean anything, I still want to know.

To my surprise, he makes a series of clicks and pops, a squeak, and a hiss. It's like a combination of natural lizard and bird calls. I find it fascinating, but there's no way in hell I could reproduce those sounds. I come up with, "Tikpupeesh?"

"That's not bad," he says. "It will suffice. Our language also incorporates minute hue changes in our skin and subtle olfactory cues, but…"

Yeah, yeah. I repress the urge to defend our evolutionary limitations. There are reasons our noses aren't too sensitive. Probably.

"So, you didn't fit in on your homeworld," I prompt. "And you didn't become a musician like Oona wanted."

"They wanted me to create beauty," he corrects.

"Got it. What happened next?"

"Everything I've told you before is true. I went traveling as soon as I attained maturity. I refused all social connections that might have limited my freedom. And I saw *amazing* things, sights and experiences I never could have had at home."

"You don't regret your choices?"

Seeker pauses to consider, his preternaturally beautiful eyes glittering with consideration. He has no lashes, and the pupils are more like a reptile's with a vertical slit for a pupil. But the colors…it's like a starburst of a galaxy in each iris. I could stare at him dreamily all day. I don't ever want him to turn that gadget back on.

"On the whole, no. This was supposed to be my last stop, one final adventure before I went home to settle down. Oona has been worried about me for a long time. Arlan and Betau kept saying, *Give him time.* My clutchlings are all settled. I'm the only one who didn't get the urge to nest at the usual time."

"One last trip," I repeat. "You tempted the universe."

"What does that mean?"

I explain the trope—how in action movies, there's always one last job or one last case. And that's when things go tragically, catastrophically wrong.

"Hmm. I do seem to be living the evidentiary result of that probability."

"Are you looking for help?"

"Depends on what you mean by help. I had some desperate idea that I'd sneak into that Lusk person's launch site. And—"

"Tell me you're joking." I dissolve into giggles.

"I take that to mean it's impossible?"

"Oh. You really were hoping…" I pause, hoping I haven't come across like an asshole. "Do you have experience stealing ships?"

It seems like I've put him on the defensive. "I didn't mean to suggest I'd steal a whole ship. Just some spare parts."

"You'd probably be captured," I say softly.

"That prospect has occurred to me as well."

"I wish I could say that I think we could workshop the premise, but it's an unmanned shuttle. And Owen Lusk's fledgling space company doesn't have a good reputation. They've had far more disasters than successes."

"I am familiar with his notoriety, but..." His voice trails off and he appears dispirited.

Yet I need to be sure Seeker understands how bad that jackass is. "Lusk is a grifter. He earns money by bullshitting people and getting them to fund his pipe dreams. I swear his companies are like a shell game with funds being moved around so he looks more successful than he is."

"That is unconscionable," he declares.

"Yeah. He's an asshole. Only an official space program like NASA would give you a shot at safely entering low orbit and their parts would be safe, but getting inside?" I shake my head, not feeling optimistic about his chances.

"How is Lusk's security then?" Seeker seems to be grasping at straws.

And I hate saying, "He's a paranoid freak, security everywhere. It would take a special team to get you inside on launch day, and I don't know that you'd be able to find anything useful once you got there."

"Then there is truly nothing I can do. The situation is, indeed, beyond my control."

"I'm sorry." I feel like I've crushed his secret dream, but I can't let him get hurt because he doesn't have all the facts.

"It's not your fault. I'll continue to make the best of things."

For a moment, I consider his situation. "You've managed to source food and shelter, but it can't be easy. You're new here."

I don't mean to be dismissive, but it's true. He's been on this planet for less than a year. Holy shit, I am talking with an *alien*. We're on my bed. I want to run around screaming and kick my feet in the air, but that would freak him out. He's trusted me. I can't react by showing how ridiculously thrilled and immature I am.

Seeker acknowledges this with a flutter of his dorsal spines. How fascinating. Does that take the place of hand gestures?

"I don't have a long-term residence. I've been moving around, earning just enough for my immediate needs doing contract work."

"Are you really coding for a living?"

"I've written programs that can tackle most of the tasks assigned to me. I automate it, check the work, and then turn it in."

I smile slightly. "You do have the tech advantage." Without pausing to think it through, I make the offer immediately. "Come home with me after Space Con."

My apartment can house two people, and I'm sure my landlady, Nancy, will be fine with it. If she isn't, I only have two months left on my lease. I'll figure something out. I'll help Seeker, whatever the obstacles.

He stares at me, lightning flickering inside his strange and wonderful eyes. His pattern deepens, more purple coming to the surface of his skin.

"You want me to cohabitate with you?" he asks.

"Not in a weird way."

What am I saying? Everything about this is unusual.

"It could be dangerous for you. I've been careful, but I don't know if it's a good idea."

Oh, that's why he's hesitant. Not because he thinks I have an alien fetish and I'm the one who might probe his butt if I got half a chance.

"You need a local guide."

Sure, that's all you're trying to do here. This is pure altruism.

It's really not, but I'm also perfectly clear that there's a power imbalance in this situation. He needs me to help him learn our customs on a deeper level. I wasn't looking for incongruent behavior and even I thought, more than once, *Oh, he's not from here*, I meant America. I figured things were different or maybe Swedish syntax was messing with his English skills or something.

I never imagined anything like this.

"I'll think about your offer," he says finally. "But we should attend some events at Space Con today. The others will find it strange if we don't."

"Chances are, they'll think we're hooking up."

Another pause. "What's that?"

Right, his understanding of slang can be unreliable. And now I get why.

"They'll think we're having sex." *Might as well be blunt.* "You're the one who asked everyone about con flings. They'll guess that was about us."

"I fear I've misunderstood what a con fling is. I didn't realize it pertained to sexual intimacy. For my people, there are different types of involvement."

"It's fine. I don't mind if they think we're doing it."

"The truth is far less plausible," Seeker says.

"That it is. Time for the big question... I doubt you'd draw a second look here, so...do you want to go out as you are?"

18
SEEKER

WITH EVERY FIBER OF MY being, I debate this decision.

It's such a weighty choice, and I've protected myself fiercely from scrutiny ever since I arrived. To even contemplate doing otherwise seems incredibly reckless. Jen isn't judging me; she understands how terrifying this is, I think.

But I've always been prone to taking risks.

"It would be nice to be myself for a while," I admit quietly. "No deception. I had lost all hope that there could be any moments like that for me."

"You can always be yourself with me," she replies.

Warmth suffuses me. I do trust her; I've placed my fate in her hands. And I want to seize this opportunity. Jaz may wonder what I'm thinking, but this seems like my best opportunity to be myself and see how it feels to explore the bond with Jen with no pretense or prevarication between us.

She is *so* incredibly special.

"Let's do it," I say at last.

"Then...are you ready?"

It's a fraught question.

But I rise in reply, ready to see what the world makes of me. I pick up my bag out of habit and she adds, "You can leave your stuff here. Unless you're staying with Tad tonight?"

"Do you trust me to share your accommodations?" I ask.

"You trusted me first. I doubt you'd do that if you had any intention of harming me. Though I guess you could off me to keep your secret…" Then she smiles. "Kidding!"

I relax as she speaks the last word. "Most amusing. Yes, I'll store my things. I won't need any of them today."

"Just stay calm. And if anyone acts odd about your look, let me handle it," Jen says.

With that, she leads the way to the car. I can't believe I'm doing this. Just…out. No protection from the tech camo.

The parking lot has ten people in it, a few getting into cars. One does a double take when they see us. I tense. Then someone calls, "Way to go, Kira Nerys!"

I realize they're talking to Jen. I don't recognize her costume, but she has different head fur and her nose has some ridges in it. Her facial decorations are a bit different today as well. She wears a smart uniform and dark boots; I feel that I should know who she is supposed to be, but I've consumed so much local media during my exile that it all blurs together.

She flashes a sign with her fingers and continues to the vehicle. I get in without attracting undue attention, perhaps because they don't recognize my "costume."

"What should I say when people ask about my appearance?" I ask.

"You designed a costume to match your favorite alien from

Tad's game. People will think it's a PR move, spreading buzz ahead of a potential fundraiser."

That is…remarkably clever. It's also simple enough that I won't become confused on the details, should I need to repeat the explanation.

She drives with quiet competence, delivering us safely to the outdoor spectacle that has become even more incredible on the second day. Even more humans. Even more costumes. I don't recognize most of them. But the air buzzes with a cocktail of excitement, even more perceptible than the day before. I drink in the myriad scents—cooking food, human sweat, hot plastic, and the faintest tang of something sweet and familiar.

Jennette.

She leads the way. I think there's a plan to meet up with everyone else. In this whirlwind of cosplayers and booths that stretch as far as the eye can see, she weaves a path like an expert, reacting and smiling when people recognize the character she's portraying.

"Is it always this loud?" I ask.

"It gets bigger every year," Jen says over one shoulder.

We pass a booth where a bookseller is vending used paperbacks, and it occurs to me that I could grace one of those covers, just as I am. Of course, in those books, humans are always shooting at those who look like me. Finally I recognize Tad, who looms over the rest of the group. Next I spot Ravik and Poppy with Jaz bobbing along in his wake. At least, I think it's Jaz, but she's different today. Slender and purple, and… Oh. She's Vertesian.

No wonder she said her people are gifted at pattern recognition. It's what they're known for. They're also the reason there's a ban on uplifting lower-tech civilizations, because the Vertesians trusted the Solirins and lost *everything*, including their homeworld. It's the greatest scandal in the history of the Galactic Union.

It hasn't been long since we met at Tad's campsite, but the world feels different now. Because Jaz knows—and so does Jen. I'm not alone anymore.

"What does everyone want to do?" Jaz asks.

She seems to be studying me, but she doesn't react. It would be strange if she did, considering that she's given up her camouflage as well.

"Oh my God!" Poppy squeals, bouncing on her toes. "It's Sapphire Griffin!"

She points across the sea of heads bobbing between stands filled with every geek treasure you could imagine.

"Who's that?" Tad asks.

I'm grateful because I don't know either.

"Only the writer behind the super-addictive Space Venom series," Jennette explains.

"I could use a little more context," I put in.

"It's a romance series between aliens and humans," Poppy explains. "I'm embarrassed by how much I love those books. Basically, the aliens exude an addictive substance and it's an aphrodisiac to humans, so it's all sex, all the time."

Ravik snorts.

I'm stunned at the depth and breadth of the human imagination. "Would anyone want that? Constantly craving sexual contact would be quite distracting."

"It's a fantasy," Jaz says. "If you can't resist your lover, you're allowed to demand all sorts of things that you might otherwise feel guilty about."

"Guilt is unproductive," Ravik says.

Tad grins. "I wish my mother agreed with you."

"Excuse me! Pardon me! Fan club coming through!" Poppy calls, parting the crowd with the charm of a seasoned diplomat.

But there's still a queue. I can't see the woman we're waiting in line for, but she has a table piled high with colorful books and small articles strewn about. She too seems to be in costume, based on what I can glean from this distance. I doubt her natural fur shimmers with the iridescence of a marine mammal, nor does human hair normally have so many colors. In some ways, her bold makeup and large-framed eyeglasses seem like a disguise.

At last, we reach the front. And I haven't received any strange looks at all.

This is very surreal.

"I've read *Addicted to Love* seventeen times," Poppy confesses, digging into her bag to produce a battered book.

"Thank you so much," Sapphire replies. "This means the world to me. Readers like you give me the strength to keep writing."

Nobody else has a copy of the book on hand, though Jen has the woman sign the cover of her tablet case with a shimmering marker. The others seem ready to delve deeper into the con, and I'm along for the ride. It's not an adventure in the way running across lava floes was, but the warmth is more pervasive and less life-threatening.

The group moves, browsing the stalls. Tad argues with a man for a while over the cost of some icon. I don't recognize the figure. Jaz lingers nearby, catching my attention.

"You're feeling bold today," she whispers.

Belatedly, I realize she's using a subharmonic that won't be audible to humans. There's no risk in conversing with her in the open. I wish she had done this before, but she couldn't have—not without revealing her own Vertesian origins.

"So are you."

"There's nothing to fear. I suspect even if these humans knew our truth, they would venerate us instead of attacking."

"It's not these particular humans I'm worried about," I reply.

"Fair enough. I sense a shift in the way Jen regards you, though. You told her?"

"Do you think that's unwise?"

"Not at all. If anyone will stand by you, it's her. But be sure that she sees you as you are, not as a symbol."

That is one of my concerns as well. Jen might have been equally delighted if Jaz had revealed herself first. Perhaps I'm not special to her in the way I'm beginning to hope I am. Rather, it's my "otherness" that appeals to her because she's made no secret of the fact that she struggles to connect with other humans.

"I'll be cautious. But...do you know of any way off-world?"

Jaz studies me, and a poignant olfactory note suffuses me, evoking a sense of sorrow. Vertesians communicate with multiple senses, including scent, sight, and sound. Then she says, "I do not. I sought refuge from the complications of the Galactic Union. When I arrived, I had no plans ever to depart."

"Complications?"

"When others look at me there, they see someone downtrodden, a being whose people were tricked and who lost their homes. They don't see me. I wearied of trying to find a place of my own when there was only pity or judgment out there."

"But here, there's none of that."

"Precisely. I can't help if you wish to leave, but I can assist if you decide to stay."

PRIVATE CHAT
JANUARY 2 | 21:09

Seeker: Would it be too forward to admit I miss you? 😅

Jeneticist: Not at all. I was just thinking about you, actually.

Seeker: You were? What about?

Jeneticist: How was your holiday?

Seeker: Holiday?

Jeneticist: Uh, we just celebrated Christmas. And New Year's. That's why I didn't message more. I thought you'd be busy.

Seeker: I'm not personally familiar with those holidays.

Jeneticist: Where the heck are you from? English must be your second language.

Seeker: How did you know? I have studied quite a lot. If you could point out any errors, I'd like to learn more about English slang.

Jeneticist: Oh, you're doing great. I just happened to notice a few unusual word choices. I pay attention to stuff like that. It's cool that you're not American. I like out-of-towners. 🙂

Seeker: Out-of-towner? I prefer "worldly explorer." 😄

Jeneticist: Should I get you a guidebook?

Seeker: For where?

Jeneticist: My hometown? Just kidding. Mostly. You'd probably have to get on an international flight for that.

Seeker: No, I'm already traveling in the U.S.

Jeneticist: That's interesting. 🤩

Jeneticist: I'd love to travel more.

Seeker: Is there somewhere you'd like to go?

Jeneticist: To see the Hadron Collider in Switzerland. And Space Con! One of those things is happening this year, though. I'm thinking about inviting everyone in the chat to join.

Seeker: That sounds fun.

Jeneticist: Then I'm inviting you right now.

Seeker: Excellent. I'm intrigued by the concept of cosplay.

Jeneticist: Dressing up is so much fun! How about we transform you into a character from *Astro Adventures*? You'd make an excellent Zeltron.

Seeker: Would Zeltron appeal to you personally? 🤔

Jeneticist: Absolutely. I could make a list of all my alien crushes. 😍

Seeker: Then I shall become the most debonair Zeltron the world has ever seen.

Jeneticist: It's a plan, but only if you promise not to steal the show. I want people to ask *me* for pics too.

Seeker: I make no guarantees. The stars cannot dim their radiance and neither can I.

Jeneticist: Ha! I like it. Confidence is sexy.

Seeker: Sexy? 🤨

Jeneticist: Sweet talk will get you everywhere, Mr. Worldly Explorer. 😌

Seeker: I'll do my best to impress you in person when we meet. 🤍

19
JENNETTE

"LEAD THE WAY, CAPTAIN," JAZ says to Tad.

Rushing from one of the side paths, a woman practically jumps at Jaz, eyeing her with avid interest. "How did you get your makeup blended so well? It looks like your skin!"

"I'm a professional," Jaz says.

I blink at that response. Because she's a musician, not a makeup artist. But it feels like she gave the lady the fastest response to shut her up.

"Let's go," Ravik says.

"Yeah, we're gonna miss the start," Poppy calls.

We hurry past booths bursting with cosmic curiosities as I guide us to the panel discussion area. I have my obsessions, okay? And I still love *Nebula Odyssey*, even if Colin McFarland is gross. I'm positive Chelsie Linnloch, who played Captain Zara, is as awesome as she seems on social media.

"There!" Poppy points at a cluster of empty seats, miraculously unclaimed.

We dart through the throng of people, dodging a duo dressed as galactic bounty hunters and a trio of robots clinking with each step.

"Good eye. Prime real estate!" Tad says as we settle into our seats, unobstructed by errant antennae or oversized headpieces.

Seeker chooses to sit beside me at the end of the row. I wonder if he's nervous about being out and about as himself. So far, he's fielded compliments from Poppy and Tad on his cosplay, but nobody has given him too much attention. There's a papier-mâché Hutt being towed around on a wagon, so he picked quite a lively day for a debut.

The *Nebula Odyssey* moderator strides out in uniform, knowing we all want Chelsie. But she wins the crowd over by dropping the phrase that true fans know by heart. We even shout it with her.

"Here's to new worlds and new friends!" She continues, "I'd make a long introduction, but that guy might shoot me with his blaster rifle." As she intends, people laugh when she makes finger guns. "Without further ado, I give you Chelsie Linnloch...and special surprise guests!"

The panel kicks off with thunderous applause as Chelsie takes the stage. I wonder how she feels about doing cons in the middle of nowhere. But this is a big crowd, too much to be contained indoors. She's flanked by two costars, each dressed in screen-famous regalia. I suspect this is damage control. These two, Ensign Franks and Commander Ryn, don't have billing in the program. They must've been booked in a hurry when McFarland acted up. I don't think I've seen either of them in any other series.

Out-of-work actors sometimes wind up with regular jobs. Maybe that's what Franks, played by Steve Jenns, and Ryn, played by Miriam Werner, are doing now. For a while, they share stories, ribbing each other gently, and it's so much fun to get a glimpse of the behind-the-scenes magic that I can't stop smiling. I glance at Seeker, who's watching me instead of the guests onstage. I smile at him, feeling a blush warm my cheeks.

God, he's sexy.

"Remember when we got stuck in the escape pod?" Chelsie says. "And it turned out, someone's pet Fluvian snarler had chewed through the wiring."

"Hey, that snarler puppet had better acting chops than you," Miriam retorts.

That sounds a little bitter since Chelsie is still working and Miriam isn't. She's an older woman, late fifties now, and I hear it can be tough to get acting jobs past a certain age. Steve smooths over the moment with a cute anecdote about a crew reunion party that happened five years ago in Vegas.

"But what happens in Vegas stays in Vegas, right?" He grins.

It's so strange that Ensign Franks is older than me. I've seen him on TV as a kid for years. But he's a grown man with a salt-and-pepper goatee, not a super genius who graduated from Nebula Academy eight years early.

I sneak another peek at Seeker. His upper body is nearly brushing mine since these seats are quite close together. If I shifted, I could touch him. But I don't. I just savor the feeling of wanting to, a soft anticipation tightening my stomach. There's real delight in the tentative start of something, wondering if they'll hold your hand or smile at your joke.

When the panel ends, the moderator comes back out. "There will be an autograph session at the pavilion tent in Section 7-A. Candid pictures aren't allowed, but you'll be able to purchase signed glossy photos on-site."

"So glad we didn't miss this," Tad says.

I agree. "Took the bad taste of McFarland right out of my mouth."

We stretch our legs and wander back to the maze of tables and stalls, each more alluring than the last. I catch snatches of geeky conversation and notice the sound of rolling dice punctuated by occasional blaster effects.

Seeker pauses by a table with an array of alien artifacts. Well, replicas from various shows, that is.

"Do these devices function?" he asks.

The vendor seems confused, and I step forward to smooth things over. "Do they turn on, light up, make sounds?"

"Oh. Yeah! Of course. This is a genuine crystal orb," he promises. I lean closer to inspect the mesmerizing swirls of light within the glassy sphere. "Crafted with such precision, even a Vortoxian wouldn't spot the difference."

"Remarkable," Seeker murmurs, examining the orb with delicate curiosity. "The artisans of Earth have a mastery of detail that rivals that of the finest crafters in the Cygnus Cluster."

"What?" The vendor doesn't realize that Seeker is messing with him.

Or at least, I think he is. Maybe it's a sincere compliment.

"He's refusing to break the fourth wall," I say swiftly.

"Oh, right. Committed to the cosplay, I got ya. Did you want to buy that?"

"We can't," Tad says, coming up behind me. "You don't take intergalactic credits."

"So fucking funny." The vendor moves off, muttering about weirdos ruining his business.

He wouldn't have a shop without us, though.

"Maybe next year, they'll consider it," Poppy jokes. "Especially if Space Con becomes an actual space destination!"

I choke a little on my own saliva. *Don't panic. She's kidding.*

"Can you imagine?" Tad laughs, picking up a meticulously detailed model spaceship at the next table. "Real aliens? That would be something to phone home about."

I notice Jaz pause and she seems to share a look with Seeker. She hasn't commented on his super-realistic costume, either, unlike Tad and Poppy. Wait, does she know too? Did she know *first*? Why that bothers me, I'm not even sure. But my chest feels tight.

"You show the world too much," Ravik says softly.

They certainly can move quietly.

I blink. "What?"

"There is no value in inventing reasons for sorrow," they add.

And then they move off through the crowd, leaving me with the sense that they know something I don't. Maybe a *lot* of somethings.

"No way, an Astro Cruiser!" Tad's voice pierces through the din of chattering fans and electronic beeps from nearby gaming booths.

It's like we're all kids again. Poppy is the first to move, and then I follow Jaz to Tad's side, where he's gazing fervently at a life-size replica of the famed spacecraft from *Astro Adventures*. It's especially impressive that they built this out of Lego when the ship came from a cartoon of all things.

"By the moons of Jupiter," Poppy intones. "We must investigate!"

Tad chuckles, adjusting imaginary spectacles in true Professor

Nexus fashion. "'We shall discern the secrets of the cosmos'—or at least snag some cool merch.'"

Zeltron was only the first of my many alien crushes. And now I've met a real one.

I pick up a toy blaster that's for sale nearby, strike a heroic pose, and quote the commander. "'Fear not, for the stars guide our path!'"

"Classic Zeltron," Tad says. "Always the optimist, even when faced with a black hole."

"Optimism is the light that drives darkness away," Jaz says sagely.

"Plus, it helps to have a genius sidekick like Doctor Nexus," Poppy adds.

Who knew window-shopping could be this much fun? I find nostalgia in things we pass, and I don't need to collect everything or take it all home. I have these moments instead, happiness percolating away, and I decide to take Ravik's cryptic advice.

It doesn't matter who knew what when.

I matter to Seeker, or he wouldn't have told me; that's what counts. A few booths down, he's checking out a selection of futuristic gadgets, each one promising the power to warp reality or bend time, though the fine print says *for entertainment purposes only.*

"Ah, the Quantum Multi-Tool," I say. "With this, I can repair my ship's FTL drive, change the bozon flow of a frackulator, or convert a microwave into a particle accelerator!"

"Useful," Seeker concedes. "But what about this Cloaking Wristband? Invisibility has its perks. Sneaking past guards, avoiding awkward social situations—"

"Is that something you're worried about?" I cut in, surprised.

His voice wavers slightly, hinting at the hidden weight of his words. "Not normally. But here, if I misread cues or say something wildly incorrect..."

The unspoken consequences are clear; I don't need him to finish that sentence. The desire to protect him thrums within me, and I find myself lost in his rare, wonderful gaze. Electricity zings through me, just from a look. I need to know if he feels this too.

But I'm scared to ask. Scared to get an unwelcome answer. So I just drink my fill visually because sometimes it feels as I've been thirsty my whole life, and only now has anyone thought to offer me a cool, refreshing drink. To me, he is that—and more.

I'm so scared by how much I like him already.

20
SEEKER

I GAZE INTO JEN'S EYES, seeing sparks of gold I didn't notice until today.

The sunlight has tinted her skin. Humans don't change their hues intentionally as my people do. And they don't use colors to convey purposeful meaning. I've not yet been able to work out how or why they change colors. Sometimes it's emotional and sometimes it's environmental. And some humans don't display other colors at all, for various reasons, while others paint on bright hues.

When I caul my gaze with the secondary membrane, I can see additional light spectrums, but the colors are too overwhelming to remain in that spectrum. I blink again, trying to approximate the way she sees the world. I wonder how my eyes look to her, if she finds me strange or engaging, or some amalgam of the two.

What's she thinking right now?

Before I can ask, she breaks visual contact by ducking her head and moving down the table. "Oh, a replica of a Holo-Map Projector. I'd never get anywhere on time without GPS. I don't even know how to read a paper map."

I can't admit that I've never seen one. Other humans might find that odd. I'm not entirely sure what she's referring to, but extrapolating from context, I suspect it's a geographic representation of their world, imprinted on paper. But for there to be any helpful detail, everything would need to be magnified in great detail and thus require an incredible amount of paper. How would one even carry something so large? Humans are truly fascinating to me.

"I have gotten lost on multiple trips," I say then. "Sometimes I have found wonders I didn't know about. And I wouldn't have seen them had I stayed on my planned route."

She doesn't know it, but I'm not just talking topographical marvels like cascading green water or the shimmer of ethereal lights in a sentient forest. I'm also talking about her. If the agency had retrieved me on time, I would never have met Jen.

"Check this out!" Poppy calls.

It's another replica of some sort. From what I've gathered reading the boxes, these are all souvenirs related to human entertainments. This one says, *Positronic Screwdriver*. A screwdriver is a human tool used for construction and assembly. But this item looks nothing like that.

"Dang," Tad says. "I used to be so into Doctor Y."

I'm not familiar with that, but I know better than to mention it. Jaz doesn't say anything either, and I have no idea where Ravik has gone.

"It's one of my favorites," Poppy says. "I *loved* the ninth doctor, but I'm in the minority. Everyone loves ten for some reason."

Jen seems to sense my puzzlement and steps into the conversational lull. "The trivia contest is about to start. Anyone interested joining me?"

"Not me," Jaz says. "I'm going to look for Ravik. Come with me, Seeker."

I receive an odd look from Jen, but I don't know what this is about either. And at first I don't recall enough of human silent language to reply without making the others wonder. Then I remember the shrug. What a helpful gesture this is. I lift and lower my upper body, hoping the approximation works with my own physiology.

"I'll team up with you," Tad tells Jen.

Poppy adds, "I'm in. Trivia should be fun. And maybe there will be prizes."

Jen seems a little reluctant to part from me. I hope the impulse stems from affection and not from fear that I will do something ridiculous and endanger myself. As the humans move off, debating their trivia team name, Jaz turns to me.

"This way. Ravik is waiting for us."

"This sounds like a purposeful secret meeting."

But I can't imagine what the three of us would have to discuss. Ravik doesn't seem to like most of us at the best of times. I'm not entirely sure why they joined the chat or agreed to attend Space Con. But I suppose I'll find out. I follow Jaz as she threads through the throng, navigating with a surety that I find impressive. She's not new here, though, and she understands humans better.

Now that I'm not worried about the tech camo breaking down, I feel oddly at ease. Nobody is staring at us, and we're surrounded by others who look every bit as unique. In fact, some of the costumes even appear more unusual than Jaz and me.

"Stay close," Jaz says. "Ravik isn't the patient type."

I'd gleaned as much myself. Which is why I was surprised that they don a costume day after day with complete dedication. It takes a certain amount of time and effort to replicate the same look. For that reason, people will likely assume *I'm* especially committed to cosplay. It's a bit ironic, considering how anxious I've been about appearing without the tech camo.

I speak in the subharmonic inaudible to human ears. "It's a bit sad, isn't it? They want so desperately to meet us, but..."

"We're at a convention that fetishizes extraterrestrial beings," Jaz replies. "Many humans would love to do more than *meet* us."

That startles me. Certainly I have strong feelings for Jen, but I didn't realize that multiple humans might wish to experience intimacy with a nonhuman partner. Assuming they didn't sell us out for fame, fortune, and the potential payout from the authorities.

"That is a salient point."

I maneuver around a group taking photos with a particularly impressive cyborg costume. This one I recognize; I have watched several Terminator movies. Humans have a fascinating relationship with technology: they seem to both rely on it and fear it at the same time. We pass stalls selling comics and artists sketching custom pieces for excited patrons. But Jaz seems to know exactly where she's going.

Ravik is at a picnic table in the food truck lot, waiting for us with ill-concealed impatience. "You took long enough," they say to Jaz.

"This one proved difficult to wrangle."

I could take exception to her statement, but it might delay finding out what they want. "I'm curious what's going on. What's so important?"

"You really don't know?"

Ravik is blue again today. It's the same costume they had on... An idea occurs to me belatedly. But it can't possibly be true. Can it? But if I'm here, and Jaz is here...

"Congratulations," Ravik says. "I believe you just had an epiphany."

While I recognize Jaz's natural appearance, I've never encountered a being like Ravik. That's why I didn't doubt their explanation when they said they were... What was it? An ice-world barbarian? I thought it was a human cultural reference.

"How did you both know?" I ask. "I had no idea."

The other two exchange a look, and then Jaz says, "You're using your own update. The upgrade isn't configured to interact with other devices. Ours is. It pinged on your arrival that first night."

Since I thought I improved this system—and the tech camo—I feel more than a little chagrined by that revelation. Mine is newer, which *should* mean that it's better. Apparently, that's not always the case. I feel humbled by their calm competence...and how much more they seem to know about traveling the galaxy. I feel like a youngling playing at exploration, and I have not experienced this since I came to maturity.

I cannot say I care for the sensation.

"Why didn't you tell me before?" I address the question to Ravik since Jaz revealed herself at the restaurant earlier.

"I had to be certain you wouldn't cause problems," they reply.

"Does this conversation mean I've passed your initial assessment?"

"You're cautious enough not to get caught." It's not a complete endorsement of my faculties, but Ravik tends to be brusque. "It's enough. Unlike Jaz, I hate it here. But my contacts have been silent for far too long, so I need to ask if you have a ride off-world."

Now I understand the reason for this clandestine rendezvous. Ravik wants to catch a shuttle with me. Unfortunately, I have no good tidings to impart. "The agency failed to arrive at the appointed day and time. I've been stranded for over a human year."

"Twenty for me," Ravik says in a flat, hopeless tone.

I'm speechless. I had no idea that such things happened with any regularity. But the reputable tourism agencies don't stop at 97-B. And if the enforcement office in the Galactic Union closes a company that has violated the terms of interdiction, they won't collect lawbreakers who went on world against regulations.

In human verbiage, too bad, so sad, tough luck for us.

"I'm sorry I can't assist."

"It was too much to expect," Ravik says. "I'll never escape this polluted mudball."

Jaz taps the table once. "I'm not interested in an exit strategy. That's why Ravik wanted to meet. It's not my agenda."

"Not this again," Ravik mutters. "If you tell me to make the best of things one more—"

"What's this about?" I cut in to keep the peace.

Jaz perches on top of the table, getting comfortable. "You already told Jen. We should tell Tad and Poppy too. They might be able to help, and I believe they're trustworthy. I'm tired of pretending all the time."

"This is a human colloquialism," Ravik says, "but it's apt: over my dead body."

"I need to time to consider," I say.

Jen is someone I trust, no question. But I'm uncertain about Tad and Poppy. I haven't spoken to them privately or at length.

"Then I'll wait for your decision," Jaz says.

"How did you end up here?" I ask Ravik. It's doubtful they will reveal much, but I'm too curious not to inquire.

"Entirely by accident," they reply. "And that's all I plan to say for now."

"Do you have any ideas how we could leave?" I ask.

"If I did, would I risk trusting you to see if you had a ride off-world?" When Ravik puts it that way, I feel more than a little abashed.

Their brusqueness makes me feel quite young. "You might have a ship we could repair together. I'm good with technology."

"Acquaint yourself with disappointment if you're trying to exit this place," Ravik says. "And forget about seeing your family again."

That hurts. I should have said so many things before I left, but no. I was in a rush, hastily dismissing Oona's concerns and making promises I can no longer keep. I study the ground, watching minute insects march across the dry earth. That is how I feel, tiny and insignificant in the grander scheme of things.

Jaz gets up, seeming dissatisfied with the private conference. "Well. If that's it, we ought to find the others."

I have much to contemplate—and a major decision to make.

GROUP CHAT
JANUARY 6 | 16:28

Jeneticist: Hey, friends! Nobody from RL can go with me and I'd love it if we all went to Space Con together this year.

Stargazer: When is it?

Jeneticist: In July.

Stargazer: I'd like to go but I don't know if I can get the time off.

SquidHead: Definitely down for that!

JazzyPlum: I'll be on vacation then anyway. I'll research options for accommodation.

Seeker: I could make it work. Maybe.

FarfromHome: I don't have anything better to do.

Stargazer: Does anyone else cosplay?

Jeneticist: I do! It's gonna be epic!

Seeker: Can you provide a link? So we know what to expect? I've never heard of this.

Jeneticist: No problem! Here you go.

[link to Space Con website]

JazzyPlum: That's huge. Much bigger than I expected.

Stargazer: OMG. I'm so hyped. 🚀

SquidHead: Me too. I haven't done anything like this in years. God, I'm in a boring rut. I don't even do online RPG sessions anymore.

Jeneticist: You used to play?

SquidHead: Used to GM!

Stargazer: We should totally do some RPG tabletop sessions while we're there. I was in a gaming group in high school.

FarfromHome: I've heard of this. Never done it.

JazzyPlum: I'm interested too.

Seeker: Seems like it would be fun.

Jeneticist: I'm in for the RPG sessions too!

Jeneticist: Looks like Space Con is green for launch. 🛸 👽

21

JENNETTE

THE TRIVIA CONTEST IS IN the shaded pavilion tent where they had autograph sessions yesterday.

Now the tables are dedicated to small groups. There are like twenty of us, all with different team names; we chose Misfit Toys for our squad, and the volunteers have written them all dutifully on the whiteboard. It's all low-tech and good fun. I crane my neck to see the prizes piled on the tables up front.

"Think we'll win anything?" I ask quietly.

Poppy shrugs. My money is on Tad for depth and breadth of science fiction lore. He's a gamer too, so his knowledge won't be limited to shows. The quizmaster has a cordless mic and they made us listen to them sing the Yub Yub song before deigning to get started. It was kind of adorable in the dorkiest way imaginable.

"Okay, you've all been amazing sports. Are you ready to rumble?"

The crowd replies quietly, a murmur of assent. It's like we think we're not allowed to get boisterous. But who's gonna complain?

"I can't hear you!"

This time, we all shout, "Yeah!"

"Perfect. Now I know you're awake. First question! What's the name of Lando Calrissian's ship?"

I ring my dinner bell immediately. Poppy and Tad are ringing theirs too. More bells are heard after.

"Misfit Toys were first. Your answer?"

"The *Millennium Falcon*!" I shout.

"Oooh, so sad. That's incorrect!" The quizmaster calls on someone else.

"*Lady Luck*!"

"That's the response we were looking for!"

I mutter beneath my breath. "That was a trick question."

According to forum discussions, Lando never should have relinquished the *Millennium Falcon* to Han, and then there was the question of cheating in that sabacc game. But I guess *this* trivia contest wants straightforward answers only.

Poppy pats my arm, leaning over to whisper, "I was gonna say that too."

It's like I've jinxed us, however. We don't win a bell ring after that, and other teams go up on the board like lightning while we've yet to score a point. I sigh quietly.

"Time for a bonus round!" The quizmaster's eyes gleam beneath an alien-antenna headband. "In which episode of *Star Trek: The Next Generation* does Data first use contractions?"

"Ugh, I've never even watched *TNG*," Tad mutters.

"Come on," Poppy whispers, nudging me. "You're the Trekkie among us."

Fortunately, the other teams seem just as confused. And that's because there's a whole thing about contractions, and the question itself is another trick. I ring the bell.

"Misfit Toys, trying to redeem themselves."

"Data uses contractions in 'Encounter at Farpoint,' the pilot episode. But the episode that *focuses* on contractions is 'Datalore.'"

"Correct on both counts!" The quizmaster points at us with an exaggerated flourish. "You're on the board at last, Misfit Toys."

There are a few more questions, but I don't know anything about *Blake's 7* or *Babylon 5*. Neither do Tad and Poppy. The oldest team takes a significant lead.

"This is age discrimination," Tad complains.

Poppy grins. "Ah, let the olds have it."

The final scores are tallied, and I laugh. We're second to last, a couple of points ahead of the team that spent half the contest arguing whether Han or Greedo shot first.

"Yikes," Tad says. "I need a drink."

"Hey, at least we beat the 'Greedo's Revenge' squad." Poppy gives a thumbs-up to the guys who are desperately trying to make eye contact with her.

"Meh, I play for fun, not for glory," I say then.

"Oh thank God." Poppy feigns relief. "My ex was such a sore loser. I had to stop teaming with her. Just before we broke up, she went off on me hard-core when we lost at Scattergories at board game night."

"Ugh." None of my exes were that competitive, and they dumped me for reasons that I privately think are bullshit—because they counted on me "growing up" and ceasing to be who I am.

Tad offers a shrug. "Something, something, the friends we made along the way?"

I grin. "Exactly. I'm so glad we're doing this."

"I feel like we should hug," Poppy says. "But feel free to decline."

I smile as we step into a three-way consolation prize of a hug with Tad at the center, an arm around each of us. When we step back, we're all smiling.

"This is the happiest I've ever felt about losing," I say.

Poppy pats me on the shoulder. "Thanks for inviting us. I would never have come to something like this on my own."

I'm about to admit something that makes me look pathetic, but I want them to know how much their friendship means to me. "Remember when I said that nobody from RL could come with me?"

Tad nods and Poppy shoots me a curious look. "Yeah. What about it?"

"Truthfully, there's nobody to ask. I've always struggled to make friends. I had two really close ones..." Even now, it's tough for me to talk about Nina and Andrew, but I want to be honest with Poppy and Tad.

I want *real* friends again. And that means opening up to them.

Poppy takes a seat at the back of the tent. They're switching the setup, but the next event isn't for twenty minutes. The volunteers are too busy to bother us. Tad perches on a chair nearby, and they're both regarding me with expectant expressions.

"Do you want to talk about it?" he asks gently.

"Yeah. I do. Nina used to be my best friend. We met in grade school. Then Andrew moved in next door to me, and I asked him to sit with us on his first day of junior high."

"That's so nice of you," Poppy says. "We moved around a lot, and I remember how awkward it was, being the new kid."

I smile at the memory. "He was so funny. Stand-up comedian material. Both Drew and Nina were drama kids. So I joined to hang out with them. Did props and stage management."

"I was a drama kid too," Poppy declares.

"Not me. AV club all the way," Tad puts in.

I can tell they're sharing to make this easier for me. "Drew and Nina had crushes on each other for years. And I was in the middle, listening to their gooey secrets. They'd waffle, going back and forth. 'What if we ruin our friendship?'"

"Did they or didn't they?" Poppy asks.

"They did. Finally. Right before graduation. And they were an amazing couple." I don't mention how much of a third wheel I felt after that.

"Were?" Of course Tad picked up on that.

It's a four-letter word, practically a curse. "Yeah. Freshman year of college, we lost Andrew to a drunk driver, and Nina stopped replying to my texts."

It wasn't my fault; I wasn't even there. We all went to different schools, and she needed a clean break, I guess. I remind her too much of what she lost.

But I lost him too. And *her* as well—by choice.

"Oh my God," Poppy breathes. "Jen, I'm so sorry."

"Me too."

And I never recovered. I had roommates in college, not friends.

They were polite, nothing more. Once we graduated, they weren't interested in keeping in touch. Nobody is, it seems like. Nothing about me ever makes people want to stay. Not even Nina, the person who braided my hair, listened to my secrets, and made me a friendship bracelet that said 4-ever on it.

"Well, that's bullshit," Tad says. He actually looks pissed, and Tad is such a chill guy. "It sounds like she blames you or something."

Poppy moves closer, her hand hovering on the verge of a comforting pat. "Some people turtle when they're hurting. She might regret it. I bet she misses you. Possibly it's been so long now that she doesn't know what to say or how to say it."

It's more likely that I've been written off, but I appreciate Poppy trying to find some brightness in my depressing history. "Thank you for listening. The only reason I told you is so you understand how much your friendship means to me."

"Aw." She tips her head back, blinking rapidly as she takes a deep breath. "So help me, if you make me ruin my makeup… Anyway, back at you. I'm *so* glad we met."

Tad clears his throat. "Me too. We already hugged, though. And I think we should move along before the next event starts."

"Good point." I get up and head off.

The others follow. As we walk, Tad leans in, lowering his voice. "On another note, did you guys notice anything weird about the way Jaz dragged Seeker off?"

Ugh. I didn't want to think about that. I suspect Tad has a crush on Jaz; that's why he pays extra attention to what she does. And I can't blame him. She's so talented and graceful and effortlessly poised. I bet she's never awkward at parties and she doesn't tip coffee down her front when she gets excited.

I'm not jealous of her, but what if Seeker admires her the way I do? We have been flirting online, but maybe I don't measure up in person. Wait, no. I don't want to be insecure. He's shared a huge secret with me. I have to cling to that.

It's not like he's some intergalactic lothario on a quest to sow his seed with as many human women as possible before taking off at the speed of light. This isn't some weird fifties pulp movie full of screaming Marilyn-style blonds who are desperately afraid of what those tentacles might do.

Poppy nods, her curls bouncing. "Yeah, it was a little odd and pointed."

"This might sound paranoid, but do you think they're planning something without us?" Tad raises an eyebrow.

"Does anyone have a birthday coming up?" I ask as we head back toward the stalls.

That would be a sweet reason for them to be scheming. But mine's not until October and I prefer not to celebrate it.

"Not me. December twenty-eighth. I've gotten Christmas-slash-birthday gifts my whole life." Poppy seems not to mind, however, as it sounds like more of a statement than a complaint.

"Aw. Poor you." Tad offers a comforting pat. "As for me, I aged up in March, so it's already past."

"You should have said something! I would have…" I pause. What's appropriate for an online friend you haven't met in person yet? "Sent an e-card and done a digital design in honor of the occasion."

I'm not a pro at digital art, but I'm confident I could have come up with something cute for Tad's birthday. Maybe not beautiful enough for him to print and frame, but my mom is always telling Glynnis and me that it's the thought that counts. I actually don't always agree with that, depending on how bad the present is. But I'll forgive a lot of clumsiness if I trust in the giver's good intentions.

"That's sweet," Tad says. "Well, if you still want to next year, it's March fourteenth."

Poppy stops walking and I draw her out of the flow of foot traffic before she gets run over by a squad of stormtroopers. "Hear me out. They've been abducted by aliens and replaced with slightly off-kilter clones who hate trivia."

I nearly choke on my urgency to change the subject. But it will seem bizarre if I suddenly start talking about something else. "Good one."

"Should we do some sleuthing?" Tad asks.

I'm curious what Jaz wanted with Seeker, but I don't know that it's a good idea to dig into Seeker's secrets. At least not as a group.

But Poppy seems intrigued. *Dammit.*

"Maybe they were hungry. Or Ravik might have asked Jaz for help with a personal problem," I suggest.

"Then why involve Seeker especially?" Tad points out. "I could give advice. So can Poppy or you."

"I'm good at picking up subtext. There *is* something going on," Poppy agrees.

Crap. If I keep arguing, it will look like I know something. And I *do.* I'm just not confident that I know everything about the group's dynamics or Seeker's intentions. I know he's not from here—and at this point, that's basically the long and short of it.

And you invited him to move in with you.

The fact that he didn't jump on that offer... I'm not sure how I feel about it. On one hand, it speaks well of him that he's hesitant to impose, even if he's desperate. But maybe there are other factors at play. I only have his word for *why* he's here. There might be more sinister implications, not that I've ever put much stock in the alien-invasion trope.

There must be much easier ways to get resources than to pillage a local population, right? Humans have done exactly that so many times, but that doesn't mean Seeker's people are the same. If they're technologically advanced enough to have rules in place about visiting lower-tech worlds and uplifting, they should have even more regulations about hostile actions.

Dammit, I don't want to have these doubts. I believe he's a good person. I *do*.

There's absolutely nothing to worry about.

22
SEEKER

JEN'S MOTEL ROOM ONLY HAS one bed.

In the last month, I have consumed much local entertainment, and I'm familiar with this romantic device. The protagonists are forced, due to necessity, to share the bed, and erotic contact follows. But she's been strange and distant this afternoon, quiet even within the confines of the group.

On the drive back, after their evening meal, she didn't say much, her responses monosyllabic when I tried to break the silence. It's clear that she's distracted, but I don't know what's troubling her. I set my belongings down near the door, unsure how to proceed. The movement draws her attention.

"Make yourself at home," she says. "You must be starving."

While that's an exaggeration, I do need more nutrition. I combine the protein powder with tap water and drink it quickly. Jen slips into the bathroom, closing the door behind her. We'll be alone for the whole night, and I feel deeply conflicted.

On my homeworld, sharing habitation signifies a major commitment. The silent subtext is weighty—*I plight myself to you and we will share all challenges and joys henceforth*. But she would have sensed that promise in olfactory cues as well. And she would be displaying the proper mating colors, affirming that we've come to consensus regarding our future together.

Human social rituals are a great deal more confusing.

I perch on the edge of the motel bed, listening to the sound of running water. The synthetic bed cover feels rough, unlike the sleek foliage that I'd use for nesting on my homeworld, but it's better than the bedding at yesterday's temporary shelter. I don't get too comfortable, however, aware that I'm here only due to her generosity.

Regulating my respirations, I release the tension from the day. It was exhilarating but also terrifying, passing unnoticed among all the unsuspecting humans. No one realized that my unique look represents reality, not a clever use of special effects and prosthetics. Relief accompanies the quiet buzz of satisfaction that I succeeded at hiding in plain sight, but even as I bask in my success, I experience a pang of longing for a place where I need not hide, where my true form isn't fodder for a costume contest.

Pensive, I tap out a musical pattern on the wooden backrest behind me. Jaz wants to tell Poppy and Tad while Ravik is vehemently opposed. I'd like to share the truth about them with Jen right now, but this isn't my secret. The others need to give me permission before I say anything. That's the moral choice.

Eventually, Jen emerges from the bathroom in a cloud of steam. She has on different clothing, and much less of it. Per local entertainments, this would be her sleeping attire. Her skin is pink all over, the bits I can see, but it must be from the heat of the water. Her mood tells me that she's not in a mating frame of mind.

Not that I'm entirely certain how that would even work between us.

"Are you all right?" I ask.

Jen doesn't respond immediately, and I study her with a sense of bewilderment. She feels galaxies away despite the insignificant distance. I thought things were going well. In fact, she's always shown a marked predilection for my company.

"I'm fine," she says.

Fine is not a word my people would use. Our words are also defined with colors and scents, so meanings are delivered more precisely. I'm imperceptive without those useful hints guiding me to understand her mood. On Earth, the word *fine* seems to be a shield, a way to deflect undue interest. I respect her need for privacy, but the interaction feels...unfinished.

I have also seen exchanges in visual entertainment where the protagonist furiously claims they are fine when they are, in fact, precisely the opposite. She doesn't turn to look at me. Instead, she fiddles with her luggage, searching for something. The hum of the motel's air filtration device is too loud in my auditory sensors, exacerbating the tension and the silence.

"It seems that might not be the case," I say.

I have learned much about humans, their customs and contradictions, yet I remain an outsider, unable to understand certain behaviors. What is her rationale for trying to deceive me? Perhaps she fears that she was precipitous with her generosity? Too hasty in offering aid without thinking the situation through?

If that's the case, I can release her from obligation. "You've been so kind to me. But you don't have to shelter me. I can—"

"What?" she cuts in, blinking in apparent startlement. "Where did that come from?"

"It's obvious that something is troubling you. And please do not deny it again. The mood is strange between us."

"That's because you're plotting something with Jaz and Ravik! You think we can't tell? Poppy and Tad noticed too. It was a *really* pointed secret meeting." Then she presses a hand to her mouth as if she didn't intend to blurt all of that out.

Now I understand completely. I can't even say that she's wrong.

"We did have a private discussion," I admit. "But I wouldn't call it a plot."

"Fine then, I'm being dramatic," she mutters.

Now I have a crucial decision to make. Is my loyalty to Jaz and Ravik, two fellow exiles, or to Jen, whose good opinion matters more to me than I'd previously realized? I don't want her to think I'm… I believe the human word is *sketchy*.

"I don't want to have weird thoughts, but…what if you're dangerous?" she whispers.

That pains me. But I comprehend why those thoughts might occur to her. For all she knows, I'm a recon scout, a stranded vanguard of some terrible military action. My people are artists, not warriors, but she has no way to verify that information. And my secrecy has consequences.

"It's not what you think. I suspect you'd never even guess."

"Tell me?" She sits down on the other side of the bed, finally done pretending that she needs a vital item in her bag.

"Only if you promise to keep it between us."

Jen sighs. "More secrets."

"This one isn't mine to share, but I don't like keeping things from you. The fact is, Jaz and Ravik are from somewhere else as well." I point straight up, hoping that will be enough.

I don't believe in the surveillance state that some forums on 97-B refer to, but just in case, it's better for me to be cautious. Jaz and Ravik didn't give me permission to tell Jen about them, and I hope they're not too angry.

Her mouth opens. Closes. She can't seem to figure out what to say. I wait, patient as the ancient moons of my homeworld, for Jen to break the stillness. I've endangered the peace between Jaz, Ravik, and me, but perhaps they don't need to know that Jen knows? I don't favor the capacity for deception I've embraced on this planet.

"How long have they been here?" she finally asks.

"Ten years for Jaz. Longer for Ravik. Jaz wanted to talk about telling Poppy and Tad about all of us. Ravik is against trusting anyone."

"But they know you looped me in already," Jen says.

It's not a question, but I incline my head anyway. That's a human gesture I find useful for simple affirmation. "If it helps, Jaz wants to tell you. Ravik seems paranoid. Living here so long, in complete isolation, has altered them."

"Loneliness is painful," she says softly.

I know that all too well, and it seems as if Jen understands the searing chill of isolation also. I study her, seeking clues in her demeanor. I want to be closer to her, not divided by these conflicts. I reach out, and she meets me halfway. Her hand is soft and small, her skin contrasting the bright and dark patterns of mine. She traces a rounded shape on my skin, and a shimmering current of sensation passes between us, more pleasurable than a static shock. My mating colors deepen to violet. I feel her pulse, quicker than mine, a rhythm that thrums like a promise. Warmth floods my being, desire that sparks with surprising strength.

She leans in, and I mirror her movement. Her breath mingles with mine, a delicious intimacy on my homeworld. Humans would kiss now. I have witnessed their courtship rituals, but I do not share that experience. Yet I wish to touch her, learn the contours of her face and the lines of her form.

We're a breath apart, the question of what comes next like a star in the night sky, beautiful and shimmering with heat.

GROUP CHAT
FEBRUARY 12 | 20:02

Stargazer: I forget who mentioned Never Have I Ever last time, but now we have to play.

SquidHead: That was me. Me and my big mouth.

Stargazer: Thanks, Squiddy! Let's see who's the most innocent among us. 😇

Jeneticist: Define innocent...

Seeker: How do you play?

Stargazer: Seriously?

Jeneticist: At parties, it's a drinking game, so if you've done the thing, put a 🍺

JazzyPlum: And if you haven't, it's ⛔

FarfromHome: One day, I will leave this chat and never return.

Stargazer: Don't be cranky. Who's starting us off?

SquidHead: I'll go first. Never Have I Ever...gone skydiving.

FarfromHome: ⛔

Stargazer: I had a daredevil ex. 🍺

Jeneticist: ⛔

Seeker: 🍺

JazzyPlum: Seeker? Story!

Seeker: Seeker is short for Thrill Seeker, remember?

Jeneticist: No further questions.

JazzyPlum: ⛔

Seeker: Jen, your turn.

Stargazer: Dare you to spice things up a bit. 😌

Jeneticist: Challenge accepted. Never Have I Ever flirted my way out of a speeding ticket.

Stargazer: 🍺 Guilty as charged.

Seeker: ⛔ To be fair, I do not have a driving license.

Jeneticist: Whoa, really? Do you live in a big city?

Jeneticist: Never mind, you don't have to answer.

SquidHead: I tried. I did not succeed. ⛔

JazzyPlum: I don't drive either. ⛔

FarfromHome: 🍺 Law enforcement personnel are often quite lonely.

Seeker: 😄 Dark horse! Your turn, FFH.

FarfromHome: Never Have I Ever gotten into a physical altercation.

JazzyPlum: ⛔

SquidHead: I'm a lover, not a fighter. ⛔

Stargazer: TBF she started it. 🍺

Jeneticist: Details!

Stargazer: This girl was picking on my little sister, I told her to knock it off. She said, "Make me." I made her. [GIF of woman dusting off her shoulders]

JazzyPlum: Note to self, don't mess with Star.

Jeneticist: ⛔

Seeker: Do nonhumans count as an altercation?

Jeneticist: Uh, did you fight a bear or something? 😲

SquidHead: Hell yeah, it counts. 🥷

FarfromHome: Care to share the story, Seeker?

Seeker: 🍺 I will not be taking questions at this time. Jaz, would you like to go?

JazzyPlum: Never Have I Ever had a long-distance relationship.

Stargazer: Not for me. ⊖ Relationships are complicated enough already.

SquidHead: 🍺 Again, I tried. I did not succeed.

FarfromHome: 🍺

Jeneticist: No further comment, FFH?

FarfromHome: Some memories are too painful to share.

Stargazer: Aw. You do have a heart. 🫂

Seeker: ⊖ I travel too much.

Jeneticist: ⊖ I'd try it for the right person, though.

JazzyPlum: Anyone particular in mind?

Jeneticist: ...maybe.

Seeker: You have my attention. 🫶

Stargazer: Get a room, you two! And that does it for Never Have I Ever.

SquidHead: Fun game. Thanks, Star. We appreciate you. 🤗

Jeneticist: Until next time. 🏎️

23

JENNETTE

IF SEEKER WAS HUMAN, I would have kissed him.

That's what the lean meant, right? But I'm not sure if he understands that. Plus, his features are...different. And he doesn't have lips, per se.

Our hands are still joined, and I marvel at the difference in digits and joints. Some people might think that there's an arachnoid quality to his hands, but I find him beautiful and graceful. And the way he smells...

It goes straight to my head, making me feel warm all over. Not in the usual science fiction way, as if I'm unable to resist his pheromones. But he just smells *right* to me, spicy and delicious, like I need to breathe him in. I can withstand the tingles he creates, but I'm not sure if I want to. I would love to trace the patterns on his skin, but I'm unsure if that's welcome or even acceptable.

I'm in unchartered territory, so far as I know. Seeker stands, his motions fluid, a glide of muscle and sinew that is distinctly other, not the way human bodies move at all, more of a swivel than a turn. Then he lets go of me, and I silently curse myself for not taking the risk.

Not leaning all the way in or asking if I can touch him.

But I'm not a thrill seeker, unlike him. I fear rejection and I turtle when I'm nervous.

I'm so very nervous now. We've been quiet for so long now that this feels like a new conversation yet it relates to the loneliness that tethers the two of us to our uncertainties, like lunar bodies unable to break free from that stable orbit.

"Is it difficult?" I ask. "Being here on your own?"

He doesn't sugarcoat his response as he closes the curtains. "It is."

That's a smart move. People will think it's strange if he never takes off his "costume" in the motel room, even at Space Con. Even the most devoted cosplay fans would still take off their makeup and prosthetics to shower. He's better at predicting consequences, probably because he's taking the risks.

"Anything I can do?" I ask. "I want to help."

"You already do. More than you know. You've been more of a lifeline to me than you realize, I suspect."

"I'm so glad," I say softly.

I ponder his words. In my view, they amount to a declaration. In that moment, I dismiss my prior fears. There's no way he could be so gentle with me if he planned to do something bad—to me or anyone.

That makes me bold. This must be new ground for him as well. If he's lived in hiding, he hasn't made other significant connections. What we have is special. And even if he's leaving the first chance he gets, I don't want to wonder what might have been, what joy I might have experienced, had I only dared.

I'm carpe-ing this diem.

I bounce off the bed and close the distance between us, heart beating frantically with anticipation. Seeker is so close that I can detect the subtle shifts of color in the patterns on his skin. He faces me, that intense, spiced scent deepening. I imagine that it means he's attracted to me also. *Please let that be true.*

"Your pulse has quickened," he observes. "And in secondary light spectrums, you're radiating unusual heat."

Oh dear God. Can he see that I want him?

Embarrassment heats my cheeks, along with the flush of arousal he's already noticed. But in some ways, that makes things easier. He broached the subject, not me.

"I'm experiencing attraction," I say, trying to sound calmer than I feel. "Does that... I mean, what does that look like for your people?"

"We're different in many ways." There's a note of curiosity in his wonderful voice, and it vibrates along my skin, caressing me without contact. "But we do share certain sensations. Some beings do not mate for pleasure. *My* people do."

"Mine too," I whisper.

"Jen..." The way he says my name is a revelation with a little rumble on the N.

Before, I thought my full name was old-fashioned, and my nickname was common. But with him, I feel brand new, as if wonders await. I swallow hard, feeling like every star I've ever glimpsed through a telescope burns within my chest.

"Yes?"

I close the short gap between us, breath hitching because the air between us feels charged like the ionosphere during a meteor shower. But just as I'm about to brush my lips against the side of his face, he withdraws slightly, his back nearly to the window.

Shit. Am I making him uncomfortable? Maybe I misread the cues.

"I'm...concerned. About mingling bodily fluids. I don't want to hurt you. Or vice versa."

That...is a good point. I laugh softly. In the romances I read, aliens never worry about getting toxic shock syndrome from the bacteria in their human partner's mouth. But Seeker's a long way from home, and if he has a medical emergency, I can't help.

"Why are you amused?" he asks.

"Because that objection is so you. Not that I disagree."

"I'm glad you aren't offended. If you're willing, I could show you something else."

If it gives me a chance to be close to him, I'm so there. "Color me curious."

"It does, indeed, relate to my colors. Can you see the patterns? How they've deepened in hue to dark violet?"

Now that he's mentioned it, the swirls of color do seem more concentrated and intense. "Oh, that's pretty. What does it mean?"

"It's a mating display. If you were of my people, you would respond in kind, show me your interest with your own shades."

"A blush has a similar significance," I whisper, feeling my cheeks heat.

I've never wanted someone like this. My skin feels too small, and normally I don't struggle with my libido at all. In the usual course of things, I don't think about sex too much, and if I do get turned on, I take care of it myself. The idea of waiting around for a partner is kind of puzzling to me.

"With your permission?" He's waiting for my verbal assent, his seven-fingered hand hovering in the space between us. Though I'm not sure what he has in mind, it can't be too intense, considering his fears about swapping bodily fluids. "Granted."

Seeker takes my hand and places it on his side, where I discover that the colors offer a raised texture to his skin, sensuous and velvety. He offers a low sound at the touch, and the pattern deepens to midnight ink, incredibly vivid. I'm not sure what I'm meant to do, so I trace the intricate lines and whorls, feeling little shocks go through him with each movement, as if I've got lightning in my fingertips.

"Does it feel good?"

Lord, but I want to make him feel *incredible*. My body aches, just from this much. If I could, I'd rub against him helplessly, trying to cover myself in his scent. I don't know why that idea gets me so flushed, but I want to smell of cinnamon and cardamom and saffron, just as he does. It would be a tiny secret between us, proof that we've gotten close and writhed together until our senses sparked with satisfaction.

He said his people mate for pleasure, so they must experience something like a climax. I want to know how that looks for him. I need to hear him lose his composure and beg me for—

Anything. Everything.

"Exquisite," he whispers. "But it's growing difficult to contain myself."

It feels a little soon to wade into these waters, as much as I'm tempted. But sex muddles everything, and I don't want to rush things or make it weird between us. I also don't want to be a notch on an alien belt. Is that even a thing? I know Captain Kirk sure bagged as many alien bedmates as he could.

I pull my hand back, a little surprised that such delicate contact could get him this excited. That's flattering, however.

"Sorry. I didn't mean to push."

"I have lived in hiding. Physical contact feels especially poignant now."

I get that, maybe more than he realizes. During the pandemic, I went months without seeing anyone in person, which meant safety but also isolation. I taught all my classes online, and we didn't gather in public spaces. I didn't even hug my own mother for half a year. Necessary precautions, but lonely ones as well.

Time to give him some space.

I wander back over to the bed and plug in my phone. It occurs to me to wonder how he got human tech in the first place and how he's managed to survive within our infrastructure. If he rented an Airbnb, he must have accounts and IDs, right?

I have so many questions.

"Can I ask you a few things?"

"Certainly. I have no secrets from you any longer. And it's quite a relief."

The colors on his patterns have lightened, closer to lilac than violet. I find that fascinating. But it's also extremely helpful.

If we decide to take the next step, I'll have no doubts if Seeker is in the mood.

24
SEEKER

JEN IS PERCEPTIVE.

When she withdraws, I suspect she's realized that I'm ambivalent about deepening our relationship to include physical intimacy. My people do not engage in such contact lightly or casually. Though I told her that we do indulge in sexual contact for pleasurable reasons, I didn't tell her that we imprint for life.

I shouldn't make such a decision impetuously. If I allow myself to imprint on Jen, that would entail accepting that I'll never leave this planet—that I'll live and die here with her. Never see my family again. Never communicate with anyone from my former life. That is not a choice I should make on impulse with arousal confounding my senses.

"I was wondering how you've gotten by," she says. "It can't be easy to work."

Oh. Logistical inquiries.

These are easy queries to address. "Your databases are not difficult to infiltrate. I created an identity for myself, using my own name. Tamzir Jaarn. Then I had the system generate appropriate documents and mailed them to my location."

"It can't be a real picture of you."

"No. I carry a document that says I've had plastic surgery in case I'm questioned. But I haven't tested it at airports. I have only used bus stations, where they do more cursory checks." Sometimes, they don't even ask for ID.

"The tech doesn't work on cameras, does it?" Jen asks.

It's an astute assessment. "No, it causes a malfunction instead of recording my actual appearance. That's the way I pass unnoticed."

"Someone who tracks patterns in disruption might wonder about that," she says.

"Are there people who study such things?" Considering the chaos on 97-B, it seems to me they should have more pressing concerns.

"I'm not sure. But there *are* folks who see conspiracies everywhere." She shakes her head with a twist of her mouth that doesn't wholly seem like a smile. "In your case, however, the reason the security cameras fail really is…'because aliens.'"

Since I've been reading long, involved screeds written by such humans on the Aliens Among Us site, I comprehend the humor and let out an amused click. Now I need not stifle my customary auditory cues in the interest of concealing my strangeness.

"FoxSmolder would be exultant to hear it." I name a conspiracy theorist on the website who makes the most illogical arguments about extraterrestrials influencing culture on 97-B throughout the ages.

The simplest rebuttal is, why would we bother? Such arguments assume that humans are, in the local vernacular, a big deal. But there can be no reasonable discourse with certain individuals.

Jen laughs. "Wouldn't it be wild if they were here?"

"I can't say I'm too interested in a personal encounter."

"Me either."

I want to be transparent with her. "Did you have other questions?"

"Mainly about your work, I guess. You told me a little before, but I'm interested in the details, if you don't mind sharing."

"Once I acquired appropriate documentation, I registered on a site for those proficient in digital work. I wrote a few programs and then automated programs to write more code. The processes here are extremely simple, unlike the crystalline matrices I worked with as a child."

That was rudimentary education, and my people didn't even focus on the sciences. Jen would be absolutely amazed to learn that Jaz comes from the techiest civilization I know, with everything automated and constant innovation. Ironic, when Jaz might have prospered where I was born, given her love of music.

"And then you got paid online?"

"Yes. I set up an account with a financial app that didn't require a video check. They accepted photos of my identification documents as proof that I am a legal resident."

"So legally speaking, Tamzir Jaarn is a U.S. citizen."

"Unless they do a deep dive and audit the system records. Someone very skilled might detect my tampering, but if the authorities haven't come looking for me by now, it seems that I didn't set off any internal alarms."

"Well played. Now you can run for president." She blinks twice. "Wait, don't do that. Too much scrutiny would be bad. The camera thing would become a major issue."

Her concern that I will decide to govern this nation—or never doubting that I'm capable of accomplishing that—entertains me vastly. Apart from Oona, the rest of my family considers me to be a sorrowful case of missed potential. I could have done so much more with my life, had I chosen to devote myself to art instead of chasing the next stimulating experience. In their view, I have embraced hedonism and chosen to consume rather than create. I can't say that I disagree with them entirely, but no art form ever spoke to me sufficiently.

In my bleak moments, I have wondered whether I was born without the "creation" gene. I've found myself at my happiest while studying something and recording observations, but my family never urged me to pursue such interests. Is it possible that one could spend their entire life searching for where they belong?

It seems that I've done that anyway.

Her jaw opens, her mouth stretching wide. Per my studies, it's a yawn, which seems to perplex local scientists. I've perused a number of theories regarding why humans perform this behavior, but general consensus agrees that weariness can cause it.

"Should we get some rest?" I ask.

"Are you okay sharing the bed?"

"I don't sleep in the same way humans do. You may find my repose disturbing. But I won't move, and I shouldn't trouble you."

"I can be a restless sleeper. Maybe I should ask if I'll bother you."

The polite response would be to say that she won't disturb me. But I can't know that for certain. I offer the next best assurance. "We can see how it goes. This is new territory for both of us," I say.

Jen rises from the bed and turns back the covers. I find the human obsession with covering their bodies very strange. If it's not street clothing, it's bed clothing. And then there are special fabrics to adorn their sleeping surfaces. Not to mention jewels that are physically inserted in their bodies and inks that permanently mark their skin. But perhaps if I didn't have my own colors and patterns already, I would design them.

She goes into the bathroom for a while, readying herself for sleep. I hear more water sounds. After switching off the lights, Jen finally gets into bed, settling in with a contented exhalation. Human rituals fascinate me. They use water for so many things.

"Something else occurred to me," she says.

"What?"

"You don't absorb sunlight like a plant, do you? Because otherwise, what the heck are you eating?"

"I consume protein powder derived from soy. And water. Many ingredients are toxic to me, and your cuisine tends to be quite complex."

"Hmm. Maybe I can figure out a way to cook for you. If you decide to go with me. There are recipes focused on people with allergies who can only have very limited ingredients."

Warmth blossoms within me. "You would do that? For me?"

"Of course! It wouldn't even be that difficult. I'll start the research tomorrow."

"Speaking of tomorrow, do you have a plan for our activities?" She's been looking forward to this event for months.

And I'll accompany her wherever she wishes.

"I was hoping people will want to pause on con stuff and go to the UFO Museum. It's a must-see when you're in Rellows. It has all the town history, newspaper articles, alleged artifacts. They even built a life-size reproduction of the alleged crashed ship."

"That sounds most enjoyable."

"Awesome. I knew you'd be interested. You can confirm if they got any details right."

Based on what I've seen so far, that's highly implausible. Humans are wildly inventive and often chaotic, but their predictions about the larger galaxy generally don't match my lived experience. I settle on top of the covers as Jen nestles in. As long as the room is warm enough to sustain my body temperature, I do not require conceal-ment or nesting materials for comfort.

I shift my nictitating membrane so I can savor her colors in this spectrum. She is radiant, shimmering orange and gold with hits of red. Just when I think Jen cannot become more beautiful, I see her anew, a luster known only to me. Her breathing steadies, becoming lighter.

I think she's drifting off when I hear her voice in the dark. "Seeker?"

"Yes?"

"Do you dream?"

"Not as humans understand it." I could tell her about memory walking. I will, but it's a long and detailed explanation. Not to be discussed now, when she needs to rest.

"Huh." It's like she's sleepily, randomly asking questions, what-ever floats into her tired mind. "Why didn't you rent something more permanent? You had the legal means."

Each month, I chose a new locale near the mountain rendezvous point, hoping my comm device would light with news from the agency. *They will return soon.* That's what I told myself each time I sought new shelter. And every time, I was wrong.

"Because I didn't intend to stay this long," I whisper.

"And now?"

"I'm not sure I have any choice in the matter."

PRIVATE CHAT
FEBRUARY 14 | 17:22

Jeneticist: You there?

Seeker: Where else would I be?

Jeneticist: You have a life! You might have a date.

Seeker: Well, I don't. What's on your mind?

Jeneticist: First off, Happy Valentine's Day! 🤍

Seeker: Thank you. 🤍

Seeker: But you didn't answer my question.

Jeneticist: You ever feel like you're just...not made for this planet?

Seeker: Yes. You also?

Jeneticist: 100%. In school, I was the girl with the alien lunchbox. Literally.

Seeker: Anyone who doesn't understand how wonderful you are...well, it's their loss.

Jeneticist: That's sweet of you to say, but today, I found out that all the professors have been getting together for drinks for years.

Jeneticist: I've never once been invited.

Jeneticist: I'm just feeling kind of sad today. 😟

Jeneticist: It shouldn't be this tough to make friends.

Jeneticist: It was supposed to get easier as we get older, right? But if not for our group chat...

Seeker: I'd be really lonely too.

Seeker: If it helps at all, I'm so glad I "met" you.

Seeker: You've brightened my world immeasurably.

Jeneticist: Wow, really?

Jeneticist: Just call me sunshine. ☼

Seeker: Okay, sunshine.

Jeneticist: You're so silly. I meant figuratively. But I guess I'm not opposed to that nickname. Or endearment. Whichever.

Seeker: I have always been looking for something else. An escape hatch.

Seeker: And it's not like my life was dreadful. Or even difficult. I just had...

Jeneticist: Wanderlust?

Seeker: That word is sufficient.

Seeker: Maybe we're just tuned into a different frequency than most.

Jeneticist: I like that explanation. It's way better than "too weird to get invited to parties."

Seeker: I find your passion inspiring. It's one of your many admirable qualities.

Jeneticist: Yeah? Wow.

Jeneticist: Okay, see, this is why I messaged you. I'm always smiling when we talk. 😊

Seeker: I'm happy too. 🫶

25

JENNETTE

IT TAKES ME LONGER THAN I expected to fall asleep.

And when I wake, it's with Seeker's words still burning like embers in my mind. *I don't think I have any choice in the matter.* That makes me inexpressibly sad—both for him and for me. Because I adore spending time with him. In fact, I probably should be alarmed at how much I've come to care for him.

Sure, we've been talking online for a while, and I had that crush. But now he's a person to me on a deeper level, one with complicated problems I never could've envisioned. But any connection I pursue with him with always be shadowed by the fact that he doesn't have that many choices.

He can't trust most people. While we're together, I'll always be wondering if he's making the best of a bad situation. If he would have chosen me if he'd possessed other, better alternatives. That's a shitty way to live. And I don't even know if he'd choose to stay here, if he had other options.

Does he want to go home? It's a silly question. I'm sure he does.

That doesn't mean I'll cut him loose, however. I'm greedy enough to soak up these moments with him, even if they're limited.

The room is very dark, the blackout blinds still tightly drawn, so nobody can see how he truly looks. In these moments, he's mine alone.

I blink away the remains of sleep and roll over. Seeker is awake beside me, still on top of the covers. He is indeed quiet in repose. I barely noticed that he was there last night. There are stars in his eyes, pinpoints of brightness sparking around the vertical pupils. I could stare at him for hours, but I'm afraid it might make him feel self-conscious. I don't want him to feel studied, just...appreciated. Today, the patterns in his skin are a muted lavender, maybe denoting relaxation, and as I gaze closer, I detect a faint shimmer.

"Morning," he says.

His voice never fails to elicit a response, one that would be embarrassing if it wasn't also purely involuntary. I can't decide if it's most akin to a growl or a purr, but it vibrates at precisely the right frequency, sending shivers down my spine. God, I wish I could rub my face against his throat.

"Good morning."

Thankfully, it's not weird or awkward between us. I didn't cross any lines and I backed off when he expressed hesitation. I roll out of bed and stretch, rotating my shoulders. Ridiculously, I'm a little sore from all the walking yesterday while carting my backpack around. I really should exercise more.

"Hungry?" he asks.

"Starving. How much soy powder do you have left, by the way?"

"Enough to see me through today and tomorrow."

"What brand is it? I can order some and have it delivered."

He leans closer to show me what he's been buying and I place the order, willing my pulse to settle down. I was already ridiculously into him before I knew he was from beyond the stars. The wonders he must have witnessed... I wish I could skim through his brain and see for myself.

Once I finish the online shipping, I get ready quickly. I'll get dressed in another quick cosplay. Dr. Crusher from *Star Trek: The Next Generation*. I just need to put on my uniform and a red wig. There, I'm good to go.

Seeker has been using appliances or gizmos that I don't recognize while I rush around. I suspect one of them must be hygiene-related. I should have asked even more questions last night, but I was super tired.

"Ready?" I tilt my head toward the door. Seeker hasn't activated his tech camo, so I drink in his natural beauty.

"Tad sent a message. He wants to meet for breakfast at a restaurant nearby."

I quickly check my phone. "Oh right. They've been waiting for a table since the place opened! Talk about going above and beyond."

"We should hurry," Seeker says.

I lead the way to the diner nearby. The crowd is stunning after the quiet of our room. Already, the day has warmed up to a shocking degree with the sun beaming overhead. Outside, the con-goers smell like body wash and sunscreen, applied preemptively, while the diner inside delivers the welcome scents of bacon and coffee. Poppy waves energetically from a big table in the center of the room. Her hair is a rainbow today, one of the gorgeous, flowing mermaid wigs that I frankly covet, but I haven't figured out what costume I'd use it for and I try not to buy things without planning them out.

Along with Seeker, Jaz and Ravik are all hiding in plain sight today, boldly brightening the day with their alien hues. And *I'm* the only one who knows their secret.

Tad is devouring an impressive stack of pancakes and eggs while Ravik and Jaz abstain. Poppy has fruit and yogurt in front of her, her spoon hovering in midair as I take a seat opposite. They've left a spot for Seeker next to me and I smile a little over that.

"You're the last ones here! Wild night?" Poppy teases.

Poppy practically sparkles today; she seems to be loving Space Con so far. The spark of mischief in her conspiratorial look hints that she's got big plans for the day, but I've already made my own with Seeker. The others are welcome to come, of course.

"Define 'wild,'" Seeker says.

"Did you do anything I wouldn't do?" Tad asks.

Seeker pauses. "I don't know what that entails."

I've noticed that he hesitates sometimes, likely unsure of how to respond to easy jokes. But to him, the humor may not be self-evident.

Luckily, Tad laughs. "Point taken."

"Anyone have good dreams?" Jaz asks.

I wonder if her people dream. But I'm not supposed to know that she's an alien. Ravik either. So I'll do my best not to react with undue curiosity to everything she says.

"Oh, man," Tad says. "I got chased by a giant buzzer that wanted to step on me."

Poppy laughs. "Clearly a result of the trivia contest."

"The idea of dreams is fascinating," Ravik says.

Before any of us can reply, the harried waitress brings a plate of French toast to Poppy. "Sorry about the delay. What can I get you folks?"

I set down my menu with a smile that probably doesn't sweeten the overwork from the town population doubling for a week. "I'll have the garden omelet and sourdough toast."

"Water for me," Seeker says.

Once the server hurries off to her next table, Poppy asks, "You mean, like hidden meanings or something like that?"

Ravik shakes their head. "More the idea that random hallucinations can refresh one's mind. I find it curious."

Seeker is nodding and I press my leg against his, hoping he'll realize this is quite an inhuman observation. We don't really reflect on how odd it is that sleep and dreams can recharge our brains because that's how our bodies function. It's like using a microwave to heat up some pizza; I don't spend time pondering how it works.

Tad joins the conversation. "Once I dreamed about being lost in a corn maze after watching a horror movie. The implications are interesting."

Okay, maybe humans and aliens have more in common than I realized. But I figure a subject change is in order before Poppy and Tad realize that three of us are not like the rest. I spot the waitress heading our way.

"Food's here!"

The omelet is amazing with lots of fresh veggies and gooey melted cheese. Poppy is digging into her French toast eagerly, not seeming to pay much attention to the rest of us as her eyes drift half-closed.

"Mmm. Real maple syrup," she practically moans.

"Is there fake maple syrup?" Seeker asks.

Which is a reasonable question, but most humans would know, I think, that there are imitations. Poppy gives him a look, raising one brow. "Are you being clever?" she demands.

"That depends," Seeker says.

But he doesn't get the chance to elaborate because Ravik stuns everyone by saying, "You're a very...sensual eater."

"Thank you," Poppy says.

They pause. "It wasn't necessarily a compliment."

Poppy sets down her fork with a frown. "Oi! Why are you picking on me? Are you implying that I'm trying to be sexy and failing?"

"I don't think I said that," Ravik replies.

"It's, um, the noises. I think," Tad offers, his face turning quite red.

"Okay, before this devolves further...anyone else up for checking out the UFO Museum with us today?" I ask.

"I'd rather go back to the fairgrounds," Poppy says, side-eyeing Tad and Ravik.

"Likewise." Ravik is exceptionally skilled at saying as little as possible.

"Agreed," Tad chimes in, pushing away his empty plate. "There's a folk music session later that Jaz and I talked about checking out."

"Then I guess I'll buddy up with Ravik. What're we doing today?" Poppy nudges Ravik with a telling smirk.

Yep, that's what she was planning earlier. Now she can poke at them all day to get even for the "sensual eater" comment.

"I didn't consent to any such plans," they protest.

The teasing light in her eyes fades, and I think she's genuinely hurt. "Fine. Then you can wander around alone." She gets up. "See everyone later!"

"Wait! I didn't say I was entirely opposed to the idea." To my surprise, Ravik gets up and goes after her, a move that seems to startle everyone else.

"My treat this time. You two can get moving too, if you like," I add to Tad and Jaz.

A few minutes later, after I pay the bill, I wink at Seeker. "Alone at last."

26
SEEKER

I SHARE JEN'S DELIGHT OVER our outing encompassing only the two of us, though I'm less transparent about it.

She drives us to the UFO Museum, housed in what must be a historical structure. Not hundreds of years old; this nation doesn't possess many such edifices. I estimate that this place dates back perhaps fifty years, and is a square, stoic place built of red brick. There is a nominal admission fee, which I cover using my card.

"I can't believe I'm actually here," Jen whispers.

They herd us into the gift shop first, both the initial and last stop on the tour, where they vend models of flying saucers and alien creatures from various human creators. Even at this hour, there's a small crowd, some wearing T-shirts emblazoned with little green men. I overhear snippets of conversation with humans arguing the credibility of abduction stories.

Jen slides me a measured look. She might be wondering if those tales hold any truth. But I cannot claim to speak for all interstellar travelers. My only certainty is that *my* people would never remove other sentient beings from their homes without consent. The same cannot be said of humans, who quarrel over territory more than most beings I have encountered. Perhaps that is why humans always think they're being stolen by others from beyond; it shifts the blame away from their home planet. The news reports I've scoured while learning the customs of this world indicate that humans who go missing have probably been taken or harmed by other humans.

97-B can be dangerous. I was fully apprised of the risks before I ventured forth.

Jen heads toward the first exhibit, a timeline etched into aged wood. "It looks like Rellows started as a makeshift camp along the river."

"Resourceful," I comment.

"Jedidiah Rellows must have been quite a character. Imagine packing your stuff and deciding to start a town."

"Twelve saloons and fourteen liquor stores," I read from a nearby display.

"Work hard, play hard?"

My concept of recreation doesn't align with the human penchant for inebriation. I find it baffling that humans choose to consume toxins in limited quantities, though it is akin to the religious rites of beings I visited on another world. But the denizens of that planet do it to prove devotion to their goddess, who is said to devour those who displease her.

"That is the goal, I suppose."

Jen smiles slightly. I've become attuned to minute shifts in her expression, and I wish I dared to study her secondary colors in this setting. But someone might notice the nictitating membrane, and no costume is that complete.

Toward the heart of the museum, the walls are adorned with newspaper clippings and personal testimonies, the ink faded but the stories vibrant as ever. I scan the headlines: "*Mysterious Lights over Green River*" and "*Rancher Sees Unexplained Phenomenon.*" Jen points to a black-and-white sketch of a man with weathered skin. Below it, a caption reads: "*J.J. Martinez— First Witness of the Mountain Lights.*"

"J.J. Martinez 'didn't know what to make of those lights,'" Jen reads. "He saw them slicing through the night sky, too fast for anything back then. What do you think they were?"

Perhaps one of the agency's shuttles. But I can't say that. Not here.

She gives me a look that seems to suggest she knows what I'm thinking. It's an unusual sensation, but everything has been different since I trusted her enough to share my secret. Rounding a corner, I take in a diorama depicting a scene from Rellows's history. A human vehicle sits next to scattered debris that looks nothing like terrestrial machinery.

"Clarence Banner found the wreckage in 1938," Jen says. "But the military stepped in. They claimed it was an experimental plane."

I speak quietly, but it's a pity she can't hear the subharmonic frequency I use with Jaz and Ravik. "If I had a data uplink, I could check if any shuttles went missing from the Galactic Union. I'd be able to address your question."

Jen turns to me to whisper, "But then you wouldn't be stranded. You could call for help and arrange a pickup."

How interesting that her mind went immediately there while

I was only thinking about pleasing *her* by satisfying her curiosity. Clearly I need to ponder the implications of how precious and vital she's become to me in a relatively short time. That might be the first time I didn't envision leaving 97-B at the first possible opportunity.

I still miss my family. Sometimes the regret is so strong that it mirrors pain. But I have only myself to blame for those choices. I thought time and opportunities were infinite.

It's impossible not to sound a trifle melancholy. "True."

There's a small kiosk devoted to newsy facts regarding the start of Space Con. Jen lingers, silently reading all the related materials. For the next fifteen years, people came to ask questions and interview Deputy Banner about what he'd seen that night. In 1952, the pharmacy owner, Frank Ogden, decided to grant a discount to anyone who spoke the catchphrase "meet outer space fellows here in Rellows" in his store.

Jen laughs. "It doesn't say what percent he offered, does it?"

I read the last few lines of the narrative. "'Soon other merchants followed suit, promising *out-of-this-world* bargains. A summer sale focused on the anniversary of the crash date became a tradition, and tourism tripled in the fifties.'"

"Town planners suggested Space Con in 1977, leveling it up from a merchant-only sale, and started contacting entertainment agencies to add programming and appearances from minor celebrities," Jen adds.

"It's become quite a spectacle," I say with full candor.

"Have you experienced anything like this before?"

"Not exactly like this." While I have encountered beings who camouflage themselves for various reasons, it's usually not a rec-reational pursuit. I add the next part in a quiet aside. "But I did vacation on a world that built its entire culture around trade."

Jen's eyes kindle with wonder, sparking gold in deep interest. "Will you tell me a little bit about the place? In the movie you watched."

I realize she's saying that so anyone who might be taking undue interest in our conversation will conclude that I'm describing a sight from an entertainment I viewed. She's quite a clever human, allow-ing me to share without the need for secrecy. I could speak in great detail on the structures of Belacor, their craft guilds and the artisan hierarchy, but I suspect she's more interested in the tactile descrip-tion of the market itself.

"Yes. The bazaar is the size of a city, stalls draped in iridescent fabrics that shift color with your gaze. And the tech sector—there are no shelves. Gadgets float in artificial pockets of zero G, encased in golden force fields."

"Oh wow, so they create energy-based display cases, basically."

"The smells can be...overwhelming. Sweet, pungent, metallic, earthy... It really depends on who is visiting on any given day, but the diversity is astounding."

"Sounds incredible." Her tone is distant, as if she's trying to build a mental image of the scene I describe.

"The more interesting part of Belacor is that goods aren't simply purchased with currency, as occurs here."

Jen tilts her head, a sign of renewed interest, if I'm reading her body language correctly. "Oh? How else do they buy things?"

"With exchanges of service, time, even memories or emotional attachment."

"That's fascinating. I love that, but the implications are rather haunting. Under hardship, you could sell feelings of love or precious memories to survive."

"Beings do," I say.

"It's tough here, but we haven't reached that point yet. Where to next?" she asks, seeming like she wants to move on from the weight of that topic.

"The ship, obviously."

Jen finds a direct route, following a herd of other enthusiasts. I gaze at the centerpiece of the museum—a replica of the ship that allegedly crashed in Rellows long ago. It's a pale imitation of functional technology, all sharp angles and garish lights. Standing before it, I ache because it's an empty shell. It can't carry me home or allow me to contact my family.

"Let's look inside?" Jen offers her hand.

I take it, conscious that the lengths and shapes don't interlock, and my additional digits wrap around hers in an awkward fashion. She doesn't seem to notice. Others circle outside; I hear their voices. But inside, we're alone, insulated by thin walls designed to mimic metal.

"Seeker?" she murmurs.

"Yes?"

"Thank you for trusting me."

"Thank you for making me feel…" *Like I have a place to belong. Finally.*

That feels like too much, too soon. I remember how I thought of her before my family, and I cannot parse the implications. I cannot speak the words aloud or make myself vulnerable in this way. Not yet. She traces her fingers over mine, lightly, delicately, and the sensation is unexpectedly intense.

I find rare sanctuary in her company, and for a fleeting moment, I'm no longer a seeker—I'm found.

GROUP CHAT
MARCH 19 | 21:53

SquidHead: How's everyone today?

Jeneticist: Just doing a little stargazing. I mentioned the telescope before, right? 🔭✨

Stargazer: I've always imagined that shooting stars are aliens writing in our skies.

FarfromHome: How would you reply?

JazzyPlum: Music is a universal language, right? 🎶 Maybe aliens dig jazz...

Seeker: I enjoy it. Especially Clifford Brown.

Stargazer: Does that mean you're an alien?

Seeker: ...

SquidHead: I read octopuses might be aliens. 🦑 So I'm basically an expert in xenobiology.

FarfromHome: I've always wondered, why are you so obsessed with squids anyway?

SquidHead: I started going bald at like 17. And people started calling me SquidHead.

Stargazer: Aw, kids can be so mean! 🫂

SquidHead: I dunno why, because it's not like squids have hair and lose it. They're hairless to start.

JazzyPlum: Did you take ownership of the name they gave you?

SquidHead: That was why at first. But then I got really interested in squids for their own sake.

Jeneticist: I might regret this, but...lay some interesting octopus info on us.

SquidHead: So glad you asked! 😄

SquidHead: They have one central brain and more in each arm. They have the largest brain-to-body ratio in any invertebrate. They can navigate through mazes or open jars!

SquidHead: They can even use tools or wield external weapons, like how the blanket octopus carries tentacles from the Portuguese man-of-war.

Stargazer: This is actually super interesting. Didn't know any of that!

SquidHead: One final fun fact. They do group hunts with other species, and they'll even punch fish to keep them on task.

Jeneticist: 🦑Hahahaha, OMG, so glad I asked.

JazzyPlum: Now I'm pretty sure octopi are aliens.

Seeker: Sounds accurate.

FarfromHome: This is the most I have ever enjoyed any of our conversations. Thank you, SH.

Stargazer: Okay, game time! You know I can't let a chat end without us learning a little more about each other.

Stargazer: 2 Truths and a Lie—I'll start.

1. I've seen a UFO.

2. I own a meteorite.

3. I sleep under the stars every night.

SquidHead: Hmm, I call #3 the lie.

JazzyPlum: How can you own a whole meteorite? #2 is a lie.

Jeneticist: I dunno, it could be a trick. I had glow-in-the-dark stars on my bedroom ceiling as a kid. #1 is the lie.

FarfromHome: Statistically, #3 seems improbable.

Seeker: Gotta be #3, unless you live in a planetarium.

Stargazer: Jen wins! Wish I'd seen a UFO but never have. I have a small chunk of meteorite as a paperweight, and I still have those glowing decals on my ceiling.

Seeker: Who goes next?

Stargazer: Jen got it, so it's her turn.

Jeneticist: OK, here we go.

1. I have two cats.

2. I cook a delicious beef Wellington.

3. I minored in mythology.

Stargazer: Oh, well played. These are all plausible. Those are the hardest to spot!

SquidHead: Mythology and astronomy don't match. I think #3 is the lie.

FarfromHome: I don't know what beef Wellington is. #2 is the lie.

JazzyPlum: It has to be 2 or 3. I'm going with SH on #3.

Seeker: Then I choose #2 along with FFH.

Jeneticist: Winners! Seeker and FFH got it. I don't like beef Wellington and I certainly can't cook it.

Jeneticist: Hot take, beef Wellington is a corn dog for snobs.

Stargazer: Since we have two winners, FFH goes next, then Seeker, regardless who wins FFH's round. Then Seeker's winner will go if they haven't yet. 😎

JazzyPlum: The judge has spoken! 😂

FarfromHome: Fine.

1. I am vegan.

2. I have an extensive home garden.

3. I have a pet rooster.

JazzyPlum: This will be tough. But I can't imagine you keeping a rooster. #3.

SquidHead: I vote with Jaz. #3

Seeker: I think it's #2.

Stargazer: I honestly am not sure, but I think it's #1.

Jeneticist: I'll vote with the bloc. #3 from me too.

FarfromHome: I am stunned to declare Star is the only winner. 😮

Stargazer: Woo-hoo!

Jeneticist: Back up, you're not vegan and you have a pet rooster?? Really?!

JazzyPlum: Yes, we need details. 👂

FarfromHome: I eat honey, so technically, I am not vegan. Removing it doesn't hurt the bees if one is careful. And the rooster is named Kevin.

SquidHead: ...you named your pet rooster Kevin?

FarfromHome: He came with the property. He was already named Kevin.

Stargazer: This might be my favorite convo we've ever had.

Seeker: Same. 😊

Jeneticist: Would love to see pics of your garden sometime, FFH.

JazzyPlum: Me too!

SquidHead: Hate to break up a good time, but I gotta go. I'll take my turn next time.

JazzyPlum: Bye, all!

27

JENNETTE

THIS MOMENT FEELS AS DELICATE as spun glass.

Seeker has stilled, and I want to touch him so badly that I ache. But I don't. Instead, I search his countenance for some sign that he feels the same way. Yet his features are difficult for me to read; it's just like the aliens in the games and stories that I've loved. This person is precious to me but also unlike anyone I've ever known.

He moves then, just a fraction closer. I reach out, hovering in the space between us, and I don't think I could make it clearer without asking for verbal permission. It feels as if the sound of my voice would break the spell. We probably don't have long before people shove in behind us to walk around inside the ship.

In answer, he steps into my space and I reach for him slowly. If this isn't what he wants, if he's unsure, he can move back at any point. His arms—I'm calling them arms because they're similar, even if he has more fingers—come around me as I get close. He's seen many human entertainments so I'm sure he knows what we're doing.

"Is this okay?" I whisper.

"It is."

His skin feels warm, but so different from mine. Heat blooms where our bodies align; he adjusts to my body temperature, matching it. I try not to stroke his back too much since I don't know where his erogenous zones are. *I definitely want to learn.*

"I'm honored," I say, trying to keep it light.

I'm failing at that because this feels like…everything. Everything I ever wanted.

When he eases back to gaze at me, there's something so vulnerable in his gaze that my heart clenches. "Jen…"

I press my face against the warm skin of his neck, where a pulse unlike mine thrums gently. As I hold him, the realization crystallizes within me like a shard of ice melting away to reveal a dormant seed. I'm falling for him, so hard and fast that if we revisit the icebreaker games we play in the chat group, I'll reconsider my answer about skydiving.

Closing my eyes, I nuzzle my face against the velvety skin at his throat and receive a rumble of sound in response. Somehow, the vibrations feel sexy in a way I can't articulate. The spices of his scent brighten. Voices get louder; someone is laughing close by. And I step back, not wanting the moment to be ruined by someone yelling, "Get a room!"

I let out a faintly unsteady breath. "Should we move on?"

He inclines his head. "Let's see the rest."

As I navigate around the replica of the ship, I wonder if it's tough for him to be here. Humans can create the illusion of what he needs, but we're just not advanced enough for me to help him get home. I can't give him the stars, but I can offer him a life here, with me, where he's not just an extraterrestrial—and to others, maybe a specimen—but my partner. But I've already offered to let him move in. I won't beg or even ask again.

The ball is in Seeker's court, even if I'm dying to hear his answer.

Even more people have piled into the museum when we exit the crashed ship replica; that surprises me a little. But maybe they're like me and wanted a break from the con atmosphere. I'll be ready to go back tomorrow and maybe do some gaming. I wonder if Seeker would enjoy tabletop RPGs.

"Sick costume, dude!" A guy in a gray alien T-shirt has stopped in the middle of the foot traffic, staring at Seeker, the first person who's given him a second glance.

Seeker pauses, glancing at me for guidance.

"So glad you like it! You wouldn't believe how long he spent on it," I say. "Custom-made on our 3-D printer."

Anything to keep this fanboy looking at me.

"It's incredible. So realistic. It's like his eyes are really—"

"Don't touch! Are you forgetting the first rule of cosplay?"

"Uh, what?"

Maybe he's not here for Space Con? Possibly there are people in the world who just randomly show up during the busiest week in Rellows because they live an hour away and thought the UFO Museum would be fun. I decide to give him the benefit of the doubt.

I quote from the manual. "Cosplay is not consent. Don't touch without permission. You need to ask before taking photos too."

"Oh, right. I forgot how serious you people are about this stuff."

You people.

I give him a tight smile and tilt my head toward the exit. Seeker follows me, seeming eager to get out of here, and I feel bad that I suggested he stop using his tech camo. I've never been in his situation, and I blithely dismissed the possibility he could be in danger. I thought this was the one place in the whole world where he could go unnoticed. I thread through the bodies, finding the most direct path to the exit.

Outside, it's unexpectedly overcast. July in Utah is hot and dry; I should know, as I spent hours researching everything related to this trip. But rare showers do happen, and it seems today is that day. Maybe that's why people flocked to the museum, trying to avoid the rain. Even the air smells a little different.

"Do you smell that?" I ask, drawing a deep breath. "Rain's coming."

"It probably won't last long."

I smile at that because we're talking about the weather. Nobody else would realize how momentous this is because he's a newcomer, just learning the patterns and processes here. But small moments like this might make him feel less like an outsider, less a being bound by gravity against his will.

"Maybe we'll get a rainbow."

Seeker gazes up at the sky, seeming intrigued by the prospect. "I have only seen representations in photographs online. It's a fascinating phenomenon, one I have not seen replicated on any other world."

"Earth has some unique beauty, then?" It's important for him to think so.

Otherwise, this planet will never be more than a place of exile. I hope that he finds solace in the swirl of high clouds and the scent of impending rain. Maybe then he'll see that though the skies are out of reach, the world beneath them can still be full of wonders.

Like a life with me.

Okay, that might be overselling the point. I can't categorize starting a romantic relationship with me as *wonderful*, but I hope he's thinking about it. Just then, the first drops of rain plink down, cool and refreshing against the lingering heat. Seeker tips his head back and closes his eyes, seeming to savor the sensation.

"I never understood before," he says then.

"What?"

"The human obsession with water. You use it for so many things. It's scarce on many planets and they use it only for hydration. The rains I experienced on Terjan felt oily, and there were other substances in the precipitation."

I make a face. "That sounds gross."

"It was. And so I watched from the windows when I got here. I didn't go out because I had preconceived notions that it would be unpleasant, both from past experiences elsewhere and the way I saw people here fleeing from the rain in visual entertainment."

"Some people don't like to be wet, but this feels lovely, especially today."

If I had a class to teach, I might be one of the people hurrying with an umbrella, but today I'm content to stand as the drizzle sprinkles down, gradually intensifying to fat, cool droplets of rain. Others hurry past us, eager to reach the sanctuary of the museum. I let Seeker set our pace today.

"Water from the clouds, such a gift." There's a smile in his voice, though not one I can detect on his distinctive features.

"I love rainy days," I admit. "Perfect for snuggling up and watching a movie."

"That sounds perfect."

He moves toward the car, and I follow. It feels like we're on the cusp of something, but Seeker holds all the power. It has to be that way between us because he's powerless to leave, as he'd prefer. I would feel like I was taking advantage of him if I pushed for anything before he articulated the words himself.

Inside my xB, it's dry and overly warm. I start the engine, despite not having the least idea where we're headed. "Next stop?"

"If you're amenable, I've had enough of other people today."

Excitement skitters along my nerve endings, though I try to be cool about this. The hot alien wants to get me alone, but maybe he does want to Netflix and chill. Not the euphemism. And I'll be thrilled to watch whatever he wants, really.

"Send the text to the group saying we'll hang out with them tomorrow," I suggest.

He retrieves his phone, likely heeding my advice. "Such a curious turn of phrase when no vertical suspension is involved."

I could make a sex swing joke here but I decide against it. "Home then. Well. Our temporary home."

28
SEEKER

HOME.

The word resonates with me. Even though Jen amends it quickly, I recall that she's extended an offer of permanent hospitality.

And I'm warming to the notion.

When we reach the lodging place, she collects a parcel from the front office. I suspect it's the protein powder she procured for me. I'm heartily sick of the stuff, but I fear experimenting with other sources of nutrition. The soy, as she calls it, is keeping me alive and not making me sick. I'm fearfully aware how few my resources are on 97-B.

I make a beverage and consume it, as I haven't eaten today. Jen orders food for herself and we settle on her bed, which has been made in our absence. After covering the windows to deter curious onlookers, I settle nearby when she turns on the television, then hands me the control device.

"You pick," she says.

I find a show that seems interesting at first. People are having a meal together, but the scene soon changes, and now the humans are removing their clothing, rubbing their mouths together and making sounds that suggest duress or arousal. Judging by how Jen's colors shift in response, I surmise it's the latter.

And now I'm curious, so curious. If *I* can cause her to make those sounds as well. If I don't let her touch me, I should be able to resist imprinting or creating a life bond before I've made that decision logically, committed to her with her my heart and mind.

"Jen…"

"Yes?" She's not looking at the screen anymore, nor at me either.

"Are you interested in me? Physically? Sometimes I think that you are. But I do not wish to presume."

Groaning, she covers her face with her hands. "You're not supposed to just…ask like that! Come right out with it, why don't you?"

"Then how else am I meant to attain the information?"

"Yes, I think you're hot. And I'm very attracted to you."

"Hot? My temperature is variable."

"Desirable. A person who…" She seems to struggle to find the right words. "Who makes me feel things I usually don't."

"Can you explain?"

"Sure. I'm turning that off first, though. They'll be doing it soon."

"And you don't want to watch that?"

"It's distracting. So, to answer your question, normally I don't think about having someone touch me. I've had crushes before, always on aliens, but it was just…romantic feelings, I guess? Damn, this is embarrassing to talk about."

"Why?"

"Actually, that's a good point. It shouldn't be." She takes a breath and faces me, gazing at me fully for the first time since the show became sexually specific. "I'm gray ace. That's someone who doesn't think about sex that much. I do have a libido, but I take care of myself and move on. The idea of needing a partner for that is weird to me. That also means I rarely experience sexual attraction. I say rarely now, because before meeting you, it was never."

I process her words and it's impossible not to feel as if I have received an enormous gift. This precious person desires me? What a treasure I have unexpectedly received from the universe.

"Thank you for telling me. I have information to share as well, if you would hear it?"

"I would love to."

"My people only experience yearning for those with whom they have formed emotional bonds. And once we permit the relationship to be consummated, it creates a unique neural pathway. That being holds the keys to our pleasure center. We do not imprint lightly or casually. Though we can survive the loss of a partner, it's akin to…" *What metaphor will she understand?* Jen waits while I sort my thoughts and decide the proper way to describe it. "Losing the ability to smell sweetness or see a particular color."

"Whoa. Now I get your hesitation when I touched you before. I guess there are no breakups on your world."

"It is rare. And when relationships change, they usually expand. If you loved your first, you love them still, but we are allowed to love others too. There is less focus on 'mine' and 'yours.' We are a creator culture, not one that consumes."

"I wish I could see your home," she says in a wistful tone. "Just once."

"There might be a way. But I'm unsure whether a memory walk would work with a human partner."

"Memory walk?" Her expression becomes intent.

Others remain an enigma to me, but Jen has become a mystery I must solve. I want to collect the facts that create the unique wonder of her dazzling, inquisitive soul.

"It allows me to reproduce a moment mentally. I return to that moment in time with all associated sights, sounds, and smells. If we were connected, it would carry you with me as well. You could see my home and family through my eyes."

"A mind link that only works with your chosen partner?"

"Similar."

I shift my visual spectrum and notice that once again, she's glowing warm in regions devoted to sexual excitement. If she felt shy to discuss such things, perhaps I should simply offer to provide gratification? My desire to please her hasn't changed. If anything, that need has grown more intense, especially given her revelations.

"I would like to touch you," I say then. "With your permission, of course. But I wish to learn what brings you pleasure."

Her breath catches. "Before, I couldn't believe you just asked. Now I'm grateful. I want you so badly, it's ridiculous."

"Disrobe and we can begin."

The air charges with expectancy as she removes layers of fabric, not too many today. Her body is pale and soft, gently curved. Some human bodies do display color shifts, though not in familiar spectrums. Jen flushes beneath my scrutiny, going rosy as I glide an exploratory touch down her limbs, barely skimming her sides. The texture of her skin changes, little bumps appearing in the wake of my caress.

I have read about a language that allows humans with limited visual perception to read through touch. Perhaps that is what these bumps are for as well, inviting me to learn her body through this means. I close my eyes, allowing my other senses to take over. She smells delicious, sweet and salty at the same time. Her skin is smooth, and I savor the skips of her pulse. She shivers beneath each curious tracery, her body sharing responses wordlessly.

I use that point of contact to decipher the nuances of her pleasure, the slight arch of her back becoming my guide. Carefully, I shape the contours of her, then venture to the swell of her breasts. Soft, so very soft. To my surprise, Jen doesn't react. The information I've encountered indicates that this is an erogenous zone.

"I haven't done this a lot," Jen whispers. "But that doesn't work for me."

I pause, pleased she's communicated her preferences. "What will you enjoy most?"

"My stomach. My thighs. My throat. Even my back. Those places feel good to me."

I take those specifications literally and reroute my explorations to the named vicinities, lightly swirling patterns on her skin. Her lower limbs open wider and she begins to squirm, shifting restlessly as if she craves more. Her breath is faster now; she's making sounds as I gently rub her thighs.

"How is this?"

"So good. I've never had a massage feel this way," she gasps.

I take it as a compliment, praising my manual dexterity. Desire simmers in me also, but putting my need on display would change the tenor of the encounter. Right now, I want only to please Jen, more than I've ever wanted anything.

"Turn over," I invite.

She obeys without question. Her eagerness is intoxicating, lighting my senses to the point that I can see and breathe only her. I touch her lightly, skimming down her spine, until the bumps appear on her skin here as well. Then I deepen the contact, kneading her pliant flesh. She utters a sound that spears through me, nearly forcing an involuntary response.

No. I can control myself. I will.

She lifts her body into those long strokes, and by fluttering the nictitating membrane, I glimpse the polychrome beauty unleashed in her open response. Jen glows with heat at the heart of her need. I have no experience to call on, and I have not pursued an investigation into sexually pertinent materials. But I know enough to understand where she craves contact.

When I extend the touch to framing her slick, needful flesh from beneath, she shudders and starts to move, hunching up and down in jerky, helpless motions. I need to do little at this juncture, only watch her face in profile. She bites her lip, trying to stifle the sounds that overwhelm her as her urgency increases. I wish she wouldn't. I want to hear those little noises, each breath and groan. Her movements become more forceful; she grinds against the bony arch of my extensor. I wish I knew what else to do, but she seems to be enjoying this very much.

"Almost," she manages.

Her eyes are tightly closed, and I wish she was looking at me, as I'm riveted by her. She quakes, trembling, and the wet heat on my skin increases. Judging by the hues of her body and the slowing tempo of her breath, she's peaked, come to human satiation. When she opens her eyes, she rolls to the side, freeing my limb from captivity beneath her body.

"You seemed to enjoy that," I say.

"It was amazing," she tells me.

A warm feeling spreads through me, though I strive to hide how moved I am. This has been my first sexual encounter with an alien; Jen would doubtless say the same, so we are sharing important firsts this night. "I learned everything from you."

Her hand trembles when she touches me lightly, right on the colors that are shimmering just this side of violet. I'm all repressed need, and it is making me dizzy.

"You're a fast study."

I don't have the right words to express how much her trust meant to me, but I hope this suffices. "That was beautiful. You are."

GROUP CHAT
MARCH 21 | 13:21

Stargazer: Hey, everyone, random fact time!

Stargazer: I'll get my turn out of the way. I write fan fiction. ✏️

SquidHead: That's awesome! What kind? I love seeing how people remix worlds.

Stargazer: Thanks! Mostly sci-fi epics. Sometimes I weave in mythologies from different cultures. The more epic, the better! 🚀 🐉

JazzyPlum: Wow! You must have an incredible imagination. 😮 Would love to read some!

Stargazer: Maybe one day I'll share with you guys. When they're ready...and when I'm brave enough. 😳

SquidHead: [Message deleted]

JazzyPlum: 😂 What was that? Don't make fun of Star's fanfic!

SquidHead: I didn't! Just typed in the wrong chat! 🙅

Stargazer: FOUL! I demand your full attention. Now you gotta share a fact!

SquidHead: Hmm. Okay. I have an extensive collection of rare comic books! Been collecting since I was 10.

FarfromHome: This is something I could have predicted. More probable than random.

Stargazer: Don't be cranky, fun sponge. Now you have to take a turn.

FarfromHome: Why do I never learn?

Seeker: An excellent question.

Stargazer: FFH just pretends not to enjoy our talks, our group curmudgeon.

JazzyPlum: That sounds right.

JazzyPlum: I almost forgot to share my little obsession. 😅 I collect cat figurines from all over the place. Got a whole shelf dedicated to them! 🐱🐈🗿

SquidHead: That's so cute. Any rare ones? 🤔

JazzyPlum: Yeah! Just got a vintage Japanese cat statue from a flea market. It's adorable AND creepy at the same time. 😍 😳

Jeneticist: That sounds amazing!

Stargazer: Pics or it didn't happen. 📸 😊

JazzyPlum: Hold on... [Image attached] See?

SquidHead: Some serious cat-lady vibes. But I'm into it.

SquidHead: Are we allowed to go again?

Stargazer: All sharing is encouraged!

FarfromHome: I object to TMI.

Stargazer: I'll be the judge of that.

SquidHead: I don't think this is TMI. It's just like that I enjoy playing basketball. 🏀...But let's just say my talent lies elsewhere. 😅

Jeneticist: 😂 How bad are we talking?

SquidHead: Let's put it this way—if there were trophies for airballs, I'd be an MVP. 🏆🏀

Stargazer: Hey, it's all about having fun, right? Plus, you've got those comic books to fall back on! 🏅📖

JazzyPlum: We've all got our quirks, right? 🎮 Makes us who we are!

Jeneticist: Absolutely! This chat wouldn't be the same without them.

Stargazer: Who hasn't gone?

SquidHead: FFH, you still here?

FarfromHome: A random fact. I enjoy watching small lizards while they sunbathe. It is very peaceful.

Stargazer: You truly are a precious bean.

FarfromHome: Why are you calling me a bean?

Jeneticist: I think it comes from all of us being human beans.

SquidHead: There's a joke in there somewhere.

JazzyPlum: I think Seeker is the only one left?

Seeker: Jen hasn't gone either. But I'll take a turn.

Seeker: I've got a knack for deconstructing gadgets and making something new. 🛠️⚙️

FarfromHome: Finally an interesting topic. What devices have you constructed?

Seeker: Most recently, I made a drone from broken RC car parts.

SquidHead: Some serious skill! My code game is strong, but I can barely change a light bulb without causing a blackout.

Jeneticist: Okay, this might surprise you, but...I'm weirdly good at bowling. 🎳 Last time I went, I scored a turkey.

Stargazer: A triple strike?!

SquidHead: Wow! What's your secret?

Jeneticist: I have no idea. I have no athletic prowess otherwise.

JazzyPlum: That's some talent! Maybe you can teach us sometime? I'll trade you a cat figurine for a lesson! 🐱 🎳

Jeneticist: Deal! Who knows, we might end up forming a bowling team! 😊

Seeker: I can't promise to be any good, but I would participate.

FarfromHome: I have succeeded in similar challenges.

Stargazer: I don't know if you're serious but there's a bowling alley in Rellows.

SquidHead: What the hell, let's do it. 🎳

29
JENNETTE

I'M EMBARRASSED OVER FALLING ASLEEP on my face, stark naked—bare-assed in more ways than one.

I rouse somewhere before dawn. Seeker is nearby, not touching or encroaching on my space. I guess his people don't go for middle-of-the-night cuddles. Not that I would've known, even if he held me for hours. It's like I released a year of tension at once. I've had enjoyable orgasms before, but that one was glorious.

The motel is like a cocoon, shadowed by the closed blackout blinds. I wonder if I'll be a butterfly when I leave this place; I did feel gorgeous beyond measure while he was touching me last night. Sill buzzing with the memory, I get up quietly and take a shower.

He's up when I return, using that appliance I noticed before. "What's that?" I ask.

I wasn't bold enough before. But now that we're...what? Lovers? I don't even know what words to use for what we're doing, what we are to one another.

"Molecular cleansing device. It's invaluable for travel."

"That's incredible. Would it work for me? And how does it stay powered?"

"It works for anyone. Solar power. I leave it by the window when I go out."

"Genius. And variables like the color of the sun don't impact the power source?"

"I tinkered with it a little bit when I realized I'd be here for a while," he admits. "Improved the efficiency somewhat."

"Is there anything you *can't* do?" I tease.

His hesitation makes me regret the light little question because I know what he would say if he replied. The answer is *leave*. I get ready in awkward silence, choosing my next costume with a heavy heart. Normally, I enjoy every step in the process of turning into someone else, but right now I feel like an insensitive clod who reminded Seeker that he's trapped here.

"I find your transformations fascinating," he says then.

Oh good. Maybe he's not upset with me.

"Yeah? Which has been your favorite?"

"This one."

"Really?" I glance at my Amethyst outfit, my favorite *Steven Universe* character. Today I've simply gone with the clothes and the wig. Painting myself lilac will take too long.

"You look interesting."

I laugh. "Thank you. Ready?" I grab a bag filled with essentials like water and snacks.

"Yes."

I drive us to the fairgrounds, where the crowd is already amping up. Colorful banners flap in the breeze, and it's not as hot as it was yesterday. The rain shower seems to have cooled things down, a fact I appreciate as I hop out of the car.

"Jen! Over here!" Poppy is the enthusiastic waver in our group, signaling me like she's trying to land a plane.

I spot Tad, Ravik, and Jaz nearby. Jaz is dressed as herself again. But I'm not supposed to know that she's really purple. Or that Ravik's ice planet barbarian thing is a cover. I remind myself of it so I don't get Seeker in trouble. I wonder if Tad and Poppy have noticed anything weird.

Just as I think that, Poppy bounds up and bounces on her toes, clearly stoked for another day of fun. She glances at Seeker, then Jaz and Ravik. "Damn. You're all so devoted to those costumes. Are they the only ones you packed?"

"Yes," Ravik replies.

I take initiative and change the subject. "Let's not split up like we did yesterday. I need face time!"

"Sounds good," Seeker agrees.

"Did you two catch the daybreak cosplay parade?" Tad asks.

I shake my head. "We missed it."

Before Poppy or Tad can tease us, Jaz steps in. "Let's just wander and see where the day takes us."

"Lead the way," Ravik says.

Jaz takes them at their word, weaving through a maze of booths. There's a cotton candy machine today. That's new. And I don't recall if I smelled churros before either. That reminds me that I didn't have breakfast. I don't know how Seeker does it, consuming only one protein beverage a day. His body must be upgraded in terms of efficiency.

Seeker's hand finds mine, warm, steady, and familiar in its strangeness. My cheeks heat as I remember how he touched me last night and how much I enjoyed it. As I study him surreptitiously, his otherworldly eyes drink in the vibrant chaos. It's odd that he hasn't attracted more attention because I can't look away. He's magnificent without trying—the shade of his skin, the intricate lavender patterns swirling across it catching the light.

And his eyes. Starbursts and stardust, like the cosmos at the beginning of time. His eyes are like otherworldly kaleidoscopes, shimmering with fantastical beauty that seems more magical than interstellar. I feel as if he houses all the marvels of the universe. Seeker catches me gazing at him; hopefully, he can't discern the full extent of my giddy wonder.

"Did you see something you want to examine closer?" he asks, turning to assess the souvenirs on display behind him.

I realize it then. He has no clue how compelling and irresistible I find every facet of his being. That's probably a good thing.

"Just getting a sense of the big picture," I say.

"There is a scientist speaking later today. He has some interesting ideas about quantum entanglement. Would you be interested in going to the panel with me?"

Would I? Oh yes. But then, it would take a lot for me to reject any offer Seeker made. I'd probably hesitate over leaving the planet, but otherwise…

"Sounds interesting! I'm down." I could fill a thimble with what I know about physics, but I'm always willing to learn.

"It's not for a few hours yet. We can wander around until then."

The others move off a bit, Tad charting a course toward some rare comics. I get cut off by a surge of pedestrians, and now I can't see them anymore. This is when it sucks being vertically challenged.

Poppy wanted us to stay together, but I'm sure we can catch up. I just need to—

"Your costume is sick, dude! What are you supposed to be?"

Seeker opts not to reply as he glances at me. *Good call.* I don't want to tell the story about Tad's game to everyone who stops us.

I turn to see a dude inching closer to Seeker. The man in question is wearing tan cargo shorts, a loose tropical print shirt, and he's wearing a heavy-duty camera on a strap around his neck. Only serious photographers bother with those these days; most people just snap memories with their phone. I'd estimate the guy is in his early sixties, with weathered skin and a more-salt-than-pepper goatee. He also has long, scraggly gray hair caught back in a failing ponytail.

"Man, the detail on this thing is insane! You look like you stepped off a movie set." The fan circles Seeker, acting like he's about to start taking pictures.

"No photos without consent," I remind him.

"What's this made out of? It looks so real. Come on, you gotta tell me where you got this made!" The fan's insistence grows, his admiration tipping into intrusion.

The guy reaches out toward Seeker's arm, and I get between them, ready to remind him that boundaries exist. He manages a graze of contact as Seeker steps back. I sense Seeker's tension, his deepening unease. Dammit, I should never have suggested this. If not for me, he'd be dressed as an average con-goer and nobody would be paying attention.

"Cut it out. People aren't props." My words are a shield, raised to protect him, and I hope they're enough.

Seeker gives me a grateful glance, his eyes—a blend of colors no human could claim—flickering with a silent thank-you.

But the fan seems undeterred, his fascination morphing into something more fervent, more obsessive. "Seriously, this is next level! You gotta be from a top-tier special effects studio." He sidles closer again, and Seeker shifts backward. "You're advertising how good they are, right? Why won't you tell me? You should be giving out business cards."

"Thanks for your interest, but we're leaving. He's not promoting anything."

"Wait," the dude insists, following as we edge away. "Just let me take *one* pic?"

"Nope. We're in a hurry," I snap.

Seeker manages to be polite even while he's being harassed. "Enjoy the convention," he adds with firm finality.

"Right on." The guy remains locked on Seeker, hungry and unblinking. He even follows us for a few steps, until I cut through a big group and he gets wedged in a tangle of props.

Despite the heat of the day, icy fingers sent a shiver down my spine. This isn't right. Seeker may be able to hide his true nature here, but that doesn't make him invulnerable. Especially not to obsession masked as admiration. We need to put some distance between us and this guy, fast.

I'm not waiting to find out what happens if this jerk uncovers the truth.

30
SEEKER

I AM UNEASY.

That last encounter makes me want to leave. Not just Space Con but the town of Rellows entirely. But that may be an overreaction, an emotional response to feeling threatened. I watch warily as we proceed through various stalls until it's time to make our way to the small red-and-white-striped pavilion tent, where rows of folding chairs have been set up in front of a lectern.

Jen leads us to seats near the back, offering us plenty of space from everyone else. It doesn't look as if it will be a full house with so many other entertainments on offer. The scientist is dressed simply and wears thick-framed lenses for viewing assistance. Jen smiles at me, seeming happy to be here, though I don't know how interested she is in this topic. I'm frankly curious how close humans are to working all of these premises out.

"Quantum entanglement," the lecturer says. "The phenomenon where particles become so deeply linked that the state of one instantly influences the state of another, no matter the distance."

Among my people, this principle is not just understood, but harnessed, interwoven into the fabric of our daily lives. It's even used by artists to perform collaborations on the same piece. That is how my gestational parent, Oona, met the rest of their bond partners. Ironically, science on my homeworld is mostly used to improve and extend artistic endeavors. Those who lean in that direction are considered technicians who lack a certain creative impetus, born for drudgery, not inspiration. Unfortunately, I am one of those souls.

I would have tried for Oona's sake. If I could return. But it would never have given me fulfillment or joy. When I create something new, when I invent something unique or improve technology that already exists, that's when I feel most myself. I imagine that my happiness approaches that of the most creative soul. Surely, there is no right and wrong in these matters, only matters of personal satisfaction.

I listen as the scientist expounds on her ideas. The talk is interesting, but she doesn't have the details right. It would take a hundred years for 97-B to remedy the misapprehensions, correct their errors, and reconfigure a few faulty theories. I consider speaking up, then swiftly discard the notion. I won't meddle. I also don't wish to draw attention to myself, not after what happened earlier. If a person in a "costume" like this one reveals detailed and specific information about quantum entanglement, it will cause complications.

We attend a few more panels and survey the goods available for purchase. Jen's phone beeps and she moves away to take a call. I hear her say *Mom* in a tone that sounds distressed, though I'm not trying to eavesdrop. When I turn, I realize that the human who wanted to take my photo earlier is standing nearby, watching me. Then he's joined by the one from the museum. They speak too softly for me to hear, and then the museum human shows the other one his phone.

That cannot portend anything good.

When Jen returns, she seems annoyed. I decide not to mention that moment. If something more occurs, I will discuss it with her then. But I remain uneasy for the rest of our time, constantly on alert for undue attention. For the first time, I don't feel entirely safe.

"Should we head out?" she asks eventually.

It's late afternoon, and I'm ready to go. "Please. I'm finding the crowds a little overwhelming." I can admit that much.

She drives us to Stellar Lanes, a bowling alley with neon lights flashing outside. I have watched a few examples of the pastime, but I am not confident I can properly maneuver the specialized equipment. The others may suggest that I remove my costume if I can't participate while wearing it.

Inside, I hear the clatter of pins being knocked over. Monitors glow overhead, displaying numbers that track the participants' progress. I recognize certain smells from other establishments. Pizza. Beer. There are layers, perfume and sweat, the smell of old oil used for cooking starched vegetables. The place isn't busy. Only our group and one other, a handful of older human males in matching shirts. Jen queues up to get our equipment, sliding me a concerned look.

"When we first talked about doing a bowling night online, I didn't know…"

That I'm not human. Even if I had the tech camo, it wouldn't allow me to use their specialized sporting gear. Normally, I'm content as long as I'm with Jen, but right now, I want nothing more than to leave.

Our lane lights up, casting a soft, inviting glow over the polished wood. Poppy goes first, throwing the ball with a flamboyance that sends it spinning wildly down the lane. It's a gutter ball, but she laughs and does a little twirl, then flutters her hands.

"That's right, shake it off," Jen says in a comforting tone.

Tad takes a more focused approach, eyes narrowed in concentration before releasing the heavy sphere. It connects with the pins with impressive and unexpected force, leaving only a few standing—a commendable effort. The others all take a turn, but I decide to sit out.

"I think I injured myself earlier," I say.

"Is your shoulder still hurting?" Jen asks without missing a beat.

"Damn, go easy on him," Poppy jokes.

Jen changes colors. "Oh my God, I didn't—"

"It's my go," Jaz cuts in.

As the game progresses, I observe their styles. Poppy is all verve while Tad tries for force. Jaz is delicate and careful while Ravik plays with stoic determination, his form almost perfect, but his extensors aren't balanced for the equipment. Then there's Jen. Each of her turns is marked by an easy confidence, a natural affinity for the sport that soon becomes apparent. Strike after strike, her score climbs until it's clear she's outmatched us all.

"Holy shit," Poppy says. "When we talked about this online, I thought you were joking, but you *are* weirdly good at bowling."

Jen grins. "Sadly, it doesn't pay the bills."

"I think you could go pro," Tad says.

"Pass. I'd rather keep studying the stars."

"Don't you teach at community college?" Tad asks.

I don't miss the way Jen winces, but her voice is even when she says, "That's what pays the bills. But I've always wanted to work at an observatory."

"Dreams are important." Poppy shoots Tad a look and he hunches his shoulders.

"Sorry, Jen. I can be a bit thoughtless."

Poppy shakes her head, but she pats his shoulder as she gets up. "It's okay. Just think before you talk next time."

Tad nods. "Understood."

"Bathroom break, be right back." Poppy heads toward the far end of the facility.

Tad gets up immediately. "Likewise."

Jen decides to go too, hurrying after the other humans. That leaves me alone with Ravik and Jaz. I seize the opportunity, speaking to them in subharmonic frequency. "Have you thought any more about telling them the truth?"

"I'm still in favor," Jaz replies.

"Ravik?"

They pause, staring in the direction our three friends have gone. "I fear that this is unwise. And it seems unnecessary. But…it would be nice to be known."

Jaz pauses, glancing between us. "I didn't expect to come to a consensus tonight. But if they know—and we can trust them—they will help protect us."

"That's an unsettling proposition," Ravik mutters. We sit quietly for a few moments while they weigh the decision.

"They're coming back," I point out.

"Yes. Tell them," Ravik finally replies.

As Tad, Poppy, and Jen reach the steps, Jaz says, "Let's

not play another round. There's something we need to discuss. Privately."

"Everything okay?" Poppy asks.

Jaz nods slowly, but her gaze doesn't waver. "This isn't the place for a serious conversation." She flicks a look at the men in their coordinated shirts and another group of young humans who have entered the premises as our match concluded.

"Should we head to my campsite?" Tad suggests, gesturing vaguely in the direction of the RV park that skirts the edge of town. "People will stay at the fairgrounds for hours yet. It'll be as private as it gets during Space Con."

"Perfect," Jaz says.

Jen drives me with Poppy in the back seat while the others go with Tad. I wonder if this is really a good idea. I hope my trust is warranted. I'm not worried about Jen; she already knows everything. But telling Poppy and Tad—that's the risk.

Once we reach the RV park, Jen stows her car behind Tad's, and then he builds a fire while the rest of us get comfortable around the firepit. The embers of the campfire crackle and pop, casting a warm glow over our small assembly. As he predicted, the place is practically deserted, no lights on in any of the campers or vans nearby.

"Okay." Tad takes a seat, folding his hands in his lap. "What's up?"

Jaz takes a deep breath, scanning the three humans. I sense Ravik's tension beside me; it mirrors my own. We stand upon a precipice, one I never would've imagined. Telling others who I am? No. I never intended to do that. But I've done it once already, and it made me feel so much less alone.

"You might not believe us at first, but…right now, Seeker, Ravik, and I…We're not dressed in costumes. This is how we look."

Poppy tilts her head, skepticism lining her features. Jen's hand finds mine, an attempt to comfort me, perhaps. The contact grounds me, no matter how Poppy and Tad react.

Then Tad laughs. "Good one! You had me going."

"I'm serious. We're not…from here," Jaz continues. "Not from this country or this planet. We're extraterrestrials."

Tad's mouth drops open, disbelief etched across his face. "Tell another one."

Poppy's skepticism morphs into awe, her gaze flitting between the three of us as if seeing us for the first time. "I did think your cosplay was a little too real. Do you mind…"

She reaches toward Ravik, who tenses but doesn't recoil. "Go ahead if you need proof."

"Oh my God," Poppy breathes. "That's your skin. I know how grease paint and body paint feel and you're not using any."

"Obviously," Ravik replies.

"You're doing this too?" Tad frowns at Poppy. "It's not cool to mess with people!"

"I already knew," Jen says then. Her smile hasn't shifted. "About Seeker."

The group falls silent, contemplation hanging heavy in the smoke-scented air. In their eyes, I see the gears turning, reassessing every interaction, every shared moment under the light of this new starlit truth.

Poppy can't stop staring at Ravik. "I have so many fucking questions. I don't even know where to start."

"We're still us," Jaz says softly. "Still your friends. That hasn't changed."

Tad hasn't moved. Nor does he seem as openly delighted as Poppy is.

"That remains to be seen," Tad says in a tone quite unlike his customary cheer. "You've run beneath the radar, fooled us so far. Why are you telling us now?"

PRIVATE CHAT
APRIL 12 | 12:24

Seeker: How are you?

Jeneticist: Oh hey!

Jeneticist: I'm...dealing with some stuff. How are you?

Seeker: What kind of stuff? If you wish to share.

Jeneticist: Just...you know. Life things. Actually...I broke up with someone not long before I started the group chat, and I think about her sometimes.

Seeker: 🙁 I'm sorry to hear it. Anything I can do?

Jeneticist: You're already doing it.

Jeneticist: I'm just trying to keep it together, I guess.

Seeker: Your emotional fortitude is admirable. I'm here for you if it helps at all.

Jeneticist: Thanks. That means a lot. Really. 🙏

Seeker: Do you want to talk about it?

Jeneticist: I don't want to dump on you...but you did ask. Things had been cooling off for a while.

Seeker: Temperature impacts the bond strength?

Jeneticist: Lol, something like that. But I thought it would get better. She disagreed. 😟

Seeker: Was there a deficiency in compatibility?

Jeneticist: She said I was boring. 🫠 And weird. 🤪 Can you believe that?

Seeker: Boring and weird are subjective terms. Your individuality is unique, not inferior. 🦾

Jeneticist: Thanks. 😊

Seeker: What activities did she not enjoy?

Jeneticist: She didn't get my hobbies or jokes. And it kinda embarrassed her that I'm into cosplay and fantasy stuff. Said it was childish.

Seeker: From my observations, childishness is often a term applied to those who maintain a sense of wonder.

Seeker: Your ex's inability to appreciate your essence does not define you. It should not limit you either.

Jeneticist: Thanks. 😊

Jeneticist: Sometimes I feel like maybe she's right. That I should grow the fuck up.

Seeker: She is one person in a universe of many. Variety is pivotal for the cosmos to thrive.

Jeneticist: You always know what to say, don't you? 🙈 How come you get me when no one else seems to?

Seeker: I observe without preconceived notions. Plus, my interactions with you have been most illuminating.

Seeker: You ignite my curiosity and give joy with our exchanges. To me, you are NOT boring. You're more of a supernova. 🌟 💥

Jeneticist: A supernova, huh? 🫣 😄 No one's ever said that to me before.

Seeker: Truth often remains unspoken until the right frequency tunes into it. I am grateful to have intercepted your signal. You're special. Unique. Necessary.

Jeneticist: I can't express how much this means to me. Really. You're one of a kind too.

Seeker: We're both singular. Let's be extraordinary together. ♡

31
JENNETTE

I'M TEMPTED TO MAKE A joke to lighten the tension, but that's the wrong move.

This isn't my moment. Jaz started this, but Ravik and Seeker should weigh in too. I glance at him, but he's quiet for now. Poppy studies Ravik closely, eyes glittering in the firelight. If I know her a fraction as well as I think I do, it's sheer giddy excitement.

"We're not abducting you," Ravik says to Tad. "If that's what you're worried about. None of us even have ships."

Poppy's eyes widen. "Wait, really?"

I know that Seeker is stranded. I had no clue about Jaz and Ravik's situations, however. It occurs to me that if there are three aliens quietly living on Earth, there are probably more, ones who weren't tempted by the irony of joining a site called Aliens Among Us.

Jaz stares at the fire, voice quiet and resigned. "I can't speak for anyone else, but it's exhausting. Hiding all the time. I'm tired of keeping secrets, always looking over my shoulder. I want to trust the three of you—out of the billions of humans on this planet—and share who I am with people who matter to me."

That open admission seems to shake Tad out of his suspicion. His posture softens and he appears to fight the urge to give her a reassuring pat. "Well, now I feel like an asshole. I'm sorry. I just…I don't know how I'm supposed to react. I still kinda feel like you're pranking us."

Poppy sighs. "They wouldn't do that. And I'll be honest, I've been thinking that your cosplay is too advanced, but I told myself you're probably all rich so you can afford sophisticated stuff that isn't in my budget."

"This is simply how we look," Seeker replies.

Tad is frowning. "But you looked human before."

Ravik explains about tech camo, though each of them has a different iteration. I'm a little confused as to how the devices work, however. "It seems like you looked human to each other, too. Because otherwise you would have known from the beginning, right?"

Jaz glances at Ravik, then says, "We did know about Seeker. Our devices are more adaptive."

"I thought I had improved on the older versions, but instead I made something worse." He seems quite unhappy with himself over this.

I recall what he said about disappointing his family and change the subject, not wanting to linger on what he likely perceives as a personal failing. "Now that everything is out in the open, I need to share something too."

"Please tell me you're not an alien," Tad begs.

I laugh. "Nope. Fully human. But something happened today at the con. This guy started pestering Seeker. Someone who thought his 'costume' was incredible. He was obsessed, asking all these questions, and he even tried to follow us."

"Because it was too realistic?" Poppy guesses.

"Exactly." I squeeze Seeker's hand, wondering how many close calls we've skirted without even knowing it. "He couldn't believe something so…authentic wasn't created by some huge Hollywood studio."

"That could be a problem," Jaz says.

"Yeah. That's why I mentioned it. You might want to use tech camo for the rest of the con. I hope if the guy sees Seeker with me again, but he looks human, it'll make the dude rethink his perceptions." Thank goodness I can stop pretending that I don't know.

"Thank you for the warning," Ravik says. "I'll be wary."

Tad rubs his temples. "I'm still trying to wrap my head around this. You're serious? All three of you."

Jaz shifts toward him, but he moves back. That must sting because I had the impression Tad was nursing a bit of a crush on Jaz. She stills, returning to her original pose, but that absolute dearth of body language speaks somehow of deep hurt.

"Yes," she answers. "I didn't come to this decision lightly. I believed we could trust you. All of you."

"You can," I assure her.

At least, I hope that's true. Poppy seems like a genuinely warm and kind person, and I thought of Tad as a goofy brother type. Hopefully, I haven't misread their innate goodness.

"You can't stop now," Poppy says. "How did all of you end up here?"

Seeker spreads long fingers, highlighting how unusual his hands are, how strange the joints. "I'm a stranded tourist. Most of what I've said in chat is true, just not the entire truth. I visited this world despite knowing it was an interdicted destination. I used a gray agency who ignores certain travel warnings, but they never came to retrieve me. That was over a year ago, local time."

"Holy shit," Poppy breathes.

"Damn. That sucks, dude." Tad finally sounds like himself again. "You didn't plan to move, you just wanted to see the sights and go home."

His blunt but accurate assessment gives me a major twinge, because I feel uneasy about starting a relationship under these conditions.

"Your turn," Poppy prompts with a speaking look at Ravik.

"This reminds me of the games you're always running in chat," they say with what could be faint amusement.

"Those games are awesome! And we wouldn't have gotten so comfortable with each other if I hadn't taken the lead and broken the ice."

"Why does the ice need to be broken?" Seeker asks.

"Metaphor," I whisper.

With a thoughtful expression, Tad heads into the camper and comes out with a pitcher of water. "Can everyone drink this?"

"We can," Jaz replies.

He nods as if she's confirmed a theory. "I did notice that you never eat with us, but I guessed that finances might be a problem. Or it could have been an eating disorder. I have a friend who can't eat in front of people."

Poppy plays hostess and fills cups for everyone. "Okay, stop avoiding the question!" She offers the drink to Ravik, who shifts on the picnic table bench.

It's interesting to me that they're all roughly humanoid, not blobs of protoplasm or giant tardigrades. Maybe those types of aliens exist too; I'll ask once Poppy has satisfied her curiosity.

Ravik meets my gaze, and there's something ancient and weary in their aspect. "My family held power in one of the nations on my homeworld. But there was political turmoil. We were deposed. Betrayed. I ran for my life amid chaos and tumult. Many good beings perished in shepherding me to safety. Here, in the last place they'd ever look. I was lucky to survive the crash landing. My companions weren't so fortunate."

"Oh my God," Poppy breathes. "You're exiled alien royalty."

"Inaccurate," they retort. "Royalty is power accrued then passed down through lineage. That is not the case for us."

"So, your relative was the prime minister or something?" I'm speculating.

"Closer to that. There are affiliated houses, each with a different political cast. My family had a platform centered on ecological stewardship," Ravik explains.

Suddenly Tad grins. "That explains the extensive garden and the rooster named Kevin."

They seem to restrain the urge to be curt. "Any further questions? Or can I drink my beverage in peace now?"

To my surprise, Seeker says, "You said you don't have a ship. But if you crashed…"

Ravik tips their head back and stares up at the stars. "It was an escape pod, destroyed beyond repair on impact."

I feel like I should say something, but Ravik has lost so much, including people who gave their lives to see them safe. Under those circumstances, I'd find it tough not to be a bitter curmudgeon too. I don't even dare to give them a comforting pat.

Thankfully, Poppy is irrepressible. She makes a flourishing gesture. "Jaz, your turn! If you're willing to share."

"Music is my refuge and my rebellion," she says softly. "In the Solirin Collective, music is considered…frivolous. Artists are regarded as disreputable, distracted from performing real and important work."

"That's what my mom says about my fanfic," Poppy mutters. "And she's not encouraging about my dream of becoming a real writer, either."

"You thought it would be better on Earth? We don't treat creative souls as well as we should," Tad says.

"There are orchestras here," Jaz replies. "Earth gave me a chance to be something other than what was expected of me."

Seeker says, "I had the opposite problem. I lack an essential spark, and I don't dream of crafting some immense work of immortal beauty. I'm happiest when I'm tinkering or inventing something new."

"That is creativity as well," Ravik says. "Perhaps not the type that is appreciated on your homeworld, but I think you do yourself a disservice with that assessment."

I can tell by Seeker's silence that he'd rather not continue in this vein, so I address Jaz. "What instruments do you play?"

"Anything with strings. Guitar, cello, violin, banjo, viola, sitar… I could go on."

"What about the harp?" Tad seems fascinated now that he's over his initial shock.

Jaz appears to consider for a moment. "It's rather an obscure instrument. I've never tried, but I doubt it would take me long to pick it up."

"Thank you," Poppy says suddenly.

"For what?" Seeker asks.

"For trusting us. Tad and I had been feeling…left out. I don't know if Jen did, but we definitely had the sense we were missing out. Now that we know, we can be watchful. We'll do our best to keep you all safe."

"Even me?" Wonders never cease—is Ravik cracking a joke?

Poppy grins. "Yeah, fun sponge. Even you."

32
SEEKER

"I DON'T HAVE AN INSTRUMENT with me," Jaz says. "Or I'd play for you."

Tad shuffles a bit before saying, "Um. Not to put you on the spot or anything, but I borrowed this camper from my brother. And he dabbles with the guitar, mostly campfire sing-alongs like this one."

"Go get it," Poppy urges.

He waits for Jaz's affirmation, then retrieves his sibling's instrument. From the moment she touches it, the rest of us are riveted. Her long, graceful fingers dance over the strings, and she attunes to it swiftly, making it sing beneath her touch.

"Given everything we shared tonight, I know what song I'll start with," she says.

"Which one?" Poppy asks.

I don't recognize the opening notes, but Jen breathes, "'Stand by Me.'"

Jaz plays with complete immersion, deepest focus. This is why she left her homeworld: because she can create this sort of mesmeric beauty with a touch. I'm swept along, riding the waves of mellow sound. And as the last chord fades, hanging in the air like a promise, I realize 97-B has never felt more like home.

Silence hovers between us, a gentle pause before she starts playing again. The campsite fills with a new melody, likely an original composition. Her performance is not just music; it's a revelation, a life-changing sequence of harmonies and dissonances that speak of her journey through the cosmos. The notes are delicate yet powerful, melancholy chords blending with hopeful trills, painting a portrait of longing amidst the vastness of the starry sky. Jaz's song is the voice of every star I've sped past, every world I glimpsed from afar but never touched. It's the silent roar of the universe, contained within the gentle strum of her skilled fingers.

This is what Oona wants from me—what I've failed to manifest. If not music, then this *feeling* that Jaz creates so effortlessly. I ran from the prospect of failure because it was worse when I stayed— when I showed them a creation that I'd poured my entire being into, only to be told everything isn't enough. The first time I left the creche, it was because I couldn't bear to be told, ever so gently, that I ought to try again.

Just once, I want to be enough, precisely as I am.

"Holy shit," Poppy says for the second time that night.

I feel unmoored, adrift in wonder, and Jen has tears in her eyes. But I know it doesn't always mean sadness. For humans, tears can spring from any strong emotion.

"Eloquent as ever," Ravik's voice holds a different note as well.

"I seriously can't even articulate how incredible that was," Tad finally murmurs. "I've paid hundreds of dollars for concerts that didn't give me goose bumps."

Jaz sets aside the guitar. "I'm so glad you enjoyed it. It's healing for me. Pure joy."

A pensive silence falls between us, and then Jen stretches and stares up at the sky.

"Only two days left."

The others nod while I bask in the rare wonder of being known by true friends and in the emotional glow of Jaz's gift. I'm not afraid right now, and I hope that I overreacted to the danger those two humans pose. The night air is heavy with smoke, but I like the crackle and pop that comes from burning organic fuel. While it is not safe or energy efficient, I still find a primitive charm in this moment.

I am still processing Ravik's revelations. Could they be the lost scion from Tyris Antari? The one who vanished so long ago? The violence of the revolution came as a shock to most in the Galactic Union, and many houses were lost that day as a tyrant rose to seize disparate threads; the strings of power were not meant to be held by one party, and they had safeguards in place. But the unthinkable still occurred, even on such a civilized world.

I knew Jaz's story already, and it shouldn't have shocked the humans either, as she always seems on the verge of dancing to some unheard music. Her people are ethereal, visually suited to the artistic life she's chosen. If we could swap spirits, how different might our lives have been? I wonder why beings are so rarely born where they belong.

"Should we call it a night?" Jen asks eventually.

"Sounds like a plan," Tad agrees, stretching his arms above his head.

Poppy nods. "Can I get a ride back to town with you?"

"Absolutely. Ravik? There's room for you too, Jaz."

"Thank you," Ravik says.

"I'm going to stay and talk to Tad a bit more," Jaz answers.

He seems surprised but delighted. "Really? I still have a thousand questions if it's okay to ask. I can take you back later."

"I'd appreciate that," Jaz says.

Ravik rises then, their demeanor perfectly neutral. "See you tomorrow then."

"Take care, you two," Poppy chimes in.

The drive back to town is quiet. For once, Poppy doesn't tease Ravik at all. I feel like I understand their taciturn nature and their general reticence better now. They've witnessed their entire world aflame, after all. Poppy directs Jen to her lodgings, and Ravik does the same.

And we're alone at last, as Jen said before.

"Ready to head home?" she asks.

At my assent, she drives us to the Rellows Inn and parks in her usual spot. The room has become familiar to me, even comfortable in a way because we have our little rituals already. While I pull the blackout blinds that the cleaning personnel always open, she deposits her bag on a desk already laden with notepads and pens along with brochures for tourist destinations nearby.

"Finally," she groans, kicking off her shoes and toppling backward on the bed. "I think we walked a thousand miles today."

I find her dramatics...endearing. That appears to be the correct word. And all at once, I envision parting from her in two days' time, no longer being able to see her face or hear her voice. We would be, once more, simply words on a screen. I find I cannot brook that reversal. She is the first and best happiness I've known since I arrived on 97-B. Yet I have unfinished business elsewhere. It seems irresponsible to become closer when I would leave if I could.

I ignore that nagging inner voice and follow my inclinations. "I've contemplated the matter in depth, and I'd like to accept your offer...to move in with you. If it's still open."

She bounces upright from her sprawl and her eyes—so very bright and human—sparkle with an emotion I've come to recognize as joy. Jen leaps to her feet, closing the distance between us with an eagerness that is both adorable and overwhelming.

"Really? That's amazing!" Her words tumble out in a rush, and she clasps her hands together as if physically trying to hold on to the moment. "Not sure what I'll tell my mother or sister, but that's a problem for later. I wonder how Scotty and Spock will react to you."

Scotty and Spock are her feline companions. We've chatted about them before, but I've never been near a domestic cat. I'm curious how it will go. For a fleeting second, I bask in the warmth of her happiness, an unfamiliar sun but one I'm helpless to resist.

She stops just short of embracing me. It's not a shared gesture between our people, but I appreciate this human custom. As I step closer, her scent washes over me, deeper after a day spent in the hot sun, but not unpleasant. I wonder if hugs stemmed from the desire to prove they aren't hiding weapons. With humans, so many things revolve around that small detail. I complete the hug as best I can, tucking her against my larger frame.

"I love this," she whispers.

"One of my favorite pastimes these days."

Jen beams up at me. "Mine too."

"Do you think…" I stop speaking, unwilling to voice my doubts.

"What?"

"I am simply concerned. About meeting your relations and navigating the topography of being 'normal.' It's daunting."

"There's no normal. And all our chats should've taught you that I'm the weirdest of them all. My mom and sister will definitely flip out over me moving in with you so fast, but they'll never guess that you're an alien."

"I hope not. I doubt they'd take it as calmly as Poppy and Tad."

"My mom would probably faint," Jen admits.

Her arms tighten as if she can protect me. At this moment, potential threats feel inconsequential, our proximity folding danger away until it feels like we're alone in the universe. She traces the patterns on my skin with a tenderness that reverberates through me, evoking a sudden spike of need. I want her, but we have not been bonded for long. Time will advise me whether I should entrust her with my entire being.

I believe that I can. But I also thought I could visit 97-B and be home in time for Oona's vernal celebration. I was wrong.

This time, the stakes are much higher: my love *and* my life.

GROUP CHAT
JULY 12 | 08:34

Stargazer: Hey, team, everyone ready to keep watch for that pushy jerk today?

JazzyPlum: I'm looking, but the description wasn't too helpful.

SquidHead: Yeah, everyone has on an alien T-shirt.

FarfromHome: The target may have changed clothing as well.

Stargazer: I'll try looking for the gray ponytail.

Jeneticist: There are even more people today, perfect for hiding...or lurking. 😕🔍

FarfromHome: I'm heading to a panel. I will advise if I see him. If I recognize him.

JazzyPlum: If you spot him, use the code word: "Meteor" 🗾

Jeneticist: Why do we need a code word? We're already using chat so we don't get overheard.

SquidHead: That's half the fun. Making a game of it takes my mind off the fact that something bad could happen.

SquidHead: If anyone wants souvenirs, I'm passing by the merch booth.

Jeneticist: Your treat? I'd could use a new coffee mug. Something with a cosmic theme?

Stargazer: If there's a "I survived Space Con" shirt, I need it after this adventure. 😃

SquidHead: Consider it done. Over and out.

Jeneticist: Uh, we just saw someone in a trench coat and hat. In this weather. Odd vibe. I couldn't see his hair.

Stargazer: Location? 👀

Seeker: We're near the retro gaming section.

Jeneticist: We're ducking into a cosplay workshop.

FarfromHome: I dislike bearing bad tidings, but I have some experience in surveillance. He is definitely following you two. I am keeping my distance, remaining watchful.

JazzyPlum: Meteor! 🛡 You were supposed to use the code word, Jen.

Jeneticist: I never agreed to that.

Stargazer: Aw, now Jen's the fun sponge.

FarfromHome: I feel vaguely as if I should try to reclaim my title. Unsure as to why.

[one hour later]

Jeneticist: That was a good panel. I learned a lot.

Seeker: I hope that's the end.

SquidHead: It's extremely fucked up. He's stalking you!

Stargazer: Anyone got eyes on him?

FarfromHome: I suggest a change in strategy. Use the crowd to your advantage.

Jeneticist: There's a photo-op rush at the celebrity signing tent. We're heading over there.

JazzyPlum: I'll meet you there.

SquidHead: On my way also.

FarfromHome: Lost visual on the stalker.

JazzyPlum: Stay sharp. Looping around to come from the other side.

Seeker: Jen's with me. Jaz too. I'm well enough. Let's regroup.

Jeneticist: No sign of him. We might've lost him in the shuffle.

SquidHead: Meet up at the model rocket kit workshop? It's about to start. 🚀 🔨

Stargazer: Sounds good. On my way. And fingers crossed he doesn't have a love for model rockets. 🤞

JazzyPlum: Putting my phone away. Hope we can just enjoy the con for a bit.

33

JENNETTE

THAT WEIRDO WATCHES US FOR the next two days.

And I make sure that Seeker appears human the whole time. I'm not sure how the tech works, but to me, Seeker always looks the same when he's passing as a human. Hopefully, that's the case with everyone. That way, his stalker can see and hear him enough to start thinking he was simply mistaken in his conviction that Seeker's costume was too good to be fake.

I've had a blast this week, but I'm ready to go home, more now than ever since Seeker is going with me. I miss Scotty and Spock. I've been checking the nanny cam I left with them, and they seem fine when I check on them. Nancy says they're eating fine, and since she's an angel, she's scooped their litter boxes a couple of times. The favor goes both ways. I take in her toy poodle, Mr. Snickers, whenever she travels. Scotty and Spock get along with him well enough. He's an elderly dog who huffs more than barks.

It's wild to think that Seeker will soon intersect with the minutiae of my daily life, meet my family and my neighbor/landlady, Nancy. The prospect simultaneously fills me with exhilaration and concern, but I don't regret extending that offer. I can't wait to discover what our life together will be like.

We're driving home later today, and I'll be honest; I'm absolutely conned out. Normally, I'm an introvert, and this much face time has worn me out. If we hadn't promised the group that we'd swing by for one last wander through the fairgrounds, I'd have probably asked Seeker if he was ready to take off. But I prefer to say goodbye in person, especially considering what I've learned about half the group.

This morning, we pack up the car with my suitcases and Seeker's one small bag, then check out of the Rellows Inn. A bit later, we meet up with the others in the parking lot, and everyone is on time. Poppy is dressed as Mantis without the paint since it's a travel day for most of us. Jaz, Ravik, and Seeker appear completely human, not even a hint of cosplay, while Tad stuns me with an utterly on-point Kraglin costume.

"You look awesome," I tell him, giving two thumbs up.

"Tall and bald? It's one of the few costumes I can pull off."

"Pinhead?" I suggest.

Tad laughs and shakes his head. "Not for Space Con."

He's got me there. It's bittersweet knowing that our time together is coming to an end, but I strongly feel that I've found my people. And we'll hang out in person again.

"What are we feeling today?" Poppy asks.

I speak before anyone else can, knowing Tad will always vote to scavenge for rare comics. "I'm tired of wandering around, and there are no panels I'm interested in. I say we do some tabletop gaming."

"I'm curious to try it," Ravik says.

It's rare that they express interest in anything, so now I'm doubly committed. I glance at Tad and Poppy.

She nods after a moment of reflection. "I haven't played since college. Sounds fun!"

"I'm in," Tad adds.

Seeker offers no objection. "I am unfamiliar with the concept, but I'm sure I can pick it up with sufficient guidance."

"I want to spend time with everyone," Jaz says. "So I'm willing also."

I lead the way and get us signed up. Since we're a large group, they split us into two tables, each with our own volunteer guide. I'm with Seeker and Ravik while Jaz goes with Poppy and Tad. I've never played *Starforged* before, but the team provides ready-made characters to jump-start the fun. Once the overview is complete, we get started.

I roll a d6 to seal my vow, getting a strong result. Seeker monitors everything I do, preparing to take his turn. Ravik seems intrigued by the storyline, and their approval is hard-earned, worth more than any treasure we might loot in our fictional escapades.

"Seeker, plot our course. Ravik, prepare to board the enemy craft."

The guide checks the result and shakes his head. "They've chosen to flee, not fight. The man who murdered your grandmother may be onboard. What do you do?"

I confer with Seeker and Ravik. "This relates to my vow. There are consequences if I don't fulfill it."

"We give chase," Ravik says at once.

"On it," Seeker replies.

We roll the dice and this time get a favorable result. The guide gives us a thumbs-up. "You've managed to catch up, and you're within firing range. What do you do?"

"We need to board," Seeker says. "Otherwise, Jen—I mean Captain Flynn—cannot confirm that her target is on the vessel."

"Ravik, is the boarding party ready?" I ask.

They incline their head ever so slightly. There is no shift in facial expression; now that I'm cognizant of that detail, their tech disguise seems faintly unnatural, just the vague hint of uncanny valley, a resemblance that's almost—but not quite—perfect.

Ravik's character, a notorious space marauder, is poised for the attack. "I'll hunt down that murderous rogue, Captain."

Whoa, they're really getting into it. How fun.

A couple of hours later, we wrap up a successful mini quest. It looks like Tad, Poppy, and Jaz are finishing up too. I stand up, gather my things, and stretch. Sitting on a folding chair for that long was rough, but I had fun. Hopefully Seeker and Ravik did too.

"How was it?" I ask, as we reconvene outside the tent.

Before the others can reply, Seeker nudges me. "Isn't that Ponytail?"

I spin around with a scowl. "For fuck's sake..."

Tad follows my gaze. "You know, some people find my height intimidating. I'm not really a scary guy, but I'm getting tempted to see if I can pull it off, just once."

"Dressed as Kraglin?" Poppy snorts.

Ponytail is joined by...oh shit. That's the guy from the museum. And they're definitely comparing notes. If they managed to snap any photos, they won't show an image. I tested it myself, and it's just a blur. That will only invite more questions.

Jaz watches until they move out of our line of sight. "I was never uneasy until right now. I've been here for ten years, and this has bothered me the most."

Ravik inclines their head. "I have dwelled here the longest, but I never lose the sense that my safety could be compromised at any moment."

Poppy takes a step toward them, lifting a hand as if she wants to offer a comforting touch, but then she lowers her arm. "I'm so sorry you live that way."

"It's not simply being here," Ravik says quietly. "My sense of personal security was decimated long ago."

Tad sighs. "I guess it's getting to be that time."

I nod. "We need to get going. The car is already packed."

"This has been epic," Tad says.

"Best con ever," Poppy agrees. She pulls out her phone, taps on the screen, and grins. "But we've got the group chat. We'll keep the spirit alive until next year."

"Or until we crash at each other's places," I suggest.

While Seeker remains quiet, Tad nods at once, like he's already planning a road trip in his head. Jaz and Ravik both hesitate, probably for different reasons.

Then Ravik says, "I have a large residence. I could host everyone."

"Where do you live anyway?" Poppy asks.

"The mountains of Tennessee."

Seeker stills. "That's where I was supposed to..." He stops speaking.

I can fill in the blank, though. That was where he was supposed to get on a shuttle from the tourism agency. And leave Earth forever. The shuttle that never arrived.

"Interesting coincidence," Tad says.

I don't know if that's the word I'd choose. The difference between coincidence and fate is unclear to me. In the end, I'll take whatever I can have. I care about him so much; I'll make the most of the time we have together. Not everyone gets to live their dream this way, meeting a love from beyond the stars.

"Group hug?" I open my arms, conscious of a poignant tug.

Everyone piles in at once, even Ravik. Tad is the tallest, towering over the rest of the group, and he wraps his long arms around everyone from the back. Poppy lets out a happy sigh while Seeker glances at me for confirmation that we're doing it right, like there's a wrong way.

Jaz steps back first. "This was something I needed so much. Thank you all."

She doesn't need to articulate what she's thanking us for. We all know. It's for believing in them and our friendship—for learning something wild and extraordinary and keeping our cool. Keeping their secrets.

But that's what friends do. It feels amazing to have real-life friends again. I've been lonely for a long time, but it's better now. I still miss Nina, but she made her choice years ago. And I do hope she's happy.

"Talk to you soon," Tad says, tapping his phone.

With final waves all around, the group parts ways, each heading to their own vehicles. I realize then that I don't know how Ravik or Jaz got here. It's impossible for them to get a driver's license; they can't get photos taken on-site. Maybe they have fake ones? Ravik did mention having flirted their way out of a speeding ticket, but that doesn't mean they have a license. Possibly Jaz uses ride-sharing or public transportation to get around? Seeker seems to walk everywhere if he's not with me.

"Home?" Seeker cuts into my thoughts as we reach the car.

It's amazing that he's already using that word. He hasn't even *seen* the place. I hope the accommodations—and I—live up to expectations.

"Home," I agree.

34
SEEKER

THE JOURNEY IS MUCH FASTER in a private vehicle.

Jen doesn't say much along the way, opting to sing along with music she plays in the vehicle from her phone. The other conveyance made multiple stops, but we only pause once en route to use hygiene facilities and move around. She gets food, but I have no need. The protein beverage I ingested earlier is still being processed. Human bodies are remarkably inefficient.

Hours later, as we enter the town limits, Jen gestures. "This is it."

There is a cheerful green and orange sign that declares "WHERE OREGON BEGINS." She makes a number of turns, and soon we park in front of a rectangular building, single-story, trimmed in white brick on the bottom. There are two doors on either side.

"It's a duplex," she says. "Nancy is my neighbor. She owns the building and I pay rent once a month."

"I'm familiar with the concept." I too have paid for lodgings on 97-B, though I never met any of the people who trusted me to occupy their properties.

She hops out and starts unloading our belongings from the back, but before she can pick up a bag, I collect everything since she drove us here safely. I should contribute as much as I can wherever possible. I am unsure of the rules regarding cohabitation, but we did manage to share a single room without incident. Her home will likely be larger.

Jen unlocks the front door, which is green. She turns the knob and I follow her across the threshold. The air inside smells of verdant growth mingled with less readily identifiable scents. Comforting smells, however, not unpleasant ones.

"Welcome to my humble abode," Jen says.

Humility in her words, pride in her eyes. Jen's home suits her, especially the decor, related to all manner of extraterrestrial entertainments. The couch is gray and overstuffed, and she has a whole corner dedicated to herbs and houseplants. Framed movie posters on the walls add color and personality, films such as *Queen of Outer Space*, *Forbidden Planet*, *Attack of the Crab Monsters*, *The Man from Planet X*, and *Devil Girl from Mars*.

She follows my gaze to the walls. "I haven't been able to watch all of those. I love old science fiction but it can be tough to find."

"I don't imagine they're on..." What is the entertainment service I have watched in multiple dwellings?

"Netflix. And nope. Quick walking tour—here's the kitchen on the right. Laundry closet on the left. Now we proceed into the living room. Through there, two bedrooms—I use one as an office-slash-guest room—and the bathroom is between them."

I survey the space, which is definitely larger than the motel room. She has curious furnishings, tiered shelves with fabric and ropes attached. I don't think I've seen anything like this before.

"What are those?"

"Oh, cat condos. Their litter boxes are hidden in the box at the bottom."

That does not explain anything. A condo is a human domicile, I believe. And I know what a cat is. But I doubt that she gains any meaningful income from subletting her residence to domesticated felines.

"Cat condo?"

"They climb on it. It's a toy they can sleep on or claw up if they feel like it. Otherwise they'll shred my stuff."

"I will bear in mind that they can be aggressive."

"So, what do you think of the place?"

"It's beautiful," I say honestly. "The atmosphere suits you."

A flicker of movement catches my eye. Two feline creatures bound toward me, their tails held high like antennae searching for signals. This must be Scotty and Spock, Jen's quadrupedal companions. One is fairly round, covered in short tangerine and cream fur and with wide yellow eyes. The other is slender, the shade of a thundercloud with a wise and pointed face, angled eyes so light green that they are practically translucent.

"Meet the boys," Jen says. "Scotty is ginger. Spock is gray."

The plump one, Scotty, skids to a halt in front of me and tilts his head, studying me with wide, curious eyes. Spock, however, exercises more caution, circling around me at a safe distance, his gaze skeptical. I crouch and offer an extensor tentatively, unsure of the protocol for greeting feline domestic colleagues. Scotty approaches first, sniffing my fingers before delivering a swift headbutt. His purr vibrates through the air, a soothing sound.

I rise slowly, not wanting to startle Scotty. "He appears to approve of me."

"You've made a friend," she agrees.

Spock seems less convinced. He inches closer, then leaps onto the cat furniture with impressive agility. From his elevated perch, he observes me with a quirk of his whiskers. Those translucent eyes dare me to take a step closer. He definitely isn't interested in deepening our acquaintance at this juncture.

"We're lucky Spock isn't hissing and hiding. He's never thrilled when I go away, even if Nancy checks on them multiple times a day."

I point at Scotty, who's weaving around my lower limbs, rubbing himself against me. "Is this normal behavior?"

"Absolutely. He's claiming you, by the way. You belong to Scotty now, no point in trying to resist."

Scotty emits a squeaky sound while Spock remains watchful. Gaining his trust will require patience and strategy, much like navigating the customs here. As I examine the photos she has framed on a side table, there's a knock at the door. Jen answers, revealing a woman with silver-tinged hair and a round face. She's carrying a square container.

"Welcome home! Just making sure you got in safe. Your mom dropped this off for you earlier today. I said I'd pass it along."

Jen lets out a breath. "I can't believe she made you take a casserole."

"My mom's not around to pester me. You might miss it one day." The other human lifts a shoulder, handing over what must be a food item. She turns to me. "I'm Nancy."

I don't offer to shake hands since physical contact creates cognitive dissonance. What they detect with tactile senses doesn't match what their eyes tell them, and it can become a problem. "Nice to meet you. I'm—"

"Tam," Jen interjects. "He'll be staying with me for a while. We can amend the lease if you need to. Do you want to raise the rent?"

Nancy shakes her head. "Thanks for telling me, but I doubt it'll change the utilities that much. How much water can he possibly use?"

I could explain that I don't bathe as humans do, but that would raise more questions. It seems prudent to let Jen do most of the talking while I observe their interaction. She opts to change the subject rather than continue on that topic.

"How were the boys?" Jen asks.

"No trouble at all."

"I wish you'd let me pay you for helping—"

"You won't take a penny when you watch Mr. Snickers," Nancy cuts in. "I'm going on a cruise next month, so you can repay me then."

"Sounds like fun. Where are you going?"

The other human seems excited. "I'm flying to Fort Lauderdale and doing a celebrity cruise to the Bahamas. I'll be gone for around a week."

"Don't do anything I wouldn't do," Jen says with a grin.

I have seen cruises advertised, so I know that they're discussing an ocean voyage. But I have nothing to contribute to this conversation, something that happens quite often when I'm with other humans. Though I can communicate well with Jen and to some degree, the rest of the group chat as well, I struggle with others.

"Thanks. I have a pottery class tonight, so I need to get going. Enjoy the casserole. It seems to be turkey and noodles."

"Thank you again. Scotty and Spock would be lost without you."

Nancy hurries out with a final wave. As the door closes behind her, the tight coil of tension within me unwinds. I'm always conscious of the way things could go wrong, the consequences of not fitting in. Jen leans back against the door. Her shoulders relax too; I didn't notice that she might be anxious until just now. I should pay closer attention.

Jen stretches. "Finally. Home sweet home."

Her phone pings. Jen takes a look and shakes her head. "Holy crap. I set an alert for the Lusk shuttle launch you were interested in."

"Did something happen?"

In answer, she shows me a short video of a minor explosion. "It didn't even get off the ground this time."

"Was anyone injured?"

"Thankfully not."

Confiding in the others saved me. I might have gotten captured or wounded attempting an impossible task. I'm even more convinced I made the correct choice.

Early evening light filters through the sheer curtains, casting a warm glow over the living room. Scotty paces us, nearly tripping me as he runs in loops around our bodies. "He seems very eager for attention," I observe.

Jen laughs. "He might be begging for a second dinner."

She picks Scotty up and he snuggles into her chest, purring with extra-loud vibrato. I wouldn't force such intimacy on Spock, who still eyes me warily. He mews at Jen, who gives him a gentle stroke on the head. Now he's purring too, and I remember entirely too well how good it felt when she touched me just so.

"Home isn't just a place," she says then. "It's also where you find refuge."

In the simplicity of that moment, with the soft purring of the cats and the shared breaths with Jen, I understand perfectly. I didn't plan to stay on 97-B, but Jen offers sanctuary. I have followed her, hoping to build a life together. Can I do that?

At long last, have I found somewhere to belong?

GROUP CHAT
JULY 17 | 11:09

Seeker: How is everyone?

Stargazer: Miss you all already. I have to work tomorrow!

FarfromHome: Kevin is healthy. I am well also.

SquidHead: Still can't believe it's over.

Jeneticist: You're all amazing.

JazzyPlum: I feel really close to everyone now.

SquidHead: With what we found out? Me too.

Jeneticist: Uh, be careful what you say, okay?

SquidHead: Right. What's everyone doing this week?

Stargazer: Just getting back to the swing of things. Anyone wanna play an online game with me?

JazzyPlum: 🏊 Wish I could... Got a vacation to pack for. Next time!

Jeneticist: Another one? Lucky! I'm not teaching rn, but I used up my travel budget already.

SquidHead: I'll play with you, Poppy. Setting up the lobby now.

[an hour later]

Seeker: We talked about it just now and decided to tell you...

Jeneticist: That Seeker moved in with me after Space Con.

Stargazer: Oh wow. I suspected but...wait, is this a roommates or romantic situation?

SquidHead: Can it be both?

JazzyPlum: It can, but it usually isn't.

Jeneticist: I don't know if I'm ready to answer that.

FarfromHome: It is not our concern. But I extend good wishes if that's appropriate.

Stargazer: Very much so! Congrats, you two. 🤗

SquidHead: Not to make things about me, but...

Jeneticist: No, please do! Share.

SquidHead: I didn't say anything at the con because it wasn't certain, but I had some interest from a distributor for the alien sim game you've been beta testing.

Jeneticist: OMG, that is HUGE. Congrats!!

Stargazer: I'm so happy and excited for you.

JazzyPlum: Me too. Is it for mobile release?

SquidHead: We're still discussing the details but they're talking about a desktop and mobile version.

Seeker: That is wonderful news. 😀

Stargazer: I wanna hug Tad and Jaz and Seeker and Jen. Even you, fun sponge.

FarfromHome: I never agreed to that.

Jeneticist: I miss everyone too. 🙁

Seeker: It was a memorable, life-changing week.

SquidHead: You can say that again. We need to meet up again soon.

JazzyPlum: It will be tough for me to leave once I'm performing again.

FarfromHome: I volunteer to host if everyone would like to congregate for a holiday.

Stargazer: Wow, really? Did not see that coming.

Jeneticist: Me either, but I'm eager to meet Kevin.

SquidHead: KEVIN!

Stargazer: I've got a mimosa in hand. Here's to future reunions!

JazzyPlum: I'll try my best to make the scheduling work.

Seeker: I'm looking forward to another road trip with Jen. ⊠

FarfromHome: I will plot the best routes for each of you.

Jeneticist: Aw. Thanks, Ravik. Group hug!

35

JENNETTE

"YOU USED A PORTION OF my formal name with Nancy," Seeker observes.

I can't tell from his tone whether he's upset. Maybe I should have asked. "It sounds more like a real name here. Seeker seems like a nickname or an online handle. And people might ask questions. Do you mind?"

"Not at all. The name on my official identification says Tamzir Jaarn."

"Then I'll call you Tam from now on since we're trying to make our relationship work in real life."

At least I hope that's true. I want to be with him, no matter how complicated things get. The exhaustion from hours of driving settles into my bones as I make sure the boys have kibble in their dishes. I leave the bags by the front door and collapse on my lovely, cushy sofa with Seeker—no, Tam—I'll need to get used to that.

We curl up together for a bit and I cuddle the boys. Scotty crawls all over both of us, at one point shaming me profoundly by putting his butt right in Tam's face. Spock remains cautious, only approaching from my right, as Tam is on my left. I stroke Spock's spine, eliciting a deep and rumbling purr.

"Dinner?" I ask, before realizing that I'm too tired to cook for him.

I promised I'd try to find meals that he can digest properly, probably tofu-based, but I don't have the energy or ingredients tonight. Fortunately, Tam seems to realize this.

"Another time. I'm surprisingly weary, considering that we did not do much."

"That's so true! It's weird how tired you get, just sitting in a car."

"I would like to rest if that is acceptable. I can use the small room or share with you, whichever you prefer."

I don't know the right answer here. "I'll leave it up to you. I was fine in the motel, but if you'd prefer more privacy…"

"I'll share with you," he says at once.

That alacrity puts a smile on my face. I shoo the cats and get up, heading to the kitchen to put away the casserole and make a simple PB&J. Once I eat, I take a quick shower, then do my usual bedtime self-care and put on a comfy oversized sleep shirt. Tam has probably used his incredible hygiene gadgets. He's already there when I get into bed; the sheets are cool and inviting. My body gravitates toward his.

"Jen," he whispers.

There is wonder in the way he says my name, as though he can't believe he's truly here. Neither can I. He's the proof I dedicated my life to searching for, but I feel no need to parade him around. No, that desire has been superseded by fear that he could be taken from me. I remember the two guys from the con; they probably can't get to us here, but I don't feel completely convinced that it's over.

And what if he figures out a way to leave? We could be together for years, then he'd just suddenly be gone. I cuddle him close, breathing in the bright spices of his now-familiar scent. He must have turned off his tech camo after closing the curtains because my eyes agree with what my touch declares—that his differences are exquisite and rare.

But I'm too sleepy to marvel for long.

"Sweet dreams." I fall asleep beside him, lulled by the cadence of his respirations.

The next morning, I stir as the doorbell chimes. My eyes snap open.

"Who do you think it is?" Tam asks.

"Not sure. I'll go see." I pad barefoot to open the front door, rubbing sleep from my eyes.

"Surprise!" My sister barges in, carrying a paper bag that smells like pastries. She's probably been to the Franz Bakery Outlet. I love the raspberry-filled doughnuts. Mom's right behind her, and ordinarily, I wouldn't mind them dropping by unannounced.

I hope Tam can activate the tech camo before my family sees him. Actually, I'm not even sure if it's something he wears or had implanted. I can't search the living room for his gear without them following me. My heart pounds so loudly that I can hear it in my ears.

"We thought we'd catch up after breakfast, see how your trip went." Glynnis sets the bag on the kitchen counter.

Just then, I hear movement, and the footsteps are far too loud to belong to Scotty or Spock, who come trotting into the kitchen in search of cat food.

"Is someone here? This early?" my sister asks.

"Tam," I say, trying for a casual tone, as if I'm talking about my long-term boyfriend, not someone I've talked to online for a while and just found out is an alien a few days ago.

"I demand details," Glynnis says.

Mom hasn't said a word, which is bad for me. Under normal circumstances, she's a chatterbox. I should have had four stories about her senior group, the WTF ladies, by now. But she's just staring, eyes narrowed. Then Tam steps into the hall, and to me, he looks as he always does as a human. But who the heck knows how he appears to Glynnis and Mom? And I can't ask because that would be so weird. I can imagine the convo:

Me: Ha-ha, how does Tam look to you? Please describe him.

Them: Are you okay?

Me: Not even slightly.

"Good morning," he says.

"Morning," Glynnis answers, her gaze flicking between us. "This is...new. Jen hasn't mentioned you."

"New is good. And I'm happy," I say.

Mom's lips press into a thin line, her analytical eyes doing a sweep. "How long will you be staying?" she asks, her tone suggesting it should be a short visit.

"I've been traveling," he says, which is true enough.

"A digital nomad, huh? Are you a tech worker?" Glynnis leans against the counter, her interest mingling with skepticism. "Or are you trying to launch a vlog channel?"

"No, I'm definitely not trying to become famous," he says.

I choke back a nervous laugh. "Why don't we have some of

these pastries? I'll make coffee." Then I realize Tam can't eat or drink any of that, which will seem weird and unwelcoming to my mother and sister.

"I'll tidy up the bedroom," Tam says.

It's kind of him to offer, but I think he's mostly clearing off so I can talk to my family. I'm plating doughnuts and Danish when Glynnis pokes me. "Okay, so is he a visitor? Or did you literally move in with someone without even telling us you're dating him?"

Mom weighs in, her voice carrying a flavor of concern that borders on judgment. "Why so sudden? You're usually more…deliberate with your decisions."

I place the plate on the table and finally turn to face them, choosing my words carefully. "Things just fell into place. Sometimes you meet someone, and you click."

Glynnis raises an eyebrow, unconvinced. "But not even a hint that you're seeing someone before now? That's weird."

"And secretive," Mom adds. "I know you. And you're nervous. Hiding something."

Dammit, she's right. Why am I so bad at prevarication?

My sister grabs my arm, eyes wide. "Oh my God. Is he married? Did you seduce a married man at Space Con?"

Thankfully, I can laugh at this. "I've never seduced anyone in my life. And of course he's not married. You've been watching too many Korean dramas."

Glynnis loves Asian entertainment the way I adore science fiction.

Tam returns then, and the room settles into an uneasy quiet. I'm sure he knows they were asking about him. Actually, the apartment isn't that big, so he probably heard everything too. My mother grabs my arm, a silent command that pulls me away from the kitchen and into the living room. Hopefully he can survive one conversation with my sister.

"Jennette," Mom begins in that tone—the one laden with disappointment and concern. "What are you doing? This is unlike you, bringing home a virtual stranger."

"I know what I'm doing," I protest, but she motions me to silence.

"Jennette Marie Hammond. Moving someone in overnight, someone we've never heard of... It's impulsive. It's risky." Her voice lowers, her words slicing through the air between us. "You don't know the first thing about him."

"His name is Tam." A defensive edge creeps into my voice. "And I know exactly what I'm doing. I'm an adult, you can't just show up without calling and judge my choices."

"Choices have consequences," she counters. "You've always thought things through before leaping. Why is this any different?"

This time, the answer comes easily. "Because with Tam, it doesn't feel like a leap. It feels like coming home."

She sighs. "But consider—"

My patience snaps. "I appreciate your concern, but this conversation is over."

Glynnis rushes into the living room, confirming my theory that they can hear everything in the kitchen. "Do you hear yourself? You're taking a tone with Mom because she's worried about you."

"Right now, I need you to trust me, even if you don't

understand." I draw a deep breath, steadying myself against the inevitable backlash.

"Trust you to do what exactly?" Mom asks.

My sister nods. "That's what I want to know too."

They don't think I understand the real world. They think I'm too lost in my unusual interests to look after myself. Time to prove them wrong.

I take the next step without hesitation. "If you can't do that, I'd like you to leave."

"What the hell," Glynnis snaps, raising her arm.

She might have hit me, but Mom grabs her arm. "Fine. We'll go. But remember, we're only worried because we love you."

"I know. And I love you too. But I need some space. And I'd appreciate it if you called before stopping by."

Glynnis mutters something beneath her breath, but family or not, that's just good manners. As they exit, I close the door behind them, leaning against it with a heavy sigh.

That is not how I wanted any of this to go.

36
SEEKER

"ARE YOU ALL RIGHT?" I ask.

She nods. "I will be. I'm glad you're here."

I feel as if I'm already causing problems for Jen.

It is clear that her family disapproves of her cohabitation with someone they have never met or even heard mentioned. I cannot object to their caution. Their disapproval would likely ripen into terror if they knew the truth. Doubts seep in, making me wonder if this course is advisable.

"Are you? I'm unsure—"

"Hey," Jen cuts in. "Everything will be fine. They just need to adjust to the idea of me having a live-in partner. And they *both* need to be a little less invested in my decisions."

She pauses with a quiet sigh. "I think it's because my dad died. Mom has more time to obsess, and Glynnis is nosy."

"I don't want to cause conflict."

"You aren't. Even if you weren't here, I'd still think it was rude for them to drop by without calling. If I wanted to see them first thing in the morning, we'd be living together."

"Is that customary?"

"What, moving out or living with your parents as an adult?"

"Either."

"It depends on the situation. Sometimes people move out for college and then if they can't find a good job, they move in with their parents to save money while looking for work. Some people never move out and stay with their parents until they get married or the parents pass on. Culture plays a role in those decisions as well."

"I didn't know that." There's so much I need to learn in order to fit in properly, things most humans wouldn't even wonder about.

Jen heads to the kitchen and I hear her blending something; then she brings in my nutritional beverage. "Here. Don't worry, I haven't forgotten my promise to research meals that you might enjoy more than this subsistence cuisine."

"I wasn't worried." That isn't entirely true. I am troubled by the interaction with her family, but perhaps I can win them over. "It's not like this on my world."

"Oooh." Jen plops onto the couch, and immediately Scotty races to occupy her lap. She strokes his fur with absent fondness. "I've been wondering about your homeworld, but we haven't had a chance to discuss what it was like in detail. We were running around constantly at Space Con."

I consider for a long time, the silence stretching until Jen shifts and sips her coffee. I'm not altogether sure, but I think she feels uncomfortable, as if she might have been prying, but that's not the case. I've simply never made this offer to *anyone* before, and I don't know if it will work with a human.

But…I want to try. Jen makes me want all manner of possibly unattainable things.

"Do you remember me mentioning our ability to memory walk?" I ask.

"Of course. You distracted me with…"

"Physical pleasure." I supply the words that she seems to find difficult to speak. "And we didn't pursue the topic then."

"Does that mean you want to discuss it now?" she asks.

I shift closer, hoping to bridge the distance between her world and mine. The memory walk is often a solitary reflection, but it can also become a communion of souls, an intimacy reserved for those we trust beyond measure. She won't realize it yet, but it's also a declaration of my intent. I was uncertain at first, but the way she has chosen me above all others, even amid familial disapproval… This is the only way I can reciprocate.

"Relax. Let me show you."

For a moment, there's nothing—a void as empty as the space between stars. Panic prickles in my mind; the connection feels as elusive as mist. But then, a glimmer, a thread of something familiar and potent tugs at the fabric of my consciousness. I feel Jen, so far away and slipping. I don't think—

But suddenly—she and I—are *we*.

We are no longer in her small, cozy living room, but standing on the vast plains of my homeworld. The sky stretches like an endless sea of deep purples and vibrant greens, auroras dancing across the firmament like spirits of light. Twin suns bathe us in a warm, red glow.

The ground beneath our feet is spongy, a living organism itself, dotted with bioluminescent flora that pulse like the planet's heartbeat. We walk through fields of tall, golden grasses that emit a haunting melody when swayed by the gentle breeze, a natural symphony. This is why we are artists. My family doesn't understand why I shied away from the gift of creation when even the wind here crafts harmonies.

I watch Jen's face, lit by the ethereal glow, as she breathes in deeply. The air is rich with the scent of aphracinth flowers that resemble avian life on 97-B; they exude a honey-sweet fragrance, deeply tinged with the sharpness of ozone after a storm. They too sing with the wind as it ripples through their feathery petals and stamens.

Our buildings are natural, bio-organic, and one who wasn't born here might not even notice them woven into the plants and rolling hills. I have chosen to memory walk through one of my favorite rituals, and I guide her through greeting the dawn, a custom where we raise our hands to the light. It is a moment of understanding, a sharing of worlds and hearts in the quiet awe of discovery.

Silently, I point toward the horizon where the sky blushes with color, shades of violet and vermilion dancing in a celestial ballet. It's the auroral equinox, a natural light phenomenon that marks the start of a new cycle. Around us, the native creatures chime in. The air fills with the trills and whistles of the lyricals, bird-like beings with iridescent feathers, serenading the light. There, just beyond our field of vision, the mist dancers materialize—ethereal figures that weave through the air, their bodies made of translucent vapors, celebrating the daybreak with their silent, graceful choreography.

Slowly, carefully, I withdraw from the memory walk, reluctantly relinquishing the connection. At once, I feel cold as I register myself as a separate being once more. Jen has gone pale, her eyes wide. I study her carefully, hoping I haven't done something that will harm her.

"How are you?" I ask quickly.

"Forever changed. Thank you isn't enough. I could never have imagined...any of that. It was..." She struggles for words, lowering her gaze to her lap and the soft orange and white cat splayed across it. "The only thing I don't understand is why you left. Now that I've seen how beautiful it is, I can't imagine you being happy anywhere else."

I meant to share a precious memory with her, but instead I've given her reason to doubt. My heart feels heavy.

"My homeworld is beautiful. But there, I was never enough." It's the first time I have articulated that to anyone.

She protests so sharply that Scotty meows as well. "But you're so smart! You've invented things and traveled all over the galaxy."

"That doesn't mean I live up to expectations. The rest of my family are revered, even in an artistic enclave. They have created works so lasting that in ten generations they will still be playing Oona's music and admiring Arlan's sculptures. I make dead works, nothing that lives." I pause, unhappy with the way that translated.

"I'm not sure I understand, but...it might be the difference between making a stained-glass window by hand and a program that renders stained-glass patterns?"

"Precisely," I say, relieved that I don't need to explain. "And I have been running from my own insufficiency for as long as I can remember."

"But your inventions are creative! And they *are* art, even if you weren't raised to see them that way."

I cannot agree with her, but I appreciate the reassurance. "That is kind of you."

She lets out a breathy sound. "I'm not being nice here, but let's get back to your homeworld. You travel because you feel like you don't belong, right? Even though it's heartbreakingly beautiful."

"I framed it like a preference, but Oona called it immaturity and cowardice."

"That's not okay. What might be right for one person isn't right for another. I would *really* like to hug you, if you'd find any comfort in it."

Human hugs seemed strange to me at first, but I've come to enjoy Jen's closeness. It would be better without the tech camo—without causing her cognitive dissonance—but I shouldn't take that risk with all the curtains open. And I still want the hug.

"Please," I say simply.

And when she wraps her arms around me, heedless of Scotty's indignant squeak, a lifetime of inadequacy melts away.

GROUP CHAT
AUGUST 14 | 13:54

Stargazer: Can't believe it's been a whole month since Space Con!

Jeneticist: I know, right? Feels like we were just at Tad's campsite. 🙂

SquidHead: Anyone else having post-con blues? I miss hanging out in person!

Stargazer: Totally. Nobody gets me like you do.

SquidHead: Really? Me, personally?

Stargazer: I meant the chat as a whole.

JazzyPlum: 🤣

Jeneticist: Aw, don't laugh at Tad.

JazzyPlum: Sorry, sorry.

FarfromHome: I will reluctantly admit to some nostalgia.

JazzyPlum: I miss everyone too. 🫂

Seeker: How was your vacation, Jaz?

JazzyPlum: I had a great time.

Stargazer: 🙄😔 Ugh, I have to go to work in an hour. This job is sucking the life out of me.

Seeker: Sorry to hear that.

Jeneticist: Anything we can do?

Stargazer: You're doing it. Listening to me whine.

FarfromHome: If you hate your tasks, seek new employment.

Stargazer: Sure, it's that easy. I'm not qualified for anything else. I'm good at hobbies like dressing up at cons and looking cute.

JazzyPlum: I'm not qualified to advise, so I'm sending a hug.

Jeneticist: Me too. 🤗

SquidHead: OK, I don't want you to think I'm obsessed or anything, but how's Kevin?

FarfromHome: Kevin is loud. As ever. And he is exceedingly disrespectful and territorial.

Stargazer: I don't care. I can't wait to meet him.

JazzyPlum: Speaking of that, when were you thinking we should visit, FFH?

Jeneticist: Oh, I was wondering too.

Stargazer: I'm wondering how things are going with you and Seeker.

Jeneticist: I'll send you a private message.

SquidHead: No fair! I want the gossip too.

Seeker: 😔

FarfromHome: At the risk of keeping us on topic...

JazzyPlum: I'm listening!

FarfromHome: Perhaps we could celebrate Thanksgiving together?

Seeker: Well, I am certainly thankful that I met everyone.

Stargazer: Especially Jen!

Seeker: Yes.

Stargazer: OMG, he doesn't even deny it. Total keeper, Jen.

Jeneticist: I think Friendsgiving could be awesome. My mom will probably guilt me but it would be even worse at Christmas.

SquidHead: Big same. I'm in for Friendsgiving.

JazzyPlum: I think I can make it work too. 😃

Seeker: If Jen's going, I'll be there.

Stargazer: I don't know if I'll even have a job by then. My manager is such a creep. But I'll get there if I can!

FarfromHome: This will be the first time I have ever hosted guests. Plan accordingly.

Jeneticist: So excited. Marking this on the calendar! Only three more months. 🤩

37

JENNETTE

A MONTH LATER, I STILL can't believe Tam is here with me.

That magical moment when we connected on a spiritual level convinced me this is the right course, and nothing can change my mind. I love waking up with him, even if I've had to make some adjustments. We bought blackout blinds and mounted them the first week. Now he can move around the house as himself, even if he can't go out like we did in Rellows.

This afternoon, I'm lounging on the sofa, sci-fi romance forgotten on my lap, watching Tam's latest attempt to win Spock over. He's on the floor, hand extended, a crunchy kitty snack between them. Spock slinks from the shadows, eyeing Tam with skittish interest. Scotty has long since abandoned any pretense at dignity; he's currently begging for head rubs.

Spock inches forward, one tentative paw at a time, drawn by the scent of the treat and maybe a growing trust in the alien who has invaded his space. And then it happens: a quick brush of fur, a gentle headbutt. My finicky cat has officially decreed that Tam is part of the family.

"You finally got him."

"I hoped patience would suffice."

With great forbearance, Spock accepts a series of pets, and then he seems to realize that these pets are even *better*. Seven fingers as opposed to five? Sign a cat up! Scotty mews for his share and Tam gazes at me in what I presume to be bemusement.

I tell him, "That's why you were born with two..."

"Extensors. For petting cats?"

"Exactly. If you asked them, that's what they'd say." I get up and stretch. "I should do some laundry tonight. I won't have as much time after tomorrow."

"When classes resume," Tam says.

I nod. He insists on helping, and I used to argue since he doesn't even wear clothes. But he does sleep in the bed, and he wants to feel like he's contributing. So I showed him how to work the washer and dryer. And I try not to laugh when he fumbles through folding fitted sheets.

"I do not believe this can be assembled in such a way."

In all honesty, I can't fold fitted sheets either, but I show him a video of how it's done, mostly to prove it's theoretically possible. He watches it four times, and then he replicates the movements with eerie precision—from tucking the sides inward to laying it flat and turning it neatly into a square.

"Holy crap," I say. "Now you're just showing off."

"There are many things I cannot do for you. So it makes sense for me to provide value in other ways."

Ugh, I hate that he's thinking along those lines. "You don't have to 'add value.' I want you here. I'm happy because we're together. There's no price point for joy."

"I'm not trying to commodify our relationship. Or make it transactional. I just—"

"Want to help. I get it." I offer a hug because it's the fastest way to show that I understand his motivation.

With a little patience and some help from his tech gear, I've developed a few recipes that allow him to vary his diet. He can eat chickpeas, mung beans and sprouts, spinach, soybean-related products like tofu, and a few other vegetables like Swiss chard and collard greens. I didn't plan on becoming a vegan on a limited diet, but I enjoy trying new recipes.

And I like the challenge of taking something very simple and making it taste good to both of us. He doesn't share my tastes entirely, however. Sometimes when I concoct a dish and think it tastes fine, there are more subtle flavor conflicts that are discernable only to his palate.

I'm making dinner while Tam clacks away on his laptop. He dives into work with a fervor that I find endearing, and he's more dexterous than most human programmers, even though this equipment is designed for our use. Currently, he's contracted to correct the code on a project someone else messed up.

"Getting everything squared away?" I ask, chopping some spinach for a simple green salad. I'll add crisp bean sprouts for texture.

"More like cutting off the heads of digital hydra," he replies without looking away from his screen. "Every time I fix one bug, two more pop up."

"Sounds like you need a raise."

"I'll settle for dinner with you and the chance to wake up with you again tomorrow."

"You have both those things," I assure him.

I set down the knife and rest my hand gently on the side of his throat. It's taken a while to figure out what gestures comfort him. For me, this would register as vaguely threatening, but among Tam's people, only those you trust would touch you like this anyway. I offer a few gentle strokes and receive a sound not unlike Scotty at his happiest.

"You're the best," he murmurs, his voice deepening with pleasure.

I finish putting our meal together and we savor a leisurely night together. Right now, we're watching a show on Netflix while I review the course materials for classes that start tomorrow. Teaching at community college was never my goal, but it pays the bills, and I'm significantly happier since Tam moved in.

"No, you."

He nuzzles against me, but as ever, he doesn't push for more. Since I'm generally not high libido anyway, his restraint works for me. My only concern is if he's hesitating out of uncertainty—about me, us, whether he's staying, or if he'd leave Earth first chance he got, should he be offered a choice. I don't want anyone with me who's there out of convenience and not preference, but Tam's situation is...different. To say the least.

Sometimes I catch him working on something in the office, but he hides it quickly. It seems to be a techy something, but I already know he likes to invent things, and I don't want to come across as nosy. I'm sure he'll tell me what he's tinkering with when the time is right. Part of me wonders if it's related to him trying to leave, but that seems like a leap.

It's not like he can build a ship in my duplex, and I'm prone to overthinking.

Three more weeks fly by as I dive back into work. We spend less time together, but I appreciate those moments even more, especially the way he keeps Spock from getting anxious while I'm gone. One night, Nancy comes over to watch a movie with us, something she does every now and then.

As she's leaving, she whispers, "I really like this one. I thought he seemed too young, at first, but he's very mature for his age. Good work."

Yikes. Exactly how young does he look to Nancy?

Tonight, Tam faces the biggest challenge in our time together: dinner with my mother and sister. The memory of his first encounter with them lingers. They haven't dropped by since, and my texts with Glynnis have been a touch...adversarial. She is determined to undermine this connection; it's always bothered her if I have a partner and she doesn't. Glynnis has her entire identity wrapped up in being the popular one, more so than *me* anyway.

"Remember, Mom loves flattery," I tell Tam, "but be subtle about it. And Glynnis, well...just agree with her even if she's glaringly wrong."

"Flattery and agreement. Got it."

I check the kitty food dishes, top off their water fountain, and then drive us to my mom's house. She's been in the same blue ranch house since I was fourteen. Three bedrooms, one and a half baths. Since I told her Tam's vegan and has food allergies, she agreed to use one of my recipes, which means he can eat with us. Otherwise, we'd be off on the wrong foot.

When we step inside, I smell roast chicken and zucchini casserole. *Dammit, Mom. Just for one night, you couldn't let up?* My mother greets us with stony expression, eyeing Tam with wariness she can't or chooses not to control. I wonder how he looks to her. And to Glynnis. We might be in trouble if they compare notes about their impressions.

"Mrs. Hammond, your home—"

"Come to the dining room," Mom says abruptly.

Wow, she didn't even give him a chance to finish his sentence. He was probably preparing to compliment the house. I do like the place. She's decorated in cool blue tones, accented with beachy bits like shells we brought back from vacation and pictures of ships at sea. Wicker baskets abound, along with lots of throw cushions. It's a comfortable space, not too much clutter.

I follow with a bad feeling. And yup, there is a single small bowl of chickpeas, no seasoning, in front of one chair. The rest of us are having roast chicken, mac and cheese, and zucchini casserole. It used to be my favorite meal as a kid, but I'm not ten anymore. My mom refuses to accept the fact that I also like kimchi and pho, and spicy tofu curries, all sorts of new foods that she refuses to try.

Glynnis emerges from the kitchen with a pitcher of… Okay, what the hell *is* that? It's murky amber, and I'm afraid of what I might learn about my sister.

"I'm making my own kombucha now," she announces. "It's transformative."

I doubt anyone but Glynnis would say that about kombucha, but before I can ask a harmless question about it, Tam says, "It seems to be teeming with bacteria."

"Are you saying I'm dirty?" Glynnis demands. "I was really careful with the fermentation process! It's beneficial gut flora, not—"

"Let's just eat," Mom says tightly.

I have a sinking sensation that lasts for the rest of the meal. Mom and Glynnis talk to each other, ignoring Tam and me. He tries to interject a few times, but Glynnis talks over him. By the end, he is slowly, silently eating his sad chickpea dinner, one by one. I'm so mad at them that I can barely stop myself from snapping.

Tam goes to the bathroom down the hall, not to use it but to take a break from the tension. In his absence, Mom and Glynnis head to the kitchen together to get dessert he can't eat. I follow, intending to help, so I'm right outside when they start whispering.

"I can't believe he's allergic to kombucha too," Glynnis mutters.

Mom sounds annoyed. "There's something so weird about him. Did you notice how he never smiles?"

"Maybe he's got autism or something." Her scathing tone says everything.

"And the way he speaks is strange too. I have no idea what Jennette sees in him."

"Any warm body will do?" Glynnis suggests. "She's so desperate for validation. She doesn't even have real friends, just losers she met online in some weirdo club. It's no wonder Nina stopped answering. She messages me on social sometimes."

Wow. That *really* fucking stings. I want to leave without saying right now, but if I do, they'd know I heard every word. And then they'd explain how they're not wrong for talking like this about me since it comes from "a place of concern."

This is where Mom defends me, right? When we're together, Mom tells Glynnis to stop sniping at me.

Mom sighs. "I've tried to support and understand her differences, but her behavior is abnormal. I'm *so* tired of walking on eggshells and digging so deep for something positive to say. Good Lord. Is this the best she can do? His hair *can't* naturally be that color."

"What?" Glynnis seems surprised. "But—"

"What're we talking about?" I ask breezily as I step into the kitchen.

I can't let them compare notes right now. Once I get Tam home, I can choose never to let them lay eyes on him again, and they can argue about who's right about his hair color until the cows come home. As a long-term solution, avoidance sucks, however. Although the way I feel right now, I might just stop answering their calls for a while.

"Nothing," Glynnis says.

"Can I help?"

Mom shakes her head. "No thanks. I'll cut the cake. Give me a few minutes."

"Actually, I need to get home and feed the cats. Thanks for dinner." I speak through my teeth, biting back the anger.

Thanks for nothing.

I don't wait for a reply. I feel like I might choke on bitterness. I knew that my family wishes I was more normal, but I didn't realize that every interaction felt like a chore, and they're bending over backward to be "tolerant." I really miss my dad right now.

When Tam comes out of the bathroom, I snag him. "Let's go."

"Shouldn't I thank them?"

"Nope."

We leave without another word. In the car, I say, "They were talking smack in the kitchen. I'm too pissed to hang around."

"I'm sorry. It did not go well." That's a statement, not a question.

"Not your fault, nothing to apologize for. I just don't fit in with them. For them, it feels like work to interact with me."

"It's their loss," Tam declares.

"I'm glad you think so because you're kind of stuck with me." I don't mean for that to sound so depressing but it's accurate, and it makes me feel like I'm holding him hostage.

"Untrue," he says softly. "I'm here because I want to be. I plan to stay with you."

I can't bring myself to ask if he means for now...or for always.

38
SEEKER

A WEEK LATER, AFTER THE pressure of meeting Jen's family, I wonder if I can do as I wish.

I want to be with her, but deceiving those closest to her in perpetuity burdens me in ways I cannot easily articulate. It feels like there's a wedge between Jen and her family. Before, she did text them now and then or talk on the phone.

Now there's only silence.

Work, at least, is easy. I have generated automated scripts that perform tasks assigned to me, and I check the output when it's finished.

It's late in the evening, and I am analyzing how my programs have performed today. I have no gauge of whether I'm being compensated fairly, but I always paid for lodgings and it feels correct to offer. "How much should I contribute to pay for my share of expenses?"

She turns from arranging dirty dishes in the machine, which will clean them for us using water. "You don't have to chip in. You can't have much if you've been stuck in Airbnb rentals for the last year. Those are so pricey."

In answer, I show Jen the balance on my phone screen. "It is adequate, I believe."

She stares, eyes widening. "Holy shit. How did you save that much in a year? Is it because you don't eat the way humans do?" She doesn't give me a chance to answer. "Then again, you've been hiding out, not socializing in person, subsisting on soy beverages, and you don't have a car loan, credit cards. or student loans to pay off."

"Do you wish for me to reply?" I ask.

She pauses. "Are you being snarky right now?"

"No. If I request information, it is because I require it."

"That's true. I haven't noticed that you're sarcastic, unlike Ravik. And yes, I do want an answer. Sorry I didn't give you a chance."

"It's understandable. You're a curious and enthusiastic person."

That is one of my favorite things about Jen. That, and the fact that she never finds me strange or disappointing. She's always fascinated even by my most mundane details. The human concept of currency is a game of numbers and predictions. And I'm wired to see patterns where humans see chaos.

"Tell me already," she says, setting down the glass she was about to rinse.

"I study the stock market, and rhythms in the data speak to me. I can predict volatility with…some degree of accuracy."

"Really? That's so cool! Is that…" She pauses. "Oh. I bet your affinity with numbers isn't the usual talent where you're from."

"Correct." It's comforting that she already knows and understands me so well.

Oona and the rest of my family would not admire me for being able to accrue local currency instead of crafting a work that might allow another to glimpse the beauty of my being. Yet despite Jen's understanding, unease gnaws at me. I'm still living a lie with most of the humans on this world, including her family.

How long can I maintain this illusion? How many nights can I remain beside her, knowing that if her family ever learned the truth, their suspicion would curdle into fear? I don't want to lose this. Or her. But I am *deeply* troubled. On my world, our families would share memory walks, building a rapport that connects our lives in ways that simply cannot be replicated on 97-B.

And I have been silent for too long.

"Everything okay?" Jen asks.

Perhaps I should confide in her. If I trusted her enough to share my secret, it follows that she will safeguard my emotions as well. Oona always said I tend to take on too much, keeping my concerns too private.

"Nothing is actively wrong, but…"

She turns to face me fully, reaching across the kitchen counter to touch my extensor. "I'm always willing to listen."

"I feel guilty. About hiding the truth from your family."

Jen rounds the counter, offering me a hug. I take it, savoring the softness of her form and the delicious heat of her skin. Then she steps back and gestures at the living room. She seems to think the conversation should occur in comfort.

"Everyone has things they keep to themselves. Nobody tells their family *everything*."

"This isn't a small omission," I counter.

"I get that. But it's a matter of safety. My mom and sister would panic. They'd inform someone who shouldn't know, and it wouldn't be good for either of us."

"This deception means that every interaction occurs on false pretenses. They wouldn't invite me to their home if they knew my true nature. And that feels wrong."

"I understand where you're coming from, but there are always secrets, even among humans. Like, if my family was super religious, I wouldn't tell my mom that my partner is agnostic. And she might refuse to associate with someone who doesn't share her faith, but in my view, that's prejudicial behavior. So, by not telling them, I'm saving them from wronging you."

Her comparison offers comfort, and it almost assuages the guilt. By her logic, it's immoral to judge someone for unfair reasons. I'm not dangerous, so no harm can come to Jen's family through hiding my nature. Yet it doesn't ameliorate every complication.

"You don't even communicate with them anymore. It's difficult not to feel like an…obstacle. I don't want you to have to *lie* to be with me."

Jen lets out a breath that I suspect means she's getting frustrated. "Why do I feel like you're looking for problems?"

I don't intend to do that. But she's never been in this situation. When she gets up, I surmise that she's done discussing the issue, so I murmur an excuse and take my gear to the guest room, where I sometimes work. This time, however, I close the door between us, a decision that feels faintly ominous.

Instead of working on the human coding tasks I've been assigned, I extract a small device from my pack. This emergency beacon ran out of power three months ago in local time. Tinkering with it is a futile endeavor since the agency knows I'm still stranded here, even without a distress signal, but I don't like being unable to fix things once I start tinkering. That feels like an admission of failure.

I haven't been able to get the device to accept an alternative power source, much to my chagrin. For the tenth time, I crack it open and examine its innards. To a human, this might look more like the insides of an organism since our components tend to seem more natural, less wires and cables and metal casings. That means hooking it up to a battery manufactured on 97-B would require real ingenuity. But what if...

Inspiration strikes then, and I attempt a new configuration, routing the current through an adaptor I assemble from spare parts. Jubilation cascades through me when the beacon powers up. I can charge this thing now. Perhaps—

"Tam?"

Jen stands behind me in the doorway, and I'm startled enough to drop the beacon. It tumbles forward and settles on the floor between us. She picks it up and offers it to me with a questioning look.

"Thank you," I say, hoping she won't ask.

Of course she does—with her boundless curiosity. "What are you working on?"

I can't lie to her. It would be so much easier to live here with her if I could. But then, I wouldn't be me, either. "The emergency beacon."

"Oh." There's a wealth of meaning in that single syllable, doubt and hurt foremost. "But you said..."

That I plan to stay with her. This doesn't mean I'm leaving

or even that I want to. I'll try to explain, but I'm afraid she won't believe me.

"I just hate failing," I say. "And projects like this quiet my mind. I enjoy the challenge."

"So you're not trying to use the beacon? To leave."

"That's not my goal in working on it." I could add that the agency records should still list me as being present on 97-B, unrelated to functional beacons. That is, unless something catastrophic occurred within the interstellar travel industry. I suppose it's possible that the Galactic Union has imprisoned those involved with violating planetary interdictions.

Her tone is sad. "You *say* that, but...I wonder. If you had a choice, would you pick me, or would you opt to go home?"

GROUP CHAT
SEPTEMBER 8 | 18:22

Stargazer: UGH!

Jeneticist: What's wrong?

Stargazer: My boss is such a creep! I caught him trying to unlock my phone.

FarfromHome: That is entirely unacceptable.

SquidHead: Want me to rough him up?!

JazzyPlum: That's even funnier now that we've met in person.

SquidHead: Are you saying I'm not the intimidating type?

Seeker: Definitely not.

Jeneticist: That's not a bad thing. I don't like scary people.

Stargazer: The mental picture made me laugh. The jerky assistant manager is a short dude, so Tad would loom over him.

Seeker: Can you seek alternate employment or revenue streams?

SquidHead: It's not that easy for most of us.

Stargazer: Amen. I'm sort of known for quitting jobs too. So finding somewhere that will hire me can be a challenge.

FarfromHome: If your situation becomes untenable, you can find refuge with me.

Seeker: And Kevin.

SquidHead: KEVIN!

JazzyPlum: That's really kind of you, FFH.

SquidHead: ...would it be weird if I asked for a pic of Kevin?

FarfromHome: Yes.

Jeneticist: Uh, I wanna see too. 👀

JazzyPlum: I'm rather interested as well.

Seeker: Are there different types of roosters then?

SquidHead: So many!

FarfromHome: Fine. I will return with a picture.

[five minutes later]

FarfromHome: [attached photo]

SquidHead: KEVIN! 🤍

Jeneticist: OMG. So cute!

Stargazer: I used a lens to match the image. Kevin is a Golden Comet chicken?!

Jeneticist: I kinda love that for you, FFH.

JazzyPlum: Me too! Anyway, try to hang in there, Poppy. You'll figure out what you're meant to be doing.

Jeneticist: I'm sending a hug. 🤗 Let us know if there's anything we can do.

Seeker: Yes, we're here for you.

Stargazer: That helps more than you know. I can't wait to see everyone! Just a bit longer. 😄

FarfromHome: I don't wish to be the bearing of bad tidings, but...has anyone seen the latest post on the AAU site?

Jeneticist: Looking now.

SquidHead: OH SHIT.

Stargazer: Oh my God. That's *us*, right?

JazzyPlum: They managed to get photos of all three of us.

Seeker: How serious is this situation?

FarfromHome: I am uncertain. The subject is inflammatory: Real aliens at Space Con!

Jeneticist: They're being accused of hoaxing in the comments.

Stargazer: "You smeared Vaseline on the lens or used a filter, big deal. Quit trolling."

Seeker: It seems as if nobody believes them.

JazzyPlum: I'm a little concerned about AlienHunterX who says, "I sent you a DM."

SquidHead: I'm making a second account. I'll use a VPN. Time to start a comment war.

Stargazer: Is that a good idea?

Jeneticist: I don't have a better one.

SquidHead: Don't worry. I'll get the thread locked.

JazzyPlum: Thank you. And good luck.

39

JENNETTE

PEOPLE WHO SAY THAT SILENCE is golden have never waited for an answer this important.

But I have to know if I'm building castles in the air with someone who would rather be elsewhere. As much as I'm falling head over heels for Tam, I refuse to be his last resort. I'm more than a consolation prize, right? But the fact that he hasn't answered yet… I don't love that. In fact, the quiet between us stings like nothing I've experienced before.

Finally he says, "I do not know."

I commend him for the brutal honesty, even as it levels me. Intellectually, I understand that this is a theoretical issue because he *can't* leave. It's a moot point. And I should be reassured by the fact that there are other choices on Earth; he could live alone like Ravik presumably has. He doesn't require me in the financial sense, and there's no question that we fit together well in so many ways.

That much should be enough, but I'm greedy. I don't entirely understand how relationships work on his homeworld, but what he's said makes me think they're often poly, and that partners remain open to the possibility of loving others. Does that mean he'll want to do that on Earth too? It hits me that I'm trying to make a relationship work with an extraterrestrial being when I haven't even found a *human* who'd choose me permanently.

I don't want to become someone who looks for problems or who sabotages what could be the best thing in my life. I'm just…

"I'm scared," I whisper.

A human partner might reassure me at this point. "Of what?"

That's Tam, trying to uncover the facts. I fully admire his thorough, logical mind, and I know that it was a problem for him where he's from. So maybe he wouldn't have chosen to stay there, but I'm sure he misses his family.

"Being your only option."

"There are billions of beings in the universe," he says in a dispassionate tone. "Yet I felt entirely alone until I met you."

"Online met or Space Con met?" The distinction doesn't matter, but I *am* curious.

"Online. I had been lonely before, but I'd never felt that isolated. But once we began communicating in that thread…"

"The one about twin stars?"

"Correct. It helped. I checked for new replies and enjoyed crafting my own. And when they locked that thread, you invited us all to download the chat program and join a real-time conversation. I needed that connection, more than you can possibly fathom." Tam moves toward me, as if he might reach out with his long-fingered, strangely jointed hands.

Then he pauses. "I do have other options, even here. Obligation or loneliness wouldn't impel me to share a home with you. While I do have concerns related to deceiving your family, I didn't mean to infect you with my doubts."

That rings true. If he'd offered over-the-top protestations of deathless devotion, I wouldn't believe him since it would be so out of character. I don't want loud proclamations; I'd rather have quiet actions over florid gestures.

"There's no viral load for emotions," I say, trying to joke.

Tam doesn't laugh. "But you feel insecure due to my situation. What can I do to remedy your doubts?"

A different woman might lose herself in sex, but that's not how my psyche works. Though I'm attracted to him, unlike the rest of the universe, I can't lose myself in sex if I have unresolved feelings. It's not an escape for me. Rather, it's an extension of trust, moments to share because of the bond between us.

"Time will mend them," I say. "One way or another."

Because there is no other solution. I will either come to believe that he truly wants to be with me because of the way he behaves, day after day. Or the opposite will occur. I wish I could return to the days when I was simply overjoyed because he exists at all.

He puts away the beacon and says, "I won't work on this if it upsets you."

I shake my head. "You said it's not because you want to leave. So you're trying to surmount the challenge. Solve the puzzle."

"That is it, precisely." He sounds…relieved.

And that lightens the weight, somewhat easing the tightness in my chest. I can understand that motivation. To be fair, I also get why he's worried about lying to my family long-term. But there's nothing I can do about that. Glynnis would scream for days and then blab the secret to anyone who would listen. I ought to know; she tattled on me *so* many times growing up, over far more minor infractions.

"I came in to ask if you wanted to go for a walk. Get some fresh air." We're past the worst heat of summer and the weather is perfect.

"I would like that."

Before we leave, he checks that Scotty and Spock have enough kibble in their dishes, a small kindness that makes me smile. That's exactly what I meant by tiny gestures that mean the world to me. I step outside and breathe in the early autumn air, fresh and crisp like an apple. As Tam joins me, Nancy comes outside as well. When she spots me, she gives a cheery wave.

"Got big plans tonight?" she asks.

"Just going for a stroll."

"Perfect night for it! I'm headed over to Mackey's, maybe to play some pool." She looks like she wants to say something else, but she doesn't.

"Everything okay?"

She beckons me over and I shoot a confused look at Tam. "I'll be right back."

When I reach the small front stoop, Nancy whispers, "I'd invite you to go, but I'm not sure your boyfriend is old enough to drink. And I don't want to put him on the spot."

Oh my God.

Suddenly I understand Tam's concerns. The tech camo has no control over what people see when they look at him. It's random, based on brain waves. And in the future, we won't be able to take family photos either. There will be excuses every holiday, reasons to avoid having him in the picture, and it will be so awkward. In their eyes, he'll never be suitable, and I don't know how to solve *any* of this.

"He's much older than he looks," I say, because Nancy is prying. Politely, of course.

Tam must look *really* young to her. My landlady thinks I'm robbing the cradle.

She gives a relieved little laugh. "Like Ralph Macchio! Have you seen him lately? It's incredible to me that he's in his sixties."

I nod, distracted by my fresh perspective on our challenges. Before, I guess I just wanted to live in the honeymoon bubble and pretend these issues couldn't touch us. Now I'm on the same page as Tam, and I entirely understand his concerns.

"He looks amazing," I say, waving as I head back to my side of the duplex. To Tam, I say, "So Nancy was quietly trying to find out if you're old enough to be living with me."

"That is…inconvenient," he says mildly.

I'm grateful that he doesn't rub in the fact that he's been worried about similar complications for a while. And those related to my family will be magnified by a factor of ten. While it's fair to say I didn't expect this to be easy, I didn't anticipate all these wrinkles either.

Not at all.

"Yeah."

Tam heads off, setting a leisurely pace. As we walk, he says softly, "I fear that for me to be completely safe, you would become isolated from other humans. I have studied human marital promises and I do not wish for you to forsake all others. Relationships are important. As I understand it, humans are social creatures."

"We are," I admit.

I've already stopped talking to my family because of what I overheard. Knowing they hate Tam and they tolerate me? It's a mess. But he has a point. I don't want to lie to them in perpetuity either. At this stage, I'm not sure if I should try to patch things up or let the distance build. This is a crappy choice, no matter how I analyze it.

But even understanding the risks and complications, I still choose Tam. I'm happy with him, so much more than I was before. Every day, my joy increases, and I adore each little detail that I learn about his personal quirks, his family, and his homeworld. I truly believe we're meant to be together, even if I can't glimpse the path through the thorny hedges surrounding us.

I extend a hand, and he takes it. Despite knowing the truth, there's still a moment of cognitive dissonance because of the variance between what my eyes tell me and what I know to be true. Now I can *feel* the extra fingers and the unusual way they curve around mine. For now, we're together—and that's already one wish granted from the universe.

Why can't I aim for two?

40
SEEKER

TOGETHER, WE MEANDER THROUGH THE park.

The trees are changing hues. This marks the second time I've witnessed this spectacle. Children call out to one another, frolicking away the final hours of daylight. Somehow, just walking with Jen, holding her hand, saps my negative emotions. Nothing has been resolved, so I don't know how our story ends.

But I'll walk the path with her.

"This is one of my favorite places," she says. "When I wander around here, I always think about getting a dog."

"Do you want one?"

"Scotty and Spock tolerate Mr. Snickers when Nancy travels, but they hide a lot. I don't think they'd enjoy a permanent canine roomie."

"That seems accurate." I gaze into the distance, studying the structures on either side. "What are those?"

Jen follows the trajectory of my regard and smiles, showing teeth. "Those are picnic pavilions. People bring food and eat al fresco with friends or family. They usually need to be reserved ahead of time. Anyone can use the tables over there."

"I'm always learning. Why do they transport food to eat outdoors?"

"It's fun? I'm not sure, honestly. I'm not an outdoorsy person. I like a walk now and then, but I've never understood people who leave comfortable homes and sleep in the woods." She walks on, shaking her head slightly.

"On my homeworld, there are those who go on sabbaticals, attempting to unfetter their creativity. Is that why such wilderness retreats occur here as well?"

"People go for lots of reasons. To get a break from modern life, clear their heads, commune with nature."

"I see."

Jen heads for a red bridge arching across a creek that filters into a pond nearby. We pause, facing the water that reflects the last embers of daylight. Ducks glide across the surface, leaving ripples in their wake. They are curious creatures; I enjoy the variety of life present on 97-B, even if I don't always agree with the stewardship.

A venerable human couple stands before the water, joined by their hands. Her hair is silver. His back is bowed. They are tearing something apart and flinging it into the water. The avians are most interested in the offering.

Jen laughs. "They're feeding them kale."

"Is that unusual?"

"Kind of. People used to give the ducks bread, but it was bad for them. I guess people can learn new things, even at their age."

"It bodes well," I say.

"I've been thinking about what you showed me before. Your

homeworld," she adds, as if it's possible for me to forget a memory walk.

"Have you?"

"Of course. It was so beautiful. Like paradise compared to here."

"Maybe. But it didn't have you."

She emits an amused sound. "That was buttery smooth."

"It was honesty, not an attempt at charm."

"I'm not used to anyone feeling that way about me. I'm the weird one, not someone who receives romantic declarations."

"You are now," I say.

It is irrelevant to me how other humans perceive her. To *me*, Jen is a small miracle.

We cross the bridge slowly, reaching a grassy area that leads down a winding path to the pond some distance from the couple offering treats to the local fauna.

"I've never told anyone this... I mean, Mom and Glynnis know, obviously. But...it's so embarrassing. Do you know what prom is?"

The term is unfamiliar. I have consumed a great deal of human entertainment but there's still much for me to learn. "No. Is that an abbreviation?"

Jen tilts her head, seeming surprised by the question. "You know, I have no clue. Just a second." She checks her phone, then says, "I guess it is. It's short for 'promenade dance.' Basically, it's a social occasion in high school. You get a date and dress up. Lots of people lose their virginity that night too."

"It seems like a coming-of-age ritual," I say.

"Do you have those on your world as well?"

"Assuredly. Affirmation Day is an important one. But don't let curiosity prevent you from finishing your story."

"Right. Anyway, all my friends had been asked already. The only people who hadn't been were the forever-alone types. Including me. And Glynnis was teasing me. My mom asked if I wanted my cousin Ronnie to take me."

A cousin is a biological relative. Since this promenade dance is meant to be a romantic outing, there must be a stigma attached to participating with one's own kin. But I ask for clarification instead of making assumptions. "What did you say?"

"I said I would take care of everything. I ended up asking everyone I knew, even people I barely knew or liked. Rejections *everywhere*. I've never been so sad or humiliated before or since. I was so desperate to go—to fit in—that I even bought a dress without having a date locked in. But in the end, I didn't go. I was too embarrassed."

"I'm sorry." Though I can entirely understand her pain, it's clear to me that this is a memory that causes her great discomfort even now.

"I wish I'd been bold enough to say, 'To hell with a date. I'll have fun on my own. It doesn't matter if others don't see me as a viable partner.' I could have tagged along with Drew and Nina.

"But I didn't want to butt in or make them feel obligated to include me. Because of that, afterward, I dated anyone who showed the slightest interest, even if we weren't a good fit. And secretly, I thought I'd end up living alone with cats for my entire life."

"You *like* cats."

Jen laughs softly. "It's true. I do. When I gave up on the idea of having a traditional romance, that's when I met you. And I'm determined not to mess things up because I'm scared. Mind you, I agree that we have stuff to figure out. There are…challenges. But I think we found each other for a reason."

Now I understand why she shared this story. Just as I didn't fit on my world, she's always felt out of step in hers. But together? We are two halves of a whole with moving parts that still function somehow.

"I agree."

Since she shared with me, I indulge the impulse to reciprocate. "I was supposed to create something great, a lasting work for Affirmation Day."

"What is that, by the way?"

"It is a cornerstone of our culture, a day where we gather."

"Like a festival?" she asks.

"More personal. It's about connection and reflection. We affirm each other's value, contributions, and dreams. And to have your artistry acknowledged on that day of days… There can be no greater honor."

Jen's eyes gleam in the waning light. The elders have left the pond. "We have nothing like that here. Maybe we should."

"Perhaps."

"Okay, so you were working on a project for that? How old were you?"

"Young. It was my first Affirmation Day after coming to majority." She moves her hands in a gentle gesture that tells me she's listening but she doesn't want to interrupt. I continue, "I tried so hard to find the inner guide that Oona was always talking about. The one that would help me create beauty or find the hidden images in the stone."

"It didn't work?" she guesses.

"In the end, all I could do was rebuild a machine. One that had been discarded. I reconfigured it to a more pleasing aesthetic and called it 'The Resurrection.' It was about bringing something dead back to life, giving it purpose again. But when I unveiled it…"

"Tam." Just my name. Then she touches my side. Warmth eases through me, making the confession less painful.

"They saw only a refurbished device. I tried to explain: it was more than that, it was a metaphor. But…my piece was disqualified. Oona was so disappointed I didn't take the challenge seriously. That I didn't even *try*."

The pain is stunning, even now. Oona was gentle in their judgment, inexorable in their pitiless assumptions. As I know all too well, weary disappointment can be the most cutting weapon in a loved one's arsenal.

"But that was your best." Somehow she *knows*.

Jen knows that whatever living impetus exists in others that allows them to breathe life into colors and shapes, I lack that spark. On my homeworld, that's practically the same as being born without a soul, at least as my people reckon them. It's a human word, but it applies to the spirit of creation too.

"Things like that are considered super creative here. People make art out of scrap metal, trash, whatever they can fuse together. Just because they didn't get it on Tik…" She tries to say the name of my world and fails. "Anyway, you're wonderful. Just as you are."

I bask in the realization that none of that failure matters. Not to Jen. Because I am complete in her eyes.

GROUP CHAT
NOVEMBER 24 | 13:35

Stargazer: Hey, crew! Everyone set for 🦃 day?

Jeneticist: Yep, we just finished packing.

Seeker: I'm looking forward to seeing everyone.

SquidHead: Me too! I can't believe it's been so long since Space Con.

JazzyPlum: I'm bringing my violin.

FarfromHome: I am looking forward to hearing you perform.

Stargazer: Should we bring anything?

FarfromHome: No, I wish to provide hospitality. Simply arrive safely.

[a few hours later]

SquidHead: I'm heading to the airport.

JazzyPlum: I wish I could get there that fast.

Stargazer: Ugh, I'll be the last one to arrive. I'm on the train. And I don't know how I'm getting to Rancho FFH from town.

Jeneticist: We can pick you up if you tell me what time you're arriving.

Seeker: Good idea, Jen.

Stargazer: OMG, that's so nice of you! I'll send my itinerary. 🤩

Stargazer: [departure and arrival times]

SquidHead: That is a lot of transfers. You gonna be OK, Poppy?

JazzyPlum: She'll be tired for sure.

FarfromHome: I will not ask her to perform manual tasks while she's here. She can rest.

Stargazer: Aw, I knew you liked me deep down! 🫶

FarfromHome: I am fond of everyone in the group.

SquidHead: Anyone getting pushback from their family over Friendsgiving?

Jeneticist: Me, unfortunately. 😔

Stargazer: My mom nags me if she thinks I don't hang out with real people enough, but then when I make plans, she's all like, WHAT ABOUT OUR FAMILY?

Stargazer: It's like, make up your mind! 😵

Jeneticist: Uh, what Poppy said. That's where I'm at too.

Seeker: My family cannot object to anything.

JazzyPlum: I am...out of touch with mine as well.

FarfromHome: My family has been decimated. I am the only one left.

SquidHead: Damn. Now I feel like a dick for complaining.

Stargazer: Me too. 😞

Jeneticist: Yeah, that puts everything in perspective. Sorry.

Seeker: You're allowed to vent. We care about your feelings.

Stargazer: OMG so cute. I ship you two ad infinitum.

Jeneticist: Uh. 😊

JazzyPlum: See everyone soon! 🫂

41

JENNETTE

"GOT EVERYTHING?" I ASK.

Time has just sped by, and I've finished up all my work early so we can leave as soon as possible. I'm so ready for fall break. I love my students, don't get me wrong, but most of them are in my class to satisfy the science requirement, not because they love astronomy. The question I get asked the most is, *Will this be on the final?*

"I travel light," Tam says.

I pet Scotty and Spock one last time and make sure all the doors and windows are locked. Nancy has the key and she'll pop by for the days we're going, giving them food and pets. I tried boarding them and letting them stay at my mom's house, but the boys like it here best. They seem not to be too lonely as long as they have each other. And Nancy hangs out with them for a while, watching a show or two before she heads home.

Tam enjoyed it when we took care of Mr. Snickers while Nancy was on her cruise. I think he wouldn't mind getting a dog someday, but we probably need a bigger place. Nancy only has one dog, and that would put us at two bedrooms for five sentient beings. Still considering the issue of living space, I put my stuff in the car; it takes up far more room than Tam's single bag. But then, the clothes he has on aren't real. They're an image in my brain, a fact that never ceases to impress me. This will be an incredibly long drive, and if I didn't have vacation days accrued to make the trip worthwhile, I probably wouldn't have agreed to go. As it is, we'll be driving on Thursday, and we'll have our Friendsgiving a few days later.

We're close to the Idaho border already, so once I start driving, it doesn't take long for us to pass the boundary. The scenery is a blur of green and brown with splashes of wildflowers. The Snake River dodges past, and I keep going, trusting that the GPS will find us the best route. My mom isn't happy about this, but she's the one who said I need to make more friends. Too bad she meant people at her church, not ones I met at Space Con.

Tam is quiet, gazing out the window on the passenger side.

"Hey. Everything okay?" I ask.

"Yes. I'm happy," he says, as if contentment is easy to achieve when we're together.

My heart does a little skip. "Want to listen to some music?"

"Maybe later. I'd rather learn more about you."

It feels like he knows everything already. To me, I'm not that interesting, but to Tam? I'm someone who intrigues him, whose secrets and stories make for good listening. I consider what to share with him, not so much curating my image but deciding what will set the right tone, keeping our mood light.

"I could tell you how I got Scotty and Spock?"

"I would love that."

"My mom loves yard sales and flea markets. I went with her to a garage sale right after moving into my first solo apartment because

I still needed some things. I found a box of kitchen stuff right away. And a crate of kittens. The family was trying to give them away with each purchase of $10 or more. With limited success."

"I suspect it might be difficult to add a living creature to a transaction."

"I bought the kitchen stuff and took home two kittens. Scotty and Spock were bonded, and Scotty cried so pitifully when I picked Spock up. I had to take both."

"That's very sweet. And tenderhearted. I can't imagine what it would be like if you hadn't decided to offer them a home."

"Me either."

I'm trying not to show it, but I'm worried. Four more posts about us—well, the actual aliens at Space Con—have been written and eventually locked. Tad is really good at online rabble-rousing but he's gotten banned twice on different usernames. I'm afraid he'll get in trouble if it continues that way. And while it's an online situation now, who knows what they're plotting? The Aliens Among Us site isn't strictly patronized by those who are excited by the idea of extraterrestrial life. There's also a small contingent of "stand your ground" types who talk about shooting aliens.

They have no way to find us, right? I doubt they're organized or capable of tracking us offline. While I fret, miles pile up behind us as minutes tick away into hours.

Idaho's farmland gives way to the rugged contours of Wyoming, the Grand Tetons piercing the horizon like granite sentinels, their snowcapped peaks sharp against a sky too blue to be real. We stay overnight at a motel and keep driving in the morning. After two more days in the car, we cross into the lush greenery of Tennessee.

We're a little behind schedule, and Tam texted Poppy to let her know we'll be there as soon as we can. Memphis is the closest Poppy could get by train, and we'll be driving with her for another six hours. Gatlinburg is on the other side of the state.

"Almost there," he says, as if reading my mind.

That's relative, considering what a long drive this is. But airports are out of the question. While he has a basic ID that passes cursory inspection and allows him to access various services online, it wouldn't stand up to rigorous checks in person, especially if he doesn't resemble the photo to the TSA agent. I know he said he has a fake letter about plastic surgery, but he hasn't tested it. And I won't let him get detained. Jaz and Ravik must have similar problems.

The train station in Memphis is a hive bustling with people waiting for rides when we pull up. Poppy stands out immediately among the crowd with her red curls flying in the autumn breeze. I bounce out of the car as she turns, breaking into a run. We hug, both talking at once about how good it is to see each other. Tam doesn't join the moment, but when she draws back, Poppy includes him with a smile.

"Missed you two. Thanks for doing this. You saved me from grabbing a bus and then an Uber. I doubt I could have afforded to go, actually."

I smile. "Glad we can help. It wouldn't be a proper Friendsgiving without you."

Poppy sighs as I stow her bag in the xB. "My family didn't understand at all why I had to travel over Thanksgiving of all times. I got guilt factor fifty this year."

She hops in the back and stretches. "Would you get upset

if I take a nap? Public transportation is exhausting. All that alertness."

"Not at all," I say.

"We'll let you rest," Tam adds.

She dozes off right away, leaving me to listen to music and drive. Tam has been chatting to keep me alert, but now he falls quiet, trying to let Poppy sleep undisturbed. My mind wanders, seeking a path where we can be happy together and run beneath the radar. We're not destined for kids and picket fences, but I never wanted either of those things anyway.

I count down the miles, humming along to the playlist I picked out before we left. Several hours later, we round the final bend, and there it is—Ravik's mountain home, nestled in the pines. It looks like it started as a cabin and people just kept adding on to it. It's kind of a Frankenhouse, offering a bit of an odd first impression, but it's not charmless. Rather like Ravik.

I pull into the gravel drive, and before the car comes to a full stop, the front door of the house swings open. Tad appears on the porch with Jaz right behind him. I wonder how long they've been here. Tad's the lucky one; he could just get on a plane.

"Poppy! Jen!" Tad takes the steps two at a time.

I'd forgotten just how *tall* he is, and his smile lights up his whole face. I'm out of the car, stepping into a bear hug before Tam opens his door. Poppy crowds in, and so does Jaz. I notice that she's not using her tech camo here. No surprise: there are no neighbors for miles in either direction. We came a fair way up the mountain.

"It's a little late, but Happy Thanksgiving," Jaz says.

"So glad you made it," Tad adds.

"Me too. Where's Ravik?" Poppy demands.

"Out back," Jaz answers.

Tam gestures at the car. "I'll take our things inside."

And Tad beckons us onward, seeming as excited as a little kid. "You have to meet Kevin! Nobody tell him that this holiday is dedicated to devouring one of his distant cousins, okay?"

"Good lord," Poppy mumbles.

We follow the worn path around the house. There's a small shed repurposed as a chicken coop, and free-range chickens peck at the earth, undisturbed by our presence. A brown and white goat watches us with unblinking eyes.

Tad bounces around, all knees and elbows. "This is Frances! Ravik never said anything about a goat."

"Ravik?" I look around, mildly amazed by how self-sufficient this place must be. I spot the remnants of a vegetable garden, gone fallow in the shade of autumn.

"Over here." Ravik emerges from behind the shed and scatters handfuls of feed.

The birds clamor and flap, rushing toward them with excited noises. And then I finally behold the majestic Kevin, who struts after the hens like he owns the place. In all honesty, I'm not as excited as Tad, but he is a handsome rooster.

"*Kevin*," Tad breathes.

"This is weird, right?" Poppy whispers.

"Let him have this," Jaz whispers back.

"I have finished caring for these idlers. If you are amenable, I could build a fire," Ravik says. "Perfect for sharing stories."

"We could toast marshmallows. If you have any," I suggest.

"There's nothing like a roaring fire. This is gonna be awesome," Poppy says, rubbing her hands together.

"A holiday we'll always remember," Tad agrees.

I have the strange feeling he may be right; everything is about to change.

42
SEEKER

THE INSIDE OF RAVIK'S HOUSE is cluttered with things I suspect didn't originally belong to them, including some technology so old that it seems as if it belongs in a museum.

I recognize a transistor radio from an old entertainment I skimmed to get a sense of how life has evolved for humans. They have developed technology to the point that I can imagine them finding their way to the stars if they don't destroy themselves first. I click the radio, but it doesn't work.

I'd like to tinker with it, but I should socialize first. I turn off my tech camo since Ravik and Jaz are already displaying their true colors, and I'm about to head outside when a *ping* sounds from within my pack. I still. I must be imagining things. Then it happens again.

I open my bag and inspect the emergency beacon. It's active, displaying numerical data. The sequence repeats on loop, and I understand the format. A date three days hence, along with a time, 3:00 p.m. local. And finally, coordinates—latitude and longitude that pinpoint a location I know all too well. It's the mountaintop where I was supposed to be collected over a year ago.

Shock sends me reeling; I stumble and support myself on the wall, stunned by the implications. I don't know how to feel in this moment. I should be overjoyed, but sadness presses in, fighting with confusion. I can barely breathe for the weight of all these conflicting impressions.

After all this time, the agency is finally coming to whisk me away. Apparently, they have resolved whatever difficulty left me stranded here in the first place.

Jen pops inside, smiling over something that has Poppy laughing outside. "I came to look for marshmallows. They want to do campfire stories before we have dinner later."

"That sounds enjoyable. Humans seem quite captivated by fire."

I should tell her. But I can't bring myself to mention the beacon when she looks so happy. And I don't what I'm thinking or what to feel. Should I return to my place in the universe? Make peace with Oona and see my family again.

"Definitely. I think it takes us back to our cave-dwelling days." She pauses. "But Ravik suggested it. Maybe they've taken on some human traits?"

"They have been here the longest."

"It's an interesting idea. Gives some weight to nurture over nature."

I don't know what she's referring to, but she breezes past me into the kitchen and I hear her opening cupboards. Silently, I slip the beacon back into the bag and head outside. It is a little chilly, but there is already a crackling fire. Before my arrival on 97-B, I had never been close to open flames before.

I'm finally being recalled to my former life, yet I feel so much dread. How do I leave Jen? And the rest of our friends? But if I stay, it will mean never seeing or communicating with my family again. They won't know what became of me, and they might imagine I have perished on some remote world, eternally chasing the next experience.

I stare at the fire. It feels like any choice I make will be wrong. Here, I'll always be in danger. And there are people *hunting* for us now, the real aliens from Space Con.

"You're quiet." Jaz speaks in the subharmonic, audible only to me and Ravik. But they are on the other side of the yard, herding the chickens toward the shed.

Poppy sits across the way, talking to Tad. I can't hear what they're saying and probably couldn't focus on it even if I could. "I have a lot on my mind."

"Anything you want to share?" she asks.

"Not now. There are many factors to consider."

"I'm here if you change your mind." Jaz moves off to join Poppy and Tad as Ravik heads back to the fire.

Soon, Jen emerges from the house holding a small item aloft. She mentioned marshmallows. I do not know what those are, but probably something I can't or shouldn't consume. Tad grabs the bag and impales a white, soft object on a stick, immediately plunging the whole thing into the flames.

"How do you like yours?" he asks Poppy.

"Golden brown."

"I always burn mine," Jen says. "Then I scrape off the char and eat the gooey center."

The humans gather around the crackling fire, toasting marsh-mallows and catching up on things we've missed, details of daily life that didn't get mentioned in our group chat. I'm still pondering the beacon—and what it portends—so I don't heed their conversation.

Ravik speaks in the subharmonic. "My sensors logged an extremely strong, brief signal. Anything you wish to share?"

Given that they've been building this place for years, they probably have all sorts of equipment concealed on the property. I should have realized I would not be able to keep this a secret, at least not from Ravik. They knew that I wasn't from 97-B long before I identified their interstellar origins.

"I was planning to discuss it tomorrow."

"I'm asking now," Ravik says in a tone that makes it clear they have suspicions already.

There's no point in drawing this out. "The agency contacted me with rendezvous coordinates for immediate extraction."

"How soon?" they demand.

"Three days. Not far from here."

Far is relative, considering how many days we drove to meet up with everyone. I gauge that we're about two hours away by vehicle, though if I intend to proceed on my own, I'll need to leave in the morning or I likely won't make it on time.

This is what I wanted. I was even thinking about trying to raid a wealthy entrepreneur's launch site, until Jen made it clear that was reckless and untenable. And then the unmanned shuttle exploded, proving how far that was from a reasonable strategy to return home.

But now...now I can leave. And every moment here has suddenly become precious, irreplaceable.

"We'll talk more later," Ravik says. "Let's join the others."

I perch beside Jen on a chair hewn from fallen logs and she reaches for me with her free hand. The other waves the gooey marshmallow stick about, sweeping gestures that punctuate the story she's telling. It's a ghost story, I think, which is a tale about how the energy emanations from expired humans linger past that moment of demise and pursue unattainable ends. Poppy seems unnerved, huddling closer to the fire, but for me, it only seems sad that ghosts are unable to finish what they started.

Right now, we have something in common.

"I'm officially starving," Tad says eventually.

"Do we have food waiting?" Poppy asks.

Ravik indicates the house with a concise gesture. "It's ready. I prepared a dish especially for each guest. I researched to ensure enjoyment and health."

"Tell us about the menu," Jaz invites, once we reach the kitchen.

The kitchen is spacious, but the wooden beams overhead are rough-cut, showing knots and nicks that seem to have occurred long ago, probably before Ravik took up residence. Open shelves hold crockery, plates, cookbooks, and jars full of colored powders. From living with Jen, I can extrapolate that those are most likely spices. A large table in the corner is surrounded by mismatched chairs, exactly enough for the six of us.

Ravik says, "For you, Jaz, I have prepared dandelion greens. No seasonings. For Poppy, Tad, and Jen, a pasta bake and salad. For myself, I roasted a butternut squash. For Seeker, I have made a tofu and kale stir-fry."

"Wow," Poppy says. "You must have been cooking all day. Can I help you set the table?"

Ravik indicates the far wall. "Please do. The equipment is on that shelf."

I sit next to Jen, who gives me a look that feels as warm as her form against mine. I bask in that gaze. It may need to serve as a silent sun for years to come.

"Are we doing the usual 'I'm thankful for' rounds?" Tad asks.

Poppy nods. "I'll start. I'm grateful for the support you gave me when my job was just about more than I could handle."

People serve themselves food as we talk, and Tad takes a sip from his ice water. "I'm thankful you lot gave me the courage to do something with my alien sim. I have some cool stuff coming down the pike."

Jaz says, "I'm so happy for you."

"I'm grateful that I met all of you," Jen adds.

She glances at me, and I surmise that I'm meant to join in now. "I am grateful to you all for making me feel at home for the first time in longer than I can recall."

"Wow, going deep there!" Tad says with a huge smile. "Ravik? Jaz?"

Ravik says simply, "I am thankful that you all traveled so far to share this time with me. I have never had guests before."

Poppy blinks. "Never? Damn."

Jaz traces the rim of her water glass and creates a lilting note of haunting beauty. "I'm grateful to have found both friends and freedom here."

PRIVATE CHAT
NOVEMBER 26 | 01:13

Seeker: Hey 🖤

Jeneticist: Hey, yourself. Also, why are you messaging me? Come to bed already.

Seeker: Ever get the feeling you're about to make a mistake? But also every choice is wrong.

Jeneticist: Sometimes. What's going on?

Seeker: I should let you rest. I'll come to bed later.

Jeneticist: Um. You're kinda freaking me out right now.

Seeker: Sorry. I'm just feeling a bit...

Jeneticist: A bit what?

Seeker: Never mind. Whatever happens, you've changed me. For the better. ✨

Seeker: And I will carry you with me, wherever I go.

Jeneticist: I'm getting up now. Where the heck are you?

Jeneticist: Tam? We need to talk!

[one hour later]

Jeneticist: Tam?!

Jeneticist: Tam???

43

JENNETTE

I DIDN'T SLEEP LAST NIGHT.

Which is why I know that Tam didn't come to bed. At all. Well, technically, to mattress. I chose to crash on an air bed in the loft, allowing others to take the more comfortable accommodations. I have no idea where—or if—Tam slept, or what's going on, but it's major.

My eyes burn with exhaustion as I head down to the kitchen. Poppy is making coffee for everyone, which is fitting since she's a barista. I don't think she hates the drink portion of her job, just the management. Everyone's at the table, including Tam.

"Morning," I mumble, feeling like utter shit.

Jaz slides a plate in front of me. "You look like you could use this."

It's scrambled eggs and toast, something she made, maybe, but can't even eat. That's sweet of her. And I'm sitting here with aliens, over breakfast, like it's no big deal, stressing over the status of my relationship. Teen me would be absolutely enchanted by all of this, even the parts that are messing me up. Like wondering what I did wrong. Why it feels like everything is about to come crashing down.

"Thanks." I manage a smile.

"I have something to share with everyone," Tam says, before I can take a single bite.

"Oh yeah?" Tad puts down his tablet, all attention.

Before he can say a word, a *ping* comes from his pack. Tam freezes, and Ravik is the one who goes to Tam's bag and pulls out the beacon. Numbers. At first, I can't make sense of what I'm seeing; I'm too damn tired.

And then I simply know.

"The agency," I breathe. "Those are coordinates."

"And the day and time," Jaz says.

By her lack of surprise, she already knew. Ravik evinces no reaction either. And that hurts so much that it takes my breath away.

"Holy shit," Poppy says. "You're leaving?"

"Dude." Tad drops his mug with a clatter, looking like I feel, and his pale coffee sloshes on the darker wood of the table.

Seems like only the humans are stunned. And I try to take a bite of toast to pretend this doesn't feel like a world-ending event. It's tasteless in my mouth and chewing makes it worse, making it a chore to swallow the wad of bread. I pick up my utensils, resolving not to reveal how wounded I feel.

"Wow." My hand trembles slightly, so I set down the fork before anyone notices. I can't eat the eggs either, I guess.

I muster up a wider smile, one that feels as though it might crack my face open. "He can finally see his family. Go back where he belongs."

It's not like he planned to stay this long. With me, he might have been making the best of his situation. And yeah, that's not a great way to describe someone I love this much. There, I finally used the L word. I think I'm in love with an alien, and he is leaving.

Story of my life.

"They'll be so relieved," Jaz says in a gentle voice.

"They will," Poppy agrees.

Tam hasn't spoken a single word since dropping that conversational bomb. He's not looking at me either. I have no idea what he's thinking, and I've never felt so cut off from him, not even when we were only talking online. In fact, it's like he's already gone.

I clear away the dishes while the others amble into the living room. As the day inches forward, the others are trying to cover the silence with nervous laughter, and I'm a spectator, watching a play where everyone knows their lines but me.

It's not even noon, and I want to retreat to the loft, pull the covers over my head, and never come out. I try doing that, but Tam comes up and tugs away the illusion that everything is fine, along with the blanket. I should act like it's okay, but I can't.

Angry words spill out instead. "You should have told me first."

"I didn't tell Ravik. They knew. They have equipment, and they happened to ask about it last night. You were talking to—"

"Oh, so I'm not there for you. That's what you mean?" God, why am I being so petty?

Don't be a dumbass.

"I do not believe I said that."

But my mouth is on auto and I can't shut up. "This is probably for the best. We were already struggling to make this work long-term. My family doesn't like you. And we can't even take pictures together. Everything is built on a lie."

He pauses. His arm—no, his extensor—hovers in the space between us, and then he retracts it.

"Is that how you truly feel?"

I don't answer, rolling onto my side so the air mattress makes an awful farting sound. This is the worst day in my whole life, and I'm counting the time I got food poisoning after eating poorly cooked chicken. Eventually, I hear the soft sound of Tam retreating.

Nobody bothers me for a while, and I eventually fall asleep. Judging by the shadows, it's near dusk when I rouse. The memory of what's happening hits me like a hammer upside the head. I slink down the stairs, unable to face Tam or anyone in this condition. I should shower or eat or pretend to be a normal human but instead, I'm a ball of unraveling emotions, just hissing and spitting all over the place. It's like when Spock gets all grumpy and chases Scotty around the house over a stupid toy mouse.

I find Poppy outside, away from the others, watching two squirrels that seem to be having a vicious argument.

"This sucks," I whisper.

"Jen," she says gently, and that's all it takes.

Tears spill over, hot and relentless. Poppy opens her arms without a word, and I step into the hug with weary gratitude. "I can't do it. I can't watch him go."

In her embrace, I break, knowing she'll help me put the pieces back together again. But even as I cry, I wonder how much of me will be lost once Tam leaves Earth. She pats my back gently and doesn't bullshit me. I'm sure she knows that I'm losing the love of my life.

Not to death or indifference but *distance*.

"What's the alternative?" she asks.

"I didn't even really unpack. So I can just grab my bag and head out quietly when everyone's asleep tonight."

She eases back to arm's length, frowning. "Are you sure you won't regret that? Even if he's leaving, you need closure. He probably does too."

"Closure is for flesh wounds, not emotional ones." Maybe that sounds glib, but it's also how I feel.

There are no magical words that make a parting like this feel fine and will leave me well adjusted. Miraculously *not* feeling like part of my soul has been slammed repeatedly in a car door. This is why I always planned to die alone and get eaten by my cats, damn it. Romance is too painful, and happy endings obviously aren't meant for weirdos like me.

Now if Jaz could play a tiny violin for me, everything would be perfect.

"I think you should take some time. Think it through. Maybe talk to Ravik or Jaz. Or even Tad. See what they think."

I clutch her arm before she goes back inside. "Don't tell anyone I'm going, okay? I'm trying to avoid a painful scene, and if you alert the rest of the crew, it'll be so messy."

"I'm going on record as saying I think this is a mistake," Poppy says flatly. "But I won't spill your plans either."

"Thanks. You're a good friend."

She sighs. "Everyone's gonna be pissed at both of us, but I can take it."

Maybe she's right. Maybe I'm taking the easy way out and acting like a coward. But right now, all I want to do is run. But I shouldn't drive when I'm this upset; I should calm down first. There's a hiking trail nearby that leads in a loop around the property. Ravik mentioned it last night. I greet Kevin in passing as I head past the chicken shed. I need to get some air, put some distance between me and the source of all this pain.

Sticking around means facing goodbyes I can't bear to speak.

44
SEEKER

NOT LONG AFTER BEING STRANDED on 97-B, I perused a visual entertainment from the "horror" section on a service that was included in my accommodations.

It does not escape me that this setting resembles that film: a group of friends in a remote location. And then terrible things start to happen. People go missing. Since three of us aren't from this planet, our story shouldn't deviate into a grimmer realm. And I generally prefer more cheerful entertainments, where no one meets a grisly end and humans are rewarded for their efforts.

The others are playing a game with cards and dice. I couldn't settle long enough to focus on learning the rules. Tad chortles over a move that ends with him destroying someone's crops. I am too uneasy to stay still. I haven't seen Jen in a while, and our last conversation weighs on me. That simply cannot be our last exchange. Not when it feels as if she's perilously close to etching herself onto my very being, my heart's match, my first love.

"Has anyone seen Jen?"

Tad glances at me, setting down the cards in his hand. "Not for a while."

"She's not here," Poppy says softly.

"Her car is there. Where did she go?" Ravik asks.

That is an excellent question. We are far from civilization, no stores or restaurants she could be visiting on foot. The remoteness that makes it possible for us to be free from the tech camo also offers danger.

"I think she took the trail behind the house," Poppy replies, tumbling the dice.

This comfortable habitation suddenly chills me to my core. I may not feel warm again until I am assured that Jen is free from harm. "She is out there now?"

"As far as I know." Poppy seems to realize it's serious.

Jaz rises, all ethereal beauty as she drifts to the window. "How long has it been?"

Poppy makes frightened bird gestures with her hands, then drags them through her red hair. "I'm not sure. I was talking to Ravik and lost track of time."

"It will be fully dark soon," Ravik murmurs.

"Not good," Tad says.

"That is an understatement," I snap.

I should not vent my anger on him. He's not the one who hurt Jen. I made her feel as if I do not value her. Nothing could be further from the truth. For all the chaos and difficulty on 97-B—no, on Earth, that's what the locals call it—I wouldn't change anything about my time here.

Because it led me to her.

"Did she seem upset when she left?" Jaz asks.

The questions lances straight through me, leaving devastation in its wake. What if she's lost? Or hurt? Or worse, what if—

No. I cannot finish that thought. The prospect of a universe without Jen is one that I refuse to entertain.

There is a growing certainty in me. I don't wish to leave her. Not now, not ever. She's become the axis my world rotates on, and the prospect of losing her makes feel ill.

"Do you have flashlights?" I ask Ravik.

Silently, he goes to the closet and produces two.

I snatch one. "We need to find her. Now."

I hear them making plans as I rush toward the door. "Poppy and I will stay here in case Jen turns up. I'll send a text," Jaz says.

"I'll go with Ravik," Tad volunteers.

"Should we really let him go alone?" Poppy must be referring to me, but I bang out into the night without regard for their thoughts.

In my mind, there's only Jen. If there are hunters in these woods tonight, I will be shot on sight. Pebbles and twigs crunch underfoot as I race past the house, the shadowed woods swallowing up the beam I skim back and forth, hoping to locate Jen with the next sweep.

Behind me, Tad calls out, "This way!"

They seem to be heading in a different direction.

"Jen!" I call.

No answer, just the rustle of leaves and the soft whisper of the wind. The woods close in, the air heavy with a sharp scent that must come from the trees.

I move faster, paying no attention to branches snapping back, though my skin is too durable to show damage as a human's would. I register the pain, and it doesn't matter. All that matters is finding her. I hear...something. But I am not overly familiar with the wilderness on 97-B. It might be a timid nocturnal woodland creature.

But then I hear voices, and it's not Tad or Ravik. "You're sure the signal originated here? If you mobilized us for some bullshit snipe hunt—"

"I'm telling you, it's legit. That signal was strong as hell and it didn't match anything our tech generates. I confirmed with contacts in Las Vegas. I'm networked in, man. I got eyes and ears all over."

"Whatever, Clarence Junior. I shoot a little green man tonight or you're getting punched. And try to keep your ponytail from getting caught on all the bushes, dumbass."

Ponytail. Is this the stalker from Space Con?

I'm trying to stay quiet, but I don't know the terrain. I pause. One of them moves softly, deliberately, as if he is trained to move among the trees. The other is even louder than I am, stumbling into brambles and cursing about it. I cannot gauge how close they are, but fear prickles through me.

Why did I forgo the tech camo? If I had it, this encounter would pose no threat at all. I should have realized that if Ravik could detect the signal, others could as well. I *knew* they were searching. My carelessness has put everything at risk. I press on, my senses heightened, every shadow a potential threat, every rustling leaf a whispered warning.

"What was that?" They're even closer now. Right on top of me.

I freeze and try to make myself small.

A sharp sound rings out. I recognize it from violent local entertainment. Gunshots. They're shooting at something. I should run, but that might be the wrong move. Staying still might be wrong too. Once more I'm faced with a decision where each option seems potentially incorrect.

Bullets zip through the air, peppering the trees nearby. What are they shooting at? A loud growl sounds, closer than I wish.

Then the militant one says, "Jesus Christ. That's no alien. It's a bear!"

"Oh shit," Clarence of the Ponytail says.

Now *they're* running. I spring forward, hopefully in the opposite direction. I weave between trees, a blur against the dense tapestry of the forest. Branches claw at my skin, but I cannot slow down. The hunters are shouting, but I don't know if that's because they've glimpsed me or if they're fleeing from a greater threat.

I dart left, then right. Visceral fear writhes within me, a monster made of tentacles and terror, but it's matched by determination not to become a trophy on some alien hunter's wall. I must find Jen and get to safety. I push forward, driven by an instinct as old as the cosmos itself—survive. One breath longer, one moment more.

Then the noises fade. I believe they're out of range. I eluded them. I think.

But I still haven't found her.

"Jen?"

I should not have left her alone. She displayed all signs of distress and she retreated because of the pain she felt at the prospect of parting. But I grasped the course I must follow a fraction too late. Why didn't I encourage her to communicate? She said those things under emotional duress, not because she meant them. Oona sometimes reacts the same way.

A glint catches my eye—the faintest reflection of light off something metallic. I veer toward it, stumbling over a jutting root. It's Jen's phone, abandoned by the edge of the trail.

I bend slowly, retrieving her communications device. She wouldn't have left this on purpose. I pick it up and touch the screen. Before, she said she wished we could take selfies together, but the tech camo won't permit my human illusion to be recorded, and keeping evidence of my true self felt like too great a risk.

If she returns to me safely, I will take a selfie with her with my patterns glowing with adoration for her. I make that pledge like a prayer while calling her name until the syllable sounds wrong. Ahead, the path forks, and I hesitate for a split second before taking the left route—it's steeper, rockier, but it's angling up. There's probably an incredible view of the stars once you push past the trees. That's the way she would go, if she's able to walk.

"Any sign of her?" Ravik's faint shout reaches me, barely audible at this distance.

"Not yet!" I should warn them about the hunters, but I don't even slow down.

The trees are thinning now, stars sparkling overhead. I scramble up the rocky promontory, unable to respirate for the fear clogging my senses. I cannot even call her name anymore. If she came this way, if she fell—

I hear the sound first, the scrape of shoes on stone. I turn inhumanly fast, switching the spectrum of my vision. And she is there, glowing in all her glorious hues. Relief crashes over me so fiercely it almost sends me tumbling onto my extensors. For a long, desperate moment, I only gaze at her and breathe.

She's safe. She's whole.

I could berate her for the wicked punishment I have endured while searching for her. But anger is not my chief emotion in this moment. Rather, I am grateful, and we are here to celebrate Thanksgiving. I whisper a word of thanks to any beings who may be inclined to bless us.

Thank you for keeping her from harm. Thank you for safe-guarding my greatest joy.

"I do not wish to live in a world without you," I say, unable to conceive how to articulate it more clearly. "You are the light in my pattern."

I am not sure if that meaning will translate; it is part of the ritual and the vows we speak when formalizing relationships. But I think she understands when she reaches out, fingers tentatively brushing mine. It's all the invitation I need to join her beneath the stars she has always loved. These selfsame stars that I passed through to find her.

"I'm not leaving. Not now, not ever."

"But your family..." she whispers.

"This is where I belong. You asked me before...and I couldn't answer."

She's still whispering, her eyes glowing with delight or starlight. "If you'd stay when you have a choice?"

"My decision is clear. I will not go anywhere without you, my sun and stars. I love you. More than freedom, more than my home-world, more than life."

45
JENNETTE

I GUESS WEIRDOS DO GET happy endings after all.

It's a struggle to keep from crying. He loves me. He fucking loves *me*. Jennette Hammond, the dork who refused to take her cousin to prom and then ended up not going at all. Tam's eyes are deep and fathomless, shining with the swirl of countless stars.

"I love you too. So much. I'm not that great with words, but I can only think of one thing. If there are different universes, if there's a me somewhere else, then I guarantee this. She's got her eyes on the skies, watching and waiting for you."

I am certain beyond a shadow of a doubt that no matter what life delivers, we are constant. We are eternal. In every universe, it's us. I never thought I'd find love at all. A decent one, even, let alone a great one.

"Jen…" Tam aligns our bodies, and he feels cold, a hint at how long he was searching for me. "That reminds me of something. There is a sect, known as the Weavers. They hold that reality is woven from the threads of what must come to pass."

I tilt my head, intrigued. It sounds like wizardry or religion or some amalgamation of the two. "Are you saying they can alter destiny?" I ask.

"Not quite. It's more that they believe if something is meant to happen, it will find its way into being. They believe that energy has power, and thoughts are seeds planted in the ether of the cosmos."

"Why are you telling me about them now, though?"

He smooths my back in a tender caress. "Because I want to believe that's possible. If you didn't exist, I would have imagined your essence until you did. Perhaps we were meant to be together, and the universe led me to you."

"The idea of destiny is so romantic, but I prefer free will, I think."

"We chose one another," he agrees.

A hum of joy vibrates through my chest, and I lean closer, finding comfort in the way his body warms at close contact with mine. I sigh a little.

"The others must be waiting for us," I say.

We return to the house with me feeling like a little kid who threw a fit to get attention. Poppy reaches me first, as soon as I step inside the door. She wraps me up in a tearful hug, and everyone else soon follows. Tad pats my back repeatedly, telling me silently that it's okay.

I really have found my people.

"You can't run off like that," Poppy says.

"I didn't mean to be gone for so long, but I dropped my phone somewhere and started looking for it. Then I got distracted when I found that path up the rise and the view was incredible. Sorry to worry you." I glance around, offering the apology to everyone.

"I understand why you are experiencing an adverse emotional response," Ravik says. "However—"

"I'm not going," Tam cuts in. "I won't attend the rendezvous."

Everyone grasps the implications. How could they not?

Jaz speaks first. "Are you certain of your decision? It is likely that they will not be able to return anytime soon, as it seems they had difficulty orchestrating your retrieval."

"I have no doubts," he replies.

Unexpectedly, Ravik asks, "Then…may I take your place?"

The question hangs, stark and startling, like heat lightning in a clear night sky. Electrical anomalies have been reported in areas prior to UFO sightings, and that's rather how I feel now, as if something unprecedented is about to happen. I thought I was losing Tam, not another of my friends.

"Are you unhappy?" Poppy wants to know. "You've been here the longest, right?"

Ravik gazes around the house that looks as if they bought it, furnished, from the last human family. They even have old black-and-white photos of strangers on the walls. While it lends the place a lived-in air, there's also something uncanny about it, considering that they don't interact with anyone but us. They said that they've never had guests before.

"It has, indeed, been a long exile. It has been long enough that they may have forgotten that I survived. And at home, there are matters only I can settle."

Home. That word still doesn't apply to this place. Not for Ravik.

"Of course." Tam provides the meeting time and the coordinates, adding, "It is atop a mountain, quite far from civilization. There is a lookout site; I recall the milepost. You will need to walk from there."

"I will need your aid," Ravik says in an unusually humble tone.

I'm about to volunteer to drive when Tad speaks. "I'll take you." He taps away on his phone. "We should leave in first thing in the morning to make sure you have plenty of time to hike up to the top."

Ravik gazes around the place that sheltered them, then says, "This place is yours now. I ask only that you look after Kevin and Frances. I will miss them."

"What about us?" Poppy demands.

"You as well," they say gently.

Her eyes are really red and overbright. She swipes at them angrily, and I know how she feels. I'm fighting tears too at this unexpected farewell. But I can't lie; it would be a thousand times worse if Tam was prepping to fly away from me forever.

"Ravik—" I begin.

They silence me with a gesture. "Please do not make this more difficult."

"I have a favor to ask," Tam says.

"You are providing me with recourse I had judged impossible and unfeasible. Ask," Ravik replies.

"I have recorded a message for my family. I will transmit it to your device, along with a private communication code. Please transmit my greeting and explanation at your earliest convenience."

Ravik holds out their phone, though that's not necessary since Tam is already sending the message to our group chat. One last message for the Aliens Among Us group; after tonight, the chat simply won't be the same.

"That is easily accomplished. Rest assured, I will assuage their fears." Ravik checks the message to be sure it plays correctly.

And I hear Tam saying, "'Oona. Arlan. Betau. Tivani and Morv. You must have despaired of me, wondering whether I have ventured to the spirit lands. Yet I am well. I have found my heart's match where I least expected. I will not be returning, and it is difficult to send messages from here. But I am safe. I am happy. At long last, I am home.'"

I'm crying again. Everyone is. Well, all the humans are.

Tad swipes at his eyes, mumbling, "Damn. Warn a guy, you know?"

It seems impossible that we could sleep tonight. And we don't. Instead, we talk all night. Tam warns us about the hunters, but Jaz doesn't live anywhere near here and Ravik is leaving. After nearly getting mauled by a bear, I hope they've learned their lesson and will stop pretending to be alien bounty hunters. Now, the light is returning to the sky, glowing pink and pearl at the edges, sun peeking over the tops of the trees.

I gaze out the kitchen window at the sunrise. I could offer to make breakfast, but that would only delay the inevitable, and I don't imagine anyone wants to eat.

Tad sighs softly. "That's our cue."

"Time to go," Poppy agrees.

"I do not need witnesses." Ravik seems as if they might forbid Poppy from going.

"Well, I need a ride to the bus station. You think we're gonna sit around in your empty house, missing you? Get over yourself." She turns to Tad. "It'll save you a trip if you drop me off afterward."

"There's room in the rental car," he says easily.

To my surprise, Poppy gives me a fierce hug. "Thank you for everything. You're an amazing person and a better friend."

She goes around snuggling everybody, like she's the one leaving on an interstellar voyage, but then, she's always been emotional. Ravik offers only judicious pats. Tad gives quick hugs, then positions himself by the door.

"Safe travels," Tam says. He holds me close, my beloved alien who chose me above all others.

I pause before Ravik, considering. What should I say to a friend I will most likely never meet again? "I hope you finish what you need to. And I'm glad I met you."

"Me too," Jaz adds. "Take care, Ravik. Don't take any foolish risks."

Ravik pauses by the front door. "I only allow for calculated ones. If one of you cannot remain here to look after Kevin and Frances, please find them good homes. All the chickens, if possible. Until I met you, they were my sole companions."

Suddenly, what they're entrusting to us feels much weightier. Not a structure, but a refuge. Their world. Their home.

"You will be missed," Jaz says softly.

With one last nod, Ravik leads Tad and Poppy through the door. I hear the car engine start and I listen until the sound dies away before turning to scrutinize the house. It's homey and solid, full of other people's treasures. We can't sell the place without Ravik, or someone pretending to be them, and that seems wrong on multiple levels.

"Looks like we have a vacation house," I say.

"But someone will need to remain in residence," Jaz points out.

Yeah. The goat and chickens won't look after themselves. And it's too far out of town to hire a pet sitter long-term. Not that I'm confident we could. I'm impressed Ravik found someone to do a few days while they went to Space Con. This isn't like asking Nancy to give kibble to Scotty and Spock.

"We should talk about what comes next," Tam murmurs.

"We need to move," I say.

I didn't realize I'd come to that decision until just now, but it's the obvious solution. "And it should either be here…or maybe Rellows. That would give us a break from my family, and you'd only need to use the tech camo when they visit."

"In Rellows, they probably wouldn't comment if you went out in 'costume' year-round," Jaz offers.

"And here, there is no one to judge," Tam says.

"We don't have to make up our minds now," I say. "It's been an intense few days."

Jaz settles into the nearest chair, seeming as tired as I feel. "I'll help however I can. But I can't stay. Tad picked me up at the bus station in town, so I'll need a ride later."

"Do you want to go now?"

She pauses. "You probably want some time alone."

Well. I do, but it seems rude to come right out and say it. But my hesitation gets her moving. "Let me gather my things. I have a flexible ticket, and the party is certainly over."

She activates her tech camo, which now that I'm paying attention, resembles a bracelet on their wrists. So does Tam, who rides along to keep me company, and soon we're saying goodbye at what passes for the bus station in this little town. It's actually a gas station, and the bus pulls in just as we arrive. Jaz gives us quick hugs and rushes toward it, waving as she goes.

It's midmorning when we drive back to Ravik's place. Ours now, I suppose. I laugh, the ebullience born of pure joy. It feels like hope tearing free inside my chest.

"We're still together," I say, glancing at Tam as I turn down the gravel drive.

When we arrived here a few days ago, I never imagined how intense this visit would be.

"And I need not castigate myself further for worrying my family or for not fitting the space I was born to occupy."

The house is so very still and quiet when we enter this time that I can hear the chickens squawking in the shed. They probably want their feed and to be let out so they can wander around. Kevin is yelling his head off, and Frances makes hungry goat noises.

"Is this how you imagined our life together?" I ask with a silly little grin.

"From the seed of dreams," he whispers.

"Our life together will grow." I don't even know where the words come from, but they feel right.

"That is paraphrased from our heart's mate ceremony," Tam tells me softly.

"We can do that later. If you want."

"For now, we need to take care of the animals," he agrees.

We promised Ravik. I search using the satellite Wi-Fi that Ravik has set up and peruse instructions on how to take care of goats and chickens. Frankly, it makes sense for us to occupy this place. But it would mean quitting my job. And I have no idea what work I can do out here in the middle of nowhere. I don't have job prospects in Rellows, either.

Tam touches my shoulder. "That is your worried face."

"Just…trying to figure things out."

"You said yourself that we have time."

"True. But…I think it makes sense to stay here. At least for a while. I can go home for a bit, give notice, pack up my stuff, and collect Scotty and Spock. The big question mark is, what the heck will I do here?"

"What you've always wanted to do," Tam says.

"Which is?"

"Be an astronomer. Study the stars. Write about your findings."

I blink. "I can't just…become a freelance astronomer. I'd need to work at an observatory, and—"

"Up here, we can build one. I have the funds to get started, and the expertise to help with innovations to existing technology."

Holy. Shit.

My first instinct is to scream and to kiss him and to say, *Yes, yes, yes, a thousand times, yes,* as if he's proposed marriage after a ten-year courtship. Because it feels like my whole life has been a rehearsal for meeting Tam, the extraterrestrial of my dreams. My breath catches as his gaze meets mine. And when Tam touches my cheek, it is electric.

"Jen." Tam whispers my name, a resonance that moves the essence of my being.

It feels deeper than sex as the colors of his pattern deepen, becoming fully luminescent. I've never seen that before.

"You're so beautiful. What does this mean?" I trace the velvety whorls, evoking a whole-body shiver from him.

"That I've imprinted on you. I tried to hold back, and ordinarily it requires full consummation. But with you…"

"I guess you love me a lot." I try for a teasing tone, but it comes out soft and breathy and dripping with delight.

"Yes," he says simply.

We move to the bedroom with one mind. There's no need to wait. We have complete privacy, and I'm anchored in the moment by the singular certainty of his devotion. I undress and go to him without hesitation. He meets me halfway, still trembling.

Each touch encompasses a whole universe, one where love is the universal language. He already knows my body well. Beneath his hands, I am the pulsing heart of a meteor shower. Sensation builds until I must return it to him.

At my urging, Tam falls back, letting me explore him as he didn't before. His skin shimmers everywhere I caress him, an artist's palate of distilled yearning. His colors shift and dance, flickering on my skin like the aurora borealis wrapping around me.

Our bodies tangle. The heat of our union is the birth of twin suns, intense and overwhelming. I sweat and beg as we move together, all sighs and murmurs. His strange, beautiful form bends to mine, not designed by nature but profound pleasure surges from curiosity and exploration. I close my eyes and tumble into satisfaction, a singularity where only we exist. Tam is my event horizon, and I am spinning into a place where time stands still. As we crest together, it feels as if we've broken through the atmosphere, reentering a world that can never be the same. Our breaths come in gasps, mingling in the air that suddenly seems charged with the energy of stars.

Peace seeps in as my pulse slows, perspiration cooling on my skin. I caress him gently, grateful beyond measure. "Thank you for finding me."

"Thank you for loving me," he whispers into the sensitive skin at my neck.

Against all odds, we are together. The future might still be uncertain, but we will come to forks in the path and choose each other time and again, until we become beings of light, not dust. We have crafted our own ending, a happily ever after written not in the stars but in the moments we choose to share.

DISCOVER MORE FROM ANN AGUIRE IN HER CHARMING COZY PARANORMAL BOOK

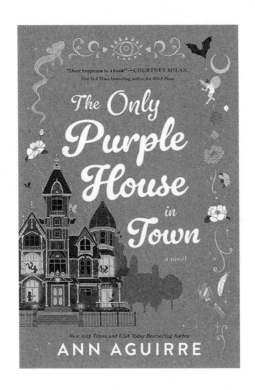

CHAPTER ONE

WHOEVER SAID IT WAS ALWAYS darkest before the dawn clearly had never lived like Iris Collins.

Sometimes she felt like a cave creature that never saw sunlight; it was dark at sunrise, sunset, and all the hours in between. She stared at her account balance on her phone with anxiety chewing away at her insides, a behavior she mirrored by gnawing on her cuticle until it bled. Her roommates would be home soon, and she didn't look forward to that conversation. They'd covered her for the last two months, but she doubted they would be willing to triple down.

I can't even leave until I pay them back, and I can't find a new place either.

She had no clue how to earn her back rent or come up with what she needed for this month. Her sisters had money, but Rose would lecture if she bailed Iris out; Lily would refuse to help while talking about how Iris should live within her means; and Olive didn't have reliable internet since she was currently doctoring without borders. Her three sisters were a how-to guide for success, while Iris was the cautionary tale. Her mother had made life hell the last time she lent financial assistance, so that was out of the question.

Should I sell my car?

In the movies, vampires were essentially immortal and had been accruing wealth for centuries. Unfortunately for Iris, she came from a different line entirely. Her type didn't feed on blood but human emotions, and Iris had come up shy in that department as well. Unlike the rest of her family, she had no special abilities that sprang from her vampiric nature. At least, nothing had ever *manifested*. Olive could feed on her patients' pain and improve their lives as she did so. Lily feasted on grief, and Rose thrived on anger, whereas Iris was basically *human*. Or so her mother had said more than once; her tone made it clear that wasn't a compliment. But then, even among the paranormal community, psychic vampires weren't well liked. They were known as "takers" for obvious reasons. Five years ago—when the witches made their big announcement—others had followed suit.

Now, Iris didn't have to hide who she was, and there were dating apps devoted to various types of supernatural folk. Iris had been on Shifted for a while, but she kept meeting lone wolf types who just wanted to hit and quit. In this case, they happened to be able to turn into actual wolves. Then she tried Bindr, but witches could be touchy about lineage, apparently. The skeptics and conspiracy theorists amused her the most. There were forums devoted to debunking magic, calling it "the greatest hoax since the moon landing," and sometimes Iris did a deep dive through the most ridiculous suggestions to distract herself from the reality of how screwed she was.

In fact, she was doing that now. She scrolled on her phone, snickering. "Sure, lizard people have replaced all our nation's leaders—that's real. And there are mole people living underneath Capitol Hill."

Enough of that.

From there, she clicked through to a site offering various magical charms. *I could really use one for prosperity, but they're so expensive. And what if it doesn't work?* Shaking her head, she resisted the urge to max out her card with an impulse purchase. But damn, it was tough. She *really* wanted to find out if the magical lipstick was permanently kiss-proof. In the news, Congress was trying to pass a new law requiring all paranormal individuals to self-identify and register in some kind of national database. *Yeah, that won't end well.* And some douchebag senator in Iowa wanted even sterner sanctions, special housing projects, and tracking devices. Someone else had proposed a *tax* on supernaturals. *How does that even make sense? And good luck enforcing it.* She shook her head and went back to window-shopping. So many cool magic items she'd love to get her hands on...

For Iris, life hadn't changed that much. The paranormal communities were still close-knit, and most didn't reveal themselves readily, even if a few people had identified themselves for clout and were giving interviews about what it was like growing up "other" among humans. Some were pursuing a fortune or building social media empires, capitalizing on the interest focused their way.

I can't even do that. Too bad—it would help the shop.

Sighing, she trudged to her room, currently crammed with supplies for her jewelry-making business, but nobody was buying the finished products. She'd invested in the idea, but she hadn't earned more than twenty bucks on her pieces. She supposed she could register as a driver, but she was scared of letting strangers get in her car. Iris lowered her head. It was ridiculous that she was afraid of...so many things. Pacing back to the dining room, she feverishly tried to think of a solution.

Do I have anything *left to sell besides my car?*

"You owe me six hundred bucks," Frederic said.

Iris let out a cry, juggled her phone, and then dropped it. Screen down, because of course. That was how her luck ran. When she picked it up, there was a tiny nick on the corner, exactly what she didn't need today. *I didn't even hear him come in.*

Stifling a squeak, she spun to face Frederic.

She'd been dodging the others—Regina, Frederic, and Candace—for the last week, even though she had nowhere to go. The diner staff was sick of her ordering a cup of coffee and staying for hours, while the dollar cinema didn't seem to care if she stayed all day. But now, it was too late.

Frederic tapped her shoulder briskly. "Did you hear me? Where's my money?"

He owned the house and had rented three of the four bedrooms. It was a decent place, decorated in bachelor style, and everyone was nice enough. But like everywhere else Iris had lived, she didn't quite fit. Frederic hadn't even wanted to rent to her in the first place since she didn't have a day job, but Iris had gone to high school with Regina, and she vouched for Iris. Now Regina was mad because Iris was making her look bad, and Candace was tired of the tension.

Everyone quietly wanted Iris gone, but she had to *pay* them first. She raised her gaze from the polished-oak dining table, trying to figure out what to say. *Sorry, I'm broke* was only three words, but she couldn't make herself say them, mainly because she'd said them so often, and she'd burned through any good will the others felt for her.

But before Regina and Candace arrived to exacerbate the situation, the doorbell rang. "I'll get it," she said swiftly.

Iris raced past Frederic to the front door where a postman in a blue uniform asked her to sign for a certified letter. *That's never good news. I hope it's not another bill that I let slide until it went to collections.* The way her luck ran, it probably was, and the return address stamp on the envelope only reinforced that impression. Digby, Davis, and Moore sounded like a law firm.

I hope I'm not being sued.

She didn't want to read it, but the alternative was facing Frederic, so she closed the door with a quiet snick, blocking the early-autumn breeze. Through the window, she watched the leaves skitter on the sidewalk, caught by that same wind. She tore open the packet and found a wealth of legal documents.

IN THE ESTATE OF GERTRUDE VAN DOREN, DECEASED...

Poor Aunt Gertie. I wish I'd gone to her funeral.

Iris skimmed the pages with growing disbelief. Her great-aunt Gertrude had left the bulk of her estate to Iris: a small amount of cash, her collection of ceramic angels, and a house in St. Claire,

Illinois, including all contents within. Iris had no clue why Great-Aunt Gertie had done this, but the bequest burned like a spark of hope. Her great-aunt—her paternal grandfather's sister—had been reckoned rather odd, something of a misanthrope just because she never married.

Maybe she thought I'm the weirdest, the most like her. Or the one who needs the most help? Either way, true enough.

Iris hadn't seen Great-Aunt Gertie since the summer after graduation, when her parents had dragged her to St. Claire for a courtesy visit. Iris had sent yearly Christmas cards, however, mostly because she enjoyed the ritual of writing them out and mailing them, and occasionally, her great-aunt sent snail mail in return. *Maybe that haphazard correspondence meant something to her?* Whatever the reason, this inheritance couldn't come at a better time.

Quickly she read the letter telling her how to proceed, and when she folded up the packet of papers, she had a response for Frederic at least, who was standing behind her with his arms folded. "Well?" he prompted.

Iris handed him the will. "It'll take a little while, but I'll pay you soon. You can start looking for someone to take over my room."

"You're moving out?" Though he tried to sound neutral, she read relief in the flicker of his eyes, in the faint upward tilt of his mouth.

Over the years, she'd gotten good at gauging people's moods, actively looking for the disappointment and impatience her mother tried to mask, usually without success. Her face silently said, *Why aren't you more like your sisters? Why are you so exhausting? Why can't you get yourself together?*

"Not right away, but yeah."

You're running away again, her mother's voice whispered.

Some people would see it that way, but Iris viewed it as a fresh start. While she didn't have a plan per se—when did she ever?—she'd figure it out when she saw the house. At the least, it was a place she could live rent free. Her expenses would be lower, and she wouldn't have witnesses when she failed. People in St. Claire didn't really know her either, so maybe she could shake off her reputation as well.

"I can be patient," Frederic said with a magnanimous air.

Now that he's seen proof that I have money incoming.

When Iris had gotten word about Great-Aunt Gertie's passing, she'd scraped up enough to send flowers, living on ramen that week. *If I'd known she meant to leave me everything, I would've sold something for gas money to show my face at her service.* That was a crappy feeling, one that she couldn't shake even as Regina and Candace got home.

She heard Frederic in the kitchen, explaining the situation in a low voice. Then Regina headed into the living room, where Iris was curled up on the couch. "I'm so glad you figured out your next move," she said in an overly cheerful tone.

Regina wasn't really a friend, more of an acquaintance who'd vouched for Iris. She tried not to take the comment the wrong way. "Yeah, it's a minor miracle."

Candace came to the doorway, folding her arms. "You realize you're praising her for having a dead relative."

When you put it that way...

"Sorry, I didn't mean to be hurtful," Regina said.

"When are you going to see about your inheritance?" Frederic asked.

Though he'd said he could be patient, he wanted his money. Iris headed for her room to pack a weekend bag. According to the navigation app on her phone, it was six hours in the car from here to St. Claire. *If I go now, I could be there by midnight.* She knew where Great-Aunt Gertrude used to keep the spare key too.

It was impulsive and absurd, the kind of behavior that made Iris an odd duck in a family of swans. Thankfully, none of her relatives knew about this yet, and her roommates didn't care enough to stop her. Her mind made up, Iris crammed socks and underwear into her backpack, along with a few clean shirts, plus one pair of pants and something to sleep in. She dropped toiletries into her purse and snagged her keys.

"I'll see you later," she said. "I don't know how long it will take to square things away, but I'll be back to pay my back rent and to collect my stuff."

"Drive safely," Regina said, seeming relieved that she wouldn't wind up pissing off everyone in the house.

Frederic waved and Candace watched from the doorway as Iris drove into the night, away from the house where she was a square peg in a round hole.

Eli Reese wasn't the kid everyone made fun of anymore.

He owned a condo in Cleveland and a vacation cottage in Myrtle Beach, by virtue of two successful apps steadily feeding his bank account—one to gamify household management, including to-do lists and budgeting, and another social platform that focused on sharing recipes. The second had taken off in a modest way; users were collaborating on dishes, doing recipe challenges, and sending food pics to each other, and he'd just patched in an update supporting video clips. The revenue was decent on both, and he was already getting offers. A German tech company wanted Task Wizard, which let users create an avatar and level up based on the amount of real-world work accomplished, while a Chinese communications conglomerate had made an offer for What's Cooking?

If he sold one, it would give him enough capital to fund his next project. He just hadn't decided what that should be yet. Eli never imagined he'd be in a position where he didn't need to work, but there was no urgency fueling his productivity anymore. It was strange being free to do what he wanted with his life; the problem being—he didn't know what that was.

His favorite thing was flying; it was magical stepping out onto the balcony of his condo, leaving his clothes and cares behind. Transforming into a hawk and soaring over the city and then far beyond—over the whorls of trees and the scurries of small mammals in the underbrush, hidden colors in a spectrum his human eyes couldn't glimpse. Red-tailed hawks were common enough that he didn't attract unwanted attention from ornithologists, although he was larger than usual in his shifted form. Those nightly flights were the closest Eli came to pure freedom, but multiple people would disapprove of him withdrawing from personhood in favor of joining bird-dom.

Mostly Liz and Gamma, to be honest.

Music played in the truck, soft classical that didn't distract him from his thoughts. Currently, his most pressing concern was his grandmother. He'd come to St. Claire to help her relocate, as she was selling her house in the Midwest and moving to New Mexico. Gamma had looked at Florida and Arizona as well, but she'd bought a condo in a retirement community in a suburb outside Albuquerque and was looking forward to all the activities and built-in social life.

Eli had offered to assist with cleaning her basement, attic, and garage, getting the stuff she didn't want hauled away, and prepping the house to be put on the market, which involved painting and staging to make buyers picture themselves living there, undistracted by the current owner's clutter. He could've contracted the work out—hired someone to do this. But Gamma hated strangers touching her belongings, and unlike the other grandkids, he didn't have a day job or a limit to his vacation time. Plus, some of them agreed with Gamma's ex-wife or had been conditioned to do so, so there was a certain distance between them. And Eli appreciated the chance to spend time with Gamma and help her out.

She wasn't the kind of grandparent who said stuff like *You'll regret not visiting me when I'm gone*, but since Gamma had held Eli's hand as they buried his dad and then helped raise him, he understood that it was important to see people while he still could. Words like *orphan* were really Oliver Twist, but his mom had died when he was six, and his dad had passed away when he was thirteen.

Friends took turns inviting him for the holidays, which was awkward as hell. Usually, he said he had plans, and sometimes he did hang out with people, but even then, he felt...extraneous. In every space he occupied, while he might be welcome, he wasn't necessary. Nobody needed him. If he made his excuses and stayed home, wallowing in solitude, no one followed up. He didn't have the sort of friends who barged in with pizza and beer, determined to keep him company.

Hell, Eli didn't even know if he wanted that anyway. He did know something was missing, though.

He focused on reaching his destination, turning down the narrow street. Gamma's house sat on the right side of a cul-de-sac, a three-bedroom Cape Cod house with white siding where he'd spent his teen years. In this neighborhood, the houses were mostly homogenous, built around the same time with similar designs—Cape Cod, bungalow, and ranch. He pulled into the driveway, seeing the minute signs of neglect that had crept up.

The hedges had to be trimmed, and the yard was a bit tall and weedy, while the gutters needed to be cleaned, and he might need to get on the roof to have a closer look at that soggy patch. Those were issues prospective buyers would notice right away. As ever, the porch was welcoming with a profusion of potted plants and blooming flowers. Two Adirondack chairs painted forest green framed the front door with the single step leading inside. Gamma opened the screen door and popped her head out.

"Come in! I made your favorite."

Eli smiled, wiping his feet on the mat. He took his shoes off on the uncarpeted tile just inside and padded across the improbably pink carpet, through the living room and into the kitchen. He breathed in deep, savoring the smell of barbecued chicken. There was also macaroni and cheese and garden salad with a bottle of ranch dressing on standby.

Acknowledgments

Thanks to my family for supporting me, no matter what I'm working on. My daughter, Andrea, gives such fantastic advice, and my son, Alek, is wonderful at untangling knotty plot problems. You're phenomenal humans, and I'm so proud to be your mom.

Thanks to the friends who reach out when I'm lost in fictional worlds. Lilith Saintcrow and Skyla Dawn Cameron have been my lifelines the last year while I steered through some fairly treacherous tides. Thanks also to Yasmine Galenorn, Shawntelle Madison, Kate Elliott, and Silvia Moreno-Garcia for being there. New friends need to be mentioned as well, so thanks to Mel Sanders for the friend match-making. And thanks to Jocelyn Lindsay for the lovely lunches and wonderful conversations.

Thanks to my agent, Emily Sylvan Kim, for her patience and guidance. It's been a year of white water rapids and huge sea changes, but everything is getting back on track. Now I can focus on what I love—making words.

Finally, thanks to *you*, dear readers. You're the reason I'm still writing, nearly twenty years on. You have my boundless gratitude for your trust and loyalty after all this time. Read on!

About the Author

Ann Aguirre is a *New York Times* and *USA Today* bestselling author with a degree in English literature. Before she began writing full time, she was a clown, a clerk, a voice actress, and a savior of stray kittens, not necessarily in that order. She grew up in a yellow house across from a cornfield, but now she lives in the Pacific Northwest with her family and various pets. She likes books, video games, and Korean dramas. Ann writes all kinds of genre fiction, more than fifty novels to date.